Jove titles by Dylann Crush

THE COWBOY SAYS I DO
HER KIND OF COWBOY

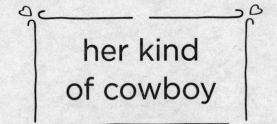

her kind
of cowboy

DYLANN CRUSH

JOVE
New York

A JOVE BOOK
Published by Berkley
An imprint of Penguin Random House LLC
penguinrandomhouse.com

Copyright © 2021 by Dylann Crush
Excerpt from *Crazy About a Cowboy* © 2021 by Dylann Crush
Penguin Random House supports copyright. Copyright fuels creativity, encourages
diverse voices, promotes free speech, and creates a vibrant culture. Thank you for buying
an authorized edition of this book and for complying with copyright laws by not
reproducing, scanning, or distributing any part of it in any form without permission.
You are supporting writers and allowing Penguin Random House to continue to
publish books for every reader.

A JOVE BOOK, BERKLEY, and the BERKLEY & B colophon are
registered trademarks of Penguin Random House LLC.

ISBN: 9780593101667

First Edition: January 2021

Printed in the United States of America
1   3   5   7   9   10   8   6   4   2

Cover design by Ally Andryshak
Book design by Gaelyn Galbreath

For Shirley, aka Babushka.
The world is a much better place with you in it.

one

"Why me?" Alex Sanders crossed his arms over his chest as he eyed the older man behind the desk. He hadn't known what to think when he'd been summoned from the cozy lounge to trek across the ice and snow of the South Pole for a meeting with his boss. A lead on a job back on the mainland was the last thing he'd expected.

"I suggested you because of your experience. You worked with penguins at that marine theme park, and your file is full of glowing recommendations from the scientists here." The chair creaked as his boss leaned back. "You mentioned you aren't interested in staying over the winter, so I thought you might be in need of gainful employment. Didn't you say you're from Texas?"

Alex nodded. He'd been working at the remote research station on the coast of Antarctica for the past six months, but with the summer season drawing to a close, he planned on hopping one of the remaining February flights and getting the hell out of there. One summer at the South Pole had been enough for a homegrown Texas boy who hadn't even owned a winter coat before setting foot on the frozen continent. His only hesitation had been not knowing where to go next.

"We've enjoyed having you as part of the team. If you want to take a season off and help my colleague out, we'll hold a spot for you, and you can come back next spring." His boss leaned forward and scribbled something down on a piece of paper. "Here's the number. Give him a call if you're interested, but I'd do it fast. He wants to get this lined up as soon as possible, and if you want to get out of here before they stop running flights, you'll need to make a decision soon."

Alex took the slip of paper, recognizing the Houston area code. "Thanks. I'll think about it."

"Think fast. I'd make the call today." He checked his watch. "You've got about a half hour left of satellite time before you'll have to wait until tomorrow."

Alex shook his boss's hand as he got up to leave. He'd lucked into this gig last year when he met a fellow rock climber in Australia. The guy had taken some time off to travel before heading back to his post at a station in Antarctica. His team was short a research assistant for their study on penguin breeding, and Alex was always up for another adventure, so he'd signed on for a six-month stint. He'd never spent that much time in one place and as the shortened days turned into long periods of darkness, he told himself he'd get out the first chance he got.

The job offer might be his lucky break. But could he really go back to the one place on earth he never wanted to see again? His sister Charlene had been begging him to come home for months. Gramps was having trouble settling into the new assisted living facility she'd found for him, and with four girls at home and a husband who was deployed, she'd reached her wit's end trying to hold it all together.

Alex wished his parents were still around to help out. But the duty had skipped an entire generation when his dad passed, and his mom didn't feel any sense of obligation to the family she'd never wanted to be part of. What the hell. He didn't have anything to lose. May as well make the call and see what might be in it for him.

Fifteen minutes later, he pulled the phone away from his ear and gave it a quick glance. The man on the other end was making such a ridiculous offer that for a moment Alex figured he might be getting pranked.

"I assure you, Mr. Sanders, this is a legitimate proposal. Our needs require someone with a specialized skill set, and my client is willing to pay generously for the assistance."

"Penguins." Alex rolled the word around on his tongue. "In Texas. For a wedding." Yeah, still sounded just as ridiculous as the first time the attorney on the other end of the phone said it out loud.

"My client realizes the unique nature of his request, but we're talking about his only daughter. He's willing to do whatever it takes to make sure she gets the wedding of her dreams."

Alex wondered what it would be like to afford to have his every wish granted. Even something so absolutely asinine as a winter wonderland wedding in southeast Texas. With penguins.

"And all I have to do is take care of the penguins for a couple months?" Alex confirmed.

"You'll be solely in charge of their welfare and training. Mr. Munyon is donating a generous amount to the Houston Marine Life Aquarium. Their current permanent penguin habitat is in need of repair. While the penguins are off display we'll have a subset of the herd—"

"It's a waddle," Alex interrupted.

"A waddle?"

"A waddle or a colony. Unless they're out on the water. Then a group of penguins is called a raft."

"How interesting. As I was saying, we'll have most of the waddle stay on-site at the aquarium. But we'll separate a few and put them in your care. By the time the wedding is over, they'll all be reunited in the new penguin habitat."

"I see." But Alex didn't see at all. "And where will the penguins I'll be in charge of be living during this time?"

"That's a loose end we need to tie up. Are you interested in the position? Mr. Munyon would like to move on it right away."

"If I take this on, I need to be near Swynton. That's where my family lives."

"That's fine. Mr. Munyon's stipulations require an address within a one-hundred-mile radius of Houston. If you find somewhere acceptable near your hometown where they can have the wedding and house the penguins, it would be a win-win. Can you let me know your answer within the next day or two?"

Alex drummed his fingers against the arm of his chair. "Let me think about it. Send over the details and I'll take a look."

"Fantastic. I'll have my assistant e-mail over the particulars. Mr. Munyon is a generous man. If you do a good job, he might be able to offer you something more permanent."

"I'll be in touch." Alex disconnected the call and spun his chair around to look out the window. A blanket of white covered the flat terrain. He'd been working in the cold long enough. If all went well he could give Charlene a hand with Gramps, cash in on the too-good-to-be-true offer he'd just received, then move onto something more lucrative. With a little bit of time left while the satellite was still hooked up for outgoing calls, he punched in his sister's number.

She answered after the first ring. "You'd better not be calling unless you're telling me what time to pick you up from the airport."

"Always good to talk to you too, Sis."

"I'm serious. Did you see my e-mail? Gramps has really done it this time. The nursing home threatened to kick him out."

Alex scoffed. "He's been kicked out of other places at least a half dozen times before. Just deliver a batch of your killer cookies to the office and they'll find a way to forget about it."

"Not this time. I even put in a call to the state director and he said Gramps has taken things too far. He's got one more strike, and then they'll ban him for good."

"What did he do?" Alex had seen a series of e-mails come through from Char last night, but after spending eight hours working outside in subzero temps, all he'd wanted to do was sit in the lounge with a tumbler of whiskey.

"You didn't read my e-mails, did you?" Her frustration trickled through the phone line and wrapped tight around his chest.

"I'm sorry. It was a long day, and—"

"They're all long days for you. And how is that? You've got no one but yourself to worry about down there. Meanwhile I'm trying to manage two jobs, an absent husband, four kids, and a man who refuses to grow up."

Alex raked a hand through his hair. "Isn't there another home nearby? Maybe somewhere we haven't tried yet?"

"Not that I know of. Either he's been kicked out or they've heard about him and won't take him." She groaned. "What are we going to do?"

That was the million-dollar question. Their grandfather had outlived his wife and kids. With no one left to look after him but Alex and his sister, Gramps was wreaking havoc all over the county. It wasn't fair for Char to have to deal with him on her own, not on top of everything else she had going on.

"I'll see what I can do, okay?"

"That's what you always say. I know you'd rather cut off an arm than come home, and I don't blame you, but . . ."

His heart cracked at the pain in her voice.

"I need you."

"I know." He let out a sigh. "I've got a lead on something

that might put me in Texas for a while. Give me a day or two to look into it, okay?"

"I'll manage for the next few days. I can't do this on my own though. You're going to have to help. Either we hire a live-in aide and let him go back to the ranch or—"

"I'll figure something out."

"Thanks." Relief vibrated through that one word, fortifying Alex's resolve to figure out a way to pitch in. It was time he stepped up, and the crazy proposition from the richest man in Texas would give him the opportunity he needed. Assuming the numbers looked good, there was no way he could say no. Not when Char needed him like she did.

His gaze traveled over the blinding white landscape. It would be nice to have a change of scenery. Even if he had promised himself he'd never have to go home again.

Zina Baxter kicked the covers off and let her foot drop to the ground. Her toes squished around in something unmistakably dog related. Something unmistakably foul. She groaned. It had to be dog poop. She thought she'd housebroken the rescue pup she'd brought home from the shelter with her last night, but it looked like they still had a way to go.

Typically the sun would have risen by now but with the slew of thunderstorms that had settled over Ido, Texas, for the past several days, Zina couldn't make out more than a few hazy outlines in the early light of dawn.

"Come on, Herbie. I thought we talked about this."

The pup hopped off the bed, the tags on his collar jangling, and appeared at her side. With a quick swipe of his tongue, all of her anger dissipated. It wasn't his fault he wasn't housebroken yet. She'd been running the For Pitties' Sake pit bull rescue for a few years now. Even the most loving pups came with a ton of baggage. The thunder and lightning during last night's storm probably set him off.

She ran a hand over the back of his head. "It's okay, bud." Then she shifted her weight to her heels and waddled to the bathroom to wipe off her foot. By the time she'd showered, cleaned up Herbie's mess, and driven the short distance to the dog rescue shelter, the sky had lightened a few shades.

Staff would be in later, but she'd taken the morning shift today. That meant it was up to her to get the dogs fed and out for a potty break. Herbie trotted alongside her as she unlocked the front door and let herself in to the crumbling building For Pitties' Sake had called home for the last ten years. A puddle of liquid greeted her.

At first she thought one of the dozens of dogs at the rescue had broken out of its kennel and had an accident. But when she flipped on the light and looked toward the ceiling, she immediately spotted the source of the leak. Her stomach twisted. Several tiles of the drop-down ceiling sagged. A line of rainwater dripped in a constant *plop-plop*, splatting onto her feet as she stood in shock.

Herbie plunged through the puddle, licking up the water and taking the opportunity to splash around.

"This isn't here to play with." Zina let out a sigh. She'd been working on an idea for a special event to increase awareness about the shelter. Now she'd have to shift all of her energy into raising enough funds to clean up this mess and make repairs. For a moment she wished she'd never taken on this project. Maybe she should have stayed in the military and never come back to Ido.

A chorus of barks and yips sounded from the back of the building. The dogs. That's why she'd taken over. And that's why she'd stayed. As she made her way toward the back where the kennels were set up, her phone rang.

"Good morning, sunshine," her best friend, Lacey, practically sang into the phone.

"What are you so happy about?"

"Gee, who crapped in your cereal this morning?"

"It wasn't my cereal. It was my bedroom floor and I put my foot in it."

"Oh, hon. Which lucky male did you take home with you last night?"

"Herbie."

"And that's the way he treated you?"

"Hey, I'm used to getting dumped on by members of the opposite sex. Just look at my last attempt at a relationship." She should have known the last guy she tried dating was cheating on her. All the signs were there, she'd just been too busy to notice.

"We still on for lunch?"

"I've gotta cancel," Zina said. "There's a leak at the shelter, and I've got to get it patched up before the rain starts again."

"Oh no. Are all of the dogs okay?" Lacey asked.

"Yeah, they seem to be. But I've got a few inches of water to sop up."

"My offer still stands, you know."

Zina shook her head. "I'm not going to pimp out my pups so you can bring in more crazy brides." Lacey had been after her to come up with some sort of puppy wedding package. Ever since she'd been elected mayor and revamped the tiny town of Idont, Texas, into Ido, she'd started billing it as the best place in Texas to tie the knot. Over the past year Lacey had come up with all kinds of crackpot ideas.

"Just think about it, you bring over a couple of the dogs to take part in a few weddings and you'll earn enough to get the roof replaced in no time at all."

There had to be another way. Zina loved her bestie, they'd had each other's backs since they were in junior high together, but this latest obsession of Lacey's had her shaking her head. "I'll figure something out."

The muffled barks turned into an earsplitting chorus as she pushed through the door from the front office to the back. "I'll have to call you later. I've got to feed the dogs."

"How about I bring lunch to you? I can stop by around noon."

"Sure." One less thing to have to think about. Although, holding Lacey at bay with her crazy ideas might take more effort than trying to figure out what to feed herself for lunch, so it might not be an equal trade-off.

"See you in a bit."

Zina disconnected and slid her phone back into her pocket. As she let the first phase of pups out to the runs in back, she searched for more damage. Besides a few small drips and drops in the supply room, the back of the building didn't seem to have any major issues. Thank goodness. She didn't think she could deal with another crisis.

Lacey might be embracing all things having to do with Ido, but Zina couldn't seem to get on board the crazy-train idea of transforming their tiny town into a mecca for demanding brides. Ever since last spring when they'd had that article in *Texas Times*, the town had been bursting at the seams with weddings and the headaches that came with them.

Lacey was in hog heaven since her sole role as mayor was to force a breath of life back into the town. But Zina, along with quite a few other longtime residents, weren't so thrilled with having a slew of outsiders descend on their small corner of Texas every weekend. Also, the wedding business had caused an increase in the number of pit bulls being abandoned to For Pitties' Sake. And that was something Zina vowed to fix.

By the time Lacey arrived at noon, Zina had run two loads of wet towels through the dryer and still had more to go.

"You really need to take care of this." Lacey glanced down at the bucket as rainwater continued to drip from the ceiling.

"I put a call in for someone to come take a look this afternoon." Zina picked up the wet towels and traded them out for a fresh batch. At this rate, she wouldn't be able to keep up. Unless she wanted to move into the shelter and work towel patrol all weekend, she needed to figure out a way to stop the leaks.

"I got you a taco dinner from Ortega's. That ought to lift your spirits." Lacey reached into the brown paper bag she'd brought with her and set the food on the counter.

Zina's stomach growled. She'd been so busy the thought of breakfast hadn't even crossed her mind and now it was time for lunch. "Thanks. You're always looking out for me, aren't you?"

A grin spread across Lacey's face. "I sure am. That's why I think you need to take me up on my offer. It's easy money."

Zina shook her head. "No way. Pimping my pups out so you can make a buck off some bossy bride isn't going to help."

"I don't see how you can say that." Lacey clamped her hands to her hips. Her wedding ring caught the light from the fluorescent overheads and sent sparkles all over the walls, reminding Zina of how much her friend's life had changed over the past year.

"I know you think it would be helping, but I don't know how any of these dogs would react if we dumped them into one of your gussied-up wedding ordeals. With my luck some drunk bridesmaid would get bit and then I'd have liability issues in addition to the leaks I've got going on now."

"But you could pick some of the most laid-back dogs. Like Buster." Lacey pointed to a square dog bed set up in the corner of the office.

A giant pit bull lifted his head at the mention of his name. His tail thumped against the linoleum, once, twice, before he let out a rush of gas.

"You want to clear the ceremony?" Zina asked as the stench of Buster's explosion wafted through the air. "Because if you're looking for a way to run off the wedding party, Buster's your dog."

Lacey wrinkled her nose and then pinched it between her fingers. "Okay, so not Buster. But surely you've got another option. How many dogs do you have here right now?"

"Too many." Zina gathered the brown bag with one hand and waved the other in front of her face, trying to fan away Buster's stench. "Let's go sit out front."

"There have got to be a few sweet ones." Lacey followed her to the picnic table in the shade of a giant live oak.

Zina handed her a towel to dry off the plastic bench. "I just don't feel comfortable with the idea."

Or any of the ideas Lacey had been coming up with lately. Transforming the town into wedding central had been bad enough, but Lacey kept trying to up the stakes. Zina had made multiple attempts to try to talk her down, but Lacey was hell-bent on putting Ido on the map.

"Fine. I'll come up with another idea." Lacey bit into her taco with more force than necessary. The shell cracked, dumping half of the contents onto the paper wrapper.

"Careful. Don't take out your aggression on the taco supreme." Zina grinned.

"Has anyone ever told you you're impossible?"

"You know you're the only person in town who thinks so."

"No one else knows you as well as I do." Lacey narrowed her eyes as she took another bite—a gentle bite.

Zina held back a response. Lacey might have a point, but holding her ground was the only thing that had ever worked for her. Until it hadn't. The one time she'd let someone else talk her into not listening to her gut, she'd almost ended up with a hole in her head. Granted, life in Ido was much different than the time she'd spent on active duty in the Middle East. But still, she couldn't be too careful, especially not with the crazies who kept dumping pit bulls around town.

As if she could read her mind, Lacey finished a sip of her soda and turned to Zina. "You have any more incidents?"

"Hmm?" Zina tried to pretend she didn't know exactly what her friend meant.

"Vandalism. Bodie told me he was out at your place earlier this week. Someone took a baseball bat to your mailbox."

"Nope. Nothing since then. They pretty much chalked it up to some kids with too much free time on their hands."

"If it happens again call Bodie first. He told me you called the sheriff's department and it took forever for them to send someone out."

Zina shrugged. "I don't want anyone to accuse me of taking special liberties."

"You're practically family. That's not taking special liberties, that's just what it is."

Practically family. The thought of Lacey with her blond hair and blue eyes fitting in with Zina's mix of Mexican, German, and Scottish heritage brought a grin to her face. Her friendship with Lacey was one of the only things she enjoyed about being back in town. That and the dogs.

She'd wished she could pick up and leave it all behind more than a time or two over the years. But her deeply ingrained sense of obligation held her back. Lacey would be lost without her. And Zina loved knowing she was actually making a difference in the lives of the dogs she was able to save. But if she were being honest with herself, like, really, truly, gut-wrenchingly honest, the main reason she stayed was that she could never leave her brother.

"Hey, are you going to be out by the Phillips House anytime today?" Lacey asked.

"I can be. I need to pick up some more towels at home and take Zeb to an appointment. What do you need?"

Lacey's eyes softened at the mention of Zina's older brother's name. "How's he doing?"

"Better."

"Remember, hon, it's me you're talking to. You can tell me the truth."

Zina set her taco down. "He's doing fine. I just wish he'd

find something to live for again. He's lost that light he used to have, you know?"

"He's lucky he has you looking out for him." Lacey nodded. "He'll find his way."

"I hope so." As much as Zina might dream about leaving Ido, she could never move away from her brother. Zeb had enlisted in the Marines right out of high school and spent five years on active duty before the transport he was in rolled over an IED. When he came home, he was a different person than the young man who'd left with stars in his eyes and the desire to follow in their dad's footsteps.

"Just give it time. Time heals all wounds, isn't that what they say?" Lacey dipped a chip into her guacamole.

Time. That was one thing she never seemed to have enough of nowadays. "You asked about running to the Phillips House. What do you need?"

"Oh, I've got some linens I picked up from the dry cleaner from last weekend's wedding that need to be put away. If you're out that way, would you mind dropping them off for me?"

"Sure." It was the least she could do. Lacey wouldn't hesitate to do her a favor. All she ever had to do was ask.

two

The unseasonable heat of a late-February afternoon drifted over Alex like he'd walked into a steam room. Unaccustomed to any amount of humidity, he tried to suck in a breath as he exited Houston's Hobby Airport. In the past twenty-four hours he'd experienced a change in time of nineteen hours and a temperature shift of over seventy degrees. In his time away, working in one of the coldest places in the world, he'd all but forgotten how he'd almost melted during his childhood in Texas.

He tightened his grip on the handle of his bag. His fingers slipped a bit. He was already sweating and he'd barely stepped outside. Maybe taking this opportunity was a mistake. Before he could go too far down that path, a horn sounded. A huge pickup truck screeched to a halt in front of him, and Charlene hopped out of the driver's seat.

"If I wasn't looking at you with my own eyes, I wouldn't believe you're here." Before he could reply, she wrapped her arms around him and squeezed tight.

His throat constricted at the sight of his sister. It had been too long. "Good to see you, too."

She pulled back and he caught a hint of tears in the corners of her eyes. He'd let her take on too much. She never should have had to deal with Gramps on top of everything else she had going on.

She flung her arm around his side and guided him toward the truck. "Have I told you how happy I am that you're here?"

He hugged her close. "How's Gramps?"

The smile faded, her mouth turning slightly downward. "He's still at the nursing home right now. But I've got to get him out of there. He's so unpredictable."

"I don't know how you do it. Raising four kids, practically by yourself. You're incredible, you know?" He had nothing but the utmost respect for his older sister. When her husband signed up for another tour of duty, she'd done everything she could to hold things together. Being so far away, Alex had no idea what kind of toll that took. But now that he saw the worry lines etched into her forehead, how her clothes hung from her thin frame, and the dark smudges under her eyes, he vowed he'd do what he could to ease her burden.

"So tell me about this job you landed. What kind of opportunity brings a guy who's spent the last six months working in Antarctica back home to Texas?"

"I'm not sure you'll believe me if I tell you." When he talked to Munyon's attorney about the job, Alex thought it was a joke. He still didn't believe it himself.

"Go on, try me."

"Okay." He waited for Char to climb into the truck as he buckled up. "I got an offer to take care of a small group of penguins."

"At the aquarium?"

"No, that's just it. They're redoing the exhibit, so I have to relocate them."

"Where?" Char asked.

"I'm not sure yet." That was the only kink in his plan.

"We don't have room for penguins. So help me, Alex, if you think you're going to—"

He twisted in his seat to meet his sister's gaze. A few years ago, he might have strung her along for a bit, just for a few laughs. But in her current situation, he didn't want to risk sending her over the edge and having to take on all of her other responsibilities in addition to Gramps.

"Don't worry, they're not coming to your place."

"Promise?" Her voice squeaked.

"Yes, I promise."

"So where are you going to put these penguins?" she asked.

"I haven't quite figured that part out yet, but I've got a couple of ideas and a few months to make it happen."

"You've got to be kidding. How many penguins are you talking about?"

"Six. A nice half dozen." Alex's blood pressure notched up as he thought about it. There should be a few things in life that money couldn't buy. Evidently a bridal party made up of penguins wasn't one of them. According to the attorney, Munyon's daughter had dreamed of her big day as a little girl. And been changing her mind ever since.

She'd started with a wedding on a private island in the Caribbean. But in the last month she'd shifted gears and now she wanted penguins. As the only daughter of a man with more money than God, she'd have exactly what she wanted on her big day, no matter how ridiculous it seemed or how much it cost.

Char let out a laugh. "I guess those summers you spent working at that marine life park are finally paying off. Where are you going to house half a dozen penguins?"

"I'm not sure yet. Know of anywhere nearby where there's room for a huge wedding and space to set up a temporary habitat?"

"You know they're putting up that wedding place over in Ido," Char volunteered.

"Ido?" Alex asked.

"I don't think I mentioned it, but Idont changed their name to Ido last year."

"Why the hell would they do that?" The only thing Idont had going for it was Phillips Stationery and Imports. That place had been around for over a hundred years and was the backbone of Idont's business.

"You remember Lacey Cherish?"

At Alex's nod, she continued. "The Phillips family shut down the import business, so she went and turned the Phillips House into a venue for weddings and events. Got the whole town to rename themselves Ido. If you ask me, that girl's got a few screws loose."

"Really?"

"Yeah. Business is booming. Although it's a pain in the ass to try to get around town. She's got a couple of weddings every weekend. Traffic can get pretty backed up along the highway."

"What's she doing with the warehouse?" Alex asked. If there was a place nearby that might fit the bill, it would save him days, maybe even weeks, of research.

"I don't know. Storage, maybe?"

His first day in Texas, and things were already looking good. "Think we can swing by the Phillips place on the way home?"

"Sure, I'll have Jordan keep an eye on her sisters when they get home from school. What do you have in mind?" Char asked.

"Just an idea. We'll see."

Zina hung another tablecloth on a hanger in the upstairs closet at the Phillips House. Lacey had been using the historic Victorian as a venue to host all kinds of events, although most of them were weddings. As she folded up the empty bag and slid it into the bottom of the antique armoire, tires crunched on the gravel drive outside.

She glanced out the window, surprised at the sight of a blue pickup truck. Usually prospective brides and grooms set up appointments directly with Lacey. Zina waited as a couple got out of the truck. The man and woman stood outside their vehicle for a moment, and then the man headed for the front steps.

Probably a couple looking for a wedding venue. She let the curtain fall back in place. The doorbell chimed as she made her way down the grand staircase to the foyer. She'd just hand them one of Lacey's cards and get on with her day.

But then she opened the door. She wasn't prepared for the sight of the man standing on the other side. Although, she wasn't sure a woman could do anything to prepare for a man like him showing up on her doorstep.

He towered over her, just like he probably stood a head taller than most other men. Granted, she was on the shorter side since she'd inherited her height from her mama's side of the family, along with her curves. His broad shoulders filled the doorframe, blocking out the light behind him.

But it wasn't his height or his build that made her take a step back. It was his eyes. Somewhere between blue and green, they locked onto her, holding her mesmerized in their grip.

She cleared her throat and held tighter to the doorframe. "Can I help you?"

"I'm looking for Lacey Cherish. Is she around?"

His voice vibrated through her, the deep baritone rumbling from her toes to the tips of her curls. Zina shook her head. "She's at the office. Are you looking for a place for an event?"

"Something like that." He grinned, and the corners of his eyes crinkled.

Good Lord, was that a hint of a dimple peeking out at

her from his left cheek? She'd been lost in those eyes, but when he smiled, his lips quirking up into a grin, her insides churned. Who was he?

"I could show you around if you'd like." She tilted her head, inviting him to step into the foyer.

"Thanks, but I'm mostly interested in the warehouse. Do you know if she ever rents that out?"

"The warehouse?" What kind of event would he want to hold in the warehouse? "I don't know, but I can give you one of her cards."

"That would be great."

"Here you go." As Zina handed him the card, her fingers brushed his. Her whole arm quivered. She shook it off, uncomfortable with the sensation.

No need to get her panties in a wad over some stranger. Especially one who was off the market.

"Thanks." He glanced to the card, then back to her. "You look familiar. Do I know you?"

"No. I'm sure I'd remember." The words spilled out before she had a chance to shut herself up. As she tried to compose herself, she thrust her hand at him. "Zina Baxter. I'm one of Lacey's friends."

"Baxter . . ." His hand curled around hers. Tingles shot up her arm. "You're Zeb's little sister, aren't you?"

"You know my brother?" Who was this guy? And how did he know her older brother? Zeb hadn't gotten out much since he returned from his tour of duty a couple of years ago.

"Yeah. I played against him and Lacey's brother, Luke, a few times on the football field. He had talent. I was surprised he didn't make it to the pros."

Yes, Zeb had talent. He also had a chip on his shoulder the size of Texas and felt like he needed to prove something, so he'd enlisted in the Marines right out of high school.

"Things don't always turn out the way we hope." Zina's

heart twisted a bit as she considered the future her brother might have had if he'd made a different choice. She probably wouldn't be standing here talking to this cool drink of water if her brother had gone to college. She wouldn't have had to take an early hardship discharge from the Army and would probably still be training dogs for the military.

No need to revisit the *coulda*, *woulda*, *shoulda*s of her past. She refocused her attention on the man in front of her.

"You didn't tell me your name." She eyed him with newfound curiosity.

"Sorry about that. Alex Sanders."

"And that's your fiancée?" Zina peered past him to the woman standing by the truck.

Alex laughed, a deep rumble of laughter that made her toes curl. And Zina's toes didn't curl easily.

He hooked a thumb and gestured to the truck. "That's my sister. I grew up over in Swynton. Just got back into town, and we're on our way home from the airport."

"So what do you want with Lacey?" Her internal radar switched on high alert, and she tried to feel out his intentions.

"I've got a proposition for her. Do you know if she's currently using the warehouse for anything?" He stepped back and turned to face the direction of the warehouse. A line of tall trees obstructed it from view.

"Just for storage right now. You have something you need to store?" *Or something you need to hide?* she thought to herself.

"Maybe." He slid the business card into the back pocket of his jeans. "I'll give her a call. It was nice to meet you, Zina."

She didn't like the way he said her name, the way he rolled the syllables over his tongue, drawing it out in his native Texas drawl. Didn't like the way it made her stomach clench or her cheeks heat. Didn't like it one bit.

"Have a good day."

"Be sure and tell your brother I said hello."

She nodded, forcing a smile. She'd do no such thing. Not until she found out what Alex Sanders wanted with Lacey. He turned and made his way down the front steps, his shoulders rolling, making her insides twist and turn around themselves like a piece of licorice candy. As he and his sister stepped on the running boards and got into the truck, she reached for her phone. Lacey would strangle her if she didn't give her a heads-up that the sex on a stick she'd just met was going to be giving her a call.

three

❤

Alex hadn't seen his nieces in person since he fled his hometown over eight years ago. They'd talked via video, but he was unprepared for how grown-up they were. When had Jordan gotten so tall? At twelve years old she looked a lot more like a teenager instead of the sweet toddler he used to sneak candy to. She barely glanced up from her phone as he followed Char into the cramped living room of the three-bedroom ranch. And that must be Izzy sitting next to her. How old was she now, eight or nine?

The television blared some cartoon featuring princesses, and the two little ones, Frankie and Dolly, sat on the ground, staring up at the screen.

"Girls, say hi to your uncle Alex." Char reached out and turned off the TV.

A collective groan rose from the floor.

"Your uncle." Char put an arm behind his back and propelled him forward a few steps.

"Hey. Dolly and Frankie, right?" He tried to reconcile

the tiny faces he'd seen on his phone screen with the two little girls in front of him. They seemed so big, so real.

"Manners," Char prompted.

The youngest, Dolly, got to her feet, tripping over the sparkly nightgown that hung to the ground. "It's a pleasure to meet you, Uncle Alex." She held her hand out as she dipped into a low curtsy.

Char rolled her eyes. "That one thinks she's a four-year-old princess. You'll get used to it."

A princess? What did he know about princesses? He took her small hand in his and bent forward as he lifted it to his lips. "It's nice to finally meet you in person, Dolly."

"Ew"—she yanked her hand back—"don't kiss it."

Char put her hand on Dolly's shoulder and spun her around. "Go put your real clothes on. We're taking Uncle Alex out to dinner tonight."

"Oh, that's not necessary." He tried to picture the six of them clustered around a table. What did one talk about with girls? Especially little girls? Life at the research station was unfiltered. He'd never had to watch his language or think about what he said before it flew out of his mouth. Char appeared to run a fairly tight ship. Wouldn't do him any good to get kicked out the day he arrived. "How about I grill up some steaks or something right here?"

"I like hot dogs," Frankie said. "With mustard and relish and no ketchup."

"Ketchup's the best." Izzy—a mini version of Char— bounced across the room, her feet barely touching the ground.

"Ketchup's gross. So's mustard. And I won't eat a hot dog unless it's a tofu dog." Jordan gave a salute from where she occupied the corner of the couch. "Hi, Uncle Alex. 'Sup?"

"She's a vegetarian this week," Char said.

"When did they get so big?" He couldn't get over how much they'd grown.

"Stick around and you can help us usher in the teen years." Char moved around the room while she talked, picking up various items that appeared to have been abandoned by their owners. "If you'd rather stay in and have hot dogs, that's easier."

"Hot dogs are fine." He tracked her as she moved from one mess to the next. "How old are they all now? Jordan's still only twelve, right?"

Char nodded. "Izzy turns eleven in a few weeks and Frankie's six. That's what happens, they grow."

He shook his head. "I can't believe it."

"Mom, can I wear lip gloss if we're going out to dinner?" Izzy asked.

"No. We're staying home for hot dogs. Besides, you know you're not allowed to wear makeup yet."

Alex stood there, soaking it in. The majority of his interactions over the past several years had been with men. The sheer quantity of estrogen in the room made his stomach queasy. "Is there somewhere I can go to—"

"You need to go potty?" Dolly asked.

"No." Alex glanced to Char but she'd already started down the hall.

"Follow me. I've got you set up in the back bedroom."

"That's my room," Izzy wailed. "How am I going to be able to work on my project if I can't get into my room?"

"Mommy says Izzy's a drama mean." Dolly nodded to herself.

"It's a drama queen, not *mean*," Izzy yelled before slamming the louvered door leading into the kitchen. It didn't stick, just bounced into the doorstop and ricocheted back and forth several times. "And I am not."

"Jordan, get over here and pick up your stuff." Char stopped to pick up a hockey stick. "She thinks she's going to play for the NHL someday. Can you believe it?"

Alex hefted his duffel over his shoulder and made his way down the hall. Framed pictures lined the walls. An image of their parents' wedding day hung at eye level. His mom beamed at his dad. His dad didn't look quite as thrilled to be taking part in what Alex later learned was somewhat of a shotgun wedding. Where was she now? He shouldn't care, but it still bothered him that she'd walked out on them.

Char's wedding photo hung underneath. She and Dave smiled into each other's eyes like they were the only two people in the world. He let out a chuckle. Suckers. Look where that got her . . . holding down the fort while her husband played Army thousands of miles away. He thanked his lucky stars he'd managed to make it to the ripe old age of twenty-eight without falling for that kind of a setup.

A few more steps and he entered a small bedroom that appeared to have a split personality. Hockey posters covered two of the walls. Wayne Gretzky peered down on him while Sidney Crosby took a slap shot to the goal. Dark blue paint peeked out from underneath the posters, and a lamp made out of hockey pucks sat next to the narrow twin bed.

"The two older girls share. Jordan's into hockey and, well, Izzy's into animals." Char leaned the hockey stick up against the corner of the room.

"You hear anything from Mom?" He tried to act casual, like it wouldn't matter either way.

"Just the annual Christmas card." Char shrugged. "I haven't talked to her in years. The return address is a post office box in Biloxi."

"Mississippi?" Alex asked.

"Yep. She'd probably send you one, too, if you ever settled down and got yourself a permanent address."

"Wouldn't be worth it." He shot his sister a grin. She knew him better than anyone, which meant she was very familiar with his inability to stay in one place too long.

"Even now?" Char folded a pair of pants and set them on one of the beds. "I figured once you'd been on the road for a while you might want to come home. Hasn't all that wanderlust seeped out of your veins yet?"

Alex held her gaze for a moment, but the hope and hurt made him look away. How could he explain his need to keep moving? She wouldn't understand. Her whole life was here in this house with Dave and the girls. But Alex didn't have anything holding him to a certain place. He never had and if it were up to him, he never would.

He glanced around the other half of the room. Pictures of kittens and puppies and . . . his gaze stopped at a large cage hanging in the corner. "What the hell is that?"

"What the hell is that? What the hell is that?" a giant bird squawked as it flapped its wings and flew out of the open door of the cage.

Alex ducked as it dive-bombed his head before settling on top of the dresser.

"Alex, meet Shiner Bock, the newest member of the family." Char picked up a discarded sweatshirt.

"What is it?" Alex evaluated the large bird as it sat and pecked at its wings with a giant curved beak.

"A parrot. Izzy traded her bike for it a couple of weeks ago to some guy driving through the neighborhood." Char pulled open a drawer, and the bird climbed onto her shoulder. "She got grounded for a month for talking to a stranger and we got Shiner Bock."

"Got Shiner," the bird mimicked.

Alex let his bag fall to the ground. "Thanks for putting me up. I promise I'll find my own place as soon as I can."

Char turned to him. "I'm so glad to have you here."

The bird cocked its head one way and then the other.

"Maybe it's good to be home."

"Yeah?" She tilted her head to the side, matching the parrot's pose.

Alex stifled a laugh. "Yeah, for a little while."

He meant it. He might have left the small world of Swynton behind when he tore out of town all those years ago. But it was nice to be back among the only family he had left. As long as he got out before everyone started to smother him with expectations.

There was a fine line between a nice visit and making a commitment. He'd be more than willing to help out while he was around. From the looks of things, Char needed it. Dave had been on back-to-back tours since Jordan was a baby. Seemed like he only had enough time between tours to come back, meet the newest kid, and knock up his wife again.

But Char could handle it. She was the strong one in the family, always had been. Alex would stick around long enough to collect his paycheck and make sure Gramps was settled somewhere before he took off again. That meant the clock was ticking and it was time to get started.

Zina pulled up Lacey's number on speaker as she made her way across town. Zeb had an appointment with his therapist and refused to take the free shuttle that provided rides for local veterans. He said it reminded him too much of being on the transport vehicle when they'd run over the IED that ended his military career.

"Hey, what's up?" Lacey asked.

"I just wanted to let you know that I ran by the Phillips House and dropped off your linens."

"Great, thanks." Lacey must have held her hand over the mic. Her voice sounded muffled as she said something to someone in the background.

"And I ran into someone interesting." Zina waited for a response. When none came, she continued. "He used to play football against your brother and Zeb."

The phone clunked like Lacey had dropped it. Zina knew her best friend had taken on too many obligations since she'd been elected mayor. And she'd added even more to her overflowing plate when she married Deputy Sheriff

Bodie Phillips last spring and became the sole contact for Ido's budding wedding business. But somehow, with everything else she had going on, she'd always found time for Zina. At least until recently.

"Hellooooo?" Zina said. "You there?"

A click came through the phone. "Go ahead. Sorry about that. You were saying?"

"I was trying to warn you that you're going to be getting a call from a guy who stopped by the Phillips House."

"A guy? What kind of a guy?" Lacey still sounded distracted. She'd lost interest in other men when she'd tied the knot with her own childhood crush.

"A hot-as-hell piece of man candy I'd like to lick in all the right places." Zina smiled to herself. That ought to get Lacey's attention.

Silence. Usually Lacey would shoot back a snappy reply to a comment like that. Instead, a deep laugh rolled through the speaker.

"Should I be worried?" Bodie asked.

Zina's cheeks burned like they'd been seared on a flaming barbecue grate. "Bodie? Where's Lacey?"

Lacey's laughter filled the cab of the pickup. "I'm right here. I've got you on speaker. You might want to curb your enthusiasm. Not everyone needs to know how long it's been since you had the chance to lick a proper piece of man candy."

Stunned into momentary silence, Zina contemplated hanging up. "I realize y'all are married now but for the love of all things holy, do you have to share everything with him?"

The phone clicked again. "I'm sorry. You're off speaker now. Feel better?"

"No. In fact, I don't feel better. Who else knows how long it's been since I've licked anything?"

"No one. Bodie just stopped by with some paperwork I

needed to sign. He's leaving now." The sound of a smacking kiss, then a giggle from Lacey made Zina's stomach churn.

"Want to call me back after you've violated your husband in the privacy of your public office?"

"No. He's gone now. I promise. Please, fill me in on this lickable man."

"Forget it." Zina pulled into the drive of the group home where her brother lived. "I try to do a good deed by giving you a heads-up and now I'll never live it down."

"I'm sorry. It's too easy to poke fun. Seriously, though, what did he want?"

"He wants to talk to you about renting the warehouse."

"For what?"

"I have no idea. But I gave him your card and he said he'd be giving you a call. My duty is done. Now if you'll excuse me, I've got to drive Zeb to his appointment and get back in time to meet the roofing guy."

Lacey clucked her tongue. "Did you get his name?"

"Who, the roofing guy?"

"No, the man candy."

"Yeah, Alex somebody. Said he used to play football against Luke and Zeb. He grew up over in Swynton and came by with his sister."

"Not Alex Sanders," Lacey said. "If you're talking about Alex Sanders, then your lickable man candy assessment is right on the money. Oh hell, he was hot back in high school."

"Well he's matured into hotter hotness and he's going to be looking you up, so be forewarned."

"Hmm. You know I'm off the market but if there's new lickable man candy in town, I think it's only fitting that you take a chance."

Zina pressed her hand to her heart as it began to thump in double time. Figures that Lacey would make a suggestion like that. "You only want me to settle down so you don't feel so guilty for being so freaking happy all the time."

"You may be right about that. It really is a downer when you shut me up when I try to talk about how great married sex is."

"I've got to go. My ears are on fire and as it is I'll never be able to take anything Deputy Phillips says seriously again."

"Just don't let him cuff you. You have no idea where those handcuffs have been."

"I'm hanging up now."

"Love you, girl."

"Love you, too." Zina ended the call. Let no good deed go unpunished. She'd only been trying to give Lacey a heads-up. Now she'd have unwelcome visions of her best friend and Bodie and a pair of department-issued handcuffs floating around in her head. As if she needed anything else to make her painfully, uncomfortably, achingly aware of how long her current dry spell had lasted.

As she shoved all thoughts of Alex Sanders out of her mind, lickable torso and all, she made her way to the front door. Zeb stepped out on the stoop, his service dog by his side. He didn't go anywhere without Semper, not since Zina had finally found an organization that could provide him with a highly trained dog to help him with his debilitating PTSD. She'd been so impressed with Zeb's improvement since he'd started working with Semper that she'd been volunteering with the group to identify rescue pups that came into For Pitties' Sake that might be good candidates to enter their training program. If she couldn't do her part by actively serving in the military, at least she could try to make those who did serve more comfortable when they returned home.

"You ready?" She glanced up at Zeb.

"Let's get this over with." He didn't even try to pretend he didn't hate the required therapy sessions he'd agreed to attend as part of Semper's placement.

"Hey, I met someone you used to face on the football

field today." Maybe Zeb remembered Alex. She hadn't planned on mentioning it, but it wouldn't hurt to ask, just in case he could provide some background info that might give Lacey an edge. Yeah, for Lacey's sake, she told herself.

"Oh yeah, who's that?" Zeb's hand shook slightly as he climbed into the front seat of the truck.

"Alex Sanders. Ring a bell?"

A hint of a smile cracked his lips in two. How long had it been since Zeb had worn anything but his usual frown?

"Sanders. Hell yeah. He rang plenty of bells in his day, if you know what I mean."

Zina held the door open for Semper to hop into the back seat, then huffed out a breath as she slammed the door. So the lickable man candy was probably a manwhore. Figured.

"What's he doing back?" Zeb asked. "Last I heard he dropped out of college, hopped a plane, and no one's seen him for years."

"I don't know. He stopped by the Phillips House while I was over there today and wanted to talk to Lacey about the warehouse. I think his sister was with him."

"Well tell him I said hi next time you see him, okay?" The trace of a smile still hanging on his lips, Zeb gripped the door, probably trying to prepare himself for the nerve-racking five-minute drive to the therapist's office.

"You ready?"

At his nod, Zina shifted into gear. She had no plans to see Alex Sanders again. He'd probably be in and out of Ido before the dust settled around his boots. No one who escaped the doldrums of small-town life and had any say in the matter ever came back for good.

four

Alex ran a finger around the inside of his collar, trying to loosen its choke hold. It had been years since he'd worn anything but a thermal undershirt or a T-shirt this close to his skin. Char suggested he dress up a bit if he wanted to pitch to Lacey. She was the mayor now after all.

The mayor.

What the hell had been going on around here since he'd been gone?

His sister filled him in on how Lacey's dad had to step down amid a cloud of controversy and Lacey had taken it upon herself to step up. The gal had gumption, that was for sure. But would she be willing to take a risk on his wild plan? He stepped into the mayor's office, figuring there was only one way to find out.

"Alex Sanders here to see Mayor Cherish." He stopped in front of the receptionist's desk.

"Take a seat, I'll let her know you're here." The woman gestured toward a set of worn leather couches.

Alex sat down and leaned back against a cushion. He

glanced at the magazines spread out in front of him. An issue of *Texas Times* stood out. He recognized the image on the cover—the Phillips House. As he scanned the article it gave him some hope. Seemed Char's version of events was right on the button. Lacey had rebranded the entire town to become a mecca for high-profile brides. The demands the oil baron had for his daughter's wedding ought to fit right in. Before he had a chance to finish the article, Lacey appeared in the doorway to her office.

"Alex?"

He stood, holding on to the magazine. If she showed any resistance to his idea, he might need it to remind her how big a risk she'd taken before.

"Mayor Cherish, it's nice to meet you."

"Don't you dare pretend you don't remember me." She brushed his hand away and gave him a hug. "You used to TP my house when we were younger."

He returned the embrace as he let out a laugh. "I wasn't sure you'd remember."

"Remember?" She pulled back and met his gaze. "I ought to have my husband take you into custody. I think there are still some pieces of toilet paper stuck in the branches of the old pecan tree my dad's got out front."

For half a heartbeat he didn't know if she was kidding. But then she shot him a dazzling smile and stepped aside. "It's good to see you again."

He let out a breath. Wouldn't do him any good to get arrested for pranks he pulled over a decade ago before he had a chance to make his pitch. "I hear congratulations are in order. You and Bodie got married last year?"

"That's right. Come on in."

He stepped past her and entered the mayor's office. Pictures of bridal bouquets, decorations, and wedding dresses covered the walls. He'd expected some sense of grandeur. Instead, he walked into wedding central.

"Sorry, I'm kind of in the middle of a big project. Grab

a chair. Tell me, what brought you in today? My assistant said you were pretty cryptic on the phone and wouldn't tell her exactly what this visit is about."

Alex took a seat and set the magazine down on the desk in front of him. If he'd been unsure of Lacey's commitment to positioning Ido as the wedding capital of Texas, his worries were dashed by the sheer quantity of wedding pictures she'd posted on the walls.

"I have a proposition for you, Mayor Cherish."

She plopped down into the chair behind the desk. "Oh, call me Lacey. And fill me in. What do you have going on?"

He cleared his throat, wishing he'd opted for a damn T-shirt and not this noose Char had knotted around his neck. "I'm looking for a place to hold a wedding."

Her eyes widened. "You're getting married?"

He couldn't help but laugh. Tying the knot was the farthest thing from his mind. "No. But I've been put in touch with a man whose daughter is. They're looking for a place to hold her wedding and have a few particular requests."

Lacey squinted as she leaned back in her chair. "So you're a wedding planner now?"

"Not exactly." Alex swallowed, forcing the lump in his throat past the tight collar.

"I'm not sure I understand what you need."

He leaned forward, putting his palms on the desk. "I've been working at a research station in Antarctica studying penguins for the past several months."

"Penguins?" Lacey crossed her arms over her chest, and a deep furrow bisected her forehead. "What's this got to do with weddings?"

"I spoke with an attorney last week who wants to hire me. He needs someone to care for some penguins that need to be rehomed while the aquarium renovates their habitat." He was royally botching this. The look on Lacey's face proved it. If her eyebrows dropped any lower over her eyes, she probably wouldn't be able to see out of them.

"I still don't get what this has to do with the warehouse."

"That's where the wedding bit comes in. You know who Tad Munyon is?"

"The oil guy?"

Alex nodded.

"Everyone in Texas knows who the Munyons are. What's he got to do with penguins?"

Alex cleared his throat but before he could get to the heart of the problem, the intercom on Lacey's desk buzzed.

"Mayor Cherish, you've got Cyrus Beasley on line one. He has a few questions about an upcoming wedding."

"Thanks, Chelsea. Tell him I'll be with him in just a moment." She disconnected, then leveled her gaze at Alex. "I'm sorry, I've got to take that call. Our local newspaper photographer's trying to convince me to let him do all of the wedding pictures at the Phillips House. Can you tell me real quick exactly how I can help you today?"

"I need a place to rehome some penguins. Just for a few months. And Munyon wants somewhere to host his daughter's wedding."

Lacey shook her head.

"Her winter wonderland wedding." Alex paused. "With the penguins."

A peal of laughter tumbled from Lacey's lips before she clamped her hand over her mouth. "I'm sorry, did you say she wants a wedding with penguins in it? We're talking about live birds, right?"

Alex nodded.

"The birds who live where there's ice and snow?"

Alex nodded again. He was starting to feel like a bobblehead doll.

"In Texas?" She pushed back from the desk and stood. "I mean, I've fielded some odd requests since we started this venture, but this takes it to a whole new level."

"I know, it's strange." Alex got to his feet. "Caught me off guard, too, when I first heard it. But he's offering a ton of money to make this happen. I was thinking, if you're not using the warehouse for anything, maybe I can create a temporary habitat for them there."

"For the penguins?"

When she said it out loud it sounded even crazier than when he'd first heard the idea over the phone.

"It's an odd request—"

"Oh, you have no idea what kind of requests I've had. I had two trapeze artists who wanted me to rig a whole circus setup so they could get married in the air, then I had a guy who makes swords call and ask if I could set up an entire Viking encampment for his wedding, complete with a forge."

"Really? So penguins aren't so off the wall then."

"No, it's bizarre." Lacey rounded the desk and perched on the edge. "I've never had anyone ask me to turn my warehouse into living quarters for marine life before."

"It would just be for a couple of months. And he's willing to pay."

"How much are we talking about?"

"Name your price." Alex shrugged. He'd been given the authority to negotiate with Lacey when he agreed to take the job. Munyon didn't care what it cost, he just wanted his daughter to be happy.

"Five grand."

"No problem."

"Seriously? To use my empty warehouse for a couple of months?"

"Actually, I may need it for three or four. The wedding isn't until August. You know, winter wonderland with the penguins and all that. But for five grand a month, I think that's fair."

"A month?" Lacey's jaw dropped open. "You're going to pay me five grand a month to house some penguins?"

"Yeah." He finally allowed himself a smile since it seemed like things were going to work out. "He'll cover all of the costs to create the habitat and then return the warehouse to its original state when we're done."

"Naturally." Lacey tucked her hands in the pockets of her dress pants and circled the desk. "And when is all of this supposed to start?"

"Well, if the wedding's in August, I'd say we need to move them in by sometime in May or June."

She nodded. "That's only a few months away. And you're going to oversee all of this? You know how to handle penguins? I won't have to do a thing?"

"That's right. In addition to my time in Antarctica, I used to work with penguins in the summers over at the big marine life park in Houston. I'll handle everything, assuming I can get full access to the property so I can keep the penguins in check."

"The penguins who will be living in my warehouse . . ."

"I'm sure they'll want to have the wedding there, too. If you could touch base with the wedding planner they've hired to get plans rolling for that . . ." He reached into his wallet and pulled out the piece of paper he'd scrawled the wedding planner's name on. "Here you go."

Lacey took one look at it and started to fan herself. Her cheeks turned red as she flipped the tiny piece of paper back and forth. "You're kidding me."

"What?" The way her face flushed, like she had a hot rash marching up her cheeks, made him wish he hadn't requested a private audience with the mayor. He couldn't let her pass out. What would her assistant think?

"It's . . ." Lacey wheezed. Her chest heaved and she looked like she couldn't catch her breath.

"Hey, are you okay?" Alex wrapped his hands around her upper arms. "Take some slow breaths, nice and easy."

She met his gaze, her blue eyes wild. "But it's . . . Chyna . . ."

"Yeah, weird name, huh?"

"You don't understand . . ." She drew in another deep breath. "Wedding planner . . . famous . . ."

Alex nodded, his pulse spiking as he tried to get her to calm down. "Breathe in . . . one . . . two . . . three . . ."

Lacey blinked fast as she broke away from his grasp. "She wants to come here?"

"Yeah, what's the big deal?" he asked.

Before she could answer, Lacey collapsed to the ground. Alex stood, totally paralyzed for a long beat, every part of him frozen in place. What if he'd just killed the mayor?

Then he dropped to his knees next to her. "Mayor Cherish?"

Zina pushed the curtain to the side as she entered Lacey's hospital room. Her friend sat propped up in bed, her back against a fort of pillows.

"Are you all right?" She moved closer to the bed and reached for Lacey's hand.

Lacey gritted her teeth, not meeting Zina's gaze. "I'm mortified is what I am. How did you hear about this? Please tell me there's not a photo of me sprawled out on the floor of my office that's gone viral on social media."

Zina bit back a laugh. "Bodie called me from the road and asked me to check up on you. He sure sounded worried."

"He had to do some training down in Austin. I told him I was fine and not to come back. Can't have him hovering around, makes me nervous."

"You really passed out in your office?"

"Flat on my ass." She finally turned her head, her eyes searching out Zina's. "And right in front of Alex Sanders."

"So he managed to track you down?"

"Yeah. He wants to use the warehouse as temporary housing for . . . wait for it . . . penguins."

Zina stepped back, her hand still clasping Lacey's. "Penguins?"

"Can you believe it? Tad Munyon's daughter is getting married and wants a winter wonderland wedding." She rolled her eyes.

"With penguins?" Zina asked.

"A half dozen of them."

"So that's what Alex is doing back in town." Zina nodded to herself. Things were starting to make sense. A little.

"It's a great opportunity. They're even bringing in, get this, Chyna Daniels as the wedding planner." Lacey let out a little squeal as she said the name. "Chyna Daniels . . . she's one of the hottest wedding planners in LA. In the world, really."

"And I'm supposed to be impressed about that, why exactly?" Zina tilted her head, suddenly very much aware of how Lacey's life had taken a different turn. While she was wrapped up in celebrity wedding planners and the lifestyles of the rich and famous, Zina had been trying to get by, keep her head above water, and ensure her dog shelter stayed dry.

Lacey sat up straighter, her eyes taking on a little bit of a wild shine. "She could put us on the map. I'm talking big weddings. The six-figure kind. The kind that could—"

"The kind that could make this town even more crazy than it already is." Zina shook her head.

"What are you talking about? This is good news for all of us."

Zina clucked her tongue, a trick her mother used to pull on her when she'd done something and should have known better. "Lacey, who's going to do your million-dollar wedding's cake?"

"Well, Jojo's been doing a great job so—"

"The flowers?" Zina leaned over the bed. Before she gave Lacey a chance to respond, she fired again. "The food? The people in this town aren't prepared to handle zillion-dollar weddings. They can barely handle the day-to-day business they've got."

Lacey pushed herself up, her eyes burning bright,

apparently ready for a verbal throwdown. "Oh yeah? What's our unemployment rate since we started the wedding venue from where it was when the Phillips Imports business shut down? Those weddings you seem to hate are giving the good people of this town jobs, paying to put food on their table, and keeping the economy afloat."

Zina hung her head. "I just think you're setting them up for disappointment. What's going to happen when Jojo's cake receives a scathing review from one of those celebrity rags? Or there's nowhere to stay because the Sleep Tight Inn is all filled up? Are you going to set up some luxury campground for guests?"

"You know"—Lacey tapped her lip—"that's not a half-bad idea."

"Oh, give me a break. This whole thing is getting out of hand. First you wanted puppies, now you've moved on to penguins—"

"Puppies and penguins could be cute together." Lacey reached for a notepad on the side table.

"Can you even hear yourself?" Zina asked.

At that moment, the curtain shifted. Alex stood there, a paper cup in one hand. "Sorry, I hope I'm not interrupting anything but I got you some fresh water."

Zina's cheeks heated as his gaze roamed over her, probably trying to figure out how she fit into the day's events. "What are you doing here?"

"He followed the ambulance over." Lacey tossed a pearly smile his way. "I see the two of you already know each other. Have you had a chance to get all caught up?"

Zina gritted her teeth as she faced Lacey. The tone she'd used was a dead giveaway. Now that she'd found her happily-ever-after with Bodie she couldn't wait for Zina to settle down with her own Mr. Right. But the problem was, Ido was only so big and there weren't a whole lot of misters to choose from. It didn't take someone with a PhD in matchmaking to figure out the kind of ideas Lacey must have whirring around in her head.

"I don't think now is the time for catching up." Zina smoothed her hand over the crisp hospital sheet. "We need to make sure you're okay. Maybe you need a painkiller"— she leaned closer to Lacey—"or a sleeping pill."

Lacey laughed off the attempt at shutting her up. "Don't be silly. I'm fine. Besides, you're not supposed to argue with a hospital patient."

Before Zina could respond, a nurse came into the room. "You're free to go, Ms. Cherish. I'd suggest making sure you eat breakfast from now on. You've got to keep your blood sugar more consistent with a baby on the way."

"Looks like you're not going to end up a hospital patient after all," Zina said.

Alex stifled a laugh.

"Wait. Did you say 'baby on the way'?" Zina asked.

Lacey's eyes went wide. "I was going to tell you."

"When?" Zina crossed her arms over her chest, all of a sudden feeling the need to put a bit of a barrier between herself and Lacey. Although, it wasn't like getting knocked up was contagious. "When exactly did you plan on telling me you had a baby on board?"

"I just found out about it a couple of weeks ago." Lacey shifted to hang her legs over the side of the bed.

"Weeks? You've known for weeks and you haven't said a word?"

"Most couples don't share the news until after the first trimester." Lacey's voice dropped a notch. "In case things go wrong."

Guilt rolled over her and Zina put a hand on Lacey's shoulder. "I'm sorry. Let me give you a ride home."

Lacey slid off the edge of the bed. "I'm not going home. I still have work to get done today. But I'll tell you what you can do."

"What's that?" Zina asked, already dreading whatever plan Lacey might concoct. There was a 99 percent chance it would involve her and Alex.

"Alex needs to take a look at the warehouse. Why don't you let me take your truck, then he can drop you at the shelter, and you can show him the warehouse on the way?"

Zina wasn't going to let herself be manipulated that easily. Not when Lacey's plan had a whole lot more to do with matchmaking than it did with being efficient. "That seems unnecessary. Why doesn't Alex drop you off back at your office and you can stop at the warehouse on the way?"

"Because I don't have time to traipse around while there's a Munyon wedding to plan. I'm already way behind." Lacey held out her hand.

"Fine." Zina huffed out a breath as she handed over her keys. "I don't know why I let you boss me around like that."

"Because you love me." Lacey flung an arm around Zina as she stood. "Now the two of you get going. I'm going to get dressed and then I've got a wedding planner to call."

Zina didn't have the energy to argue. Giving in to Lacey was always the path of least resistance. Besides, she was still reeling with the news that her best friend had managed to keep a secret of epic proportions from her for weeks. She shot a glance toward Alex, who'd been a silent witness to their entire exchange.

"Come on, Sanders, let's go." So much for him not sticking around. She tamped down any lingering sparks of interest. Now that Lacey was pregnant, she'd probably double down on her efforts to get Zina matched up with one of the few single men in town.

Zina might let Lacey get her way when it came to insignificant struggles like where to order takeout and whose turn it was to drive. But if she tried messing around with Zina's love life, she'd be in for a rude awakening. Whether Alex Sanders was lickable or not, Zina decided there was no way in hell she'd be another bell for him to ring.

five

A few minutes later Alex held the door for Zina as she climbed into the front seat of his brother-in-law's truck. Since Dave obviously wasn't using it, Char told Alex he could borrow it while he was in town.

He gave the door a gentle push to close it as Zina got settled. She didn't seem too thrilled at the idea of showing him around the warehouse, but if he wanted to get started on constructing a temporary habitat for those birds, he needed to get a move on. At least Lacey seemed to be on board. Hopefully the wedding wouldn't get too out of hand. They'd started by requesting penguins. How much crazier could it get?

"Thanks for being willing to show me around." He glanced to Zina, who stared straight ahead. "How long have you been living in Ido?"

"Too damn long." She clipped her seat belt and gave him a smile. "Sorry if I came across as being a little difficult. Lacey has a way of taking over and expecting the rest of us to fall into line."

He chuckled as he turned the key in the ignition. "My sister's kind of like that."

"Does she live around here?"

"Yeah we grew up over in Swynton. Although, I spent plenty of time under the lights at the stadium here in Ido."

Zina nodded. "And you're back in town now to take care of some penguins?"

"Seems that way." He couldn't hold back his smile. He liked the curvy, dark-haired woman in the seat next to him. She had attitude. And based on the way she talked to Lacey, she didn't take a bunch of shit from people. Reminded him of some of the badass women he'd met in Antarctica. "How did you get involved in the dog shelter?"

She gave a brief history of her experience in the military as a dog handler. "And then I came home and decided to take over For Pitties' Sake. Now we seem to be a hot spot for people to dump their unwanted pit bulls."

"My sister said something about a local dog-fighting ring?"

"Bodie thinks he's closing in on them, but they keep moving their operation, and I get stuck with the leftovers. I don't understand how people can be so cruel to an animal." She shifted her gaze to straight ahead, but not before he caught a hint of hurt in her eyes.

"That sounds kind of dangerous. You ever think about a different line of work?"

"Running away only makes them think they've won."

Spoken like a true warrior. His opinion of Zina rose by a few notches. "Sometimes the best bet is to retreat for a bit and come up with a game plan."

"You've never been in the military, have you?"

He shook his head as he navigated the truck down the drive to the Phillips House.

"If I don't stand my ground, people will think it's okay to walk all over me."

"I see." He said the words but he didn't see. Not at all.

To him, there were few things in life worth risking everything for.

The truck stopped in front of the warehouse and before he could make his way around to open Zina's door, she'd hopped out. By the time he met her on the concrete pad by the door, she'd leaned down and removed a key from underneath a potted plant.

"That doesn't seem so secure." If he planned on housing the penguins here, he'd have to talk to Lacey about beefing up her security.

"There's not much in here that anyone would want." Zina unlocked the door and pushed it open.

Alex followed her into the front office space, where several desks had been stacked and piled against the wall. "I take it she's not using the space for anything but storage right now?"

"That's right." Zina moved toward a door at the back of the office and then stepped through.

Alex followed, his eyes adjusting to the dim interior. Tall ceilings rose above them. The warehouse was a blank slate, just waiting for someone to create something useful out of it. Immediately his thoughts went to how best to utilize the room. There was plenty of space for a water feature, which would be vital for the penguins. They wouldn't need anything too spectacular since they'd only be there for a while, but a saltwater pool and some ice were going to be required.

"What do you think?" Zina asked. "Do you think you and your birds could be happy here?"

He let his gaze float around the room before settling on her and matching her smile with one of his own. "Yeah, I think we will."

Zina tried to squelch the nervous jitters coursing through her as soon as Alex smiled at her. He had a nice smile. The kind that used to work its way into her core and made her want to turn on the charm. But that was a long time ago. She hadn't acted slaphappy over a man in years and she wouldn't start again now. No matter how being around him made her stomach churn.

And thanks to Lacey she was riding shotgun in his brother-in-law's truck while he drove her back to the shelter.

"Turn right up here," she directed. With him at the wheel next to her, she was almost reminded of being on a date. But the last time she'd been on a real date, she'd still believed in happily-ever-afters. Which meant that was a hell of a long time ago, before reality had given her a giant kick in the ass.

The shelter came into view. Her heart expanded, opened up like a freaking blooming flower seeking the sun every time she saw it. The shelter was the one good thing she'd managed to do with her life. Keeping it afloat took more than a full-time effort but she wouldn't have it any other way.

"You can just let me off in front." She unclipped her seat belt as the truck slowed.

"Don't I get to come in?" Alex asked.

"You want to?" He didn't strike her as the type who'd want to chill out with the dogs. He seemed like he had much more important things to do, especially if he was going to get started on creating a penguin habitat out of nothing.

"I've got a little time to spare. I'd love to meet some of your dogs." He killed the engine. It was settled. He was coming inside.

Zina led the way.

"So are you open to the public?" He stood behind her as she unlocked the front door.

"Yeah. That's the only way we get dogs adopted out. But I'm short staffed so if there's no one around to work the desk, we have to lock up." She pushed the door open, and he put an arm out to catch it, insisting she go first.

They entered the foyer and she immediately went to the pile of wet towels on the floor. The ceiling was still leaking and she'd been waiting for two days now for someone to come take a look.

"You got a leak?" Alex asked.

"Yeah. Whole roof really needs to be replaced. I'm supposed to be getting an estimate soon. The guy's canceled on me two days in a row." She shook her head as she set her purse down behind the counter.

"I take it that's not exactly in the operating budget?"

"You got it."

"I know how that goes. I used to do some work for a nonprofit and we were always having our funding pulled."

Neither said a word as the reality of that statement sank in. It was rough being at the mercy of donations and sponsors. Maybe Alex did know a thing or two about her situation.

"You want to meet some of the dogs?" she asked.

He nodded, his eyes lighting up a bit.

"Okay, but it's about to get really loud." She pushed into the back area where the kennels were. The dogs began to bark just like they did every single time she entered the back room. "You'd think they'd get used to me coming back here."

"What?" He leaned closer, unable to hear her due to the noise.

"I said, you'd think they wouldn't bark every single time I come back here."

"One good thing about penguins"—he nudged his chin upward—"no barking."

She couldn't help but smile as she reached Buster's cage. The dog's head rested on top of his paws. He wasn't one to bark; he barely lifted his chin as they stopped in front of his kennel.

"This is Buster." She wrapped her hand around the bar on his cage. His tongue slowly lapped at her fingers. "He likes belly rubs, watching reality TV, and hot chocolate with lots of marshmallows."

"Really?" Alex let out a laugh. "How do you know that, exactly?"

"I take a different dog home with me each night so they get some time out of the shelter. It's good for them to be exposed to what it's like to be in a house instead of a cage. Some of them have spent their whole lives in kennels like this."

"Why?" Alex stuck a finger through the squares of the cage. "Why get a dog if you're only going to keep it locked up?"

Zina used to wonder the same thing. But then she learned about dog fighting. "A lot of these pups came from dog-fighting rings. They're raised for the sole purpose of competing for their owners."

"Isn't that illegal?" Alex's brow furrowed.

Zina's heart squeezed at the show of concern. "Yep. But it doesn't stop them. Sometimes one escapes or gets dumped somewhere and we find them. Then they get rehabilitated and have a chance at a good life with a family and a real home."

"Wow. What made you want to run a dog rescue?"

"I've always loved animals"—she unlatched Buster's cage—"and when I found myself back in Texas I wanted to do something that would make a difference." If she didn't turn the conversation soon, they'd be trekking over some sensitive territory and she wasn't ready for that yet, maybe not ever. "You want to pet him?"

At Alex's nod, she swung the door of Buster's crate open. The dog, who could have passed for comatose a moment before, jumped to his feet and sprang out of the crate. He attacked Zina first in a flurry of slobbery kisses. Then he turned his affection on Alex. By the time Zina caught

Buster's attention and got him into a sit-stay, Alex had been knocked onto his back by the overzealous pup.

"He must like you."

"Really?" Alex got to his feet, wiping slobber off his chin. "I'd hate to see what he'd do to someone he didn't like."

"Buster, come." She held out her hand, and Buster moved forward a few feet, then sat in front of her. "That's better."

"Are they all so . . . enthusiastic?" Alex asked.

"No. Buster's one of my ambassadors. He usually makes a good impression on people."

"What's his story?"

Zina shrugged. "I don't really know. He showed up one day undernourished with a bunch of scars on his nose and one ear ripped to shreds. I'm not sure if he was part of a dog-fighting ring or if he was just a stray. We got some weight on him and taught him some manners. He's been available for adoption for a few months but hasn't had any takers."

Alex ruffled the short hair behind Buster's good ear. "Seems like a lovable guy."

"He is. If we can teach him how to behave himself, he might qualify for a program I'm putting together that helps veterans get acclimated to life after the military."

"Oh yeah?"

"Yep." It was still in the planning stages but Zina was hopeful her partnership with the nonprofit would pan out. Helping the dogs was one thing, but if she could manage to help the dogs and some of her fellow military men and women—then she might feel like she hadn't been wasting her time in the middle of nowhere while life seemed to pass her by.

"What's going on over there?" Alex pointed to the bucket sitting in the middle of the floor.

"Another leak. Hopefully I'll get the guy out here to take a look at it before we have another storm."

"I'd be happy to check out your roof," Alex offered. "Do you have a ladder around?"

"You know about roofs?"

"Yeah. I worked for a roofing crew for a few months to make enough cash to travel. Can't be anything too difficult."

Zina shrugged. "All right then. That would be great if you could take a look."

"Where's that ladder?"

"Let me get it for you." Zina led the way outside and around the back of the building to where a tall extension ladder lay sideways on the ground.

He grabbed it and propped it up next to the building. "Where's the leak coming from?"

She pointed to the roof. "I've got two of them. One in the front office area and another one that's getting worse over in that corner."

"I'll take a look." He checked to make sure the ladder was level and then started up to the roof. Once he reached the top, he turned around and his eyes grew wide as she climbed up after him.

He offered a hand as she cleared the roofline. She took it, sliding her hand into his. The feel of his skin on hers ricocheted through her. He may have felt a little flicker of something, too. The way his mouth parted as their fingers twined made her think he might not be so immune to her touch, either.

"You didn't have to come up here. I could have filled you in." He stood next to her, not letting go of her hand.

"It's better for me to see for myself." She didn't mind. In fact, she enjoyed the way his palm felt against hers. It led her to imagine how the rest of him might feel pressed against her.

"You said it's leaking from this corner?"

She nodded and reluctantly let her hand slide out of his as he stepped to the edge of the roof.

"Feels spongy over here. Has it leaked in this spot before?" As he leaned over, placing his hand near the darkened circle to get a better look, the roof shifted underneath him.

One moment he was there, the next he was gone.

Zina screamed, her pulse thundering through her ears as she rushed to the edge of the gaping hole he'd left in the roof.

Alex sprawled across the ground below, covered in debris.

"Don't move, I'm coming." She almost lost her footing as she rushed to the edge and scrambled down the ladder. She never should have let him go up on the roof. How many times had she told herself it wasn't safe? Especially not with a known leak. She'd be lucky if he didn't sue her.

As she flung the door open and raced through the office to the back of the building, her heart pumped so fast she thought it might explode right out of her chest. He had to be okay.

Finally, she caught sight of him. He'd fallen on top of a pile of baby mattresses that had been donated to the shelter to use as beds for the larger dogs. The breath she'd been holding slowly dissipated. Maybe he wasn't dead. *Please don't let him be dead.*

"Are you all right?" She leaned over him, searching for broken bones.

"Wow, did that look as uncool as I think it did?" He struggled to prop himself up on an elbow.

"Are you hurt?" Her hand closed around his and she helped him come to a seated position.

He patted his hand over his torso, his legs, and his head. "I think I'm okay. How far did I fall?"

They both looked up at where a man-sized hole let the afternoon light in through the roof.

"I think it's about eighteen feet," Zina said. "Are you sure you're not hurt? Do you need to go to the hospital? See a doctor? Are you going to sue me?"

"Sue you?" He scowled. "I'm the dumbass who offered

to take a look at your roof. You should probably sue me for making the damage worse."

She sighed, the tension flooding from her system, leaving her shaky and a little unsteady on her feet.

"But don't sue me, please?" Alex gave her hand a squeeze. "I'm pretty sure I'm not insured for that kind of thing. And I promise I'll help you fix it."

She shook her head. "I think I'll wait for the professionals to handle this. You've kind of done enough."

"I can at least get a tarp up there to tide you over until your repair guy comes through."

"Did you hit your head?"

"No, I don't think so." For a moment his forehead creased and he patted his hands over his head. Finding no reason for concern, he shook his head slightly.

"Well, you must have if you think I'm going to let you go back up there. I'll get someone out here tomorrow if I have to drag him here myself."

Alex shifted on the stack of mattresses and put his feet on the floor. "If you change your mind . . ."

"I won't. But I do appreciate the offer." Zina leaned over to brush some slivers of wood from his shirt. "You've got stuff on your back."

"I'm just glad those mattresses broke my fall. Thank God they were there."

Thank God, thank her lucky stars, thank everything in the universe for making sure Alex had a soft space to land. She couldn't afford the claim on her insurance, not to mention what Lacey would do to her if the biggest wedding in the history of Ido fell through because she'd taken out the penguin guy.

Alex got to his feet and wiped the remaining bits of insulation from his jeans. He took a few steps toward the door leading to the front office, when a loud cracking noise exploded from the ceiling.

Zina looked up in time to see a whole section of the ceiling collapse. She yelled, her feet frozen in place. Then something crashed into her, sending her sailing across the room.

Alex covered her with his body, his broad chest pinning her to the ground. A cloud of dust rose around them and she coughed, more from his crushing weight than from the aftermath of the ceiling falling.

"Are you hurt?" He pushed up onto a hand.

Her lungs filled with air, making her chest rise and fall. His gaze settled on her face. She could tell by the heat flooding her system that her cheeks were red, and she flip-flopped back and forth from wanting to push him off her completely and pulling him into her to take advantage of that pouty bottom lip she'd been admiring.

"Zina?" He pushed up on the other hand, hovering over her. "You're not hurt, are you?"

"I'm fine." Flustered at exactly how flustered he made her feel, she willed herself to pull it together. Her roof had just collapsed, and all she could think about was how his tongue might feel sliding against hers.

"I'm sorry. Here, let me help you up." He staggered to his feet and held out a hand.

She hesitated, not wanting to expose herself to more contact. His touch, his heated gaze, his voice . . . the combination made her want to throw caution to the wind and dive headfirst into the attraction.

Shaking her head, she scrambled to her feet, sending all inappropriate thoughts about Alex scattering like the pieces of her roof that now blew around the concrete floor. "What am I going to do now?"

A shrill ring came from Alex's pocket, and he pulled out his phone. "It's Lacey."

"Don't answer it." That's all she needed was Lacey to remind her she should have had the roof repaired last time it leaked.

"What do you mean don't answer it? I have to." His brow crinkled as he held the phone to his ear. "Hello?"

Zina dusted off her pants. It was no use. At least the pups were okay. The section of roof had collapsed over the supply area. But she'd need to find a place to move them where they'd be safe until she could get the roof repaired. The only place she could think of that had space had just been leased out to the man pacing across the concrete floor on the other side of the room.

By the time he hung up, Zina had a plan. A good plan.

"Sounds like Lacey wants to meet with us at her office in the morning. Are you available around ten?" Alex asked.

"Did she say what it's about?"

"The wedding, I guess. Now what are you going to do about these dogs?"

"About that." Zina braced herself for a bit of a battle. "I have an idea."

"Okay, let's hear it." Alex gave her a smile.

She wondered how long that would last when he heard the details of her proposal. "So it looks like I'm in need of a space to hold the dogs until my roof gets fixed."

"I think we've already agreed on that." He leaned against a tall shelving unit that held extra bags of dog food that had been donated.

"And you happen to have some empty space that you won't be using for a few months." Zina summoned her biggest, brightest smile. "Win-win, right?"

"Whoa, wait a minute. I need to get a penguin habitat built if we're going to have a shot at pulling off this wedding."

"We?" Zina scrunched her nose. "There's no 'we' here. That deal is between you and Lacey. What 'we' need to figure out is where we're going to move the dogs since you single-handedly ruined their shelter."

"Wow, single-handedly? From the looks of it, your roof was in pretty bad shape before I stepped foot on it."

Zina rolled her eyes. "Fine, you're right. But you've got

space and I have a need. A huge need. Can't we work something out?"

"How long do you think it will take to fix the roof?"

"Not long. Insurance should cover it. Shouldn't take more than a few weeks at most. The dogs and I would be long gone before your penguins move in."

Alex glanced to his feet. "I do feel partly responsible for ruining your shelter."

Zina held back a grin. He was going to go for it; she could tell by the way his mouth screwed up in that cute angsty scowl.

"But we have to run it by Lacey first. I haven't even signed any paperwork. Technically the space is still hers."

He was right, of course he was right. But Zina feared Lacey wouldn't be as easy to convince. With a sense of trepidation, she dialed Lacey's number.

Less than five minutes later Zina disconnected the call—the shortest, most accommodating call she'd ever had with her childhood best friend. She was up to something. She'd been way too easygoing, way too quick to agree.

"I guess it's settled then." Alex glanced at his watch. "I've got a few hours before I need to get back to my sister's. You want some help moving those dogs?"

"That would be great." Something was off but she didn't have time to ponder it. Not now when they were losing daylight and she had two dozen dogs to move before dark. Who was she to look a gift horse in the mouth? Even when that mouth usually couldn't stop yapping at her? Maybe Lacey was in such a good mood about the big wedding that she didn't care what Alex did with the warehouse.

For the first time in a long time she'd found herself in a bind she hadn't been able to work her way out of on her own. She hated having to ask people for help. Although she never minded providing it and was the first to step up when someone else was in need, it never sat right with her when she was forced to accept help from others. Lacey joked that being too self-sufficient was her greatest weakness. Zina preferred to think of it as a strength. That was just the tip of the iceberg when it came to the differences between them.

She let her gaze drift over Alex as he hefted a couple of bags of dog food onto his shoulders to carry out to the truck. Maybe she'd finally found someone to help champion her cause. Either way, she'd taken care of the problem at hand. Tomorrow would bring a whole set of new ones, so she ought to be grateful for Alex's help while it lasted.

An hour later she'd retrieved her truck from Lacey and pulled up next to where Alex stood, leaning against the side door to the warehouse.

He met her as she walked around to the tailgate. "Where do we need to put everyone?"

"I figure I can put the pups in the back third of the warehouse while you and your penguins take over the front. Does that sound okay?"

He shrugged. "As long as they don't get in the way of building out the penguin habitat."

"I'm going to schedule a huge adoption event to try to find some of them homes." Zina lowered the back of her truck. "If I can get the numbers down, maybe I can move them to my place temporarily if the roof isn't fixed in time."

"Don't you need zoning permits or something?"

"Thankfully she's got some connections at the sheriff's department and city hall." Bodie stepped close, joining the conversation. "Hey, long time no see."

Alex took Bodie's hands and Zina stepped back, not wanting to get in the way of the testosterone surging between the two men.

"Yeah, it's been a few years."

Bodie let go first. "So you're the reason my wife ended up in the hospital?"

Alex bristled and Zina wanted to laugh. She was familiar

with Bodie's sense of humor but obviously Alex didn't have a clue the other man was joking.

"Um, how do you figure?"

Bodie shifted his weight from one foot to the other. "You came into town and told her you were delivering some fancy wedding planner on a plate. Chyna somebody? I'm surprised she didn't have a heart attack on the spot."

"Oh." His shoulders visibly relaxed as he realized Bodie wasn't about to knock him out of his boots. "Yeah, what a coup, huh?"

Bodie scratched his chin. "Hope it all goes well. I wouldn't want Lacey to get all worked up and put the baby at risk."

Zina stepped in. "Bodie, stop issuing idle threats. You're going to scare him off before we even get the penguins' swimming pool built."

"I ever tell you that you suck the fun out of everything?" Bodie grinned. "How about you help me get these dogs inside?" He gestured to Alex, who followed him over to his truck.

Zina huffed out a sigh. The last thing she needed was two men fighting over alpha dog status as she tried to hold things together. She had more to worry about than whether Alex got his feelings hurt. Like how she was going to provide an outdoor space for the dogs to get exercise since there wasn't any kind of fencing around the warehouse. It would take forever to let them out a few at a time. She'd have to see if she could rustle together some extra volunteers or put up some sort of temporary enclosure.

With a list of to-dos forming in her head, she gathered the next crate and carried it into the warehouse. Alex and Bodie had sectioned off the back third of the space and set the kennels up in long lines. She didn't have crates for all of the dogs, so she'd have to rig some makeshift pens for the better-behaved pups. Her temples began to throb at the sheer undertaking it would be. All of this work for something temporary.

But who else would fight for the pups? If it hadn't been for rescue dogs like the ones from For Pitties' Sake, her own brother would never have recovered as well as he did. With a renewed sense of purpose, she headed back outside to pick up another crate.

six

The next morning Zina arrived at the warehouse just after dawn. She needed to check on the dogs and make sure they'd all survived the night. By the time she'd taken them out a few at a time and filled everyone's bowl with breakfast, she didn't have time to run home and change before her meeting with Lacey. It wouldn't be the first time she showed up at the mayor's office looking like a hot mess.

As she slid the key under the flowerpot, tires crunched on the gravel. What was Alex doing there? He got out of the truck looking like he'd just hopped out of a magazine spread. His hair curled up at the edges, still damp from his shower. Faded jeans molded themselves to his thighs and he'd pushed the sleeves of his shirt up, giving her a chance to appreciate his strong forearms.

She patted at her hair and tried to adjust the topknot that had shifted to more of a side knot and sat lopsided on her head.

"Good morning." Alex headed her way, two cups of coffee in his hands. "I figured I'd find you here."

"I had to check on the dogs." Zina longingly glanced over her shoulder, wondering if she had enough time to duck back into the warehouse and try to freshen up. Or at least shove a stick of gum in her mouth. She'd barely even had time to brush her teeth.

"Coffee?" He held a cup out.

"Yes, please." Grateful, she took it, letting the scent of the strong brew bolster her spirits. "I hoped I'd have time to run home and get cleaned up before our meeting with Lacey, but . . ."

"I think you look great." One side of his mouth quirked up in the most adorable way.

"I think you knocked your head harder than you thought yesterday." She might joke, but inside she glowed at the compliment. Zina shook off the shivers running up and down her spine. The only thing she wanted from Alex was for him to come through on the wedding plans. That was all. She just needed to keep reminding herself of that. It was too easy to get caught up in his smile.

"As long as we're both here, do you want to ride over to the mayor's office together?" Alex gestured to his truck. "The cab's still warm."

"I've got to pick up some dog food from the feed store on my way back."

"I don't mind. I'm meeting with a contractor out here this afternoon, so I've got time."

"Who did you decide to go with?"

"Toby Townsend. Lacey recommended him. You know him?" Alex asked.

"I know everyone around here. One of the joys of living in a small town." She pulled her jacket tighter around her shoulders and walked around to the passenger side door.

He did a good job of making small talk and by the time they turned in to the parking lot at city hall, they'd discussed the weather, the unfair misconceptions about pit bulls, and whether Alex should look to South America or Latin America for his next job when he left Ido.

As they reached the door to the mayor's office, Lacey's assistant stepped out, her eyes rimmed red.

"Chelsea, what's going on?" Zina immediately went to comfort her while Alex looked on.

"I'm just running to get some tissues. We're all out." She swiped at her eyes with the back of her hand.

"What happened? Why are you so upset?" Zina asked. Chelsea wasn't the kind to wear her heart on her sleeve. Something or someone had to have upset her.

"It's that wedding planner Lacey's talking to on the phone. I accidentally dropped the call and she wasn't happy about it."

Zina put an arm around the younger woman's shoulder. "I'm sure Lacey knows you didn't mean to. Things like that happen all the time." She glanced at Alex, hoping for confirmation.

"Yeah, all the time." He nodded.

"I'll be okay. But y'all might want to get in there with Mayor Cherish. She's got that woman on speaker and it sounds like she wants to climb right through the phone and wring her neck."

Alex passed through the doorway into the reception area. Zina gave Chelsea one more pat on the shoulder before she followed him. A loud voice came from behind the closed door of Lacey's office.

"Should we go in?" Alex asked as he stepped toward the door.

Zina pressed her ear against the thick slab of wood and held up a finger. Lacey said something about working together. Her voice was calm, even toned. *That's right, rein her in. Don't let her get the best of you.* She smiled, nodding as she pulled her head away from the door. "Sounds like Lacey's got it under control."

Alex reached for the handle. "But we should still go in, right? I think we're supposed to be on this call."

Zina stepped back. "Go for it."

He turned the knob and pushed the door inward.

As he did, a screech came from the speakerphone. "You've got to make this happen. If you won't work with us, we'll find someone else."

Zina tried to peer around Alex as he filled the doorway. Lacey sat behind the desk, her hands clasped together, the whites of her knuckles showing. "I can assure you, we're doing everything we can to accommodate you. In fact, our penguin handler just came in to join us on the call." Lacey gestured to the chair opposite her desk.

Alex sat down, relaxing against the back of the seat.

"Alex Sanders, meet Chyna Daniels, Ms. Munyon's wedding planner." As she made the introduction, she rolled her eyes. Zina recognized that look. It meant Lacey was holding on by a thread. A thread that might unravel soon.

"Hi, it's nice to have a chance to talk to you." Alex glanced to Zina and nudged his chin toward the chair next to him.

"So you're the man in charge of the penguins?" The screechy tone shifted and came through the phone like honey sliding over a piece of warm corn bread just out of the oven.

"That's right." Alex's lips quirked up into a half grin. Zina waited for the fallout. Surely he didn't think he'd charmed the banshee solely with his baritone?

"We've got a problem. My client wants to move up the wedding."

Lacey cleared her throat. "I've been explaining to Chyna that we need more time than what she's proposing. Surely we can find some common ground . . . a compromise?"

Alex's shoulders rolled. "I'm sure we can figure something out. The bride is entitled to her special day, isn't she? Whatever you and Ms. Munyon need. We'll make it happen."

"That's more like it. I knew there had to be someone

reasonable in town. Why don't you give me a call later, Mr. Sanders, and we'll work out the particulars?" Chyna suggested.

Alex beamed.

But Lacey looked like she wanted to reach across the desk and smack that smile right off his face. "I'm not sure you understand, Alex. Ms. Munyon wants to move the date up quite a bit, she's asking for—"

"Whatever it is, we'll make it work." He shrugged.

Lacey leaned against the back of her chair and crossed her arms over her chest. She shook her head. "All right then. The two of you seem to have things under control."

"I think we do," Chyna said. "I've got to go. Big meeting with another bride this afternoon. Of course I can't say who it is, but do the initials O. W. mean anything to you?"

Alex treated them to a deep chuckle. "You go take care of your business in LA. I've got it all under control here."

"Please text my assistant to arrange a call for later. I'm looking forward to meeting you in person, Alex."

Lacey bit her lip while Alex glanced between them, a smug grin on his face. "Will do. You have a nice day now."

The call disconnected and Lacey eyed Alex like he was public enemy *numero uno*. "What the hell was that?"

"What?" He glanced from Lacey to Zina.

Zina felt a sliver of pity for the man because she knew what was coming. Lacey was about to go WWE on him. She might not drop Alex into a gutwrench powerbomb but she was about to give his ego a badly needed bruising. For a moment Zina wished for popcorn and a longneck so she could further her enjoyment of the show that was about to go down.

"Not only did you undermine my authority, but you just made a promise to someone regarding *my* town." Lacey rose to her full height, her movements slow and deliberate.

"You said we needed to do whatever we could to keep Ms. Munyon happy. Based on the way the conversation was going it seemed like you were about to lose us both a very valuable client." Alex crossed his arms over that broad chest of his, totally unaware of the verbal thrashing headed his way.

Lacey rounded the large desk and then stopped in front of him. "You sure you want to stick around for this, Zina? It's about to get gory."

Zina scooted to the edge of her seat. "Wouldn't miss it."

With a nod, Lacey turned her attention back to Mr. Smug and Stupid. "Do you have any idea what you just promised?"

Alex shrugged. "She wants to move the date up a bit. No big deal."

"A *bit*." Lacey leaned against the desk and crossed one foot over the other. She might look calm and cool on the outside, but Zina could tell there was an internal volcano about to erupt.

"What's the problem? I'm meeting with the contractor today. He'll probably only need six to eight weeks to install everything. I just need a month or two after that to get them trained and we'll be fine."

"So that's two months to get the dome installed, say, another two months to train them, and then you'll be ready?" She held up four fingers.

"Yeah. Sounds about right."

"Well according to what you just committed us to with Chyna, the wedding will be happening in a little over six weeks." Her eyes narrowed. She was going in for the kill.

Alex sputtered. "What? I didn't say we'd be ready that soon."

"Unfortunately, you did. Now, can you answer one question for me?"

Alex looked to Zina, his eyes sending an obvious silent cry for help. She gave him a sweet smile, then turned her gaze to the bulletin board behind Lacey's desk. Tons of images from magazines, printouts, and photos covered the large surface. Looked like the wedding business was becoming the mayor's sole focus.

"What's that?" Alex leaned over, his forearms on his knees.

"How are you going to make it all happen?"

"Me?" Alex exploded out of his chair, his hands raking through his hair. "That would be impossible. There's no way—"

"I have every bit of faith that you'll figure it out. Because that's what you just promised Chyna."

"I said no such thing." He paced the small confines of Lacey's office. "I'd never agree to that."

"Yes, you did. And now it's going to be up to you to make this happen."

Zina couldn't help the smug grin from spreading across her face. But as her smile grew, a tiny thought chipped away at her mind. Six weeks until the wedding meant she needed to get the dogs moved out as soon as possible.

"Wait a sec." She leaned forward and met Lacey's gaze.

"Yeah, I was waiting for you to realize what this means for the dogs. We're going to need to move them. There's no way Alex can get his penguin habitat built and bring in the birds if you've got a ton of dogs living there." Lacey shuffled a few papers together. "I printed up listings for some alternate places. Unfortunately none of them look ideal, but we'll have to figure something out."

Zina took the pages and riffled through them. "These are all over the place. Swynton . . . Bellsview . . . even Beaumont."

"Like I said, we're going to have to figure something out." Lacey took in a deep breath and lifted her gaze to meet Zina's. "There's something else, too. Something I need to ask you to do for me."

"What?" Whatever it was, Zina would have her back. Lacey ought to know that. They'd always been there for each other.

"The doctor's putting me on bed rest. I fainted again last night and he wants me to take it easy, at least until I get through the first trimester."

Zina's heart raced at the news. With everything Lacey had going on, how could she afford to take time off? "How long will that be?"

Lacey glanced from Alex, who seemed to have gone mute at the talk of pregnancy, to Zina, who clenched her hands together so hard they hurt. "Oh, about six weeks."

Alex groaned, his hands clasping behind his neck. "This isn't good. Dammit. How are we going to make this work?"

"That's where Zina comes in." Lacey's lips shifted into an encouraging smile. The same kind of smile she'd used when she tried to teach Zina how to ride a horse. It was her *you can do it* and *just keep going* smile that was supposed to inspire confidence. It didn't work then and it wasn't going to work now.

Zina's knees bumped together, and her hands began to shake. "Oh no."

Lacey reached out. "Give me your hand, Z. You've got this."

"No, no, no." If she said it enough times, she'd wake up. All of this would be a bad dream. The shelter roof collapsing, Alex Sanders coming to town . . . she'd close her eyes and wake up in her own bed with Buster the farting dog next to her. In an attempt to make it happen, she clenched her eyes shut tight.

"That's not going to work, sweetie." Lacey's voice pulled her back.

"I can't." Zina opened her eyes.

"You have to. For the dogs, for the town. We don't have a choice. There's no one else."

Alex must have realized if she didn't say yes, he'd be on his own to face the formidable Chyna and her unrealistic demands. He sat back down and leaned forward, his elbows on his thighs. "I'll help. We'll work as a team. That's the only way we can turn this around."

A team. Her and Alex? She'd never heard such an awful idea in her life. The *no* balanced on the tip of her tongue. Hovered there, just waiting for her to open her mouth. But then Alex hit her with that dreamy blue-green gaze. She shifted her glance to catch a ridiculously hopeful expression on Lacey's face.

Somehow the *no* fell away. "Fine."

Her stomach clenched as she spoke, already regretting her agreement. It wasn't fine. It was a horrible, awful, terrible idea. They'd never be able to pull this off.

Alex rode the rest of the way back to the warehouse in a state of shock. For someone who rarely made commitments to anything, much less anyone, he sure had wedged himself into a jam.

"You okay?" Zina glanced over, and he could feel her gaze settle on him.

His cheeks burned. How could he have let himself be so cocky, so sure? All he'd wanted to do was make things right for Lacey. But she had to step down. He and Zina were in this together now. For better or for worse.

"I'm not sure what happened in there," he admitted.

"I do. You overpromised something you're going to underdeliver. And not just you, now it's 'we' since you pulled me into it."

She made it sound so simple, so final. "How can I fix it?" He turned to face her as best he could in the front seat of the truck.

"I guess you've got two options."

Good, she was willing to help. He'd do whatever she told him. "Go on."

"Number one." She held up her pointer finger and cast a

quick glance his way. "You call Miss High-and-Mighty and tell her you made a mistake. That after considering everything, you realized that there's no way you can give the bride the wedding of her dreams on such short notice."

"You think that's what I need to do?" His stomach clenched at the thought of backing out on the infamous wedding planner. "What kind of fallout do you think we'd get if I went that route?"

Zina shrugged. "I'm not sure. She might decide you're telling the truth and convince the bride that she needs to wait."

"Or?"

"Or she could cancel the whole thing, which puts all of us in a bit of a crisis, don't you think?"

He groaned. "What am I supposed to do?"

"There's always option two."

"Which is?"

"Get your ass in gear, beg everyone you know, everyone you've ever met, and every stranger you come across on the street to help you make this happen."

He groaned louder. "I have no idea what to do."

"I'll tell you what you shouldn't have done." She looked over again, no hint of humor in her eyes.

"What's that?"

"You shouldn't have put your foot in your mouth. You shouldn't have undermined Lacey. You shouldn't have made a promise before you knew what you were getting yourself into."

He bit back the sharp retort that threatened to fly out of his mouth and took a deep breath instead. "That's great advice. But it's about ten minutes too late. How about we focus on the future instead of dwelling on the past?"

"Can you pull over here? I have dog food to pick up." She pointed up ahead.

He brought the truck to a stop in front of the feed store, then got out and followed her inside. The building looked like an old barn that could collapse at any moment. An older man with a grizzled beard sat behind the counter. One strap of his overalls fell across his chest. Zina didn't hesitate; she wrapped the man in a hug, the smile on her face genuine.

"Hi there, Coop. You said you've got some dog food to donate to the shelter?"

"I heard you were in a bind. Figured a few bags of food might help."

"It always helps. But I don't want to take anything you can make money on. You need to keep your own rescue going."

He grinned, revealing a smile that was missing a front tooth. "You've got a good heart, girl. We've got to look out for each other, us animal lovers."

"You're right about that." She ran her hand over the back of an orange tabby cat that hopped up on the counter. "Coop runs a cat rescue."

Alex didn't think she was still speaking to him after the exchange they'd had in the truck. "That explains the cats." He glanced around. Cats in all ages, sizes, and colors roamed the store.

Coop rounded the counter and shuffled toward the back. "Got it saved over here for you."

Zina motioned for Alex to follow. "He saves any bags that pass the expiration date or break open during delivery."

"That's nice of him."

"Sure is. Like he said, we look out for each other around here."

Alex wondered what she meant by that. Sure seemed like a jab at him in some form. They reached the back of the store, where a tall pile of dog food bags were stacked against the wall.

"Now, Coop. What's wrong with those bags?" She leaned closer, looking at a label. "They're not expired and don't have any holes. You can't donate those, you should put them out on the floor."

"Would you just take 'em off my hands? I want to help." The older man reached for the bag on top.

"I can't. I appreciate your willingness to pitch in, but you need the sales."

Alex didn't wonder for a moment who would win that battle. His money would be on Zina. All of it. Every single time.

The older man pulled something out of his pocket and sank it into the bag of dog food. "Well, will you look at that? Seems this one's got a hole in it. I can't sell that one. You'd better take it."

"Coop." Zina's voice came out low, threatening. "Cut that out now."

"This one, too." He stabbed another bag. "Am I going to have to attack the whole stack or would you do me the favor of taking these off my hands?"

Zina's expression changed. Alex watched the glow spread across her face. "You know I don't appreciate it when you self-sabotage to help me out."

"Just this once. You were such a help to me when I was about to lose it all, and I heard about what happened at the shelter." He turned to Alex. "You should have seen what she did when my building was on the line. They wanted to shut me down but Zina helped me file to become a nonprofit rescue for these poor kitties. She's an angel, don't you think?"

Alex studied the "angel" next to him. For someone who projected such a tough exterior, she appeared to have a whole lot more going on inside than what she wanted the world to see. "I agree."

"You two stop it." Zina's cheeks flushed. "I'll take it. Just this once though. For the pups."

"For the pups," Coop agreed.

"Can I help you get this loaded?" Alex asked.

"That would be great." Zina hefted the top bag into her arms, being careful not to lose any kibble through the hole Coop had cut into it.

Alex grabbed a bag under his arm and tossed one over

his shoulder, then followed her out to the truck. "He seems like a nice guy."

"He is. Too nice. The man would give you the shirt off his back if you asked him for it."

Alex didn't need the shirt off anyone's back, but he did need to rally the people of Ido if he wanted to make good on his promise to be ready in time for the Munyon wedding. "Is he any good at wrangling penguins?"

Zina scoffed. "You can't be serious about trying to make that date."

"What's the alternative? You said yourself that if I back out now, I risk them pulling out of the wedding. I can't afford to have that happen." He hung his head. "Not to mention y'all are counting on me."

"Wait. What's that?" Zina cocked her head to one side as she set the bag down on the tailgate.

"What?" He let the bags fall from his grip and slid them to the front of the bed.

"Is that the sound of a heartbeat? I wasn't sure you had one in there." She poked at his chest.

He captured her hand in his. "I'm not some heartless money-grubber who's only out to make a buck, you know."

"Good." She squeezed his hand. "Then you'd better start recruiting. Coop's devotion can be bought pretty easily. He's a sucker for a good fried catfish dinner down at the Burger Bonanza."

"What about you?"

"What about me?"

"What are you a sucker for?" He caught her other hand in his and held them both together. "You're the one who can make or break this."

Her chest rose and fell as she took in a slow breath. "You're giving me too much credit."

"Don't kid yourself. I've seen the way you get things done. Folks around town notice it, too. They've got nothing but praise for you."

Her jaw clenched. "You've been asking around about me?"

"Nothing bad. Just wanted to know who I was getting involved with."

"Oh, now we're involved?" She eyed him through those long lashes and he wondered what they'd feel like fluttering against his cheek. Or better yet, his chest.

He took a half step closer until only a few inches separated them. "Would you like to be?"

The moment stretched, his heartbeat pounding through his ears.

Her gaze lingered on his lips and she opened her mouth like she wanted to say something but then closed it just as fast.

Every part of him screamed not to fuck up the fragile alliance he had going with the one woman he needed to help him succeed. Every part of him but one.

"I'd like to kiss you now. Would that be okay?" He couldn't believe he had the nerve to utter the words.

Zina lifted her gaze to meet his. She nodded, the movement so slight, he wasn't sure if she meant it.

Only one way to find out. He leaned in, brushing his nose against hers. His breath caught at the contact.

She angled her head, lifting her mouth to meet his. Their lips touched. His whole world spun out of control as he reached behind her, cupping the back of her head with his palm. She tasted like the peppermints they'd grabbed from the candy dish on Lacey's desk on their way out.

Before he could take the kiss deeper, a horn blared, reminding him they were standing on the side of the road.

She pulled away, her gaze searching his. "What was that?"

Honestly, he didn't know what the hell had just happened. He couldn't exactly tell her the truth, which was that he felt like a piece of him that had always been missing just slid into place. "Depends. Do you regret it?"

"That's for me to know and for you to maybe find out."

She pulled her hand away, but the tinge of pink flushing her cheeks made him think she might have enjoyed that kiss just as much as he did. "How about we get the rest of that dog food? I've got a couple dozen hungry pitties to feed and don't you have that appointment with the contractor this afternoon?"

"Sure do." He followed her back into the feed store to pick up another load.

There was something about her that tugged at a piece of him deep down inside. She knew what it was like to be left. From what he'd learned about her story, her mom died a few years ago and her dad bailed when Zeb came home a broken version of the hero who'd gone off to war. They were two of a kind. The only difference was she stuck around to fight her battles while he made himself scarce, hoping to outrun the wounds of his past.

All of a sudden he was sorry the wedding date got moved up. If only because it meant he wouldn't have a reason to stick around Ido once it was over.

seven

Alex somehow made it through the initial meeting with the contractor even though he had a hard time concentrating after that kiss. He made plans to meet with the man again the next morning, then hightailed it across the river separating Ido from Swynton. He'd promised Char he'd be back to watch the girls before she left for her part-time job at the country club.

Spending time with his nieces would be the perfect opportunity to prove he wanted to pitch in and help while he was in town. He cranked the wheel to turn in to the driveway but stopped short when he noticed a van already taking the spot. A decal on the side read ANGEL HANDS NURSING HOME. The name rang a bell. Wasn't that the one where Gramps had been staying?

Alex's breath hitched as he thought about what that might mean. According to Char, Angel Hands was just about their last resort. If Gramps had been kicked out of one of the last places willing to take him, how would that affect Char?

He swallowed hard. How would that affect him? He'd been more than willing to contribute a little dough here and there to smooth things over and keep his grandfather in care. But if the old man kept pissing people off, where would he go?

The front door opened and a short guy in blue scrubs scurried out. A lamp sailed through the door behind him, followed by Gramps. "Get out and stay out."

Alex had barely made it out of the truck when the van screeched to a halt beside him before grinding into gear and taking off down the street. What the hell was going on? He turned toward the door where his grandfather leaned against the doorway. Char stood next to him, her hand wrapped around his arm, tugging him back into the house.

Alex hadn't laid eyes on his grandfather in years. Not since Alex's dad died and Alex had dropped out of college, loaded his backpack, and cashed out his savings account for a one-way plane ticket to Oslo. Gramps had frowned and told Alex he needed to stick around. Alex had grinned back at the older man and kept right on packing. He'd promised himself then that he'd never come back, wouldn't let the people who were supposed to love him the most be the weight that dragged him down.

Somehow Alex remembered his grandfather being taller, more intimidating. Not like the stooped, scowling stranger who glared at him as he walked up the drive.

"Alex, thank goodness you're back. I've got to leave for my shift. Jordan can pretty much handle the other girls, but . . ." Her gaze bounced back and forth between him and Gramps.

"Hey, Gramps." Alex thrust his hand forward.

The old man grunted and turned away, shuffling toward the easy chair Char kept in the corner of the living room.

"The nursing home brought him over. He can't stay there anymore." Char twisted her hands together. "What are we going to do?"

Alex took in a deep breath through his nose. "You go to work. Gramps and I probably ought to have a heart-to-heart."

"What good will that do?" Char whispered.

"I'll just explain to him, guy to guy, that he needs to step up and hold himself in check. He can't expect you to put everything on hold and take care of him, not with everything else you've got on your plate."

She shoved her hands to her hips. "You think I haven't tried that before? Ever since Nana died he's been unbearable. He keeps saying he wants to go home, but he can't stay out at the ranch all by himself."

Alex smiled as he thought about his grandmother. She was tough—never let him get away with anything—but she was also the only one who'd ever been full of hugs and smiles and fresh-baked cookies. What would Nana do if she were here?

"You go get ready for work. Gramps and I will clean up this mess, get some fresh air, and see if we can sort something out." He nodded to himself, confident he'd be able to get Gramps to see things his way.

Char rolled her eyes before she disappeared down the hallway.

Alex glanced out to the sidewalk, where the lamp had shattered into a bazillion pieces, and then wandered into the kitchen in search of a broom and dustpan. His niece Frankie sat at the table dipping her baby carrots into the jar of grape jelly, the damn bird sitting on her shoulder.

"Hey, Frankie, where's your mom keep the broom?"

She sucked the jelly off the carrot in her hand and then dipped it back into the jar. So much for no double-dipping. He kept having to remind himself he wasn't living the bachelor life anymore. At least not while he was bunking up with his sister and her kids.

"Frankie?"

She didn't respond, just kept dipping the same carrot into the jar and sucking all the jelly off.

"She can't hear you." Dolly, his youngest niece, teetered into the kitchen in her plastic heels, a feather boa wrapped around her neck. "Frankie got her headphones on." She lifted a gloved hand to point at her sister.

Alex squatted down to meet Dolly at eye level. "Thanks, sweetie. Can you tell me where your mama keeps the broom?"

Dolly shuffled to the narrow space between the fridge and the wall. "In there."

"And the dustpan?" he asked.

"We don't got no dustpan. Jordan broke it."

No dustpan. He could improvise. Spotting an oversized piece of thick paper on the counter, Alex reached for it. "Come on, Gramps. We're going outside to clean up your mess."

The old man didn't budge, just sat in the chair in the corner, unblinking as some kid show played across the screen. Alex leaned over and pushed the power button. The ten-year-old, Izzy, groaned. "Uncle Alex, I was watching that."

"Sorry, kiddo. Gramps was too invested. Now come on, let's get that broken glass cleaned up before one of the girls gets hurt." That must have done it. Gramps hefted himself out of the chair and made his way to the front door.

Alex kept one eye on his grandfather and one on Dolly to make sure she didn't follow them out onto the driveway. "What were you thinking?"

Gramps tugged his Dallas Cowboys hat lower over his eyes. "Wasn't thinking at all. You try living in a place where they don't let you have any privacy. Not a bit. Probably got cameras watching me twenty-four seven."

Best to humor the old man. At least he'd gotten his butt up out of the chair. "Probably, Gramps."

Alex began to sweep the shattered ceramic pieces of the lamp base into a pile while Gramps stood nearby. By the time he picked up the bigger pieces out of the grass, Gramps took a seat on the bench Char had sitting on the concrete porch. Alex bent down, trying to use the piece of paper he'd picked up as a dustpan.

After several trips back and forth from the giant metal garbage can Char kept on the side of the house, he was done. "Thanks for the help, Gramps. You want to take a turn around the block and get some fresh air?"

Gramps gazed up at him and then dropped his head.

"I've got to go in and wash up. You'll be all right out here for a few minutes?"

"I'm old, not incompetent," Gramps said.

Alex let out a chuckle. He wasn't cut out for the job of humoring Gramps back into line, but it wouldn't be the first time he took on something beyond his ability or way above his pay grade.

As he reentered the house, he felt like he'd walked in on World War III, Sanders-style. Izzy stood in the kitchen wailing with Char in front of her.

"What's going on?" Alex asked.

"She lost her report. It was right here on the counter and now it's gone." Char turned toward her daughter. "No more excuses. If you don't get that turned in tomorrow, you'll get another red tag and you know what that means."

Izzy turned to Alex, her eyes brimming with tears. "Uncle Alex, did you see my report?"

His heart plummeted to his feet. "What did it look like?"

She held her arms out. "It was about this big."

"Was it white?"

Her head bobbed up and down.

With a sinking feeling drowning all hopes of a peaceful night, he summoned a brave grin. "Looks like you and I are going to be making a trip to the store after dinner to pick up a new piece of poster board."

eight

Zina held the beer bottle to her lips and took a nice, long draw. What a day. Between the surprise that she was going to be in charge of the Munyon wedding and the lip-lock with Alex, she wanted to lose herself for a little while in a local beer and a platter of chicken nachos while watching the high school basketball team take on their rivals from Swynton on the local station.

"Go, Beavers!" Zeb shifted on the stool next to her.

Zina turned, her mouth full of the giant bite of cheese-covered chips she'd just eaten. It was one thing to get her brother out of the house for their weekly dinner together, but she didn't expect him to actually engage in anything beyond a stilted conversation. The fact he was cheering for the home team put a smile on her face.

Before she could swallow and comment on his enthusiasm, her phone rang.

Lacey.

Hadn't they had enough excitement for one day? Zina turned it facedown and grabbed another chip.

The phone rang again and Zeb pointed to it. "Aren't you going to answer your phone?"

Zina groaned and held it to her ear. "I'm at dinner with Zeb. What's up?"

"Can you swing by the house tomorrow morning? Kirby wants to talk to us about starting a transportation service. I think he found an old limo or something and wants in on the wedding business."

Zina took a swig from her beer. "Did you not hear the doctor? You're pregnant."

"Yeah. But it's not a death sentence. I've got months ahead of me before I have to start worrying about an actual baby."

Lacey might have finally lost her mind. Zina had heard other friends talk about pregnancy brain. Evidently it was a real thing. "You're pregnant. Incubating another human. There's an alien being growing inside you." She waited for some aha moment to wash over her friend.

Instead, Lacey cleared her throat. "Doc said as long as I take it easy I can still work from my bed. That means I have plenty of time to make sure Ms. Munyon gets the wedding of her dreams and still be ready to welcome baby P into the world."

"Baby P?"

"Yeah, like a pea pod. Bodie thinks the 'P' refers to Phillips, of course. But I know it really means 'P' for pea pod."

"You're crazy. Like certifiable, you know?"

"There's a lot riding on this. I've got to make sure this wedding goes off without a hitch. It's our chance to put Ido on the map."

"Déjà vu. You do realize you said those exact same words last year when you were working with Adeline Monroe on her big wedding. Or don't you remember what a shit show that turned out to be?"

Lacey's laugh pealed over the phone line. "I got a husband out of it, didn't I?"

Zina shoved another chip in her mouth, bracing herself for the inevitable speech that surely would follow. This was the perfect segue into Lacey's favorite topic of conversation: Zina's love life.

"You know, Bodie's got a new guy in his department. What if I order in and the two of you come to the house for dinner next week, and—"

"No."

"But he's perfect for you."

Talking around the bite of nachos, Zina managed to ask, "What makes you say that?"

"He wants to settle down. He's got a pension already going with the department and he's super stable. Bought his own place just outside of town and has plenty of room for—"

"For what?"

Lacey paused. "For pets and babies and horses if you want them. Come on, aren't you tired of living paycheck to paycheck? You deserve some downtime, someone to take care of you for a change."

Zina took a calming breath in through her nose. "You know I love you, right?"

"Of course."

"And you also know that my love life is a no-fly zone. Seriously. Cut it out, okay?"

"Maybe you're not interested since you were locking lips with a certain penguin trainer this afternoon."

Zina just about choked on her chip. "Where did you hear that?"

"Kirby said he caught a glimpse of the two of you standing there in broad daylight on the side of the road. If you've already got your eyes set on Alex, that's fine. Bodie's coworker was just a suggestion."

"What is it with married people wanting other people to get tied down so bad? We never had conversations like this when we were both single."

"That's right. We used to stay out until the sun came up

and thought peeing in public was being efficient," Lacey said. "Times change."

Zina eyed another chip. "What time do you want me to come over tomorrow?"

"Early afternoon? Say one?"

"I'll see you then." She hung up and set her phone back down on the bar. Times may change but she didn't. She'd never allowed herself to imagine the kind of things Lacey yearned for. Being on her own for so long, she knew the only thing she could expect out of life was what she took from it. She didn't deserve a happily-ever-after any more than the next person.

Dreams were just that . . . dreams. Her dreams had gotten her nowhere in the past and she'd finally stopped believing in them when she had to put in for an early hardship discharge from the military so she could come home and deal with her brother. Zeb was doing better now thanks to the Pets for Soldiers program she'd managed to get him into. But he might not ever be able to live on his own. He'd always need her to check in on him, make sure he kept up with his meds, and that the horrors of his military career didn't pull him back down into the darkness.

And that was precisely why she could be the honorary aunt to Lacey and Bodie's baby, and care for the hundreds of poor pit bulls that made their way through the rescue and feel good about the difference she was making in others' lives. But dreaming about finding the kind of happiness Lacey had found? That was a waste of time.

Alex pulled to a stop in front of the Burger Bonanza. Somehow he'd managed to burn the macaroni and cheese Char had set out for him to make for dinner. He was still trying to figure out how he'd accomplished that. Might have had something to do with accidentally leaving the burner on while he tried to break up a fight over whose turn it was to brush the blond Barbie's hair.

Didn't matter. What mattered was he had to feed four kids and Gramps, buy a piece of poster board, help Izzy salvage her project, and get everyone settled down for the night before Char got home. He'd tried to order pizza but there was only one place that delivered and they had an hour-long wait. He figured he'd be better off just running to the burger joint in Ido to grab everyone a bite. Everything would seem better on a full stomach.

"Everyone out of the truck. One, two, three . . ." He tapped the girls on the head as they piled out. Gramps stood on the sidewalk, the three older girls clustered around him. "Where's Dolly?"

Izzy shrugged. Frankie messed around with something in her bag while Jordan's fingers skimmed across the screen of her phone.

"Gramps? Where's Dolly?" Alex peered into the back seat of the truck. It wasn't that big. Nowhere for a kid to hide, not even one so small as his four-year-old niece.

Gramps shrugged and shuffled toward the door of the restaurant.

Dammit. The last time he'd seen his niece she'd been twirling around in that sparkly nightgown on the front lawn.

"Maybe you left her at home." Jordan didn't look up from her phone as she followed Gramps toward the door.

No. He couldn't have left her at home. Could he? Char was going to have his balls on a skewer if he lost her daughter. And on his third night in town. "Gramps, take the girls inside and get a table. I'm going to run back and see if Dolly's at the house."

Izzy rolled her eyes. "Uncle Alex, Mom's going to be mad."

"You know, you don't have to tell your mom everything." He ushered the girls toward the door. "Jordan, you got this?"

She held the door open while Gramps and her sisters filed past. "Yes, Uncle Alex."

"Good. I'll be back in a minute." He rounded the front of the truck and practically dove into the driver's seat. How could he have misplaced a kid? Visions of what his sister would do to him flashed through his head on the short drive home. Char was like a mama bear. Cuddly, easy tempered, and sweet as honey until something bad happened. Then she would rise up, bare her teeth, and rip apart anyone and anything that threatened her family.

As the truck screeched to a stop Alex jammed it into park and breathed a huge sigh of relief. Dolly sat on the front stoop, her head in her hands. The sparkly pink dress was spread out around her.

"Hey, baby girl. You okay?" He sat down next to her and put a hand on her shoulder.

She glanced up, big, fat tears rolling down her cheeks. "You left me."

His heart cracked in two. Like someone pounded a chisel into it and busted it open. "I'm so sorry. Everyone was in the truck. I know you were with us. I counted heads. But when we got to the restaurant, you weren't there."

"I had to get my tiara." She lifted a hand to touch the rim of the plastic crown sitting crooked on her head. "A princess can't leave home wiffout her crown."

Alex took in a deep breath, trying to fill his lungs. "You ready to go get some dinner?"

She nodded.

He slid his thumb under her eyes, wiping the tears away. "You scared me, Princess Dolly."

"I thought grown-ups didn't get scared." She gazed up at him with such trust in her eyes, it almost split his heart into quarters.

"Sometimes we do." He took her hand in his. "Now let's go get you a giant milkshake."

"Can I have strawberry?"

"You can have whatever you want." He lifted her up and set her in the back seat. She settled herself in her booster and he shut the door behind her, his head pounding.

He wasn't used to being responsible for anyone but himself. Thank God Dolly was okay. Tonight was a reminder that he needed to pay closer attention if he didn't want to get his ass kicked by taking on new responsibilities.

Ten minutes later he and Dolly joined the rest of the family in a giant corner booth. He wanted a beer, a huge, frothy mug that would ease the tension bunching his shoulders and help him forget how he'd almost lost his niece. But he glanced around the table at his nieces and ordered a sweet tea instead.

While he waited for the waitress to bring them their drinks, his gaze swept around the room. Not much had changed since he sat in this same booth with his gramps and nana all those years ago. He wondered if Gramps remembered. It seemed like the man had turned in on himself when his wife died, lost his will to keep putting one foot in front of the other. Maybe Alex could help him get a little spark of the fire he used to have burning inside him rekindled. For Char's sake. And the sake of the gaggle of girls that surrounded him in the cracked vinyl booth.

As he tried to come up with a way to cheer up Gramps, a deep, throaty laugh captured his attention. Someone at the bar was having a good chuckle over something. They probably hadn't burned mac and cheese and abandoned a four-year-old earlier in the evening. As his gaze stopped on the pair at the bar, his breath caught. Granted there weren't too many places in town to grab a bite to eat, but what the hell was Zina doing here tonight?

"Excuse me for a minute?" Alex scooted out of the booth, leaving Gramps alone with the girls. He could keep an eye on them for a quick minute from across the restaurant.

None of them even looked up. Jordan was on the damn phone. Izzy had covered her paper menu with a kaleidoscope of drawings, Frankie dug through the bag that seemed to be glued at her hip, and Dolly had lined up the sugar packets and was waving her wand over them like she was casting a spell. Gramps cupped his mug of coffee between his hands and stared across the room. They'd be okay for the couple of minutes it would take him to see what Zina was up to.

As he approached, he couldn't help but notice the guy sitting to Zina's right. Was she on a date? He almost turned back, but as she leaned over to grab her purse she saw him.

"Hey, what brings you into town tonight?" She straightened and set her purse on her lap.

"Dinner with the family." He gestured over his shoulder.

"Looks like you brought the whole crew." Zina glanced toward the table.

"Yep, my plus five."

She tapped the shoulder of the guy next to her. "Zeb, you remember Alex Sanders, don't you?"

Zeb turned around, a slightly older-looking version of the football star Alex remembered from high school. "Hey, man."

Alex clapped him on the back and Zeb shuddered. Zina put a hand on her brother's arm. "It's okay."

Shit. Alex heard Zeb came back with PTSD. "I'm sorry, I didn't think."

"He startles easily," Zina explained.

"I'm fine." Zeb shook her off and thrust a hand out to Alex. "How have you been?"

Alex took it. "Great. It's really good to see you again."

"You, too. Is that your family over there?" Zeb asked.

Alex released his grip and nudged his chin toward where he'd left Gramps and the girls. "Yeah, my nieces and my grandfather. They don't get out much."

Zina laughed. "That explains it."

"What?"

"Why the little one is mainlining sugar."

Alex looked over in time to see Dolly sneeze, wipe her nose on her sleeve, and empty several sugar packets into her mouth. He did a double take as his heart seemed to gallop through his chest. "Oh no. I'd better get back. Just saw you over here and thought I'd say hi."

"Hi." Zina wiggled her fingers at him.

"See you around." He left Zina and her brother at the bar and took quick strides back to the table. "Dolly, you can't eat that."

She stuck out her lower lip as he swiped the packets from her hand and moved the ceramic container away from her reach.

"She only likes to eat stuff that sparkles," Jordan said without looking up from her phone.

"Gimme that." Alex snagged the phone from her hands. She looked up, her eyes wide. He'd lasted almost exactly seventy-two hours before he lost his temper. The entire experience just reinforced the decision he'd made long ago. He wasn't cut out for the family life. He did best when the only person he had to think about or be responsible for was himself.

Jordan crossed her arms over her chest and clamped down hard. Dolly licked her finger in an attempt to pick up as many sugar granules from the table as she could.

Alex sucked in a breath and tried to come up with something to say. Frankie beat him to it. "Uncle Alex, Shiner wants a snack."

Shiner . . . he racked his brain trying to remember who the hell Shiner was. A loud squawk came from the bag at Frankie's side. The bird shook his head as he emerged and climbed up Frankie's arm.

"What the fuck . . . ," Alex started.

"What the fuck . . . what the fuck . . . ," the bird mimicked.

Conversation around them ground to a halt. Even the waitress stopped in her tracks as Shiner Bock climbed onto the table.

"Can he have a salad?" Frankie asked, unaware of the inappropriateness of bringing their pet bird out for a burger.

Before Alex had a chance to react, Shiner Bock bent down to take a drink out of Frankie's shake. The glass toppled, sending mint chocolate chip liquid all over the drawing Izzy had been working on.

"Shiner Bock, you ruined my picture!" Izzy tossed a purple crayon at the bird, who flapped his wings and strutted across the table.

"Gramps, a little help here?" Alex muttered under his breath. He pulled a handful of napkins out of the dispenser in an attempt to sop up some of the shake currently dripping off the edge of the table. Besides Izzy's cries, the restaurant was quiet, too damn quiet.

"Let me help." Zina appeared on his right with a towel she must have snagged from behind the bar.

"Jordan, can you grab the bird?" Alex asked.

"No way, he bites."

"He just doesn't like you because you tease him." Izzy flung a packet of sugar at her sister.

Dolly screeched. "You're taking my sparkles."

"I'm so sorry." Alex turned to Zina, who'd wiped up the sticky mint-green liquid and now held Izzy's drawing in her hand.

"It's okay. Why don't you get the bird out of here before the health department gets word of this?" She nudged her chin toward where Shiner Bock had managed to make it to the booth behind them and stood nibbling at a french fry on a woman's plate.

"Frankie. Grab the bird," Alex said.

"I can't get out." She slapped her palms on the table, where she sat sandwiched between her sisters.

Alex leaned over, put his hands under her arms, and then lifted her up and over the table. "Get him quick, okay?"

She nodded as she reached for the bird. Shiner Bock was faster though. He flapped his wings and awkwardly sailed from the table to where Zeb sat at the bar. Zeb backed away, knocking into the man behind him, who managed to spill an entire pitcher of beer.

The bartender wavered between making a grab for the bird and trying to stop the liquid from racing down the bar. The beer won. Alex's hands clenched into fists. What had he gotten himself into?

Zina handed him Izzy's drawing that still had shake dripping from the bottom. Then she snagged another towel from the edge of the bar.

Shiner Bock flapped his wings as he watched her approach, his beady eyes following her every move. As she reached for him, he hopped down the bar, racing past diners and those who were there to drink the stress of the day away. Zina almost had him, but then his claw landed in Zeb's side of refried beans and Shiner Bock paused to lick the food off his foot.

"Beans, beans, magic fruit," the bird squawked as he nibbled at his claw.

Zina stopped and glanced over her shoulder at Alex. As her gaze met his, she let out a laugh. The icy dread sliding through his veins warmed up a few degrees. He rounded the line of booths and with some silent hand gestures between them, they closed in on the unsuspecting bird.

The patrons manning the barstools scattered, leaving nothing between Alex and Shiner Bock but a few feet of hardwood flooring. Alex clucked his tongue, trying to get the bird's attention as Zina crept up behind him, her towel at the ready.

"Here, birdie." Alex kept his voice calm and steady, even as Zina closed the last few feet between them.

As the towel sailed over Shiner Bock's head, Zina wrapped her hands around him, capturing him in her grip. The customers clapped and the sound of silverware clinking on plates resumed. Alex breathed out a sigh of relief, grateful that the bird had been caught and a major crisis averted.

Frankie ran up to his side, the bag held out in front of her. "I'm sorry, Uncle Alex. Shiner Bock is scared of the dark and didn't want to stay in the bag."

He squatted down in front of her. "You can't bring animals into restaurants, honey."

"That's what Mom says. But she's not here so I thought maybe you would say it's okay." She put her hands to her cheeks.

"We'll talk about it when we get home." He took the bag from her and met Zina at the bar, where she cradled a quiet Shiner Bock against her chest. "Thanks for pitching in."

"Are you okay?" Her gaze flickered over him.

"Yeah, I'm fine." He opened the bag and waited while she settled the bird inside. "Just a minor setback. All's well."

"You sure?" She narrowed her eyes like she didn't believe him.

Why did it seem like people were always second-guessing him? A prickle of annoyance zipped along his spine. "Yes. Why do you ask?"

"Well"—she glanced down to where Shiner Bock adjusted his position in the bag—"you're here to take care of penguins, but you don't seem to have much of a way with birds."

He fought the urge to shoot her a certain kind of bird. But hell, she was right. "I guarantee you, I'm better at handling wildlife than the domesticated kind."

Zina grinned as she nudged her chin toward the table where his nieces squabbled. "For your sake, I sure hope so."

nine

Zina turned away from Alex and made her way back to the bar. So she'd questioned his ability to work with birds. It seemed only natural to wonder about his experience when he couldn't even manage a domesticated parrot. If he was that unsure of himself around a pet, how would he be able to handle the wild penguins Lacey was hell-bent on bringing to town? Did he even have experience with penguins at all?

He'd given Lacey some story about how he'd been working at a remote research station in Antarctica of all places. Could be he'd made the whole thing up so he could make a few quick bucks. Based on how he handled the bird, he probably didn't have much hands-on experience with penguins or any other kind of mammal.

"Well that was exciting," Zina said as she settled onto her barstool. "You weren't planning on finishing those nachos, were you?"

Zeb glanced down to where a trail of beans led from the plate to the platter sitting next to him. "Um, no."

"You ready to go? We might want to get out of here before they blame us for the bird disturbance."

"Sure." Zeb drained his tea.

She slid some cash across the bar to cover their meals. By the time she'd shrugged on her jacket and followed Zeb out to the parking lot, Alex was getting the brood of kids he'd brought with him all buckled into their seats. She hesitated, not wanting to have to walk past his truck, but it sat right next to hers. Finally, she let out a sigh. Since when had she ever let some guy determine her actions?

Never.

So with a little extra bounce in her step, she crossed the gravel lot. He looked up as she got closer. The resignation on his face mirrored the way she felt inside. Not nearly enough time had passed since their last interaction.

"Got everyone squared away?" she asked as she pressed the unlock button on her key fob.

"Yep. They were kind enough to box up our order for us. We're going to fly away home now. That's probably the last time you'll be seeing any member of my family roosting around here."

"That's too bad. I hear they have all-you-can-eat wings on Fridays."

He stared at her like he wasn't sure if she was joking or not. That's what her weird sense of humor often got her—people who didn't know what to make of her. "It's a joke. A bad joke. Get it? Wings because you had trouble containing your bird?"

He scoffed but his smile told her he could appreciate her sense of humor. "I didn't have trouble. Shiner Bock just had ideas of his own."

"You named your bird Shiner Bock?"

"You got a problem with that?" He clamped his hands on his hips. She might not be interested in looking at every single man as a possible mate, but even she had to admit she didn't mind checking him out. It was impossible not to.

Tousled hair the color of the sand on the Galveston coast. His eyes hovered between blue and green, going from the color of turquoise in the bracelet her mom had left her to a much darker blue color like the fields of bluebonnets that lined the highways in the spring.

"No, no problem. Just an odd choice, that's all."

"I'm sure you've named some of your rescue mutts some odd names now and then." He leaned his backside against the truck and she almost let herself get sucked into the flirtatious undercurrent that seemed to pull at her.

"Nope. We don't typically name our rescue pups after alcoholic beverages."

"That's too bad. You could have had a Fireball or maybe even a Cosmo."

"Oh, we do have a Cosmo but he's named after a TV character."

"Let me guess. Kramer? On *Seinfeld*?"

"Yeah. Are you a fan?" She had the complete series on DVD at home. It was one her brother liked to watch over and over again.

"Of course. No soup for you."

"Right. The soup episode."

"It's a classic. So what other shows do you like?"

Zina shook off the warning that she probably should stop sharing tidbits of her personal life. Alex had a way about him that made people feel comfortable, made them let down their guard. But instead of backing away, she leaned into it.

"I'm a closet fan of *Gilmore Girls*."

His lips twisted and his brow crinkled. "Can't say I've seen that one."

Common ground. Hmm. What dude shows had she seen recently? "How about reality TV? The ninja warrior show?"

"Oh, I love that one. Even thought about trying out sometime."

"You have?"

"Yeah. Does that surprise you?"

She nodded. "Most guys with your, um"—she let her gaze travel up and down his full six-foot-plus frame—"build don't seem to do very well."

His eyes sparked. "What's wrong with my build?"

Now she'd done it. That's why she didn't make a habit of talking to strangers. Especially good-looking, quick-witted guys who never seemed to have any trouble twisting her words around and getting her to sound like a complete and utter idiot. "There's nothing wrong with your build. It's just that—"

"I get it. The guys who win those competitions aren't quite so bulky. It's too bad I'm cursed."

Zina's mouth went dry. If being cursed meant he was built like a Chippendales dancer, then she wished with all her might she'd get infected by the feminine version of the same curse at some point in her life.

"Uncle Alex, Frankie's letting Shiner Bock out of the bag." Izzy leaned out the window.

"Coming." Alex turned back to face Zina, his eyes crinkling up at the corners. "I need to get going."

"Uncle Alex is in charge tonight, huh?"

"Yeah." He hooked a thumb toward the truck. "Sorry, I didn't have a chance to properly introduce you. Zina, meet Jordan, Frankie, Izzy, Dolly, and Gramps."

The older man stuck his arm out of the passenger window and waved. "Mortimer Sanders, but you can call me Morty."

Zina nodded. "Nice to meet you all."

Alex glanced from his grandfather back to her. "Will I see you around the warehouse tomorrow? The contractor's coming back to take some measurements and start putting together a plan for the temporary habitat."

"Where else would I be? Thanks to Lacey I'm running

point on the Munyon wedding and thanks to you, all of my dogs are living there right now."

Alex shook his head and then let it drop. "Why do I get the feeling you don't like me very much?"

"What?" Zina wasn't used to being the recipient of such direct questions. At least not since she'd come back to Ido. The military was full of people who didn't bother pussyfooting around, but since she'd moved back she'd been subject to the passive aggressiveness of well-meaning small-town residents. The sheer directness of his question made her do a double take. "What gives you that impression?"

"Gut instinct."

Her gaze traveled to his lean midsection. He was probably hiding a six-pack underneath his thermal shirt. Maybe even a twelve-pack. For a split second she wondered just how firm his abs would feel under her palms. Their brief kiss earlier hadn't given her enough time to find out. Suddenly, hot prickles flooded her cheeks.

"Look, it's not that I don't like you." She plastered a practiced look of sheer indifference on her face. "I barely know you. I'm just looking out for Lacey, and I don't want her to get burned."

"You don't think I'm legit?" He cocked a brow. Probably a look he'd used all his life. The kind of look that made women's panties melt and bras fall off and led to hours of sweaty aerobic activity that ended with another notch in his bedpost.

Zina squashed down the immediate attraction and focused her thoughts on Lacey. Trusting, naive Lacey, who believed everyone had a vested interest in seeing her plan succeed. But Zina knew that most people only wanted to participate in someone else's success as long as they benefited as well. And that's why she was leery of Alex Sanders.

"I need to go and you obviously have more important

things to do than stand here and try to convince me of your honorable intentions." She turned to walk the last few feet to her truck.

Alex reached for her arm. Heat radiated from his touch, even through the sleeve of her shirt. She looked at his fingers wrapping around her forearm.

He immediately released his grip. "Sorry. I just want you to know that I'm not looking to mess with Lacey. This offer was too good to pass over. I'll be around long enough to get through the wedding, then I'll head out. In fact, I just heard about a job at a resort down in Ecuador that sounds promising."

"Mm-hmm." Zina scowled as she reached for the handle of her door.

"You'll see." Alex gave her another grin, a toned-down version of his last smile.

She'd see. That's the one thing she knew for sure. She'd see because she'd be watching him like a freaking hawk.

"Uncle Alex, we still have to finish my project you ruined." One of the girls stuck her head out of the window.

"You don't happen to know where I can get a piece of poster board, do you?" His shoulders slumped. "I accidentally used Izzy's project as a dustpan. Her mom's at work until late, and if she doesn't get her project turned in tomorrow, she gets an orange tag."

"A red tag, Uncle Alex. There's no such thing as an orange tag at my school."

"See?" He shrugged his shoulders. "I can't even keep my colors straight."

Against her better judgment, Zina let down her guard. "What does she have to do?"

"Draw the life cycle of a couple of things. A butterfly, and maybe a tree." He shifted his keys from one hand to the other. "We'll figure it out."

Zina glanced toward the passenger seat of her truck,

where Zeb sat adjusting his earbuds. "You know what? Zeb is an excellent artist. I could ask him if he's willing to help."

"Really?" Alex's eyes sparkled. "You sure it wouldn't be too much trouble?"

She should make up an excuse. No good would come of spending more time with him. He'd just admitted he was only sticking around through the wedding. It wouldn't make sense to put herself out there or let herself get attached. But instead of retracting the offer, she matched his smile.

"Sure, let me ask him."

"How did you learn how to draw?" Izzy sat next to Zeb at Char's kitchen table, trying to copy the swift, sure strokes of his pencil as he sketched out a very detailed monarch butterfly.

"I taught myself. Lots of practice." Zeb's forehead furrowed in concentration.

"Why don't you give him some space?" Alex suggested.

Zina's hand landed on his arm. "He's fine. He'll let her know if she starts to bother him, won't you, Zeb?"

"Yep, sure will."

Zeb had already sketched out the first four stages of a butterfly's life cycle before the girls had finished their takeout. Inviting him and Zina back to the house had been a brilliant idea. Not only would Izzy get her project done in time, but Alex would get a chance to spend some more time with Zina.

"Everyone done with dinner?" Alex reached for the paper wrappers from the burgers and empty french fry containers his nieces had left at the table.

"Let me help with that." Zina picked up cups and crinkled napkins. "Trash under the sink?"

"Thanks." He held the cabinet door open for her. "I need

to make sure Frankie put the bird back in his cage. I'll be back in a sec."

Zina nodded as he turned. She'd never get tired of watching him walk away, not with the way his backside filled out a pair of jeans. She waited until he'd disappeared into one of the doors at the end of the hall, and then wandered after him, wanting to check out the dozens of family pictures decorating the walls.

She recognized his sister in several of them, along with a younger version of Alex. He still had the same dimple on his left cheek but his eyes weren't nearly as bright now as they were in the faded photos from his youth.

"That's my son, Charlene and Alex's father." Alex's grandfather stood behind her, pointing a shaky finger at the large family photo she'd been looking at. "You know what it's like to lose a child?"

Zina shook her head. "I can't imagine."

"Sucks the life right out of you. Dragged my wife to an early grave." He lowered his hand. "Here they are at Disney World. Took us two days to drive to Florida but it was worth it for the smiles on those kids' faces."

"You have a beautiful family," Zina said.

"Doesn't feel much like a family anymore. Charlene doesn't have time to catch her breath, and Alex can't seem to run far enough or fast enough to get away." He shook his head.

"You're not giving away all the family secrets, are you, Gramps?" Alex joined them, a smile making that damn dimple pop.

"He's just showing me how cute you used to be." Zina turned her attention back to the photos on the wall. A small photograph of a young boy in his underwear with a cape flung over his shoulders caught her eye. "Is this you?"

Alex glanced at the picture, his cheeks flushing just the slightest shade of pink. "No, that can't be me."

"It sure as hell is you." Morty lifted the frame off the

wall and passed it to Zina. "He used to run around naked with nothing on but that cape. Called himself Captain Jaybird."

Zina pressed a hand to her lips to try to keep from laughing. "That's adorable."

"Hey, I was like four in that picture."

"You must have been pretty tall for a four-year-old." Zina tapped on the glass. "You sure you weren't older than that?"

"Maybe six." Alex's eyes shifted away from the picture.

"Boy hated to wear clothes. He was naked all the time." Morty raised a brow. "I'm pretty sure you were about ten here. Your grandmother had to wrestle you into a pair of briefs or you would have had the neighbor girls running away screaming."

Zina could only imagine what grown-up Alex might look like in a pair of skimpy briefs. The mere thought made her heart pound and her cheeks heat. There was no way he'd send women screaming at the sight of his naked ass now unless they were running toward him.

"Give me that." He grinned and reached for the picture.

Zina held it behind her back.

"I'm going to go lie down." Morty ambled down the hall, leaving the two of them alone.

"You sure you're up for wrestling?" Alex stood in front of her, a smug grin on his face.

"You want it, come and get it." Zina backed down the hall, the picture clenched in her hands.

His arms circled her, drawing her against his chest as his fingers fumbled to free the frame from her grasp. "That can't be me. It's probably a picture of my brother-in-law when he was a kid."

"So you're denying you liked to run around naked?"

"I wasn't naked, I had on a cape." He backed her up, sandwiching her between the wall and the concrete planes of his chest.

"So the picture is of you." Zina bit her lip, trying not to laugh right into his face.

"What if it is?" His gaze dipped to her lips. "It's not like I still run around with my ass hanging out, pretending to be something I'm not."

The tone shifted. They'd started off teasing, playful, but there seemed to be a lot more meaning to his words now.

"What do you mean 'something you're not'?" she asked.

"Nothing. Can I have the picture back?"

She let her arm drop to her side, her fingers still holding the frame. There wasn't room between them for a sheet of paper, much less a picture frame. "You know, not all superheroes have to wear a cape."

One side of his mouth quirked up in a half-hearted grin. "And not all little boys outgrow wanting to run around naked. At least not if they're in the right company."

Her eyes widened even as heat sparked in her core. Kissing the man on the side of the road in a moment of weakness was one thing. But letting herself take the bait he offered now would be a huge mistake.

"I'd better get going." She dragged her gaze away from his mouth.

"Mm-hmm." His hand closed around the picture and he took it from her. "A lot of people around here seem to think you're like a local superhero."

Zina scooted a few inches away, her back still up against the wall. "Anyone who says that is either drunk, crazy, or lying."

He didn't respond right away. Just stood there grinning at her. "See you tomorrow?"

"Tomorrow," she whispered, still caught up in the intoxicating feeling of being too close to him. If she wanted to, she could reach up and press her lips against the little divot at the base of his throat, the place where his heartbeat pulsed.

He lowered his head toward hers and pressed his lips

against her cheek, the contact too fleeting, not nearly enough to satisfy the building desire. "I've got to go get the girls to bed."

She jerked her head away, shaking off the haze. "Yeah. I need to get Zeb home. I've got another early morning tomorrow."

"Maybe we can talk about my underwear then if you really want to."

Zina laughed. "You're something else, you know that?"

But as she drifted down the hall, her thoughts still lingering on Alex and just what he might look like in nothing but a cape, she wondered if something else might be just what she was in the mood for. If something else might be just what she needed.

ten

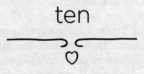

The next morning Alex woke to the sound of a siren. He startled, jumping up from the air mattress Char had blown up and set in the middle of the living room. He'd been displaced from his short stay in the back bedroom when Gramps moved in. He grabbed his jeans and stuffed in one leg, then the other. Was it an ambulance? Surely Char would have woken him up if something happened to one of the girls.

As he pulled his T-shirt on over his head, Frankie came into the room. "There you are."

"What's happening? Is everyone okay?" Alex rushed to his niece, who calmly took a bite of a banana as she stood at the foot of his makeshift bed.

"Yeah. Mom said to wake you up so I sent Shiner Bock in to do the job."

Alex glanced to his right. The damn bird sat on top of the credenza, shaking his head and plucking at his feathers. "You're kidding me."

Frankie shook her head. "He can make all kinds of

noises. Watch this." She held a small piece of banana out to the bird. "Shiner, cry like a baby."

The bird bobbed his head and then began to wail. Alex would have sworn there was a newborn infant somewhere in the house.

"See?" Frankie held her finger out to the bird, who took a delicate nibble of the banana.

"I see. Is there a way to turn him off?"

Frankie's brow drew down over her eyes, making her little forehead crease. "He's a bird, Uncle Alex."

"Yeah, I know." He reached out and pulled his niece in for a hug. "What time is it, anyway?"

Frankie shrugged her shoulders as she twirled away. "Time to go to school. Mom says we're leaving in five minutes."

"Okay, thanks."

She reached for the bird, who climbed onto her hand and then waddled up her arm to rest on her shoulder. "Jordan made waffles. Mom says you better come and get some before Dolly feeds them to her stuffed animals."

"Be there in a sec." He waited for her to disappear through the doorway before reaching for his phone.

The contractor had confirmed their meeting for this morning. He didn't have any time to waste if he wanted to get the penguin habitat constructed in time for the wedding. For a moment his thoughts wandered to his interaction with Zina last night. She was like the pit bulls she rescued— tough and protective of the ones she loved.

The fact she was suspicious of his motives rankled him a bit. It shouldn't matter what she thought. He was going to be stressed enough as it was without any outside interference. But he'd made it this far in life by winning people over. He'd just have to work a little harder to gain her trust.

"I heard there were waffles." He entered the kitchen to find the aftermath of an explosion of flour all over the kitchen counters. His jacket hung on the back of the chair he'd used last night. Somehow it had also suffered the wrath of whoever had taken out their aggression by making breakfast.

"We had a little accident with the baking mix," Char said.

"Really? Who's responsible? I think someone deserves to be tickle tortured for that." Alex held his hands up and wiggled his fingers.

"It was Jordan." Dolly giggled and pointed her wand at her older sister.

"Don't even think about it, Uncle Alex." Jordan jerked the spatula out of the bowl, sending a glob of raw waffle batter right at his shirt.

The batter splattered against his chest and then plopped onto the floor. Alex glanced from his shirt to Jordan, whose eyes had gone wide.

"Sorry about that." She thrust the spatula back in the bowl.

"No problem, kiddo. What's a little salmonella poisoning among family members," he joked.

"Coffee's on. Mugs are in the cabinet in front of you. It's the only way I survive." Char tossed him a towel and offered a sympathetic smile.

He grinned back. Then Dolly pushed past him, her plate tipping just enough to spill syrup down the front of his pants. He jumped backward, knocking over the pitcher of orange juice. It raced across the counter, dousing his notebook in liquid.

"For fuck's sake."

"For fuck's sake. For fuck's sake," the bird mocked him.

"Oooh, Uncle Alex is going to get a consequence." Izzy covered her mouth with her hand.

Silence descended. The only noise came from Jordan's phone in the form of a video she'd been watching while she monitored the waffle iron.

"Alex, can I talk to you?" Char turned away from where she'd been packing lunch boxes. "In the living room?"

He glanced from Jordan to Frankie. They both looked away. Izzy shook her head and Dolly clucked her tongue. He was a grown man. Why did he suddenly feel like he was about to get grounded by his sister?

Char moved down the hall and stopped inside the living room. "What's going on?"

He slid his hand over his shirt. "I'm covered in breakfast. Is it always like this around here?"

"Yeah, it pretty much is." Her shoulders slumped. "Which is why I can't have Gramps moving in, too."

He wanted to offer some sort of comfort but wasn't sure how. "We'll figure something out. Once I get paid from this gig, I'll have plenty to pitch in and find Gramps a new place to go."

"How did we end up here?" Char lifted her head. Her lower lids brimmed with tears.

A hollow feeling grew in his gut. While she'd been trying to make a life for herself and her family, he'd been partying around the world. Tossing back beers at the Hofbräuhaus in Munich, watching the gals put on a show at the Moulin Rouge, and doing his best to single-handedly support the economy of several islands in the South Pacific.

"We're going to make this work." He reached out and put a hand on his sister's shoulder.

"Since when? You're only going to be here long enough to cash in and then you'll be off again on another adventure." She shrugged his hand away and ran a finger under her eye, wiping away any hint of emotion.

"I'm sorry. I wish I could have been here for you more."

"You don't mean that." She leveled him with a direct gaze. "You've never been able to stay in one place."

His cheeks tingled. He knew she'd been struggling. He'd known it for a while. Every time they chatted via video, he'd get an idea of just how busy her life was. But when he'd been on the other side of the world, it had been easy to ignore. Char could handle anything. She was the strong, stable one. He was the one who took the party with him wherever he went. He'd never grown roots, never wanted to, not the kind that Char had put down.

"I'm here now."

"Yeah, but for how long? I can manage the four kids, the husband who's never home, working two jobs to try to keep groceries on the table. The choices Dave and I have made have led us to where we are and we'll deal with that."

He nodded.

"But I can't take on Gramps all by myself."

"I'm here to help. I won't leave until we find a solution. One that works for both of you."

"And watch your language."

"I'll try. I'm not used to being around impressionable ears but I'll do my best." He glanced down at his clothes. "Now I've got to change before I go meet with the contractor. Can I do anything to help you get out the door this morning?"

"Actually"—Char bit her lower lip—"Dolly's day care provider canceled for today and my calendar is packed at work. Think she can hang with you?"

"What, like all day?"

"Yeah. She only has preschool three days a week and goes to day care the rest. But there's some virus sweeping through and I could really use a hand."

Alex swallowed the no that tried to squeeze past his lips. "Yeah, of course. I'd be happy to watch her."

"Great. Thanks." Char leaned over and pressed a quick kiss to his cheek. "I'll make sure she and Gramps are ready to go."

"Wait. Where's Gramps going today?"

Char stopped in the doorway and turned around real slow. "With you. He can't stay here on his own all day. My house can't take it. Last night I caught him trying to order pay-per-view."

"Okay, Gramps, too." It was going to be a real party

trying to get work done with a multigenerational audience today, but that's what he'd signed up for.

"You're a lifesaver."

He didn't feel like a lifesaver. He felt like a life ring, bobbing around in the ocean trying to stay afloat until someone bigger and braver came by to take over. But he'd promised to pitch in, so he vowed to make the best of it.

Twenty minutes later he'd changed clothes, snagged a quick breakfast of lumpy waffles, and was ready to head out. Char had already left to take the three older girls to school and get to work.

"Dolly, Gramps, time to go." He'd tried drying his notebook with a hair dryer but the pages still stuck together. There had to be something else sitting around he could use. While he waited for his niece and his grandfather to turn off the TV in the other room, he pulled open one drawer after another, looking for something he could write on.

"I'm ready, Uncle Alex." Dolly skipped into the room, her plastic dress-up heels clunking along the floor.

"Oh, sweetheart, we're going to a warehouse today. Why don't you run back to your room and change?"

Her lower lip jutted out. "But I want to wear my princess dress."

He checked his watch. They were short on time but if she hurried, they wouldn't be late. "I just don't want you to get dirty. Warehouses can be a tricky place for princesses, you know."

Dolly's brow furrowed as she whirled around and stomped out of the kitchen.

"Gramps!" Alex opened the last drawer. He scooped up a pen and notebook and shoved them into his bag.

Gramps shuffled into the kitchen. "I'd rather stay home."

Alex shook his head. "Not gonna happen. Char said you need to be supervised today."

"I pressed the wrong button last night. Thought I was getting that new Bourne movie."

"You can tell that to Char later. Right now I need you to get it in gear or I'm going to be late."

Gramps frowned and muttered to himself as he moved toward the hall closet. Alex checked his watch again. He needed to start this project off on the right foot.

"Dolly! Come on, hon. We've got to go."

She clomped down the hall in some sort of footwear that was too heavy to be the plastic princess shoes. As she entered the kitchen, his head felt like it might explode.

"I'm ready, Uncle Alex." The voice sounded like his adorable niece, but the creature it came from didn't look anything like the four-year-old he'd sent back to change a few minutes ago.

"What the hell did you do to yourself?" His heart skipped a beat, then another as he took in her makeover. She'd wrapped herself in toilet paper from head to toe. All except for her face, which peeped out from the white shroud.

"What the hell. What the hell." Why did the damn bird only repeat swear words? That was a question for another day. Right now he needed to get Dolly cleaned up and out the door.

"Now I won't get dirty."

"Come on, we'll unwrap you as we go." He grabbed her under his arm and swept her out the door behind Gramps, the bird squawking as they slammed the door.

Zina checked her watch again. The contractor Alex hired to start work on the penguin habitat had been pacing for the past fifteen minutes. If Alex didn't show up soon, she'd have to lock up and tell him to reschedule. She had quite a few errands to run before heading to Lacey's for their meeting. As if the whole idea of creating a wedding around penguins wasn't ridiculous enough. The least Alex could do was be considerate of her time. It's not like she was on board with this stupid idea to begin with. Any lingering warm feelings toward him had faded the longer she stood there waiting for him to arrive.

She was about to start turning off lights, when a vehicle pulled into the gravel parking lot. Finally. Alex deserved an ass chewing for keeping her waiting this long. She opened her mouth, ready to deliver when he entered the front door.

"Where the hell have you been?" she asked, ready to meet his gaze with a glare of her own.

Instead, a child walked in. Barely three feet tall and wearing some sort of shredded toilet paper gown with thick-soled boots, the girl opened her eyes wide.

Alex appeared behind her. "Language, please."

Zina startled. She didn't like being caught off guard, especially when her mood had gone sour from waiting so long.

The contractor thrust his hand at Alex. "Good to see you again."

Alex gave Zina a smug grin as he took Toby's hand. "Thanks for meeting me out here. I'm sorry I'm late. We had a wardrobe issue."

"My daughter's got a mind of her own also, so I completely understand."

Zina crossed her arms over her chest, ready to interrupt the moment of male bonding. "Should we check out the back?"

"Let's do it." Alex walked ahead of them, leading the way with his hand on his niece's shoulder. "Dolly and I are eager to put some plans in place, aren't we?"

The girl nodded. "Uncle Alex says I can pet the penguins when they move in and help feed them."

Zina rolled her eyes. Who else would want to feed the penguins? Ido had already turned into a tourist mecca with all the weddings. What kind of crazy visitors would a penguin habitat bring in? She'd have to talk to Lacey about that. Maybe they could keep it on the down low until they got closer to the wedding.

"Gramps, you want to wait out here or come to the back with us?" Alex asked.

"I'll wait here." Morty slumped into a chair and set his chin in his hands.

"Suit yourself." Alex opened the door to the warehouse. "Shall we?"

Zina followed the small group into the cavernous space. She didn't know exactly how big it was but Lacey had said they could fit a regulation-sized football field inside, so there was plenty of room for whatever half-baked idea Alex might come up with. She stood to the side while he counted off steps.

"I figured we can bring in a temporary dome. That way we don't have to insulate the entire space. We'll need to keep the temperature regulated for the penguins."

"Of course." Townsend jotted down a few notes.

While the men volleyed ideas back and forth, Zina's gaze wandered around the warehouse. They'd moved all of the shelving to one side, so the vast majority of the space was open, making it seem even larger than it probably was.

Dolly spun and danced in a wide circle around them, her shoes thunking on the concrete floors. Zina remembered her from the restaurant last night. She'd been dressed in sparkles and a tutu then. "I like your shoes."

"Thanks." Dolly spiraled closer. "Uncle Alex said I would get dirty here, so I wrapped up."

Zina stifled a giggle. So that's why the kid was outfitted in layer upon layer of toilet paper. "Don't you have a jacket or something you could have put on instead?"

Dolly stopped spinning and wobbled slightly. Zina put her arm out to keep the girl from falling over. "If I wore a robe, you wouldn't be able to see my sparkles."

"I suppose you're right."

"Do you like sparkles?"

Zina thought for a moment. "Yeah, I like some sparkles from time to time." The truth was, she'd rather dress in camo than adorn herself with glitter and jewels. But Dolly obviously preferred to shine, and Zina would never take away someone's right to sparkle.

"Mama says I'm obnextus."

"Obnoxious?"

"Yeah, that's what she says. But Daddy likes it. He says I'm his little princess."

"I'm sure your daddy's right." Zina smiled at the girl. She'd felt like her daddy's little princess once upon a time. The memory made her stomach twist. She missed her dad, especially in moments like this when she was reminded of the special bond between a dad and his little girl. She'd been a daddy's girl from the beginning. That's why she'd gone into the military in the first place—to follow in her father's footsteps. But when Zeb came home a damaged shell of the eager eighteen-year-old who'd gone off to serve his country, her dad hadn't been able to handle it. He'd taken a civilian assignment on the other side of the world, and Zina hadn't heard from him in over a year.

"Uncle Alex says you have puppies here. Can I meet one?" Dolly glanced up at her.

"Sure, but one at a time. They get pretty crazy when they have visitors." That was an understatement. So many of the pitties at the rescue had such little socialization with people, especially kids, that they went absolutely crazy with excitement when exposed to a new person. Most of the animals had acclimated to having her around, but new dogs came into the shelter just about every day and there was no way to predict which ones might be used to kids and which ones needed to stay separate.

"Daddy said we could get a dog someday when he's home all the time."

"Oh?" Zina asked. "Where's your daddy now?"

Dolly twirled, making the toilet paper flop up and down. "He's in Ganistan. Mommy says it's far, far away."

"Afghanistan?"

The girl's forehead wrinkled. "I think so."

"Yeah, that is far away. I went there once."

"Is there lots of sand?"

Zina chuckled, immediately taken back to where the sand blew across her face all day, finding its way into cracks and crevices she didn't even know she had. "Yeah, there's lots of sand."

"Like at the beach? I like the beach."

"Not quite like at the beach." The beach had the ocean, where you could take a quick dip and wash off the hot stickiness of the day. The sand in the Middle East was relentless. It found its way into her hair, her nose, and the cracks between her toes. No matter how many times she rinsed off, she'd still find it everywhere. Not to mention how many pounds of sand she probably ate since it seemed to coat everything at camp, including the food.

"Who would you like to meet first?"

"Do you have any puppies?" Dolly asked.

Zina mentally raced through the dogs in residence. "Not really. We don't get a ton of puppies unless one of the mama dogs we rescue is pregnant."

"That's too bad. I love puppies."

"Yeah, they're super cute. I do have a dog that just came in who's about six months old. That's kind of still a puppy. Would you like to meet her?"

"Yes, please." Dolly took her hand, her tiny fingers wrapping around Zina's, making her feel a strange sense of protectiveness inside.

Danger zone. Zina wasn't used to caring for small children. Big children, either. She hadn't spent too much time around kids at all. Maybe entertaining Alex's niece for a few minutes would be good for her. It would give her a heads-up on what it might be like when Lacey and Bodie delivered their little bundle of joy.

Zina led Dolly into the back section of the warehouse. "They're going to bark a lot when we go in. Not because they're mad or anything. They just get excited when they get visitors."

Dolly nodded as she pulled her hand away and covered her ears.

"You ready?"

The little girl smiled up at her. "Yep."

"Here we go." Zina stepped past the shelves. A chorus of barks and yips erupted. Tails wagged and dogs came to the front of their kennels, hoping for a treat or a chance to head outside and play with their friends.

Zina smiled at the volunteers who'd come to help the dogs settle in as she led Dolly toward the space they'd designated for the younger dogs. Sometimes the older pups got too wild with the smaller ones, so they kept them separated until they put on enough bulk to handle themselves.

She stopped in front of the kennel of a female who'd been brought in the previous week. The pup had passed the health exam but was a little shy around strangers so needed to be socialized a bit more before she'd be eligible for adoption.

"What's her name?" Dolly asked.

Zina checked the tag on the front of the kennel. "Looks like they haven't given her one yet. Would you like to name her?"

Dolly's eyes lit up. "Oh, yes, please!"

"Great. Let me get her out so you can get to know each other better." The door to the kennel swung open and the pup took a few tentative steps toward them, her tag wagging. Zina slipped a leash over her head and led them outside.

"Can I pet her?" Dolly asked.

"Of course. Just let her sniff your hand first so she can get to know you."

Dolly held her hand out toward the pup, who took a few shaky steps forward. She sniffed at Dolly's hand, then her tongue swept out of her mouth and covered Dolly's fingers. The little girl giggled. "Oh, that tickles."

Zina didn't try to hold back her own laughter. "She likes you."

"I like her, too. Can we call her a princess name?"

"Sure." Not particularly partial to sparkles and glitter herself, Zina wasn't sure what constituted a princess name but if Dolly wanted to come up with something, that would be fine with her. She'd run out of dog names a long time ago. Every time she had to give one of the rescue pups a name, it made her just a little sad to think of how many dogs she'd had to find names for over the years. And now, with the shelter in need of repair, she might have to stop taking in new ones until they could fix the roof.

"How about Aurora?" Dolly asked.

"Oooh, that's a nice choice." Sounded a little fancy for the gray-and-white pittie who stood in front of them. But if it made Dolly happy, then Aurora it would be. "Want to walk her around a bit and let her get some exercise?"

Dolly clapped her hands together. "Oh yes."

Zina's heart lightened a little at the enthusiasm in Dolly's smile. Had she ever been that young, that bright, that full of happiness? Probably at some point. Before her mom passed and she had to grow up overnight and take on her brother's care. Would she have grown up to be so naive about the responsibilities of the world if she'd never had to fill in for her parents?

Dolly raced ahead. "This way?"

Zina held Aurora's leash. "No, let's go around back where there's plenty of grass."

Dolly followed, skipping along like she didn't have a care in the world.

For a moment Zina envied the little girl. But then she screwed a stake into the ground and clipped the tie out to Aurora's collar. The dog raced around the yard, excited to have some freedom. Dolly ran after her, two girls at play even though Aurora lapped the little girl.

After several minutes of running, Dolly collapsed against Zina, her breath huffing in and out. "That was fun."

"I'm glad you enjoyed it. Should we go inside and check on your uncle?"

Dolly looked up at her. "Can Aurora come, too?"

"Of course. She deserves a little fun time out of her kennel. Let's go find her some treats and we can see if she knows any tricks yet."

"Where did she come from?" Dolly asked. "Did her mommy and daddy not want her?"

"Oh, it's not that way with dogs. She probably got adopted into a house that didn't realize how big she'd get or how much energy she'd have." That was the typical reason most of the dogs were abandoned. Pit bulls were a fantastic breed for people who knew how to handle their curiosity and boundless energy. But so many dog owners didn't appreciate the amount of exercise they'd need and she found herself with more dogs than she could handle. And that didn't count the number of poor animals they'd found abandoned—the ones who'd most likely been part of the dog-fighting ring Bodie was trying to end.

But all of those points were way over Dolly's little head. So Zina took her by the hand and led her back inside the front office of the warehouse in search of some dog treats.

A few minutes later, Alex came through the door and interrupted their impromptu training session with Aurora. "I think we've got a tentative plan. Want me to fill you in?"

"Sure."

"Gramps, can you keep an eye on Dolly while I show Zina our plans?"

Morty took the bag of treats and waved them on.

"Thanks." Alex held the door for her and they walked back into the warehouse. "So we'll bring in a temporary dome. That way we're not trying to refrigerate such a big space."

"How big of a dome are we talking?"

"Just big enough for an ice feature and the pool."

Zina bit back a laugh. "An ice feature?"

"Yeah. They'll need something familiar to keep them cool. Nothing too dramatic. We'll make some snow and—"

"This is ridiculous. You know it's going to cost you a fortune to keep the snow from melting."

"I don't think it'll be a problem," Townsend said. "My team's handled stuff like this before. We did a whole snow globe feature for a Christmas in July event in Dallas a few years ago."

"Fine. So snow and ice aren't an issue. What about this pool? Where are you going to set that up? Are we talking kiddie pool, or—"

"Salt water, of course." Alex grinned—the kind of grin he might give a child if he were trying to explain some complicated issue.

"Of course." Zina shook her head. "How much is all of this going to cost?"

"Don't worry about expenses. Mr. Munyon made it perfectly clear he's more than willing to pay for whatever it takes to give his daughter the perfect winter wonderland wedding of her dreams."

Zina gritted her teeth to prevent from saying something she might regret. She was there for Lacey, not to try to get everyone to realize what a waste of time, money, and energy this was. How many pups could she house for the amount of money Mr. Munyon was willing to throw away to rent a dome for a couple of months? She could probably redo the whole roof for what he was spending on renting the warehouse alone. The thought made her sick to her stomach.

"I'll work up a proposal and get it over to you by the end of the day tomorrow," Townsend said.

"That sounds great. We're in a time crunch so the sooner the better." Alex shook the man's hand again.

Zina swallowed the bubble of apprehension rising in her throat. How had Lacey and Alex talked her into this? The voice of reason had never mattered much to her friend, not when she was focused on something she thought was important. Zina agreed that something had to be done to save the economy of the town, but why did it have to be weddings? Couldn't they have come up with something else instead? Something with less sparkle, less wasteful disregard for tossing money aside, and maybe a more altruistic goal?

A loud crash came from the front of the building, followed by the sound of someone stumbling through the door.

"Uncle Alex! Gramps fell down!" Dolly shrieked from the doorway.

eleven

◡

Gramps lay on the floor of the office. "Dammit, help me up."

"What happened?" Alex stopped and squatted next to the older man. "Are you okay?"

"I'm fine. Just wanted to get a closer look at that picture over there." He nodded toward a black-and-white photograph hanging on the wall by the door.

"You've got to be more careful, Gramps."

"I know." He took the hand Alex offered and pulled himself to a seated position. "I ever tell you I used to work out here?"

"No." Alex shook his head as he helped his grandfather to his feet. "When was that?"

"Too long ago to remember. I was there when they took that photo though. Right around the time I married your grandmother. Wanted to see if I could find myself in it. Those were better times."

A mixture of hopelessness and resignation laced through

his grandfather's voice. Char was right. Gramps needed a new cause, something to get him excited about the time he still had ahead of him. Right now he seemed so caught up in the past.

Alex reached up and pulled the picture from the wall. The sun had taken its toll on the faded black-and-white photo.

"Here you go. Can you find yourself?"

Gramps studied the photo for a moment, his finger slowly moving over the nameless faces who peered up from long ago. "Here I am."

He pointed to a smiling man who stood tall and proud in the back row.

"That's you?" Alex squinted at the man who bore little resemblance to his grandfather.

"Hey, I used to be a real catch. How else do you think I got the attention of the most beautiful woman in the world?" He glanced up, his watery eyes making Alex think he was living more in the past than the present. "I'm talking about your grandmother, you know."

"I figured." Alex clamped a hand to his grandfather's shoulder. Gramps was the kind of man who needed a purpose. No wonder he'd been driving folks at the nursing home crazy. The poor man was probably bored out of his mind. "I've got an idea. How about helping me with this project?"

"What kind of help do you need? I don't know anything about penguins." Gramps handed the photo back.

"Maybe not, but you used to be pretty good with your hands. Didn't you build the ranch house by yourself?"

"That was a long time ago, son." Gramps hung his head.

Alex didn't like the slump of his shoulders or the defeat in his tone. "You still have all of your tools?"

Gramps shrugged. "You'd have to ask your sister about that. For all I know she sold all my stuff when she made me move into that first home."

Alex's stomach twisted. Gramps had worked construction for over fifty years. His tools were his life. Would Char really get rid of the one thing that might make their grandfather feel competent in his later years? "I'll ask her about it. If they're gone, I'll get you new ones."

"Don't bother. She did what she had to do at the time. Probably wouldn't have any use for them anymore anyway."

Alex cast a glance at Zina, who appeared to be studying the tips of her cowboy boots with renewed interest. "Well, I still need a hand. You in?"

Gramps lifted his shoulders in a resigned shrug. "Sure. It's not like I have anything better to do."

"I wanna help, too." Dolly skipped across the office. "What can I do, Uncle Alex?"

"Hmm." He tapped a finger against his lips. "Can you be in charge of decorating?"

"For the wedding?" Her eyes shone.

Oh hell, he better put a damper on that idea before Dolly jumped to conclusions that she'd be solely responsible for decorating the entire wedding venue. "I was thinking the penguin habitat. They'll probably be missing home, so if you could draw some pictures of snow and stuff, it would make them more comfortable."

"But snow is all white." Her lower lip threatened to jut out. "How can I draw snow?"

Zina stepped in. "Maybe you could cut some snowflakes out of paper."

"I don't know how. Mama doesn't let me use the scissors anymore."

"That's because you gave your sister a haircut in her sleep." Alex tucked a finger under her chin. "I bet she'd let you use scissors if I helped you."

"Do you know how to cut snowflakes?" She looked up at him, her blue eyes full of hope.

"Not exactly, but—"

"I do," Zina volunteered. "I'll help you cut snowflakes

and we can hang them from the ceiling of the dome. How does that sound?"

"Oh yay!" Dolly clapped her hands together. "Can we make them sparkly?"

"Of course."

"With glitter and diamonds?"

Zina laughed and met his gaze over the top of Dolly's head. "Well, glitter for sure but we'll have to see about the diamonds. I'm not sure Mr. Munyon's budget, generous as it might be, will be big enough to cover that."

Dolly took Zina's hand. "When can we do it? Now?"

"Maybe later," Alex said. So this was what it felt like to be a *buzzkill* all the time. "We've got to stop and check out some apartments on the way home."

"Aw, Uncle Alex, can't I stay and make snowflakes?" Dolly gave him her best puppy dog eyes.

He considered himself fairly immune to children but found himself melting under her pointed pout. "Not today. I've got an appointment with the manager at the Pecan Hollow Apartments."

"Oh, you don't want to stay there." Zina's lips pursed and she shook her head.

"Why not? The price is right."

"Yeah, if you don't mind sharing your apartment with cockroaches the size of rodents."

Dolly stepped back. "Gross."

"Fine." Alex pulled out his phone and deleted Pecan Hollow from his list. "I've still got two other options."

"Which ones?" Zina pressed.

"Doesn't matter. I need to find somewhere by the warehouse. I've got to be close to the penguins and"—he lowered his voice—"that damn parrot is driving me crazy."

Zina let out a laugh. The sound lifted his spirits just a tad. She *was* capable of laughter, good to know.

"There are plenty of cheap apartments over in Swynton," she suggested.

"That's too far. What if I have an emergency in the middle of the night?"

"A penguin emergency?"

"Yeah."

"Like what?" She cocked her head. "One of them drowns?"

He didn't like the attempt at humor. Not at the expense of the penguins. He had yet to meet them, but he already felt protective.

"For your information, it's impossible for penguins to drown." That ought to shut her down for a little while.

"What if they have a heart attack underwater?"

"Not likely."

"I don't get it. What kind of middle-of-the-night emergency might require you to rush in and save the flock?"

"It's a colony or a waddle, not a flock." If she was so insistent on mocking him, the least she could do was to get her vocabulary correct.

"Uncle Alex." Dolly tugged at his shirt.

"Just a second, sweetie. I'm talking to Miss Zina." He refocused his attention on the feisty woman in front of him. "I'm not worried about the penguins, I'm concerned about someone trying to break in and mess with them."

"Oh, gotcha. Lacey said she's got some state-of-the-art security setup around the house."

"Yeah, but that doesn't monitor the warehouse, does it?"

"Uncle Alex?" The persistent tugging on his shirt started to get to him. He wrapped his hand around Dolly's and gently pulled it away from his shirt. "I'd prefer to be close by. Do you have any other suggestions on where I should look?"

"I'll have to think about it," Zina said, a hint of a smile playing across her lips.

He focused on those lips for a moment. Full and ripe and begging to be kissed again.

"Uncle Alex?" Dolly pulled her hand away.

"What is it?" He finally looked down in time to see the toilet paper she'd wrapped herself in start to disintegrate.

"I had to go potty." She looked up at him, tears threatening to spill over her long, full lashes.

"I'm sorry, sweetie." His heart squeezed. To hell with it. Then he glanced to Zina. "Please tell me there's a bathroom nearby?"

"Of course. Let's go up to the house and get you cleaned up." Zina held out a hand for Dolly to take.

Alex sighed. Thank God she was here. He wouldn't know what to do with Dolly if he'd been on his own. He'd had plenty of experience around animals and their offspring, just not much experience around human kids.

"You coming?" Zina looked back at him over her shoulder. She moved toward the door, Dolly shuffling along beside her, leaving him no choice but to follow.

They crossed the drive and trekked toward the house. The Victorian-style three-story towered above them. They climbed the steps to the wraparound porch, their feet thumping on the wooden stairs. Alex paused, waiting for Gramps to catch up.

"Y'all go ahead inside and I'll wait for Gramps." He gestured toward the door, hoping that Zina would have time to take care of Dolly's issue before Gramps made his way across the drive and the lawn to the house.

Zina rolled her eyes as she fit the key into the lock on the door and pushed it open. "Come on, Dolly. There's a bathroom on the second floor where we can get you cleaned up."

Dolly cast a glance back at Alex before letting Zina lead her into the house. Poor kid. She'd be in safe hands with Zina though. All he'd do was make it worse. He'd never had to help a kid with a wet pants issue before. Never even changed a diaper except on a penguin who'd had a debilitating case of diarrhea. Served it right for digging through his bag and downing all of the chocolate bars one of the Swiss scientists had brought back from a recent trip home.

He held out a hand to help Gramps up the stairs but the old man brushed it away.

"I remember coming here back in the day."

"Oh yeah?" Alex humored his grandfather.

"The parties they'd throw here." Gramps settled into a wicker chair on the porch, his face lighting up. "Your grandmother and I met at one of those parties."

"Really?" He hadn't heard much in the way of family history over the years. He'd never been interested, and by the time he realized he ought to pay attention, his mom had taken off, his dad had passed away, and he figured the info was lost for good. Char had the family pictures and photo albums, but he'd never wanted to pore over them the way she had when they were little. Now he wished he had. It would be nice to have some sort of sense of history.

"Your grandmother came down those steps like an angel." Gramps lifted a shaky finger to point to the grand staircase just inside the front door. "It was love at first sight."

Alex followed his gaze to the steps, where Zina came down, followed by Dolly, who was dressed in some sort of flowy wrap. The two of them giggled at something, giving the impression they'd just become the best of friends.

"Everything better?" Alex asked. Dolly had been a sight to behold in sparkles and toilet paper. But now she seemed to be wearing a towel or a sheet of some sort.

"We found a short robe to put on her, but I think she'll probably want to go home and change, especially if you're dead set on apartment hunting this afternoon."

Alex reached for Dolly's hand. "Thanks for your help. I couldn't have done it without you."

"Oh, I bet you could. You seem like the kind of guy who can step up when necessary." Her eyes held a glint of humor, but he could read between the lines enough to know that she was telling him not to fuck this up. Like he needed any added pressure from her. He was already feeling the overcommitment closing in on him from all sides.

He held Dolly's hand and gestured to Gramps. "Let's go. We've still got a lot to do today."

Zina dangled a plastic bag from her finger. "Here are Dolly's wet things. I suppose I'll see you over here again tomorrow?"

He snatched the bag and held it out in front of him. "Yep, see you tomorrow." Tomorrow and the day after that and the day after that. And on and on until he made it through the wedding and got Gramps settled. He'd been handing out promises like they were pieces of candy, making more commitments in the past three days than he had in the past three years.

There was something about being home again that made him want to step up. He'd better figure out what it was before he found himself promising more than he'd ever be able to deliver.

twelve

⎯⎯⎯⎯ ♡ ⎯⎯⎯⎯

"Hello?" Zina let herself in through the front door of Lacey and Bodie's house.

"We're back here on the porch," Lacey called.

"Want to tell me why you've got a hearse parked in your driveway?" Zina helped herself to a cup of coffee before heading out to the four-season porch. "And why aren't you in bed?"

Kirby stood as Zina stepped out onto the porch. "Good afternoon, Ms. Zina."

"Hey, Kirby. Is that your new set of wheels out front?" Kirby was eccentric, but relatively harmless. His ancestors had made a fortune on oil back in the day, so he'd never had to hold down a job.

"Sure is." He beamed and glanced to Lacey. "I was just talking to Mayor Cherish here about starting up my own business."

Zina lifted a brow and glanced to Lacey. Her eyes had taken on that shiny glazed look—the one Zina knew all too well. She'd seen it the day before when Alex committed them to moving up the date of the wedding, which meant Kirby was up to something.

"Is that right?" Zina took a seat on one of the cushioned chairs. "Are you putting in a new funeral home?"

"No, ma'am. I'm startin' a limo business." He nodded as he resumed his perch on the edge of his seat. "Weddings need limos, now don't they?"

Lacey turned the shiny eyes on Zina. "I was trying to explain to Kirby that a limo business typically offers limos, not hearses, as a mode of transportation."

"The hearse is just the first step." His mouth screwed into a frown. "I plan on expanding my fleet."

"Where did you get a hearse?" Zina asked.

"That auto auction they have once a month over in Cramden. I've got my eye on a school bus that's coming up next month." He reached for his mug.

Zina met Lacey's gaze, trying to sort out how she was supposed to respond. Usually her bestie handled crazy-ass requests with a combination of humor and grace. That wasn't a skill Zina possessed.

"So a hearse and a school bus?" Zina asked.

"That's right. I figure that will give me a good start. I'm prepared to offer y'all a steep discount for becoming your preferred transportation vendor." He eyed them over the rim of his mug.

"That's certainly a generous offer." Lacey gave him a gracious smile, but the way she gripped the arm of her chair showed she was anything but relaxed. "But the wedding parties we have coming to town seem to prefer a more traditional mode of transportation like a classic white stretch limo."

Kirby's face fell. Zina's chest tightened. How could Lacey handle a job where she was constantly having to turn people down?

"You know, I've seen some interesting new trends," Zina offered.

"Like what?" Lacey shot her a look of annoyance.

"Like party buses or pickup truck limos. Maybe keep your eyes peeled for something like that at one of your auctions." Zina shrugged at Lacey. "You wanted me to check out all those wedding websites."

Kirby stood, his jaw set. "Got it. So if I can come back with something trendy or something more classic, you'll let me work with y'all?"

"We'll consider it." Lacey set down her mug. "Zina, can you walk him out?"

"Sure." She led Kirby to the front door.

"Thanks for seeing me this afternoon. You've given me a lot to think about." He nodded at her as he propped his cowboy hat on top of his silver mane. "I'll be in touch."

Zina watched him climb into the rusty hearse before she shut the door.

"What in the world was that?" Lacey's voice came from behind her.

"What was what? Did you see how crushed he looked?" Zina turned. "Does Bodie know you're entertaining crazy old men on the porch?"

"No. What he doesn't know won't hurt him."

"At least sit down and put your feet up. Doctor's orders." Zina put her hands on Lacey's shoulders and turned her back toward the porch.

"Tell me how the meeting with the contractor went this morning." Lacey sat down and propped her feet up on the wicker coffee table.

"Fine. Alex seems to think he'll be able to pull it together. He's looking for a place to stay by the Phillips House though. Says he wants to be closer in case there's a penguin emergency."

"Of course. Tell him to take one of the bedrooms upstairs. I should have offered earlier."

"You want him to move in?" Zina didn't like the sound

of that. Having to work on the wedding and share warehouse space with him was one thing, but if he were living at the Phillips House, she'd be exposed to his damn dimple all the time. And she was having a hard enough time resisting already.

"It's fine. We have a few smaller events booked but no one's renting out the bedrooms until after the Munyon wedding. Do you want to tell him or should I?"

"Why don't you?" Zina might need to start limiting her interaction with the penguin handler. She couldn't afford to get attached, not to someone who wasn't going to be around for the long haul.

"Will do." Lacey grabbed a thick binder from the table next to her. "Now, I need to go over the details for the wedding so you know what to expect."

"Let me get a refill first." Zina reached for her mug. If she was going to have to take over as wedding planner, she needed to be fully caffeinated.

"Oh, you might want to make a fresh pot. Bodie won't let me drink anything but decaf."

"You gave me decaf coffee?" Zina asked. No wonder she hadn't felt that kick of caffeine. She moved into the kitchen to make an extra-strong pot. If she was going to have to take on the binder along with avoiding Alex and managing the dog rescue, she was going to have to have all of her wits about her . . . every last one.

thirteen

Alex couldn't keep from smiling as he drove the distance back to Char's. He'd been worried about pulling the wedding off by himself. With Zina's help it was sure to go off without a hitch. Her ability to get things done was obvious based on her level of success at the dog shelter. And now he even had a place to stay. He couldn't wait to tell Char his good news about moving out.

He eased the truck to a stop as he pulled into the driveway. Lacey's call couldn't have come at a better time. Moving into the mansion would solve a lot of his problems. Everything was starting to smell like roses, or at least a lot less like a huge pile of crap.

"What's for dinner, Uncle Alex?" Dolly chimed in from the back seat. She'd been quiet on the ride home.

"I thought maybe we'd order pizza to celebrate."

"What are we celebrating?" Gramps growled. "You moving into a mansion to work on that crazy penguin habitat?"

Alex shook his head. "It's all going to work out, Gramps."

Gramps didn't seem impressed by his commitment. "If you ask me, you're in over your head."

"Well, good thing no one's asking you." He'd told Char he'd help with Gramps, and it was becoming clear that the old man needed some sort of purpose. Once upon a time his grandfather had been full of smiles. He was always the first one to crack a joke or pull a prank. But since Nana had passed, he'd become bitter and quiet. The sooner they got him sorted out with something to do, the better. Maybe helping out with the penguins would lighten up his mood a bit.

Before they could get out of the truck, Char came through the front door and headed their way.

"Hey, how was your day?" she asked as she pulled open the back door of the truck. "Did you find a place to live?"

"Yeah. Lacey Cherish offered to let me move into the Phillips House while I'm working out there."

"What?" Char reached for Dolly and lifted her youngest out of the truck. "Why would she let you do that?"

"I'm going to be spending a ton of time out there working on the Munyon wedding."

Char clenched her jaws together. So hard that Alex could tell he was about to get a browbeating from his older sister.

"I'm going to get to make snowflakes and they have dogs out there, too," Dolly volunteered.

"Why are there dogs at the Phillips House?" Char asked.

"Cuz Uncle Alex broke their ceiling," Dolly said.

Char's brows lifted. "What ceiling?"

Alex let out a breath. "The other day I climbed up on the roof of the dog shelter to check on a leak and fell through."

"Are you okay?" Char put a hand on his shoulder, her attitude switching from pissed to concerned.

"He's fine. But I heard that poor woman's roof sure isn't." Gramps eased himself down from the truck.

Alex winced as he recalled the gaping hole in Zina's roof. But it was all going to be okay. He'd get the wedding done, help pay for her deductible on the roof, and still have plenty left to get Gramps settled in before he took off on a new adventure.

"I don't even know what to do with y'all." Char shook her head from side to side.

"Well you won't have to worry about me anymore. I'll start moving my stuff over to the Phillips House tomorrow." Alex had enjoyed spending some time with his nieces but would be happy to have some space of his own.

"Gramps, too," Char said. Her voice was firm, leaving no room for arguing.

"I figured Gramps would want to stay with you until we got this whole thing sorted. I asked him to help with the habitat, but don't you think he'd be more comfortable sleeping here?" Alex's blood chilled, his face tingled. She couldn't be serious about him taking Gramps with him. The Phillips House wouldn't be a good place for him. The bedrooms were on the second floor. Surely Char wouldn't expect Gramps to be able to navigate the steps.

"I think I'd like it out there," Gramps said, the faintest hint of a smile materializing on his face. "The air's fresher and there aren't as many people around. Plus, that way I'll be able to help you on that project like we talked about."

"It's settled then." Char grinned as she met Alex's gaze. "I'll help you get packed."

Alex hesitated as everyone else disappeared into the house. Things had taken a turn sideways. He hadn't seen that particular change of plans coming. For a moment, frustration boiled up inside. He'd be better off walking away now. The reason he'd stayed away for so long was that he didn't do well working with others. Having to take Char's and Gramps's opinions into account when making his own plans wasn't something he was used to.

But maybe it was something he needed to do more often. His interactions with Zina had taught him that sometimes people had to put their own needs aside to focus on others.

He'd never been one to live his life that way in the past. But maybe he could try for the next couple of months. Fine. He'd take Gramps with him to the Phillips House and hopefully get him to help with the construction. But he'd also make sure he got his grandfather out to visit that home he'd heard about.

He stepped into the house. Gramps sat in the easy chair, his eyes glued to the cartoon on the television again. Dolly had set up a tea party for all of her stuffed animals in the middle of the living room floor.

"Where did your mom go?" Alex asked.

Dolly's nose crinkled and she wheezed a few breaths before letting out a giant *achoo*. "Do you want some tea?" She wrinkled her nose and held up a tiny plastic teapot.

"No thanks. I need to talk to your mom about something."

"She's in the back, making sure she packs up my stuff so she can get rid of me tomorrow." Gramps's expression didn't change. "It'd be better for all of us if you'd let me just move back to the ranch."

For a split second Alex wondered how his grandfather felt about being shuffled around. The man had spent his whole life working hard to provide for his family, raise his kids. What would it feel like to have outlived them all and have nothing left to live for?

What the hell was happening to him? He could practically feel his insides turning to marshmallow fluff. The more time he spent at Char's, surrounded by her and the girls, all of them looking to him to fix things, make things better, the harder it was going to be to extricate himself from their lives later.

So instead of seizing the moment to settle Gramps's concerns, he headed down the hall. "Char? Where the hell are you?"

"Where the hell . . . where the hell . . ." Shiner Bock

strutted along the top of the dresser in the bedroom where Jordan and Izzy usually slept. At least, until they'd been displaced by Gramps.

"I can't tell you how grateful I am that you're here." Char folded Gramps's shirts into neat squares and set them into the suitcase on the bed. "I think it will be so much better for him to stay with you. Not to mention, the girls will get their bedroom back, and—"

"Am I doing the right thing?" he asked.

"What?" She paused, a pair of Gramps's baggy old briefs in her hands. "What do you mean?"

He rolled his head from shoulder to shoulder, trying to ease some of the tension away. "Gramps is pissed. All he wants is to move back to the ranch."

Char dropped the underwear. "We've been over this. There's no way he can live all the way out there on his own. I tried that with him. He fell while he was trying to move some stuff around in the barn and if the mailman hadn't found him, who knows how long he would have laid out there?"

"I know. I just wish . . ." His voice trailed off as he thought about how to share the feelings of guilt he'd been trying to process.

"Wish what?" Char pressed.

"Forget it. It's just weird being back." He couldn't quite put into words what had been bothering him. Some sense of misplaced guilt? That's probably all it was.

"I'm here if you want to talk. You know that, right?"

"Yeah, I know." But he had no intention of wasting his breath on words. Words weren't going to build a penguin habitat. And that needed to be his sole focus over the next couple of weeks if he wanted to get back to his way of normal.

fourteen

$\heartsuit$

Zina got out of the truck and held tight to Buster's leash. It had been his turn to spend the night last night. He was such a good dog, she had half a mind to adopt him herself. Maybe she would if he didn't find a family during the big adoption event she had coming up that weekend. She'd managed to avoid making a commitment to any of the pups up to that point, but where had it gotten her?

It was her favorite time of day. The sun hadn't woken up yet, and the town was still quiet. So was the warehouse. With Alex and Toby working until the late evening hours on the penguin habitat for the past two weeks, she'd embraced any chance she got to enjoy the peace and quiet.

That was the main reason she preferred the early morning shift . . . so she could have a chance to think while she went about the routine of feeding the dogs and letting them out a few at once. Thinking time had been at a premium lately, especially since it seemed Alex was standing around every corner, muscles bulging, dimple winking, lips curling into any number of smiles.

Seemed like she'd memorized all of his smiles, and he had quite the collection. Her favorite had to be the cocky-into-vulnerable-grin combination. He didn't share that one very often. She'd seen plenty of the plain ol' cocky grin. If she didn't know better, she'd assume that was the only one he had. But when he let down his guard, especially around one of his nieces, the unsure, unconfident, vulnerable part of him came through. That was the Alex she'd started falling for. Which was no good at all.

The way he'd barged in, taken over the warehouse, and kept making assumptions should be driving her crazy. But she could tell it was all a front. Hopefully he'd be long gone before he let down his guard for good. Because he was the kind of man who could ruin her if she let him.

She opened the door, and Buster went in first. The lights were on in the back of the warehouse, where she kept the dogs. Her stomach clenched. Did someone forget to turn them off last night?

Before she had a chance to check, the thump of a deep bass came from the radio she'd set up in the back. Morty's voice punctuated the silence. "Who let the dogs out? Me! Me!"

Zina clamped her hand over her mouth to keep herself from laughing out loud. She crept closer, trying to see if he had the moves to go with the song. But then Herbie barked and ran over to greet her.

Morty reached out to silence the music.

"Good morning." She bit down on her bottom lip at the shock on his face.

"How long have you been here?" He whipped a comb out of his back pocket and ran it through his hair.

"Not long."

"Good, that's good. I just came out to lend a hand. I'm an early riser so I figured I'd pitch in with the dogs." He smiled but didn't make eye contact.

Zina was afraid she might lose her semblance of control

if he did. "Thanks. You don't have to keep doing that though."

"I don't mind. Makes an old man feel useful." He nodded, slipped his comb back in his pocket, and called to Herbie. "I got them all fed. Do you mind if I take a couple out back so they can get some exercise?"

"That would be great. Thank you."

He disappeared through the back door and she let out the laugh she'd been holding back. What would Alex think about his grandpa jamming with the dogs? She unclipped Buster from his leash and filled a bowl of kibble for him.

As she bent to set it down on the ground, Alex came through the door.

"Hey, have you seen my gramps?"

"He's out back with a couple of the dogs. What are you doing out here so early?" The sun had yet to peek over the horizon. This was supposed to be her "me time" before the Sanders men got going for the day.

"They're bringing in the pool feature today, so I wanted to make sure everything's ready. Gramps isn't bothering you or getting in the way, is he?"

"No, he's been helping. This is the third time this week he beat me to the breakfast routine."

"Good." Alex grinned, and dammit, there was the slightest sliver of vulnerability in the depths of those ocean-blue eyes.

She commanded her heart to stop the funny squeeze-fluttery thing it was doing. "He's really good with the dogs."

"He's been helping a lot with the habitat, too." Alex moved to the workbench he'd set up along the wall and set out some more of his gramps's tools he'd collected from the ranch. "He seems, I don't know, happier since we moved in here."

"And how about you?" She cocked her head. "Are you acclimating to being back in Texas?"

"I guess I am. It's been nice getting to know my nieces,

even if they thought I was a lot cooler when I lived by the South Pole." His eyes crinkled at the edges when he smiled.

"Kids will keep you humble."

"Well, then humility is about to become my greatest strength. Did you get coffee yet?" He held out a thermos.

"Not yet. I was hoping to bum some off of your grandpa after I fed the dogs." She took the mug Alex handed her, grateful for the incoming kick of caffeine.

"It's been nice spending some time with him. Makes me wonder what it might have been like if I hadn't left in the first place."

Zina sensed the opportunity for a few minutes of real talk, not the flirtatious banter they'd been slinging back and forth for the past two weeks. "What do you think would have happened?"

He shrugged. "Probably would have finished college, then gone on to vet school like I'd planned."

"And it's too late for that now?" she pressed.

He opened his mouth like he wanted to say something and then closed it again, just as fast. "Hey, I think Toby's here."

Saved by the contractor. Zina silently cursed the man for his unintended interruption.

Alex spent the rest of the morning working side by side with Toby and his crew. Finally, just after one, he sat back and wiped his arm across his forehead. Somehow the sweat still trickled down to his eyes. At least the water feature was installed. He'd rigged the hose to start filling the pool. Toby promised to have the dome set up by the end of the week and then they'd be ready for the penguins.

All he needed now was for Zina to get those dogs out of there. The insurance adjuster was giving her a major run-around on the settlement to get the roof repaired, but she'd promised multiple times to get the dogs moved out before the penguins moved in.

He didn't know what he'd do if she didn't come through. Dogs were a lot more adaptable than a half dozen penguins. With any luck her numbers would go down after the adoption event she had planned this weekend. He'd even been roped into volunteering to help, starting with giving all of the dogs a bath. Anything he could do to clear the warehouse of dogs and the sexy do-gooder who'd been driving him crazy.

He felt bad for how much time she was spending with those dogs. Losing the shelter made everything worse for her. What used to take her an hour to do in the mornings now took about three times as long since she had to take the dogs out one or two at a time on leashes instead of letting them run free in a fenced-in yard.

"Hey, Alex. Can you get the door?" Gramps asked.

"Sure." He pushed open the door so Gramps and the two dogs he had with him could make their way through. Alex followed. "What are you doing?"

Gramps held tight as the dogs tugged in opposite directions on their leashes. "Come on, girls. We're going this way today." He increased his pace and the dogs moved to stay ahead of him.

"Gramps?" Alex increased his pace to keep up. "What's going on?"

"Just pitching in. I don't want to be thought of as deadweight around here."

"Who called you deadweight?" Alex immediately tensed. Did Lacey say something about them staying at the house?

"No one. But a man can feel when he's not doing his fair share. That girl needs help with the dogs and I've got the time, so I'm pitching in."

Alex stepped back as the trio passed him. Was he seeing things or was Gramps holding his head a little bit higher?

There seemed to be a new bounce in his step as well. Maybe the old man had found some purpose. If that was the case, Alex was glad. He could only imagine what it might feel like to have his best days behind him. Although, if he didn't pull this wedding off, his best days might be behind him, too.

Maybe now that Gramps had something to help with, he might not be as down. One could hope. That reminded him. He hadn't called for an update on where Gramps stood on the waiting list for a while. He picked up his phone and pulled up the number to the nursing home over in Cramden. Gramps might not like it, but even he would have to agree that once they were done with the wedding, he couldn't go back to Char's. It just wasn't a long-term solution. Once Alex figured out where he was headed after this, Gramps wouldn't have a choice but to make peace with the fact he couldn't live on his own anymore and get used to some-place new.

He waited for someone to pick up the phone.

"Water's Edge. How can I help you?" The voice on the other end of the phone held no warmth.

"I'm calling to check up on where my grandfather's name falls on your waiting list," Alex said.

"Name?"

"Mortimer Sanders."

"Hold, please." An irritating rendition of a song he vaguely recognized blared through the phone. Alex tried to curb his annoyance while he waited.

With a jarring click, the woman was back on the line. "I'm sorry but we don't have a Mortimer Sanders on the list."

"That's impossible." Alex put his hand to his forehead. "I called a couple of weeks ago and added him myself. There's got to be a mistake."

"Hold, please." The music came back on the line.

His stomach flip-flopping, Alex didn't have a choice but to stand by.

"I see we had Mortimer Sanders on the list but he was removed last week. If there's nothing else I can help you with—"

"Wait. How's that possible? I didn't remove him."

"Well someone did. Says here an Alex Sanders called."

Alex's head swam with the mix-up. "But I'm Alex Sanders."

"Is it possible you made the call and then forgot?"

The sass in her tone rubbed him the wrong way. "No. That's not possible. Can I talk to your supervisor please?"

"She's not available now but I'd be happy to take a message."

Alex questioned the authenticity of that statement but left his name and number. As he made his way back to the warehouse, he wondered how his grandfather could have been removed from the list. Char wouldn't have done it. Which left one person who would have known.

"Hey, Gramps, can I talk to you for a moment?" He tried to keep his smile friendly and not give in to the rising frustration.

"I'm busy at the moment. What's on your mind?" Gramps stood next to Zina, watching as she scooped out kibble and filled a dog's dish before sliding it into its crate.

"I'd rather chat in private if you don't mind." No need to air his family's dirty laundry in front of Zina. She already probably thought he was a lost cause based on how he'd destroyed her dog shelter.

"I don't know why you can't just speak your mind right here. You afraid you're going to piss off one of the dogs?"

"Fine. I wanted to keep it just between us, but why did you remove your name from the waiting list at Water's Edge?"

Gramps scoffed. "That place? The only water they're on the edge of is a man-made pond they filled with runoff. I don't care what you and your sister say, I'm not going back into another home."

Zina's eyebrows shot up and she let the scoop fall into

the bin. "I'll catch up with you in a bit. Sound good?" Alex didn't miss the way she dropped a hand to his grandfather's shoulder.

Gramps covered her hand with his and gave her an authentic smile, not one of the tight-lipped grimaces he'd been sending Alex's way. "Don't let my persistent grandson scare you off."

"Do I look like the kind of woman who spooks easily?" she asked.

"No, you sure don't." Gramps let out a chuckle as Zina walked away. "That girl is somethin' else. Why, if I were a few years younger . . ."

Alex couldn't agree more. Zina was full of surprises. The way she handled Gramps, the comfortable way she'd been around Dolly, there really wasn't much she couldn't do. Before he went all soft thinking about Zina and the way her lips quirked up at the corners when she found something amusing, he shook it off.

"We're talking about the wait list."

"You know, you should ask her out." Gramps nodded. "She's a real catch. Don't find women like that nowadays. They're all soft and wishy-washy. Not like your sister. And not like Zina. Those two are cut from the same kind of cloth."

"In that case, I'm out. I definitely don't need someone like Char in my life. I already have to put up with her trying to boss me around."

Gramps chuckled. "Your grandmother was like that. All bark and no bite. She'd threaten all right. But when it came down to it she was a softy."

Alex remembered. But he wasn't in the mood to share a tender moment of reminiscing. He needed to figure out why Gramps thought it was a good idea to take himself off the wait list.

"You know I'm not sticking around after this wedding, right?" Alex asked. "I got a call from Mr. Munyon's attorney. When I'm done here, he wants to hire me for another project he's got going down in the Caymans."

Gramps shrugged. "Not my business what you do with your life."

"That's right." Good, maybe they saw more eye to eye than he thought.

"Not even if you are messing it up."

"Excuse me?" Alex crossed his arms over his chest. "Why the hell do you think I'm messing up my life?"

"You keep running but you're not going to find what you're looking for." Gramps let out a sigh.

"And what exactly is it you think I'm looking for?" He wanted to know.

"I can't tell you that. You'll have to figure it out for yourself."

Alex rolled his eyes and huffed out a breath. "If you're done spouting your mumbo jumbo crap, can we talk about why you called the nursing home and took yourself off the wait list?"

Gramps didn't bat an eye. "I'm not going."

"You don't have a choice."

"Son, you've always got a choice, and I'm not spending the rest of my days at Water's Edge." He made air quotes around "Water's Edge" like he wanted to further drive his point home.

"You can't stay with Char. We both know she's in over her head with those girls."

"You're right. I don't want to stay with Char. I'm going to live on my own."

Alex wanted to shake the man's shoulders . . . anything so he'd see the light and realize he was past the luxury of being able to make those kinds of decisions for himself. But Alex figured he'd humor him, just for a bit. "Where are you planning to go?"

Gramps shrugged. "I've got a perfectly good place that's already paid for."

"It doesn't work that way. You can't stay out at the ranch by yourself. I'm calling them back and adding your name to the list."

"Do what you've got to do," Gramps said as he unclipped the first dog from its leash. "And I'll do what I need to do."

Alex shook off the thinly veiled threat. He didn't have time to worry about Gramps and the very real risk of him going rogue. He was about to be up to his ears in penguins and pit bulls, and he needed all the help he could get.

"Okay, Gramps. Let's make a deal."

"Now you want to bargain?"

"You help me with the penguins and pitch in with the dogs. If you can stay out of trouble and don't take any spills, I'll talk to Char about maybe letting you go back to the ranch."

"I think that's only fair." Gramps shrugged but didn't try to hide the satisfied grin.

"I'm still putting your name back on that list. If you have any health issues, you've got to take the spot at Water's Edge."

Gramps didn't nod but the slight incline of his head signaled he'd got the message, loud and clear.

Alex was tired of arguing. It seemed to be the only thing he'd done since he got back. He left his grandfather to deal with the dogs and went looking for Zina. What had possessed him to agree to help her bathe the dogs that afternoon?

fifteen

Zina hooked the leash to Buster's collar and handed it to Alex. "We'll take this slow. Some of the dogs don't enjoy having a bath but I want them all to look their best for Saturday, so try, okay?"

Alex took the end of the leash and looped it over his hand. "Can you tell me which ones don't like to get wet?"

He looked so unsure of himself she wanted to laugh out loud. But she didn't want to scare him off so she bit back her grin. "I'll give you the easy ones."

"Gee, thanks." He appeared to be less than thrilled at the task ahead. She didn't blame him. Bathing the dogs was a pain in the ass and she usually relied on her volunteers to take on the brunt of it. But with so many dogs to take care of, they were busy walking and feeding the ones who remained inside.

"Buster loves his baths. He'll be a good one to start with." She leaned over and scratched the big lug behind his good ear. "You take it easy on Captain Jaybird, okay?"

Buster's tail thumped against the grass in agreement.

Zina wished someone would open their hearts to him. He'd been at the shelter the longest, about six months at that point. He wasn't the cutest dog they had available. Not with his shredded ear and the scars crisscrossing his nose. But he was one of the sweetest, despite his tendency to let loose a little extra flatulence every once in a while.

"Here goes nothing." Alex moved over to where she'd hooked up the hose. He turned it on and began to spray Buster.

Zina laughed as the dog jumped and spun, trying to bite the spray of water. Then she turned to get the next dog out of her crate. The young female that Dolly named Aurora didn't seem too sure about the bath based on the way she cowered at the back of her kennel. "It's okay, sweetie. I think you'll like it."

She carried the pup out to where Alex stood with his hands full of soapsuds. Buster must have had at least a few inches of bubbles coating his back. He looked like an abominable snowman under all the white. "You might want to go easy on the shampoo."

"Yeah, I figured that out after I'd sudsed him up," Alex said. "You're right, he seems to be enjoying himself."

The dog stood still, his eyes half-closed like he'd reached some state of internal Zen. Alex turned the spray on to rinse him off. When he was done, she took the hose and he grabbed a towel to run over Buster's back.

"Your turn, little girl." Zina set Aurora down on the grass and turned the water pressure down so just a small dribble of water came out of the end. The pup sniffed at it. Her curiosity was a good sign. Zina held it out to her while her pink tongue lapped at the water.

"You're really good with her." Alex moved closer, Buster's leash in his hand.

"Lots of practice with scared animals unfortunately." She held her hand up to shade the sun and take a look at him. His shirt was soaked through thanks to Buster. While she watched, he lifted the hem and pulled it over his head.

"Didn't think I'd get so wet." He turned and flung his shirt onto a bench.

Zina drew in a deep breath as her gaze roamed over the defined muscles of his back. What did the man do to keep cut like that? Life wasn't fair. She'd give just about anything to run her hands over those shoulders.

"Everything okay?" He'd turned and was making his way back to her.

"Huh?" Pulled from her illicit musings, she glanced down. The pup had moved, meaning she'd been dripping water onto her jeans for the past several moments, creating a nice wet patch at the apex of her thighs. "Oh no."

She immediately tossed the hose to the ground, which released the kink she'd formed to make the water flow slower. The hose twisted and turned, spraying water everywhere.

"Catch it." Zina reached for it, coming up empty-handed.

Alex let go of Buster's leash and stepped on the hose, then bent to grab it with both hands. His laughter bounced off the building and echoed around her. "I got it."

"Good job." Embarrassment flooded her face with heat. Even though water dripped down her hair and she shivered slightly, her cheeks flamed.

"What happened?" He kinked the hose again, preventing the water flow.

"I don't know. I guess I was distracted."

"Mmm." His brow furrowed. "By what, exactly?"

Oh hell, he knew she'd been checking him out. She could tell by the hint of humor that sparked in his eyes. Nice eyes. Eyes she wouldn't mind gazing into for a few minutes or a few hours or even a lifetime. Best not to go there. She shook off any warm fuzzies that threatened to encroach on her bubble of safety.

"I think Buster must have let one rip."

"So you were distracted by the farting dog?" He moved closer.

"He's really got a problem. Have you heard him? I think it's why he hasn't been adopted yet."

"I didn't hear it." He moved even closer, his hand reaching for hers. "I think you're lying."

She bristled. She might exaggerate or stretch the truth from time to time, but she wasn't a liar. At least she hadn't been until she met him. Her stomach clenched. He'd called her out and she'd fibbed. Time to own it. "Fine. He didn't fart. I was distracted by something else."

"What?" He moved past the invisible barrier she'd erected to keep people out of her personal bubble. Nothing happened. Where had all of her defenses gone? In that moment she realized she was powerless against this man with the blue-green eyes and amazing abs.

She huffed out a breath and glanced to the ground. "You. Happy?"

He put a finger under her chin, searing the spot where he touched her. Nudging her chin up, he forced her to meet his gaze. "So you're saying I distracted you?"

She rolled her eyes. "Yes, fine. You distracted me."

"Wow. If taking off my shirt affected you that much, I wonder what this might do." He leaned in, pressing his lips to hers.

Zina stumbled forward but he caught her, his arms clasping around her like a vise. She'd always considered herself immune to men. Sure she enjoyed their attention sometimes, but she'd always been able to put attraction aside when necessary. Like most things in her life, she made it bend to her will. But there was no controlling the surge of desire that overwhelmed her as he took the kiss deeper.

His tongue ran over her lips, making them part like he held the secret key. She fought against it even while her arms wrapped around his midsection, pulling him tighter against her. She battled the desire to melt into him even as she angled her head to give him better access. What was happening to her? She'd never been so powerless when it came to controlling her attraction.

He pulled away, keeping hold of her arms to steady her.

She wobbled slightly, already aching to feel his lips on hers again.

"Careful there."

"I'm fine." Another little white lie. "Why don't you tie Buster up and let him dry in the sun while you . . . hey, where's Buster?" Alex had let him go to wrestle the hose. Now the dog who typically spent all day every day lounging around had hightailed it out of sight.

"I'll find him." Alex stalked to the faucet and turned off the water. "Buster?"

Zina tucked Aurora back inside her kennel so she could help with the search. They had enough problems finding stray dogs around town. She couldn't afford to have one of her pups go missing. What if he got picked up by someone who was involved with the dog-fighting ring? They might never see him again if that happened. Fear propelled her, fueling her desperation to find the missing dog.

"Why don't you head that way and I'll go this way? Alex pointed to the stand of trees that surrounded the warehouse.

"Call me if you find him?" She moved off in the opposite direction, no longer caring that her jeans stuck to her body and that her hair still dripped water down her shirt.

Alex shook his head. He'd really blown it this time. Not only did he give in to his attraction to the woman who'd been haunting his daydreams, but he'd lost her favorite dog. Despite Buster's gastrointestinal problems, the dog had grown on him. If something happened to him because of Alex's actions, not only would he never be able to forgive himself, but he may as well kiss any chance of kissing Zina again good-bye.

For some reason that bothered him. As he entered the stand of trees, brushing branches to the side, he vowed not to let thoughts of how it felt to finally kiss those full lips again get in the way of his goals. He needed this job. He needed the cash. He needed to get out of town before he got too attached.

"Buster! Where are you?" Branches swiped at his bare chest and arms as he wandered deeper into the trees. What if he didn't find him? That wasn't an option. "Come here, buddy."

He stepped on a branch, causing a sharp snap. He'd never be able to hear anything if he kept barging through the bushes like a twenty-point buck. He slowed his pace, pausing every few feet to listen. A whimper came from his left. He picked through the underbrush, following the soft sounds until he reached the spot he thought they were coming from.

A fallen log blocked his path. He leaned down to peer inside. There was Buster, snuggled around a squirming pile of some sort of animal. Alex eyed the dog. "Come here, Buster. Come on out."

The dog looked at him and curled up tighter, protecting whatever he'd wrapped himself around.

Alex pulled out his cell. He wasn't about to stick his hand in there and get it bitten off. The phone rang once and then Zina was on the line.

"Did you find him?" Worry sliced through her voice.

"Yeah. He's in a log and he's got something with him."

"Is he hurt?"

"I don't think so. I'm sending you my location via text. Just follow the dot and you'll find us."

"Okay. I'm on my way. And, Alex?"

"Yeah?"

"Thanks."

"You're welcome." He disconnected and sent a quick text to mark his location on the map. While he waited for Zina to show, he knelt down to try to figure out what Buster was so keen on protecting. "Hey, bud, what have you got there?"

Looked like a nest of rats or something. Every once in a while one of them moved, causing the rest of them to squirm around. Alex's stomach did the same, twisting and turning as he tried to figure out how they were going to get Buster out of the dead log without a fight.

Finally, the sound of Zina crashing through the woods reached him. "Alex? Where are you?"

"Over here." He moved toward the direction of her voice until he caught sight of her. "He's right here."

"Thank goodness." She reached for him as she got closer. "Where?"

Alex led her to the fallen log. "Down here. And he's got something with him. I don't know what they are but when I tried to get closer, he growled at me."

Zina knelt down and looked in the tree. "Hey, Buster. What have you got there?"

The dog whapped his tail, a much different reception than the one Alex had received. What a fair-weather friend he had in Buster. Apparently Zina had the magic touch.

She ran a hand over the dog's giant noggin. "Let me see."

Buster lifted his head, revealing the pile of critters.

"Oh, Buster." Zina pulled her hand back and pressed it to her chest.

"What?"

She looked up at him, shock registering on her face. "They're puppies."

"Puppies? Are you sure? They look like baby possums or rats or something. I would have been able to tell if they were puppies."

"Have you ever been around newborn puppies?" she asked.

He didn't have to think about that. No, he hadn't. But he never expected puppies to look like rats.

"We've got to get them back to the shelter." She gave Buster's collar a gentle tug. "Good boy. We can take it from here."

"What can I do to help?"

"Here, take Buster's leash." She handed him the end of the leash. Buster exited the log willingly. Even he could tell that Zina was better prepared to handle the situation. Smart dog.

"I wish I had something to put them in. They can't be more than a couple of days old." She glanced around. "I guess I'll just carry them in my shirt."

Alex's lungs spasmed. If she took her shirt off, he'd lose it. He glanced away, studying some leaves on a nearby branch.

"There." Zina turned to him, her shirt still in place. She held the bottom hem up, creating a little bit of a sling to carry the puppies back. "Let's go."

"What about the mom?" Alex hesitated. With puppies that young, there had to be a mama dog nearby.

"I don't know. They look pretty tiny, so I'm not sure if she's been around. If we want to save them, we need to get them back to the warehouse."

"Okay. Lead the way." He followed her through the trees, wondering how this might affect the timing on getting the dogs relocated. He hadn't had a chance to count but there had to be at least four or five of the little critters.

Zina emerged from the woods and speed walked across the lawn to the warehouse. "I wish I had all of my stuff from the shelter."

He held the door for her as she entered. "What do you need?"

"Well, we need to get them warmed up right away." She nudged her chin toward a chair. "Sit."

"You talking to me or the dog?" Alex asked.

"You. Sit down and hold a couple of them up against your chest."

He slumped into the chair and let go of Buster's leash. Zina handed him a squirming pup, who squealed as it was removed from the pile of its siblings. He cradled it in his arms. She handed over another one.

"How long do you need me to sit with them like this?" It wasn't entirely unpleasant except for the way their tiny nails scratched against his pecs.

"Until I figure out what to do. I've got formula over at the shelter. I've got to go back."

"Isn't there somewhere closer?"

"I guess I can grab some from Coop. These pups need to eat."

"I'll go." Alex stood, juggling the two pups in his arms. "You stay here and I'll go get what you need."

"You sure?" She'd set the other pups down on a towel and pulled a heating pad out of a box.

"Yep. Just let me grab my shirt. You make a list and I'll get everything you tell me to, okay?" For the first time in as long as he could remember, he wanted to help. And not just do enough to get himself out of an uncomfortable situation, but really, truly help someone in need.

"Okay." Zina took the pups and placed them on the towel with their siblings. He counted six. Six more dogs that would need to be moved. How did she do it? As soon as it looked like she was making progress, some other dogs would show up and she'd have to start all over again. He shook his head as he walked toward the door.

Thirty minutes later he'd run to the store and come back with everything Zina had on the list. She took the two bags of supplies and started barking orders. He followed her lead as she mixed up formula and began to feed the pups.

"Give me one, I can help." He held out his hands and she set a tiny black-and-white puppy in his palm.

"They're going to want to wolf it down but you've got to make sure they go slow. Otherwise they'll just get sick."

Minutes passed, then hours. He went back and forth between feeding one pup and then trading it out for another. By the time they'd all been fed, it was time to start over again.

Zina was relentless . . . kept plugging away, taking a break every now and then to feed and exercise the other dogs.

Alex wasn't going to be the reason one of the pups didn't make it, so he kept up with his job.

After she'd gotten the other dogs taken care of she joined him on the warehouse floor, where she'd spread out a few layers of blankets. She'd settled the pups in a laundry basket with the heating pad underneath, then collapsed on the blanket next to him and let her head rest on his shoulder.

"I hope they all make it." She let out a sigh that sounded like it contained all of her frustration.

He tilted his head, resting his cheek against her hair. "They will. They're lucky they've got you in their corner." With her fighting for them, he couldn't believe they wouldn't make it.

"I'm so tired." She nestled closer.

He put an arm around her shoulder and pulled her down to where her head rested in his lap. "Why don't you try to get some sleep?"

"I can't. I've got to make sure those puppies make it through the night."

"I'll keep an eye on them. I promise I'll wake you up if I need you for anything."

She shook her head. "I can't let you do that."

"Tell you what. It's uncomfortable as hell out here. Why don't we bring the pups in the house and I'll watch them while you rest?"

Her eyes closed. He almost laughed. He bet he could get her to do just about anything while sleep tugged at her consciousness.

"Come on." He got up and put his hands under her arm-pits to tug her to a standing position. She didn't resist.

"Okay, but only for a little bit."

"Whatever you say." He tucked the feeding supplies into the laundry basket and picked it up. With the basket on his hip and one arm wrapped around Zina, he led the way through the dim lighting of the warehouse and across the drive to the house. The lights were off on the lower level, which meant Gramps had turned in.

Alex opened the front door and led Zina up the stairs to the bedroom he'd been using. He herded her toward the bed. She fell onto it, already asleep. He set the basket down and slipped her shoes off her feet. Then slid her lower half under the covers.

By the time he plugged the heating pad in and made sure the pups were settled, it was time for another feeding. This had to be worse than handling a newborn. It was like a newborn times six. He did kind of like it though. Three girls and three little boys. While he held the smallest one in his arms and dropped the formula into its mouth, it let out a contented sigh.

Maybe he could get used to caring for something else. If he wasn't ready to deal with people yet, he could find enough space in his heart for an animal.

He settled the last pup back in the basket, changed out the towel for a clean one, and then wondered whether or not he should go downstairs to try to catch a few winks on the antique sofa. As he leaned over to turn off the bedside lamp, Zina cleared her throat.

"Where do you think you're going?"

sixteen

Zina patted the bed next to her. "You look like you're about to drop. Why don't you lie down for a little while?"

"Here?" His eyebrows shot up.

"No. In the warehouse." The corner of her mouth ticked up. "Of course here."

"I didn't want to disturb you. You looked so peaceful." He leaned against the bed.

"You're not disturbing me. The only thing I'm disturbed about is figuring out where those pups came from. Now sit." She patted the bed again.

"Fine. But the next feeding is in an hour." He washed his hands in the bathroom sink, then sat down on top of the comforter.

She flipped over to face him. "I'll take that one. You need to rest."

He yawned as he leaned back onto the pile of pillows. "I don't mind. It's been . . ."

"What?" She propped her head up on her hand, eager to hear his take on caring for the pups. "It's been what?"

His eyes closed and he clasped his hands over his abs. "Kind of fun. They're so helpless and needy. I've never held an animal's life in my hands like that. They're so dependent on us."

Zina nodded. "You're going to be taking care of the penguins though."

"That's different. The penguins I've worked with weren't babies. Those puppies are just a few days old. It's thrilling and terrifying, all at once."

She felt like that every day about the dogs she cared for. It was a constant ache inside that only softened when she was able to find one of her dogs a new home. She wondered if Alex would still feel that way after he lost a pup. She'd learned over the years that she couldn't save them all.

A hint of a smile played across his lips as his breathing regulated. She wouldn't ruin it for him. He might find out soon enough that loss played a big part in her chosen line of work. She set her alarm for an hour and closed her eyes. Visions of Alex and puppies played through her head. She opened her eyes again. He wasn't going to stick around long enough to see them grow. Why was she so hung up on the guy?

The bedside lamp cast a warm glow around them, making her feel like it was just the two of them. Being nestled away in this corner of the Phillips House, where no one knew where she was, gave her a certain sense of boldness. That had to be the reason she reached out and ran her finger along his arm. He sighed in his sleep and turned onto his side to face her.

She watched his chest move with his breath, imagining what it might feel like to snuggle up against him. How the sexy five-o'clock shadow might scratch across her skin. How his arms might wrap around her like they did earlier. As she lay there, her fantasies playing out in her mind, he cracked an eyelid.

"What are you doing?"

Caught off guard, she felt a wave of heat flush her cheeks. "Nothing. I couldn't sleep. Did I wake you?"

"Nah." He rolled onto his back and tossed his arm over his head.

He'd taken off his shirt again while he was feeding the pups, and she let her gaze roam over his defined abs, the bulge of his biceps. A prickly sensation started in her gut and moved downward as she took in the sight of him.

"You should get some rest. You haven't slept at all yet," she said.

"That's true. But I can't sleep."

"Why not?"

"Honestly?" He tilted his head to face her.

She nodded, both afraid to hear what he might say and eager to see if he would admit to having the same kinds of thoughts about her that she'd been having about him.

"I keep thinking about that kiss."

The sensation in her gut expanded, sending heat radiating throughout her core. "Me, too." Her voice came out soft.

"Really?" He tucked his elbow under his head and rolled over on his side.

"Yeah." The admission came out much too easy. But the ball was in his court. While she waited to see what he'd do about it, her pulse kicked up.

"Any chance you might want to do it again?"

She bit down on her lip to prevent herself from shouting out her agreement. It wouldn't do her any good to get involved with a guy like Alex. He'd be leaving as soon as he could—he'd told her that much himself. Not to mention both of them needed to put all of their focus and efforts into pulling off the wedding. There was no time for a fling.

But instead of shooting him down and making a case for why it would be an epically bad idea, she reached out and ran her fingers over his jaw. He closed his eyes as she traced the contours of his cheek, grazed his eyelids, and settled on his mouth.

His lips parted and he nipped the tip of her pointer finger. A jolt of desire slammed into her core. Any resistance she clung to disappeared as he sucked her finger into his mouth, surrounding it with wet heat. She let out a little moan.

He sucked hard and she couldn't help but imagine what it might feel like if he focused his mouth on another part of her anatomy. One much lower and more sensitive than where he'd currently zeroed in his attention. She scooted closer to him and pulled her finger from his mouth before she pressed her lips to his. Warmth flooded her system as his hand went to her hair.

She flung her arm over his side and ran her fingers up the smooth skin of his back. His shoulder rolled, and then he flipped her onto her back to hover over her, his muscles flexed. She put her hands on his biceps, enjoying the way they strained to support his weight. The whole time his mouth met hers, his tongue seeking a way past her lips.

As her heart beat double time she opened for him. His tongue scorched hers, then he lowered himself next to her. One arm went around her back, pulling her close, while the other played over her shirt. His fingers raced up her ribs, leaving a trail of goose bumps. She shivered as her need doubled, tripled, making her bolder. She shifted her leg, sliding it between his. Her feet moved up and down his calves as her knee slid even higher.

She wanted to stop. Giving in to the feelings she had for Alex would only cause pain in the long run. She'd always been able to separate physical desire from her emotions. What had changed? If they did this, there would be no turning back for her. He'd leave and she'd end up more alone than she'd been before. If she let him in, opened her heart, he'd leave a hole a mile wide.

So she did what any smart, self-sufficient woman would do. She lowered her hand and cupped him through his jeans. He moaned and slid his hand under her shirt. His fingers moved up her rib cage until they stopped at the edge of her bra. He pulled back. His gaze met hers.

"You really want to do this?" His voice came out husky, gravelly, so sexy she could feel herself edge toward the brink of something magical, fantastical, terrifying.

The question hung in the air between them. Seconds ticked by. His brow furrowed while he waited. She had the power to end this. To make sure she didn't lose a part of herself.

But then she nodded. His lips curved into a smile and she committed it to memory so she could pull it out later when she was sure to play this scene over and over again in her mind. The moment that she jumped with no safety net. She'd either get caught up by Alex or crash.

As he rolled her onto her back and began to kiss his way down her neck, across her collarbone, his hands lifted the hem of her shirt. She silently urged him on. Her fingers played with his hair, ran over his shoulders. Then her shirt went over her head. His mouth settled at the spot between her breasts. Her breath hitched, her hips bucked, and she arched into him.

He chuckled, his breath warming her skin. She wanted to flip him on his back, bite her way down his chest, and get on with it. But she made herself still and tried to enjoy the warmth of his tongue, the heat of his breath, and the way his touch sent shivers up and down her spine.

He moved his mouth from her bare skin to the cup of her bra. Then he ran his tongue under the lacy edge, meeting the sensitive skin of her breast. She shifted, aching for the same sort of contact lower. His mouth moved and his teeth scraped against her nipple through the fabric of her bra. She cursed padded cups, vowing to never ever buy them again.

"Tell me what you want." His voice rubbed along her nerve endings, exposing them one by one.

She took his hand and lifted it to her mouth. As those icy blue eyes searched her gaze, she kissed each one of his fingertips. He smiled as he watched her. Then she lowered his hand between them, pushing it past the waistband of her jeans.

His eyes sparkled. "You ready for me so soon?"

As his fingers explored, she unbuttoned her jeans. "I've been ready since the day we met. Just wondering why it's taking you so long to catch up."

His mouth parted like he wanted to say something. But he licked his bottom lip instead. "Are you calling me out for not moving fast enough for you?"

She shrugged as best she could. "Call it what you want."

His finger slid into her and she clutched the bedspread with both hands, trying to remain unaffected, even as he stroked her.

"All right. Let's take this to the next level then, shall we?" He pulled his hand away and she wanted to cry at the loss of his touch.

Before she could make a move, he'd unbuttoned his jeans, slid them off, and reached behind her for the clasp of her bra. She whispered her thanks to the universe that the man couldn't resist a challenge. Then his mouth found her breast and she couldn't think at all.

So sweet. Her skin tasted like she'd bathed in a mix of sugar and honey and maybe even maple syrup. He couldn't get enough. And what was with the attitude she'd been flinging at him? Alex didn't care what kind of inner demons she was battling inside. He just wanted to take her. With every ounce of his being he wanted to possess her, drive her crazy, and fuck the cocky attitude right out of her.

He smiled as he sucked a nipple into his mouth and she arched into him. She might try to pretend she wasn't as desperate for him as he was for her, but her hips didn't lie. And she'd been bucking and grinding against him for the better part of the past ten minutes.

Moving down her stomach, he pressed kisses against her skin, his sole focus on reaching the apex of her thighs and driving her crazy with want. Yeah, he probably should have given a quick thought to the fallout of tonight's tryst, but she certainly seemed willing. Whatever happened, he'd have to face it tomorrow. Now wasn't the time for preliminary regrets. Now was the time for action.

He didn't have a condom, so he wouldn't be able to go all in. But he could deliver satisfaction another way. And she certainly seemed like she'd be a willing recipient of his tongue. He nudged her legs apart and hooked her knees over his shoulders. She spread before him, unashamed and eager. Her willingness made him so hard it bordered on painful. And he couldn't get enough.

As he watched her white knuckle the covers, he lowered his head and swiped his tongue along her entrance.

Her hips shot off the bed. He put a hand on her navel, forcing her down, then pinned her in place while he explored. With her eyes clenched, she tried to move her hips but he kept his palm in place. His tongue worked her over, edging her closer and closer to her release until her body went taut. Her hands moved from the sheets to his head. One wrapped into his hair and tugged. He could probably get off just watching her get off. She bit her lip, preventing her moan from escaping, but he could feel it rip through her.

Finally, she stilled. Her eyes opened and she sought out his gaze. "Come here."

"Who, me?" he joked, already climbing up the bed to lie next to her.

She kissed him, her mouth hot on his. Then she wrapped a hand around his length. His eyes rolled back in his head. Their tongues swirled together as she began to stroke him. Her other hand reached down, cupped his balls, and damn if he didn't want to let himself go. But he held back, trying to extend it as long as he could. He moved his hands to her breasts, toying with her nipples as she gave him the best damn hand job of his life. She seemed to know the perfect line between pleasure and pain and gave him just enough, taking him so close to the edge that as hard as he tried, he couldn't stop the wave of release surging through him.

His hips pumped back and forth and he was lost to her touch. He had to give her credit, she didn't pull back at all. When he'd finished, his body still, he glanced over at her. She smiled, a sweet, knowing smile that rocked him to his core.

"Well that was fun."

He grinned back. "Fun?"

"Yeah." She got up from the bed and walked to the bathroom, her hips swaying, making him wish like hell he'd had the forethought to carry a condom with him. Next time he'd be better prepared. He almost laughed at that thought. How the hell could he ever have been prepared for the petite firecracker named Zina Baxter?

The faucet turned on and then off again and she came out of the bathroom with a wet washcloth. "We better get cleaned up. My alarm's set to go off in about five minutes to feed the pups again."

He took the washcloth and wiped himself off while she pulled her shirt on over her head. On his way to the bathroom he glanced over at the pups, sound asleep in their laundry basket. "Should we wake them up to eat or let them sleep?"

She peered over the edge of the bed and glanced at the pups. "They do seem pretty content."

Content. That was the feeling that had settled in his chest. It was unfamiliar, so he hadn't known what to call it. He was content for the first time in as long as he could remember. Tomorrow would bring a whole new set of problems but for tonight, in this moment, he didn't want for anything.

"Let's let 'em sleep." He climbed back onto the bed and pulled Zina close. "And maybe we can catch a little shut-eye before they wake up."

"I thought you couldn't fall asleep." She nestled against his chest.

"That was before."

"Before what?"

He nudged his nose into her hair as he spooned against her back. "Before you wore me out. Now shh."

"You're very demanding all of a sudden."

She had no idea. The kinds of demands he wanted to place on her had nothing to do with sleeping. But he needed to rest. Especially if come morning he was going to figure a way out of the mess he'd gotten himself stuck in. He chose not to respond but pulled her tighter instead, cupping her breast with one hand and holding her hands in his other.

Sighing, she settled into him, the fullness of her ass pushing against his crotch. This he could get used to. But he wouldn't let himself. Too much time had shown him that he wasn't worth betting on. He had a wanderlust inside him so strong that nothing, not even the soft curves of a woman like Zina, could release that pull.

He wondered, what would it be like to wake up every day with the same woman in his arms? To go to sleep every single night knowing exactly where he stood and where his place was in this world?

He thought about it, expecting that same sense of tightness to fill his chest. When it didn't, he should have relaxed. Maybe whatever this thing with Zina was had loosened the curse around his heart. But thinking that this was where he was meant to be, to stay, did make his heart pound. Damn, he had it bad either way. She sighed, the tension leaving her limbs as she drifted off to sleep.

He tried closing his eyes, tried letting sleep claim him, but it was no use. One of the pups let out a soft whimper. Then another. They sounded off like a chain reaction, connected by some sort of invisible thread that held them to one another.

Gently, he pulled his arm out from under Zina and rolled

to the side of the bed. He might not be able to stick around but at least he could let her get a few hours of sleep.

He got the puppy formula ready and reached for the pup making the loudest noise. It settled against his chest, sucking on the dropper. Why couldn't life be this simple? Demands were issued, needs were met. His whole life had been an epic shit show in screwing up that simple flow. He didn't know where he might stand with Zina come morning, but wherever it was, he wanted to be ready.

seventeen

Zina rolled over in bed and opened her eyes. For a moment she tried to figure out where she was. Then it all came back to her. The pups, Alex's lips on hers, Alex's lips on her . . . *oh shit*. She pulled the covers away to reveal her bare legs, bare thighs, and bare booty. Her cheeks heated. Even though she was alone in the room, his room, she reminded herself, embarrassment crawled over her skin.

She flung herself to the edge of the bed. The puppies probably needed to eat. But the laundry basket was gone. She located her jeans and her bra on the floor and struggled to get dressed. There was no time for rest. She had to figure out what to do with the puppies and how to get her dogs out of the warehouse if Alex really thought he was going to be able to make the new timeline the wedding planner demanded.

As she rounded the bend in the staircase and headed toward the kitchen, she caught a glimpse of Alex's legs through the crack in the doorway. He was barefoot, the hem of his jeans barely touching the top of his foot as he sat in one of the chairs at the kitchen table.

"So what's she going to do with all of them?" his grandfather asked.

She should clear her throat or knock on the door to let them know she was there. But a part of her wondered what he was going to say . . . if the night they'd shared would have any kind of impact on his response.

"I don't know." His voice lodged in her chest, warming her from the inside out.

"It's a shame how people treat these dogs," his gramps said. "Keep 'em around while they have value, then toss them aside like yesterday's news when they're done with them."

"Is that what you think Char and I have done to you?" A hint of hurt laced through Alex's words.

Zina didn't want to eavesdrop, but her feet stood rooted in place.

"May as well be. I think me and Herbie got something in common, right, buddy?"

Herbie wagged his tail and licked the old man's hand. Zina noticed the tidbit he passed under the table. She'd always had a no-food-from-the-table rule when it came to her dogs. Looked like Alex's grandfather didn't seem to think the rules applied to him.

"Good morning." She pushed through the door and tried to paste a smile on her face. Maybe Alex hadn't shared that she'd spent the night. Maybe she still had a shred of pride intact.

"Well aren't you looking like a peach this morning?" Alex smiled from across the table. He held a puppy in his arms. "Gramps made coffee. Help yourself."

She moved to the counter to grab a mug, hoping coffee might flush away the awkwardness of a morning after. It would have been uncomfortable enough between the two of them without Alex's grandfather joining in the mix.

Just smelling the pungent brew cleared her mind a bit. She opened a cabinet in search of a mug.

"Let me give you a hand." Morty pushed back from the table and moved toward the coffeepot.

Zina stepped back to get out of his way. Herbie followed him from the table, probably hoping for another nibble.

"Here you go." He handed her a mug. "Cream's in the fridge if you want it. Sugar's on the counter."

"Thanks so much." She fixed her coffee, then took a seat at the table. "How are the puppies this morning?"

"Good. They all made it through the night." Alex gave her a grin, one that settled her concern for the pups and also created an uncomfortable warmth inside her stomach.

"Thanks for taking care of them. I need to get them over to the vet today. Maybe we can find a surrogate mama dog to nurse them."

"They can do that for dogs?" Morty asked. "The pups will take to a new mom, just like that?"

"If she's willing, yes." Zina caught an undercurrent of tension pass between Alex and his grandfather.

"Too bad it didn't work that way for you, son."

"That's not fair." Alex bristled. His muscles tensed and for a moment Zina thought he might launch himself across the table.

"His ma wasn't exactly the nurturing type." Morty lifted his mug toward Zina. "Too bad we all can't pick our kin, huh? Did Alex tell you he was in school to become a vet?"

"He mentioned it." Zina took a sip of her coffee.

Alex got up from his chair, set the pup down in the basket, and stalked out of the room. Morty shook his head. "He's a good man but he doesn't know how to grow roots."

She didn't know how to respond. Was he directing his comment at her? Did he expect her to say something in return? "Oh, I um—"

"He's got a good heart. As soon as he finds something

worth sticking around for, he'll make a good father and husband someday." The older man gazed into his mug.

Zina gulped down a giant swig of coffee and set the mug down. "I'm going to get the pups out to the warehouse. Have a good day."

She didn't wait for him to reply. Armed with the laundry basket of puppies, she covered the distance from the house to the warehouse in record time. She didn't need to know Alex's whole backstory. Didn't need to know he came from what sounded like a broken home or that he had mama issues. She balanced the basket on one hip while she wrestled the door open. One of her volunteers saw her struggling and rushed over to lend a hand.

Zina filled her helper in on how to care for the pups, then left to run home for a quick shower and a change of clothes. She still had that adoption event scheduled for tomorrow and needed to get ready. Whether she liked it or not the penguins were coming and she had to make room.

As she pulled out of the parking lot and onto the main road, her cell rang with a call from Lacey. "How's the mama to be this morning?"

"Not good. Not good at all," Lacey answered. "Where are you?"

"On my way home to grab a shower. We found some puppies in the woods by the warehouse and I spent all night feeding them." *And doing unmentionable things to your penguin handler.* She decided to keep that part to herself.

"Bodie's at your place."

"My house?"

"Yeah. A call came in last night. Someone saw something strange going on over there. I couldn't reach you, so he went over to check it out."

"What happened?" Her heart jumped into her throat. She tried to swallow her fears back down but the knot of worry wouldn't budge.

"I don't think the roof collapsing was as much of an accident as we thought. There may have been some foul play involved as well."

"What do you mean?" Zina pressed on the gas, eager to get home and figure out what Lacey was talking about.

"Someone doesn't like the fact that you're helping all these pit bulls. I think they're trying to warn you to stay away."

"That's crazy. I've been working at the rescue for a few years now. No one's bothered us before."

"Yeah, but Bodie's getting close to figuring out who's behind the dog-fighting ring. Maybe the two are related."

Zina's mind spun with possibilities. She'd originally thought Bodie's dad and grandfather might be behind the dog-fighting ring. But when they were arrested last year for smuggling huge amounts of Cuban cigars into the country, she gave up on that idea. Since she'd teamed up with Bodie to take on the cast-off pitties he came across, they'd received some publicity about the shelter and the dogs. Maybe the people behind the dog-fighting ring were feeling threatened.

"Tell me what happened." Zina needed to know what would be waiting for her when she got home.

"They redecorated your house, hon." Lacey's voice went all quiet. "It's not safe for you to stay there anymore. I want you to move in with us for a bit."

Her heart kicked up its pace and began to beat so hard and so fast she thought she might pass out. "I can't stay with you, you're on the other side of town. It would take me forever to get to the warehouse. And even longer to get to the shelter once we get that fixed up."

"Well you can't go home. You'll stay at the Phillips House." Her voice held a finality Zina had heard before. But it had rarely been directed at her. It was her mayor voice, the one she used when she wasn't going to take no for an answer.

"I can't stay there, you've only got two bedrooms and

they're both in use," Zina ground out. Not to mention that's where Alex was. And based on what went down between them the night before, trying to maintain her distance with him so temptingly nearby might prove to be too much for her to handle.

"The men can share a room. We'll bring in an air mattress if we have to. But you're not going home and that's final." Lacey's voice bordered on shrieking.

"Settle down, mama. No need to burst an eardrum. Let me check in with Bodie and we'll make a plan from there, okay?" It didn't fail to register that she was the one who should be freaking out right now, not Lacey. Maybe this pregnancy was changing her friend in more ways than met the eye.

"All right. He's waiting for you there. Call me after?"

"I will. And, Lacey?"

"Hmm?"

"Thanks for worrying about me. You know you're a giant pain in my ass but I do love you." That was an understatement. The pain-in-the-ass part. Lacey wasn't so much a giant pain in her ass, she was more like a boil that was about to burst.

"I just don't want anything to happen to you."

"It won't. I know how to take care of myself." And she did. She'd been in the military, stationed overseas. Where she'd had to always be on alert, sleep with one eye open, and all that.

"But you don't have to take care of yourself all by yourself now. That's what friends are for."

The sentiment hit her harder than it should have. She'd blame it on the lack of sleep and the stress she'd been under for the past several days. Wiping a tear away before it fell, she took in a breath. "Gotta go, I'm almost there. I'll call you later."

As she pulled into her own drive, Bodie's sheriff's truck loomed before her.

eighteen

⌣

Alex couldn't believe his grandfather. How dare he bring up the past, especially in front of Zina? He could still taste her on his lips, still feel the way her hair slid through his fingers as he kissed her.

He pulled some clothes on and headed down to the warehouse to check on preparations. Toby was there, doing a final walk-through of the dome. He'd already filled the large aboveground pool. Alex had checked with the aquarium on exact requirements and had dumped enough salt in the bottom to make sure the penguins would feel right at home.

"Think you'll be wrapping up today?" Alex asked.

"Yeah." Toby fiddled with the thermostat. "It's done. Now all you need to do is get the temp down to where you want it and bring in the ice and snow."

"I can't believe you were able to get this done so fast."

"Where there's a will, there's a way, isn't that right?" Toby clapped him on the shoulder. "I'm just going to make a few final adjustments."

They were doing everything they could to make sure they'd have things ready. Now that the habitat was finished, he'd have such little time to get the penguins trained. Good thing they were coming from the aquarium where they'd participated in plenty of training sessions, so they were used to working for treats. He hadn't been able to make it over to Houston to see them in action yet. The director said he could come by anytime and hand select the penguins he wanted to have at the wedding. With everything under control, today seemed as good a time as any to head over. Maybe the girls would want to go with him.

He pulled out his phone and dialed Char. If memory served, she had a rare day off and might enjoy having some time to herself.

"Hey, what's up?" she answered, her voice a little breathless.

"I need to head to Houston to check out those penguins. Thought maybe the girls would want to go with me and we could give you a day to yourself. What do you say?"

"Really? I was just starting to clean out the girls' bedrooms. Do you know Frankie keeps all kinds of food under her mattress to train Shiner Bock?"

He stifled a chuckle. That didn't surprise him at all. Frankie loved that damn bird with a fierceness. She'd do just about anything for him. "I believe it."

"I wanted to ask you a question about Shiner."

"What's up?"

"I think Dolly's allergic. Is there any chance he can move out to the Phillips House with you?"

He groaned. "First Gramps, now the damn bird, too?"

"Just long enough for me to see if it makes a difference?"

"Yeah, fine."

"Thanks. Frankie will be heartbroken if we have to give him away. And I'm sure they'd love to go with you to the aquarium. What time?"

"How about an hour?"

"That'll be fine. I'll have them ready."

"Sounds good."

"Hey, Alex?"

"Yeah?"

"Thanks." She disconnected.

He tucked his phone back into his pocket and headed back to the house. That gave him just enough time for a shower, another few cups of coffee, and a talk with his grandfather about appropriate breakfast conversation. Gramps still sat at the table, where Alex had left him.

"Hey, we need to talk."

Gramps looked up. "Haven't we talked enough for one day?"

"You should have thought about that before you went and brought up things from the past."

"You can't change what kind of person your mama was." The old man gave a slight shake of the head. "But you can change what kind of man you want to be."

Alex forced down the anger rising in his chest. "You have no business talking about my mom like that. You don't know what happened back then."

"I know a lot better than you do. What were you, five? Six? When she left, you couldn't have been more than first or second grade."

Five. He was five years old when he came home from kindergarten one day to find his dad passed out in a recliner in the family room and his mom long gone. She'd left a note saying she was going to stay with her sister and would come back for them when she got a job and found them a place to live. That was the last time he'd heard from her.

"How dare you bring that up in front of a stranger?"

Gramps scoffed, laughed right into his mug of coffee. "I'd say you know that woman better than the vast majority of other people in this town. Do you think I couldn't hear the two of you going at it all night long? She ought to know what she's in for, don't you think?"

That was it. The man must have lost his mind, at least the part that had still been working. Alex stomped out of the house, leaving him to his memories and judgments. He'd sacrifice that extra coffee and head to Char's early if it meant getting away from his grandfather.

As he passed through town, he caught a glimpse of the Burger Bonanza sign. He may as well stop in and grab a cup of coffee to go.

A few minutes later he leaned against the counter while he waited for the waitress to stop by and grab his order. He hadn't spent much time in town since he'd been back—he'd been busy from dawn till dusk trying to get the warehouse ready for the impending penguin arrival. As he sat there waiting for his fix of caffeine, he let his gaze roam over the place. Same booths. Same countertop. Same cantankerous cook slinging burgers in the kitchen. It was comforting on some level to know that no matter how long he'd been gone or how far he traveled, places like this would always stay the same.

Kind of like his grandfather, he supposed. Maybe he'd been too rough on the man. Alex kneaded the back of his neck as someone slid into the booth behind him.

Must have been two people based on the way they traded muffled words back and forth. Alex didn't pay them much mind until he heard a phrase that set off a chain reaction of protectiveness. "Stupid, dog-loving bitch."

They could be talking about anyone but his mind immediately went to Zina. He fought the urge to whip around and set them straight. But that wouldn't do any good. So he sat there in silence, straining to pick up tidbits of the conversation. The waitress came over to take his order, and he decided to stick around and try to figure out what they were talking about. While she chattered away at him, he missed out on a good chunk of what was being said. He swore he heard the word "pity." But it could have been "pity" or "pittie." Laying into a man for mistaking something he said wouldn't do any good, so he waited.

The talk between them stopped when their food arrived. Alex was left to sip on his coffee and hope they started up again before he had to leave to get to Char's. He tried to turn his head and catch a glimpse of them without being too obvious as he signaled the server over for more coffee. All he could see from the corner of his eye was a pair of well-worn steel-toed work boots and a hand before the man shifted farther into the booth. Dammit. The man did wear a ring though. Looked like something he'd see on a biker. He could have sworn it was a skeleton.

He pulled out a few bucks and slid them under his saucer, figuring he'd get up and go to the restroom. That would give him a chance to sneak a quick look at the men at the table behind him. Before he could stand up, a palm landed on his shoulder.

"Alex Sanders." A woman stood next to him, her other hand held out for a handshake.

"Do I know you?" He instinctively reached for her hand, barely catching a final look at the two men as they exited through the front door.

"Suzy Mitchell, damn glad to meet you."

"If you'll excuse me for a moment . . ." Alex hopped off his stool and ran to the door, trying to catch a glimpse of the two men who'd been at the booth behind him. He made it to the window just in time to see a large black dually pickup truck fishtail out onto the main road.

"Mr. Sanders?" Suzy had followed him to the door, a friendly smile on her face.

"You didn't happen to catch sight of those two men, did you?" He moved back toward the stool where he'd been sitting, stopping on the way to see if maybe the men had paid with a credit card and left a receipt sitting there.

"Sorry, I didn't. Can I ask you a quick question though?" Her lips were bright orange, just a few shades different from her hair.

"Sure." Alex had no idea how the woman knew his

name or what he might be able to help her with, but his chance of getting more info on the two men was lost, so he managed a smile as he grabbed his jacket.

"I hear you're doin' some work out at the Phillips House?"

"That's right."

"Well, I wanted to introduce myself. I'm the town florist. You be sure to give me a call if you need flowers for that big wedding coming into town."

"Oh, they've got a wedding planner from LA making most of the arrangements, but I'll mention it to Lacey."

She nodded. "I heard you're going to have some penguins. One of 'em gets out of hand and you need to have something mounted, I can help you with that, too."

"Mounted?"

She pulled a rolled-up magazine out of her back pocket. "Taxidermy and flowers, those are my two specialties. You can see right here I was a centerfold back in the day."

He squinted, not wanting to look at the spread she held out.

"Do my own mounts, full body if you want. I figure penguins can't be too different than some of the other animals I've worked with."

Alex peeked between his lashes at the image of Suzy surrounded by woodland animals. His stomach churned. "Oh, we're set there. No need to mount the penguins."

"You let me know if you change your mind." She held out a card.

He slid it into his back pocket. "I sure will."

"Oh, one more thing?"

Alex cringed, wondering what other businesses the taxidermist florist might be dabbling in. He was almost afraid to ask. "Yes?"

"Is it true you're having a dog adoption event out at the Phillips place today? My nephew lost his dog to cancer last year and I was going to send him over."

"We sure are. Starts at three." Alex checked his watch.

Speaking of the adoption event, he'd promised Zina he'd help. If he wanted to get back in time, he'd better get a move on.

"Thanks. I'll let him know." She grinned again as she stepped past him.

Alex downed the rest of his coffee and headed toward the truck.

Twenty minutes later he pulled into Char's driveway. The girls crowded around him, apparently eager to get to the aquarium.

"Uncle Alex, is it true we're going to get to pet the penguins?" Dolly asked.

"Can we teach them how to play soccer?" Jordan passed a soccer ball between her hands.

Izzy took his hand and tugged him toward the truck. "Let's go. I want to draw them."

Char gazed at him over the top of her daughters' heads. "You sure you're up for this?"

"Um, yeah." Truth was, he was already having second thoughts. But he'd offered and it was something that needed to be done sooner rather than later.

Char lifted Dolly up so she could climb into the back seat. "Have fun."

"Did you decide what to do with your free time?"

"Sure did. One of my friends is meeting me in town for lunch and then we're getting manicures at the salon." Her smile made the hours that stretched ahead of him worth it. "Where's Gramps?"

"Oh, we kind of had it out this morning. He's back at the Phillips House."

"You can't leave him there by himself all day." Char's forehead creased.

Alex couldn't imagine spending the morning at the aquarium with his nieces and his grandfather. "He'll be fine. Where's he going to go? He'll putter around the warehouse, pet some dogs, and maybe get his head out of his ass while he's at it."

The girls giggled.

"Sorry. I shouldn't have said that." He and Gramps had exchanged some harsh words but the old man was right. He always was.

"Come on, Alex. This isn't what we talked about. If you won't take him with you, I guess I'll have to cancel my plans." She reached into her pocket and pulled out her phone.

"Fine." He let out a sigh. "We'll swing by and pick him up on the way. Happy?"

"As a clam." She leaned over and wrapped an arm around him for a half hug. "You're a good guy. Despite what everyone says."

"Gee, thanks."

"You're welcome. I've got to get going. Y'all have fun."

Fun. Right. With his four nieces and his grandfather at the aquarium. If that was fun, then Alex decided he'd been doing it wrong. He herded the other girls toward the truck and got them loaded in. As he drove back to the Phillips House, he thought about whether or not he ought to call Zina and warn her about the men at the diner. Based on what he'd heard, he didn't even know if they'd been talking about her. They could have been talking about someone else.

It would be better to relay that kind of news in person, not over the phone. But if something happened or he got a sense she was in danger at all, he'd hunt those two men down and figure out what they were up to. Satisfied he had a plan, he slid a smile onto his face and cranked up the tunes. Today was about the girls and the penguins and the cranky old man he was lucky to have as his grandfather.

nineteen

Zina took tentative steps forward, walking toward the place she'd called home for the past four years. The front picture window had been smashed in. Just broken glass. That she could live with. It could have easily happened from a baseball that went too far. Didn't mean she was the target of some underground dog-fighting ring organizers.

Bodie had his back to her as she came up the walk. He was talking into the walkie clipped to his waist. She must have scuffed her boots on the sidewalk, because he turned.

"I'll be in touch." He clipped the mic to his belt and raised his brows. "Lacey get ahold of you?"

"Yeah. What happened?"

He moved toward the front door and she followed. "Best I can tell, someone threw a brick through your front window."

"You sure it wasn't a baseball?" she asked, futile hope making her voice come out an octave higher than usual.

He grimaced. "Pretty sure. We found the brick."

"Oh."

Bodie pushed the door open and entered the house first.

Shattered glass covered the floor and spread over the couch. The couch she probably would have been sitting on if she hadn't spent last night with Alex.

"There was a note tied to the brick. I need to take it into the lab and dust it for prints but wanted you to see it first. Maybe you recognize the handwriting?" He picked up a clear baggie from the table and held it out to her.

A creased piece of paper filled the bag. She glanced to Bodie as she took it. "'Forget about the dogs or else'?"

"I guess they didn't want to waste any words. Do you recognize the handwriting at all?"

Zina shook her head. Looked like a first grader had gotten ahold of a black Magic Marker. It wasn't so much handwriting as it was thick black letters scrawled across a standard piece of notebook paper. "How are you going to figure out where it came from?"

Bodie took the bag back. "Like I said, we'll dust it for prints. The guys were out here earlier looking for tire tracks and footprints. I'm not hopeful anything will come of it. You must have had a ton of visitors lately."

"Hardly anyone ever comes out here. What makes you think otherwise?" That didn't make sense. The only people that had been to her place lately were her and maybe Lacey.

"You've got a bunch of footprints around your house."

"That's crazy. The only people who've been around my place are me and Lacey, and I guarantee she hasn't been casing the joint. Not since she's supposed to be on bed rest."

"Hmm. Interesting." Bodie tipped his cowboy hat back and scanned the interior of the house.

"What's interesting?"

"Means we're probably not dealing with an individual. There are probably a few of them. I'll need you to check your belongings and see if anything's missing. Then you can grab what you need. I'll have to mark this off as a crime scene since it's pretty obvious we're not dealing with a standard act of vandalism."

"Sure. Whatever you need to do." Zina tried to seem agreeable on the outside but inside she was everything but. How dare someone think they could scare her away from her own home. She rummaged through her stuff, checking to make sure her mama's wedding ring still sat in her jewelry box and her .357 was still hidden in its case under her bed.

Bodie waited out front while she packed up what she'd need to be away for who knew how long. He'd better hope he found the people responsible. Because if she figured it out first, she'd just as soon wring their necks for the pain they'd caused her, not to mention the animals she spent her days and nights trying to protect.

"Got what you need?" He pushed off from where he'd been leaning against the side of his truck.

"I think so. Any idea how long I'll need to stay away?"

He shook his head. "I wish I knew. I'd say plan on at least a few weeks. If you need to come back for anything, just let me know and I can meet you out here or bring it to you."

"Okay."

"Hey"—he reached for her hand and gave it a squeeze— "I'll figure out who's behind this."

"I know." She held the emotion at bay, not wanting him to see her break down.

"In the meantime, you're welcome to stay with Lacey and me. We'd love to have you."

Zina nodded. "I've already had this conversation with your wife. I've got to be closer to the dogs. Y'all live too far away."

"She told me you'd say that. But the offer stands, okay?" He gave her a half-hearted smile. "I'll call you if I hear anything."

"Thanks."

He waited while she tossed her bag in the back of her truck. Her tires spun on the gravel as she executed an awkward three-point turn and hightailed it down the drive, leaving her home behind her.

By the time she got back to the warehouse, she only wanted for one thing . . . a shower. She parked in front of the Phillips House and entered the first floor, calling out for Alex or his grandfather. Neither answered.

Alex wouldn't be happy about giving up his room, but he was staying for free so he didn't have a choice. She pulled out a fresh change of clothes and locked the bedroom door. Then she turned on the hot water and prepared to wash away the stress of the day that had barely started.

While the warm water flowed down her body, she considered her options. Stay at the Phillips House until everything blew over and Bodie figured out who was behind the threats. He'd been working on this case for over a year already. The likelihood that he'd be able to bust up the dogfighting ring and put an end to the threats seemed about as likely as the odds of her settling down with Alex and starting a brood of their own.

She could stay at the Phillips House as long as she needed. Lacey wouldn't rush her to find a new place. But she had to move the dogs as soon as possible since Alex's precious penguins would be arriving soon. Which meant she needed to come up with a different temporary solution.

By the time she'd rinsed off, towel dried, and pulled on a fresh pair of jeans, she had a plan. First step, get through the adoption event this afternoon. She had twenty-eight dogs she needed to rehome. It was time to get the word out. And the best person to work with her on that was Lacey. Whether she liked it or not, Zina was about to do whatever it would take to get Lacey to put that circle of influence she'd been curating to good use.

twenty

> ❦

"Can we see some polar bears? And maybe pet the dolphins while we're here?" Dolly held tight to his hand, dragging him away from the ticket counter.

"I don't think they have polar bears at the aquarium." He tried to check the map in one hand while she tugged and pulled at the other. "First we need to find the penguins."

"Can we watch them feed the sharks, Uncle Alex?" Frankie pulled on his shirt. "Please?"

"Yeah, we'll have time for all of that. But first, we have to find the penguins." He lifted his head from the map, doing a head count. Ever since the night he'd left Dolly at home, losing one of the girls was his greatest fear. Char would never forgive him if he came home one short. The smell of popcorn filled the air. It had been years since he'd been to a place like this.

"Can we get ice cream?" Jordan spoke up from behind him.

"Yeah, sure. Here, get your sisters an ice cream while I figure out where we're going." He pulled a twenty out of his wallet and watched while the girls joined hands and made their way over to the ice cream cart. "Gramps, do you want ice cream?"

No response.

He turned around, trying to locate his grandfather in the sea of strollers and kids. The old man sat on a bench about twenty yards back, fanning himself with the baseball cap he'd pulled off his head. Alex kept an eye on the girls while he made his way back to his grandfather.

"You okay?"

"It's hotter than Hades out here. Aren't there any exhibits inside? Who visits a place like this on the hottest day of the year?" Gramps pulled his short-sleeve button-down shirt away from his body.

Alex glanced up to where the sun hadn't even reached its peak yet. A hint of a breeze blew by. "It's not even noon. You sure you're okay?"

"Aren't we going to go inside?"

"Yes. The whole reason we came out here was to see the penguins. Come on, let's get you out of the sun. How about an ice cream to help you cool down?"

Gramps nodded and let Alex take his elbow. They walked back to where the girls stood in line. After ten minutes of waiting and five minutes of Dolly changing her mind on what flavor she wanted, they found a place to sit and enjoy their cones before heading inside.

"Thanks for the ice cream." Izzy smiled as she licked at her cone. It had already started dripping down her hand.

"Yeah, thanks, Uncle Alex." Jordan, Frankie, and Dolly echoed the sentiment. Dolly's shirt already held more ice cream than was left on her cone. Char might not be thrilled when he returned her daughters much messier than when he'd taken them, but hopefully a day of "me time" would lessen the reaction.

As he sat at the table, surrounded by family, Alex wondered what it would be like to have kids of his own. The

thought hadn't crossed his mind before. He'd always figured he'd be happy being an uncle and leaving it at that. But
after spending the night caring for a basket full of puppies,
he considered the possibility. Having someone, or something, so dependent on him made him want to step up and
meet their needs. He'd always been a one-for-one kind of
guy. This one-for-all and all-for-one never resonated with
him before. But what if it could?

He glanced over at Gramps. He'd had a son and look
where that got him. Alone with no one but two bitter grand-
kids to look after him. What would life be like if his dad
hadn't passed away? If his mom had stuck around?

He shook the thought right out of his head. Didn't do any
good wasting energy thinking about what might have been.
The best course of action was to focus on the here and now.
And the future. That meant putting all of his attention and
efforts into making sure Munyon's daughter had the best
freaking wedding money could buy.

"Y'all done yet? There's a penguin show in a few minutes." He wondered what the show would consist of. He'd
worked around penguins for a while now, and while they
were smart birds, they were also stubborn buggers. Beyond
their flapping their flippers for a fish, he wasn't sure what
kind of tricks they'd be willing to perform.

With the ice cream polished off, he picked up the napkins from the table and tossed them in the trash. He waited
while Jordan took her sisters into the bathroom to wash off
hands and cheeks and chins, and then they all headed in-
doors to find the penguins.

The theater was half-full with only a minute to go until
showtime. Alex got the girls situated, just as the show
started. It wasn't really a show, more like a training session.
The birds swam through the water, rang a few bells, and ate
a bunch of fish.

The girls clapped along with the crowd at the end of the

display. "Now who wants to go meet the penguins?" he asked.

"I do." Frankie skipped down the concrete steps toward the tank.

"I have to go potty." Dolly's mouth screwed into a precocious frown.

"Again?" Jordan asked. "I just took you."

Dolly shrugged.

"Jordan, can you take your sister to the bathroom? Gramps, go with them and make sure they come back? Izzy and Frankie can stay with me." He didn't want to split up the group, but he had to get a few words in with the penguin trainers while he had the chance.

"Fine." Jordan took Dolly's hand and stomped off in the direction of the bathroom.

"Gramps? Keep an eye on them, okay?" Alex nudged his chin toward the girls.

"Yeah, okay." Gramps shuffled off behind them.

"Now let's go meet those penguins, shall we?" Alex pointed down the steps.

Izzy took off toward the tank, leaving Alex to follow. Taking care of some penguins for a couple of weeks had to be easier than trying to corral four girls and a grumpy old man. On the way down to the front, he noticed a few cracks in the concrete and a couple of places where the tank of water had been patched up. No wonder the director was willing to make a deal with Munyon. His penguin amphitheater was in massive need of repairs. The habitat probably matched.

He stood at the edge of the tank until one of the staff came over. "Do you have a question?"

Alex held out his hand. "Hi, I'm Alex Sanders."

"Nice to meet you. What can I do for you?"

"I'm taking a handful of your penguins for a couple of weeks."

"That's right. The wedding. You're the scientist from Antarctica, right?"

Alex didn't bother to correct him and tell him he was just a grunt who'd happened upon the job. "Are you in charge here?"

"Supposedly. What do you need?"

"I was told I'd be able to pick the penguins that would be coming to Ido for the wedding?"

The man's mouth turned down into a frown. "Don't you think you're a little late for that?"

Alex's chest tightened. "What do you mean?"

"We sent them over this morning. I was told the habitat was ready and the director needed them over there as soon as possible."

"But I haven't even met them yet." Alex's heart thumped. "You're telling me a half dozen penguins left here this morning and are on their way to Ido?"

"A half dozen?" The guy's eyes narrowed. "I've got twelve of my birds on their way to you. I'd like to know what you're doing here and who's going to be there to meet them."

Twelve birds? Alex took a moment to let that information rattle through his head. "What time did they leave?"

The guy checked his diving watch. "I packed them up right before the show started. Maybe a half hour ago, tops."

"I'll handle this." Alex reached for the girls' hands. "Come on, we've got to go."

"You mess with my birds and you'll be hearing from our lawyer." The trainer's voice bounced off the concrete, following Alex down the stairs as he tugged his nieces toward the bathroom where he hoped to find Gramps and the others.

He wanted to yell back that the guy could get in line. By the time the wedding was over, there would probably be a long list of people who wanted to sue him. As he shuffled the girls to the truck, he tried to call Zina. She'd be at the warehouse. She could stall the driver and give him enough time to get home and figure out what was going on. There had to be a mistake.

Zina had almost finished setting up for the adoption event. Alex said he'd be there to help, but she hadn't seen him yet. She should have known better than to get her hopes up that he might come through for her.

At least her volunteers had shown up, along with a small crowd of people thanks to Lacey making some last-minute calls. It would be bittersweet to see the pups go. She always felt a little bit of a loss when one of them went off with their new owners. But it was for the best. All of the dogs deserved new homes—somewhere where they could get the unconditional love they deserved.

Maybe someday she'd finally get to see for herself what that felt like. She shook off the mood that had settled over her, and made the rounds, checking on the dogs and volunteers to make sure everything was in order. The last time they'd tried to hold a big event like this, a group had shown up to protest having pit bulls around town. Things had settled down since then but thanks to the brick that had gone through her front window, she was prepared for just about anything.

"Hey, Zina, I've got a guy interested in Buster." One of the regular volunteers approached.

"Really?" Her stomach turned over at the thought of Buster leaving. But it was for his own good. Zina tried to act nonchalant as she walked toward Buster's kennel. The "guy" was Jasper Taylor. They'd gone to high school together but she hadn't seen much of him since she'd moved back.

"Hey, Zina." He gave her a smile as he leaned toward Buster's crate. "Long time no see."

"Jasper, what are you doing out here today?" As far as she knew he still lived outside town. His family ran a huge commercial pecan orchard or something like that.

"My aunt Suzy said you were having a big event, so I figured I'd come check it out. I just had to say good-bye to Justice. Lost him to liver cancer last fall."

"I'm sorry. Have you met Buster yet?"

"Just through his kennel."

"Let me give you a proper introduction." She stopped when she got to Buster's kennel. "He's one of my favorites."

"Seems like a good guy."

"He is." Her favorite dog wasn't going to go home with just anyone. "He needs someone who will make sure he gets his exercise. He's a big couch potato."

"That's what I love about this breed. They're huge snugglers."

Zina opened the door to the kennel and clipped a leash on Buster's collar. "Let's take him out where he's not distracted by the others."

They walked past a few people who were checking out other dogs. Buster followed, his tail wagging. They reached the door, and Zina pushed it open. Sunlight streamed in and she shielded her eyes. Something big and dark sat in the middle of the drive, blocking the cars behind it.

"What in the world?" she muttered to herself.

"What's going on?" Jasper asked.

"I have no idea. Here, you want to take Buster around the lawn and get to know each other?" She passed him the leash, intent on finding out who had driven a semi into the middle of her dog adoption event.

"Thanks. We'll stay close."

Satisfied that Buster was in good hands, she turned her sights on the truck. A man got down from the cab, a clipboard in hand. Zina met him halfway to the building.

"Can I help you?" she asked.

"I've got a delivery here for an Alex Sanders." The man held out the clipboard. "If you'll sign, I can unload the cargo."

"What is it?" She glanced at the clipboard. Something about live animals jumped off the page. "Wait, you don't have penguins in that truck, do you?"

"Sure do. Where would you like me to put 'em?"

Zina's heart leapt into her throat. "Nowhere. We're not ready. You'll have to take them back."

"Lady, I just drove all the way from Houston. There's no way I'm taking them back."

"But . . ." This was Alex's problem. He was the one who ought to be fixing it.

"Can you sign please? Once I leave here I get to go home for a few days."

"Hold on a minute. I need to make a call about this."

He huffed out a breath and rolled his eyes. "Sure, take all the time you need."

Zina handed the clipboard back, then pulled her phone out of her back pocket. It didn't turn on. She'd forgotten to plug it in last night since she'd been so busy with Alex. Speak of the devil . . .

Alex came rushing up the drive with his nieces and his grandfather in tow. "What's going on?"

"Expecting a delivery?" She thrust her hands to her hips.

"I wasn't. But I was just at the aquarium and they heard we were ready for the penguins, so they went ahead and sent them over."

"Seriously? What are you going to do about it?" She gestured to the line of cars waiting to turn in to the parking lot. "I've got people trying to get in here to meet the dogs. You know, the dogs you need me to get out of here."

He put his hands to his temples. "Just give me a minute."

"I don't have a minute."

"I'm on it." He leaned down and pecked her cheek. "I'll figure this out and then be in to help. Girls, why don't you go with Zina?"

"Can't we meet the penguins, Uncle Alex?" Dolly asked.

"Later. Just go with Zina, please?" He gave Dolly a gentle nudge toward the warehouse.

Zina took Dolly's hand. "Come on, you can help me round up the dogs. They probably shouldn't be out here if your uncle is about to parade some penguins across the parking lot."

She took a few steps toward the warehouse, when she heard a chorus of oohs and aahs. Too late. The driver had opened up the back of the truck. A crowd of people stood on the drive, staring and pointing and smiling at the back end of the semi. Those were her people. They'd come to meet the dogs, not ogle Alex's penguins.

Before she could complain, a loud bark came from her left. Buster. He charged the crates the driver had started unloading from the truck. Jasper ran after him.

Zina stumbled toward the dog, trying to grab onto his leash. Buster had always been a giant lug of a beast who usually wouldn't move from his bed unless she offered him a treat. But now, he looked like one of those dogs who performed in agility competitions. He hopped the small makeshift fence they'd erected around the building and made a beeline for the penguins.

"Grab him!" Zina instructed anyone who might be near enough to snag his leash as he flew by. Alex sprang into motion, hurdling over one of his nieces in an attempt to intercept Buster before he reached the crates. The dog ran past, seemingly intent on reaching the birds. For a split second time seemed to stand still. Zina imagined what Buster might do to the poor birds. If someone didn't stop him, everyone who'd come to meet the dogs available for adoption might bear witness to a bird bloodbath.

"Buster!" Dolly pulled something out of her pocket and waved it in the air.

Zina strained, trying to see what she had.

"Want a treat?"

The dog stopped in midair, spinning around like he'd hit an invisible wall. Then he bounded over to Dolly and sat down right in front of her. The child was an angel from heaven, sent down to save her. Zina was sure of it. In the few seconds it took her to reach Buster, Dolly had him eating out of the palm of her hand. Literally.

"Dolly, you're a lifesaver." Zina wrapped an arm around the little girl and pulled her in for a side hug. "Thanks so much for catching Buster."

"He likes cotton candy." Dolly smiled up at Zina, her mouth covered in a mix of pink and blue spun sugar.

"How did you know that?" Zina bent down to make sure the leash was securely attached to Buster's collar.

Dolly looked at her like she was the dumbest adult on the face of the planet. "Everyone likes cotton candy."

Alex let out a nervous laugh. "Who knew?"

"Thank goodness Dolly seemed to." With the crisis averted, Zina's attention moved to the number of crates the truck driver had lined up on the driveway. "What are you going to do with them? You said six. There are more than six there."

"There was a little miscommunication about the number." Alex's foot tapped on the gravel drive. "Give me a minute. I need to go inside and make sure the dome is ready."

"You can't leave me out here with . . . with . . ."

"Ms. Baxter?" Cyrus Beasley, photographer for the local paper, stood next to her, a camera hanging from his neck.

Zina wanted to follow Alex into the building. Maybe together they could figure out what was going on and how to salvage the adoption event. But instead she stood in the center of the chaos and turned toward Cyrus. "Yes?"

"Is it true your dogs are going to be sharing living quarters with some penguins? How long do you expect them to be in town?" He held his phone in hand, waiting for her to respond.

She stared at him as the question sank in. Dogs. Penguins.

Living together. This couldn't happen. The penguins weren't supposed to arrive for another week at least. She was supposed to have time to find the dogs homes before then.

"Ms. Baxter?" Cyrus lifted his phone, holding it closer to her face. "The residents of Ido want to know what's going on right under their noses here. Are the penguins going to be safe sharing quarters with your pit bulls?"

twenty-one

"I didn't know they were coming." Alex paced the length of the kitchen.

Zina uncrossed her legs and then recrossed them the other way. She didn't believe him. He could tell by the way her jaw set. The softness he'd seen in her just last night was gone.

"I'm sorry. We'll figure this out."

"No, you'll figure this out." She finally spoke. "And by the way, why is the parrot here?"

Alex glanced toward the bay window where the girls had insisted he set up Shiner Bock's cage. "Char thinks Dolly might be allergic and wanted to see if moving him out here would make a difference. As for the penguins, fine, I'll figure this out on my own." So far all he'd been able to do was put the penguins up in the front half of the warehouse. He'd had to use the shelving units to separate them from the dogs. The old Phillips warehouse was turning into a bit of a zoo.

"All the time we spent planning the adoption event." Zina let out a loud sigh. "Wasted."

"It's not wasted. You still found homes for a few of the dogs, right?" He tried to remind her of the good that had come out of the day.

"Buster. We found a home for Buster and that's it." She held a puppy in the crook of her arm. He'd never meant to make more work for her. All along the only thing he'd wanted to do was help her out.

"Well, at least that's one dog who's going to a good home." He gave her his best winning smile.

She frowned back. It had taken all afternoon and into the evening to get the penguins and the puppies settled. Gramps had gone to bed a couple of hours ago while Alex and Zina had still been shuffling kennels around in the warehouse.

"You hungry?" he asked. "I can whip up something for us to eat."

The look she gave him let him know she had less faith in his ability to make dinner than she did in his ability to remedy the penguin and puppy situation.

"What? I've been feeding myself for years. I think I can handle it."

"You burned macaroni and cheese."

"First of all, that wasn't totally my fault. And second, I've never burned a quesadilla."

"You seem pretty sure of yourself. Go for it."

He'd show her he could succeed at something, even if it was only heating up two tortillas with some cheese between them. Determined to prove himself, he scoured the fridge for possible ingredients. He hadn't had to fend for himself at the station. They had cooks to take care of feeding the masses. But before that he'd been pretty good at managing on his own. He grabbed the eggs, cheese, some sausage left over from breakfast, and the tortillas.

Zina rose from the table, the puppy sound asleep in her

arms. "I'm going to go put him in the basket and wash up. Try not to catch the place on fire while I'm gone, okay?"

"Very funny." Alex let his gaze linger on her retreating behind. When she disappeared from view he pulled the cutting board out of the cabinet and chopped up half of a green pepper he'd found in the fridge. Next, he dropped a pat of butter into a skillet and sautéed the peppers, then got to work on the eggs. By the time Zina came back he was just putting the finishing touches on two sausage, egg, and pepper quesadillas.

"Wow, the smoke alarm didn't even go off." She smiled as he slid a plate in front of her.

"One gourmet quesadilla. Can I get you anything else?" He'd already poured the remains of the orange juice into two glasses and cut up whatever fruit Gramps hadn't eaten yet into a quick fruit salad.

"This actually looks really good. Thanks."

"You're welcome." He took a seat next to her and let his gaze linger on her as she took the first bite. Her shoulders didn't seem as tense and she didn't look like she wanted to kill him anymore.

"Mmm. This is good. Maybe you're not such a failure in the kitchen after all."

"One bad experience and I'm going to have to live that down the rest of my life, aren't I?"

"Your 'bad experience' was burning mac and cheese." Zina held a triangle of quesadilla up to her mouth. "That's pretty hard to overcome."

He shook his head. "I had to rescue Barbie from my nieces."

"So you admit you get easily distracted by women?" She swallowed the bite in her mouth and took a sip of juice.

"Not all women." He couldn't help but notice the way her throat moved as she swallowed. He'd had his lips on that same spot. Was it just a few hours ago? Thinking about how it had felt to lie next to Zina in the big bed upstairs made him shift in his seat. This thing between them, whatever it was, seemed to flip-flop back and forth between frustration and desire. He didn't know which feeling was sitting closer to the surface with her tonight.

"Hmm. I suppose Barbie is one of a kind. Good thing she's not here tonight. This is really good."

He smiled at the compliment. "So do you have any specialties?"

"What, like in the kitchen?" The tilt of her head, the way she glanced over at him, told him she was flirting. Maybe desire was winning and he'd convince her to stay over again tonight.

"Sure. In the kitchen . . . or feel free to name any talents you might have in other rooms of the house as well."

"Other rooms?" She grinned back at him. "Like I'm great at starting a load of laundry?"

"Not what I meant." He watched as she took a particularly large bite. Melted cheese oozed from where it sandwiched between the tortillas.

"Oh, I know what you meant. I just don't like to play into your conversation traps." She hitched a brow as he wondered what she meant by that.

"My conversation traps? Say more." Leaning back against the chair, he crossed his arms over his chest. Zina's mind was an interesting playground. She didn't respond the way he expected her to most of the time. It was refreshing and if he were being completely honest with himself, which he rarely did, it was also a bit intimidating.

"You know . . . where you send some flirty bullshit my way and expect me to volley it back to you."

"Oh." Wasn't he charming? He'd always thought so. Most women seemed to like the banter, the flirty foreplay. Maybe it wasn't him that was the problem. Maybe it was Zina.

"It's okay." She set her elbows on the table. "I kind of like it."

"You like what? The flirty bullshit?"

"Bullshit, bullshit," Shiner Bock piped up.

Zina laughed. "No. The quesadilla."

Damn. He should have seen that burn coming. Ready for a complete change of subject, he tried to get to know her a little better. "So you grew up in Ido?"

She shook her head. "My dad was in the military. I was an Army brat. We moved here when he retired so my mom could be closer to her family in Mexico."

"And you've lived here ever since?"

"Yeah. Except for my stint in the Army."

"How long did you serve?" Trying to get personal info out of her was like trying to milk a bull.

"Only a few years. I had to file for a dependency discharge to come home and take care of my brother."

"Zeb?"

Zina nodded. "He was in the service, too."

"I really thought he would go all the way to the NFL. He was good."

"Better than good." Her mouth set in a grim line. "I wish he had. Then maybe he wouldn't be so messed up."

"What happened?"

"I told you he's got PTSD. I think anyone who's been stationed in a war zone ends up with some level of trauma. But Zeb wasn't the same man when he came home."

"I'm sorry." Against his better judgment, he reached out and put his hand on hers.

She tried to laugh off his concern. "Sorry for what? It's not your fault."

"Of course not. I just mean I'm sorry he's had to . . . I mean, sorry both of you have had to deal with this."

"He's family. You do what you've got to do, right?" She shrugged and nibbled on her last triangle of quesadilla.

Family. Do what you've got to do. She made it sound so simple, so cut-and-dried. Here she'd given up her military career to come home and take care of her brother and he balked at the idea of having to deal with his grandfather for a few weeks.

"So who takes care of you?"

"What?" Her eyebrows drew together.

He wanted to kiss away the little wrinkle that furrowed her brow. "Who has your back? Who's your family?"

She leaned back from the table. "Lacey for one. She and Bodie are about the only family I've got left. We do all right around here though. Sometimes family doesn't necessarily mean the people who share your blood, you know?"

He nodded like he knew what she meant, but the truth was, he hadn't been very good family to anyone—not the people he shared genes with or anyone else for that matter.

"Thanks for the late dinner." Zina pushed back from the table and carried her plate over to the sink.

He scarfed down the last couple of bites and joined her next to the sink. "Do you want to stay over tonight?"

The blank look she gave him made him rethink the invitation.

"I just thought, since it's late and you've got the puppies here . . ." Hell, maybe he'd misread the entire situation. She seemed pretty into him last night.

She closed her eyes for a long moment and rubbed at her temple. "Sorry, it's been such a strange day, I forgot to tell you."

"Tell me what?"

"I've been forbidden to return to my place, so we're going to . . . well, we're going to be roommates."

A heaviness settled in the pit of his stomach. "Excuse me?"

"With everything going on I forgot to mention it. Seems someone tossed a brick through my front window last night and Bodie won't let me go home. Looks like you're stuck with me until I get the dogs out of here." She caught her lower lip with her teeth. "Is that okay?"

"Okay? Um, yeah, of course." An image of the men

from the restaurant this morning played through his head. He needed to talk to Bodie, tell him what he'd overheard. "Are you all right?"

"It's a little unnerving knowing that someone has it out for me."

"Come here." He held his arms open and she snuggled against his chest. "Gramps and I won't let anything happen to you. Not while we're around."

"I can look out for myself you know." Her voice was muffled against his shirt.

He pulled back to meet her gaze. "I have no doubt you can. But as long as we're working on this wedding, we're part of a team, right? Which means we're in this together."

"Until you leave for your next job."

"What are you talking about?"

Zina looked away. "Your gramps said you got an offer to work for Munyon. Something about checking out some investment property he's looking at and joining his team?"

"It's not a done deal." He needed the wedding to go well before anything was finalized.

"But you're considering it?"

"I'm keeping my options open." He'd be an idiot not to jump on it. Munyon owned land around the world. Alex could go to work for him and enjoy the benefit of a paycheck while still not having to settle down anywhere.

She pulled his head down and pressed her lips against his.

"What was that for?"

"I guess I'm keeping my options open, too."

His mouth spread into a smile. "Does this mean you're not going to make me sleep on the couch?"

twenty-two

Zina tossed the thin local paper down on the table. It made a very unsatisfying *whoosh*, making her wish she'd been reading one of Lacey's huge bridal magazines or a hardcover book instead. The harsh *thunk* of a thicker volume would have better matched her mood.

"What's wrong?" Morty lifted his gaze from his mug of coffee.

"They didn't even mention the dog adoption event. All of the news, if you even want to call it that, revolved around those stupid penguins." The penguins who weren't even supposed to be arriving for at least another week. Alex had left early that morning to drive into Houston to meet with the director of the aquarium. At least he seemed as concerned as she was about the mistake, not that there was anything anyone could do about it now.

He chuckled. "Folks around these parts probably ain't ever seen a penguin in real life before. Not unless they went to the zoo."

Zina huffed out a breath as she lifted her mug to her lips. "I suppose. But why couldn't we have gotten through the adoption event before they brought the dang birds over?"

She shot a glance to Shiner Bock. The Phillips House was going to the birds. Literally. "And sending twelve instead of the six we were expecting? Now all anyone wants to talk about is penguins."

"It'll all be over soon."

"Not soon enough." She got up from the table and stalked over to the sink. With Alex gone for the day, she was in charge of both the dogs and the penguins. He'd shown her how to feed them and clean up after them. With any luck he'd be back before the evening feeding. "I'm heading over to the warehouse to take care of the animals."

"I'll come with you." Morty pushed back from the table and stood. "I want to check on those little pups you brought in the other day."

"They're doing great. Greta took them in like the rock star mama I knew she'd be. They're nursing right alongside her brood."

Morty nodded. "We could all learn a lot from the way animals treat each other, don't you think?"

Zina held the door for him as they made their way onto the porch. "How so?"

"Acceptance. Willingness to see each other for who we are and where we come from. Miss Greta doesn't know those pups from Adam. Yet she's taken them in and is giving them a home, a family. Seems like if more people acted like dogs, the world might just be a better place."

Hmm. He might be onto something. Nine times out of ten she'd much rather spend time with her four-legged friends than a human. She turned her attention forward and pulled the door closed behind her.

"Oh no." As they approached the warehouse, a sinkhole seemed to materialize in her stomach, sucking all of her hope for a drama-free day right down the drain. A couple dozen cars sat in the parking lot, and a line of people stretched from the front door and wrapped around the side of the building.

"Good thing you've got backup this morning." Morty ambled ahead of her, apparently excited at the idea of having to turn the crowd of people away.

Zina increased her step to catch up to him. "What do you think they want?"

"To see the penguins, of course." He looked at her like she didn't have a working brain cell in her head. "I told you they probably haven't seen one in the wild before. This is their big chance."

"I don't think I'm up for this today. I've got to start making some calls to see if I can find a place for my dogs to go until I can get the roof repaired. Alex doesn't think it's such a good idea for them to be sharing space."

"Nonsense." Morty waved a hand in the air. "How much do you think we can charge for all these fine folks to meet a real-life penguin?"

"Oh no." Zina's heart pounded like a brass knocker on a wooden door. *Boom-boom-boom.* The echo reverberated through her limbs. "We can't charge people to come in and meet a penguin."

"Why not? You need to raise money to fix your roof, don't you?"

She did. If she could get the roof fixed up, she could move the dogs back to the shelter before the wedding and not have to worry about rehoming them in such a hurry. She considered the idea for a moment. A short moment. It did have some merit to it. Whom would it hurt if they showed off the penguins for a bit? Alex wasn't around— he'd left the two of them in charge. No harm, no foul in her opinion.

"I don't think Alex would like it." That was a lie. He'd

be furious if he heard she'd pimped out his penguins. Zina flip-flopped back and forth. It was a bad idea. Something was bound to go wrong. It always did. But instead of shooting down the crazy idea, she decided to embrace it.

"What Alex doesn't know won't hurt him, right?" The older man gave her a wink as they reached the edge of the crowd.

That sealed the deal. She was in. Wasn't Alex the one who went through life with the motto "You only live once"? Well, if he hadn't said exactly that, he sure seemed to embrace the idea.

The crowd parted as she reached the door and slid her key into the lock.

Morty leaned over and mumbled to her, "Just leave this to me. You go get everything ready and we'll be pulling in a mint before you can say *cock-a-doodle-doo*, young lady."

Zina didn't want to be the one to break it to him that penguins didn't crow like roosters. Maybe Alex was right to think his grandfather needed to be in the care of a home. But then he put his hands to his mouth in a makeshift megaphone and shouted out directions.

"Listen up, everyone. Yes, we've got a dozen of the best-trained penguins in the world. If you want an up-close and personal encounter, it's going to cost you twenty bucks apiece. Taking a picture with one bird is going to run you an extra ten. Give us about fifteen minutes, and we'll let you in one small group at a time."

Wow. Did Alex know his gramps might have been a circus ringmaster in a previous life? She yanked the door open and then pulled it closed behind her. If her dogs had to share space with the infamous birds, at least they could get something out of it. She made the rounds and fed the birds, then cleaned out their pen as best she could. Thankfully she wasn't on the morning shift for the dogs. But if they had that many people moving through the building, she ought to have an ambassador pup at the table in case anyone wanted more information or felt moved to make a larger donation to the rescue.

But who would be well behaved around the birds? She moved to the back of the warehouse to see who might be in a good mood today. Not Herbie. And Greta was on nursing duty. Maybe Aurora. She was sweet and gentle and could probably be trusted not to eat their main attraction.

Zina walked over to her kennel. The pup's tail began to wag, thumping against the raised dog bed. "Hey, girl. Feeling friendly today?"

Aurora nudged her nose through the front of the kennel. Yeah, she wouldn't give anyone any trouble. Zina opened the door and clipped her leash to her collar. Operation "Raise Money for the Pitties by Exploiting the Penguins" was well underway.

Ten minutes later the first group came into the warehouse, led by Morty. Zina fumbled and bumbled her way through the information she'd looked up right before they came in. They met the bird—the one some clever aquarium worker had named Thelma. Gramps posed the family around Thelma for a quick picture and then ushered them out the door. He handed Zina a wad of cash.

"Tuck this under the table somewhere, will you?"

She glanced around, looking for somewhere to stash the cash before the next group came in. Finding nothing suitable, she tucked it into her sports bra as he opened the door. Another group, another info dump on emperor penguins, another hundred bucks. And so it went. Zina gave Thelma a break after the first couple of groups came through, and ended up rotating through all of the penguins at least once. She skipped Gilligan on the second round. That bird was goofier than the crazy character he was named for.

By the time Morty announced there was no one left outside, Zina was more than ready for a break. They were just about to count up the cash when the warehouse door opened. Alex came in, his boots clip-clopping across the concrete floor as he stalked toward the two of them.

"What the hell's been going on around here today?" Oh, he was pissed. She could tell by the set of his jaw and the heat that blazed in those baby-bluish eyes.

"What do you mean, son?" His gramps might as well have been an award-winning actor, too. He turned from the table to face his grandson. "We've been taking care of your birds"—he hooked a thumb toward Zina—"and this one's dogs. It's a virtual zoo around here."

"More like an animal exhibition from what I hear." Alex dropped his hat onto the table. "I thought we were trying to keep a low profile?"

"By 'low,' you mean what, exactly?" she asked. It wouldn't be fair for Morty to take the heat on this one by himself. Selling out the penguins might have been his idea, but she hadn't argued against it very long.

"I was in Houston." He paused, most likely for dramatic effect. "Houston."

Zina clapped. "Yay, you survived your trip into what most Texans consider the armpit of the state and lived to tell. What do you want, a medal?"

"No." He rounded on her, shifting his anger from his grandfather to her. His glare hit her smack-dab in the center of her chest. "I want to know what's been going on. Why are there pictures of the Ido penguins trending on social media?"

The color drained from her face. She knew it because it all pooled in her gut, creating a woozy feeling in her stomach. But she tried to play it off. "What do you mean?"

He held his phone out, tipping it toward her. One of the families who had been through their penguin meet and greet stared back at her. There was Thelma, right in the middle. They'd tagged the Phillips House and hash tagged #PhillipsPenguins in their post.

"I guess you wouldn't believe me if I said someone

broke in to photobomb a feeding session?" Her voice softened as the words drifted out of her mouth. She waited for
a quirk of his lips, for that easygoing smile of his to appear.

"I can't believe you did this." He turned away, shaking
his head.

"Hey, now." Gramps stepped in. "It was my idea."

"No, Morty. We're both to blame. I guess I don't see
what the big deal is though. Thanks to Cyrus and that article in the paper, people already knew they were here. We
made some people very happy and put a small dent in the
amount it's going to take to fix the roof of the shelter."

"Part of my agreement with Munyon was that we'd keep
the damn penguins under wraps as much as possible until
right before the wedding. He's the kind of guy who wants
to make a splash. Now that it's leaked, hell"—he paused to
scrub a hand over the scruff on his chin—"the whole project might be at risk."

"Why didn't you tell me that?" Zina's heart stopped for
a moment. If the wedding fell apart, she'd lose out on the
cash he'd promised to help pay the high deductible on the
shelter. That wasn't an option.

"I didn't think I had to. What the hell were you
thinking?"

Gramps moved closer to Alex. "We were thinking we
had a good opportunity and we took it. We're all to blame
for this. You should have told us."

"Who would have thought you'd turn them into a road-
side attraction within twenty-four hours?"

Zina nodded to herself. "So it's okay for you to make
commitments like agreeing to move up the wedding date
without talking to anyone about it, and taking on double the
birds, but we aren't allowed to make any decisions without
consulting you?"

"It's not like that." He'd turned to face her, his shoulders
slumped.

"Fine, handle them how you see fit. You're the one in

charge, Mr. Sanders. From now on you can call all of the shots." Before she said something she'd regret, she retreated to the back of the warehouse.

Alex didn't come after her. She could hear him arguing with his grandfather. Maybe she'd been too quick to open herself up to the man candy with the gorgeous eyes. She thought he might be ready for change. Based on the way he'd overreacted, she was wrong.

twenty-three

Alex grabbed another bucket of sardines. With the promise of fish and the sound of the clicker training tool he'd picked up at the pet supply store, he'd made fairly good progress on getting the birds to waddle down the red carpet he'd laid out as a makeshift aisle. Now all he needed to do was to get them to stand still when they reached the end. He hadn't done much actual training of penguins since he'd spent summers at the marine life park. Even then, he'd only been an assistant.

"How's it going?" Zeb peeked his head around the corner of the temporary shelves they'd set up.

"I've been better." Alex dropped the bucket to his side. One of the penguins moseyed up and tried to stick her beak inside. "Hey, no fish yet for you."

Zeb came closer, a cardboard box in his arms. "You got a package from someone named Chyna. Zina asked me to bring it over to you."

He and Zina had yet to make up over his accusation about the penguin exploitation. Since she'd moved into the mansion, he'd gone from king of the master suite to trying to fit his six-foot-three-inch frame onto the antique sofa in the formal living room.

"She say what it is?" Alex asked.

"Nope." Zeb set the box down on a table. "Want me to open it for you?"

"Sure." What would Chyna be sending him? He hadn't heard much from the wedding planner in the past few days, although she seemed to appreciate the pictures he texted her of how the training was going.

"What's this?" Zeb held up what appeared to be a string of glittery snowflakes. "There's a note."

Alex reached for it and scanned the handwritten card. Unbelievable. Seemed Chyna wanted the penguins to accessorize with snowflake necklaces and bow ties. What would she come up with next?

"Come here, Thelma." Alex held out a sardine, capturing Thelma's attention as he slid the necklace over her head. The bird didn't seem to mind as she scarfed down her treat.

"You think this is going to work?" Zeb held out a silver sparkly bow tie.

"I have no idea." Alex took it and located Gilligan, the tallest male penguin in the group. "Come here, Gilligan. Let's see how handsome you look in a bow tie with your tails."

Zeb shook his head. "This is nuts, you know that, right?"

"Yeah. It was nuts to begin with. Now we're nearing the line of absolutely ridiculous, wouldn't you say?"

"Is there anything you want me to relay to my sister?" Zeb asked.

Where should he start? He'd tried to apologize for overreacting but hadn't been able to find the right words.

"Just tell her I'll try to get the birds to cooperate with their new wardrobe." It was easier to leave it at that.

"You know, for what it's worth . . ." Zeb stopped, although he looked like he wanted to say more.

"What?"

"I don't know what's going on between you and Zina, but she seems happier when you're around." His big shoulders rolled. "I just wanted you to know."

Alex's chest squeezed tight. "Thanks."

"Are you planning on sticking around? Like after the wedding?"

"I've got a lead on a job that will probably have me traveling all the time." Alex lifted a shoulder in an apologetic shrug. "So probably not."

"Yeah, that's what I figured." Zeb nodded. "See you around."

"See ya." He waited until Zeb disappeared around the corner again, and then silently cursed himself for the way the conversation went down. It's not that he didn't want to stick around. The more time he spent in Ido, the longer he wanted to stay. He could easily see himself settling in, moving out to the ranch with Gramps, and giving things a real chance with Zina. But he didn't know if he could. What if he started to feel stuck? What if things didn't work out and he missed the chance to take the job with Munyon? There were too many unknowns. The possibilities spun around in his head until he couldn't see straight.

He handed out the rest of the sardines to the motley crew of penguins. "Let's call it quits for today, okay, gang?"

The penguins milled around, waddling in their small group at the end of the red aisle runner. He'd taken to chatting with them while they worked. Not that he expected them to talk back, but it was better than spending all of his time alone.

"You done for the day?" Gramps came in with Herbie on a leash.

"Yeah." Alex secured the last penguin. "Want to grab a burger or something tonight?"

"Nah. Your girlfriend's got me working with one of the dogs who might be a candidate for that veteran program. Her brother's been helping."

"She's not my girlfriend, Gramps." Alex shook the idea out of his head. He and Zina had shared some amazing time between the sheets together. But that was all it was. And hell, they weren't even doing that anymore. She was still pissed at him. Once the wedding came and went, so would he. That was his MO, the way he'd lived all of his life. Onto the next adventure.

"Well I don't know what you young folks call it then. Is she your booty call?"

"Hell, no." How did his grandfather even know what a booty call was? "Have you been trying to order pay-per-view again?" Lacey would kill him if she ended up with a huge cable bill. She'd already been generous enough to let them stay rent-free.

Gramps waved off the question. "Why don't you take that non-girlfriend of yours out to dinner tonight? You've both been burning the candle at both ends. Might be good to take a break."

Alex let his chin drop to his chest. "Yeah, I'll think about it." It wasn't a bad idea. He probably should spend a little time making up for the way he'd overreacted about their penguin stunt. His grandfather had been coming out of his shell more and more since they'd been at the mansion together. He might actually have a good idea from time to time.

"Good. That woman deserves to be treated well." Gramps disappeared back behind the barrier.

He had a point. With the penguins crated and fed, Alex didn't have any other responsibilities until morning. Maybe he and Zina could find a middle ground, somewhere between the physical attraction and their apparent mutual desire to strangle each other. He might even be willing to make a little conversation. Truth was, he missed her.

When he got back to the mansion, he knocked on the door to the bedroom she'd stolen from him.

"Come in."

She sat on the edge of the bed, kicking off her shoes. "You need something?"

"I'm done for the evening. Wondered if you might want to head out and grab a burger?" He tried to sound nonchalant, like it wouldn't matter to him one way or another if she didn't want to go.

"Where?"

That was a good sign; she hadn't shot him down immediately. "Up to you. There's the Burger Bonanza. Or if you'd rather, we can go to Ortega's."

"I don't know." She pulled her feet up onto the bed and leaned against the ornate wooden headboard. "I just got back from running Zeb home. I'm kind of tired and was thinking I might just stay in tonight."

He gestured to the spot next to her. "Care if I sit down?"

"Be my guest." She pulled her feet up underneath her to make more room.

The mattress creaked as he sat down. "I think we should talk."

"Should?" Her eyebrows lifted, causing a series of lines to crisscross her forehead.

He dug deeper. This woman tested him in ways he didn't ever consider. "Let me try that again. I'd like to talk."

"About what?" She drew a throw pillow against her stomach.

"About us."

Her eyebrows rose even higher and she let out a soft laugh. "There's an 'us' now?"

"Come on, I'm trying here." He reached out to cover her hand with his.

"Trying what? To make yourself feel better?"

"No. I'm trying to have a conversation. I'd like to apologize . . ." Hell, this was harder than he thought it would be.

"For?" she prompted.

"For being an ass about the penguin thing." He knew

now he'd overreacted. There hadn't been any fallout and he'd gone a little overboard.

"Okay. Go for it."

"I just did."

"Did what?"

"Apologized."

She rolled her eyes. "No you didn't. You said you'd like to apologize."

"Right."

"But you never actually said it."

"Said what?"

"Forget it." She tossed the pillow aside and hopped off the bed.

"What just happened?" He glanced from the pillow she'd discarded to where she stood looking out the window. "I feel like I missed something."

The floor-to-ceiling curtain swayed as she moved past it. "You did miss something."

He got off the bed and took cautious steps toward her. "Care to fill me in?"

She turned. "An apology usually involves something beyond saying you want to apologize."

"What?" He was stumped.

"The actual apology. The 'I'm sorry' part." She shook her head while giving him a major eye roll. "You can talk around it all you want but it doesn't count for anything unless you actually say the words."

Like a ray of sunshine fought its way through the clouds, comprehension began to enlighten his brain. She wanted him to say the actual words. That was all. He faced her, reaching out to brush her hair behind her shoulder. "Zina . . ."

"Yes?" The word came out on a huffy sigh. Like she'd reached the end of her rope and just let go.

He took both of her hands in his. She didn't squeeze back but she didn't pull away, either. A good sign under the circumstances.

"Are you ready for this?" He licked his lips, suddenly a little unsure of how she might respond.

"I suppose so." Her chin tucked down, close to her chest. The hair he'd pushed over her shoulder fell over her eyes.

"I'm sorry." There. He'd said it. He'd apologized and the ground hadn't shaken underneath him. A gaping hole hadn't appeared in the floor and swallowed him up. He did a mental run-through of all of his bodily systems. Everything seemed to be in check. Maybe life didn't end when a guy had to say he was sorry.

"I accept your apology." She glanced up at him, that hint of flirtatious sass creeping back into her smile. "And I'm sorry, too. For exploiting your penguins and risking the wedding. I didn't think it through."

A sigh escaped his lungs. He didn't realize how tense he'd been. Making up with Zina released a weight from his shoulders. It seemed easier to breathe. "About that burger . . ."

"Give me ten minutes to freshen up, and I'll meet you downstairs."

"Deal." He squeezed her hands before he let them go, then he headed downstairs to wait.

While he sat on the duvet, scrolling through the pictures he'd taken of the penguins that day, Gramps came through the front door with Herbie trotting behind him. "I thought you would have gone on that date by now."

"Zina will be down in a minute. Thanks for the suggestion."

"You're welcome. I'm glad to see the two of you have patched things up. It's been getting pretty damn boring watching you mope around here like a lovesick pup."

"Excuse me?"

"Don't try to play games with me. I've seen the way you look at her."

Yeah, like he wanted to toss her over his shoulder and rush her upstairs. Doubtful Gramps meant that kind of look. "Maybe we need to get your glasses checked."

"I don't need my glasses checked and I don't need you telling me what to do. Have you talked to your sister about me moving back to the ranch yet?"

"I mentioned it."

"And?" Gramps pressed.

"It didn't go well. She said even if you move back out there, we'll need a backup plan. You'll have to have someone checking on you on a regular basis. Char's got her hands full as it is and I'm not going to be sticking around."

Gramps glared. "You didn't say anything about that when we made our deal. I'm doing my part by helping out around here. I expect you to do yours."

"I'm trying." Alex hadn't been to the family ranch in years, but if Char said it was too much for Gramps to handle on his own and too far outside town for her to be able to stop by and check on him on a regular basis, he believed her.

"Who put you in charge? You think because you're younger, that gives you the right to decide what I do?" Gramps patted his leg, and Herbie nudged his nose into the old man's hand. "My wife's still there. That's where I belong."

Alex hadn't heard Gramps talk like that before, especially not from the heart. He lowered his voice and reached out to put his hand on his grandfather's arm. "I know you miss her."

"You don't know shit." Gramps slapped Alex's hand away. "Until you've given your heart, your soul, your whole self to the love of your life, don't you try to talk to me about what you know about love."

Alex looked up to see Zina standing on the bottom step. He hadn't even seen her come down the stairs. His breath caught in his chest at the look on her face.

She glanced at Gramps, her brow wrinkled with concern. "Maybe we ought to stay in tonight. I can throw a salad together real quick, and—"

"You two go have fun." Gramps shook off his dark mood like a duck ruffling a little water off its feathers. "I'll be fine. Sometimes this old man needs some quiet time to reflect on all the blessings he's had in his life."

Zina moved across the foyer to take Gramps's hand. "Your wife was a very lucky woman to be loved so much."

Gramps gave her a smile before he headed toward the stairs. "Herbie will keep me company tonight, won't you?"

The dog trotted along behind him, his tail wagging a mile a minute.

Alex waited until Gramps reached the landing, and then slid his gaze to Zina. "You ready?"

"So where are we headed?" Zina gazed out the window as Alex raced down the county road.

"I thought we'd go into Swynton. There's a sports bar not too far from Char's. I need to stop and pick up some stuff at her place after if that's okay with you."

"I've got no plans tonight." She glanced at his profile—the strong jawline, the hint of scruff covering his chin, the full lips he'd had all over her a few nights before. "I'm all yours."

His head snapped her direction.

She smiled in return. It was time to make up. Living under the same roof and being at odds was taking a toll on their non-relationship.

"All mine, huh? You sure about that?" His gaze bounced back and forth from her to the road in front of him.

"The only thing I'm one hundred percent sure about is that there's no way I'm going to get all of the dogs rehomed before you have to double down on the wedding plans."

"What are we looking at?"

"Best-case scenario? I might be able to place another dozen or so in a shelter up in Beaumont until the roof gets fixed or they get adopted, whichever comes first." There was no telling how long it might take for the pups to find a new home. Some of the dogs she'd had in the past only stayed long enough to get their medical clearance before they found homes. Others, like Buster, had been with her for months before he'd found his place.

Alex ran his hand over the steering wheel, letting it rest on the top. "So that would leave us with about a dozen dogs at the warehouse?"

"Give or take one or two. But I can move them back out to my place once Bodie gives me the okay."

"No." His tone left no room for negotiation.

"Excuse me?"

"Someone out there is trying to scare you. You're not safe until Bodie figures out who it is and what they want. I know you think you can take care of yourself, but—"

"I *can* take care of myself." She backed up against the door of the truck. "And I don't need you or Bodie trying to tell me any different."

"That's not what I meant. I know you can look out for yourself. But you don't have to. You've got me."

"I've got you?" She barked out a laugh. "What makes you think I want you?" Ouch. She didn't mean to come across so harsh. Truth was, she did want Alex. Wanted him in the worst way. Wanted him to be there when she woke up in the morning. Wanted him to be there when she went to bed at night. Wanted him to stay. But she couldn't tell him that.

If it were up to her, he'd never have any inkling of the way her feelings had snuck up on her while she wasn't paying attention and tied up her heart in hopes and dreams and wishes she had no business entertaining.

His eyes shifted. She'd hurt him with that last remark. She could tell by the way his pulse ticked along his jaw and the way he held the steering wheel just a little too tight.

"It doesn't matter whether you want me or not," he ground out. His voice took on a serious edge. "I'm here and

I'm not going to let anything happen to you or the dogs while I'm around."

She hadn't seen this side of him before. He usually deflected any effort at trying to hold a serious conversation. But tonight he was dead serious.

"Look, Alex." She let out a frustrated sigh. "I don't mean to burst your bubble or dash your dream of being the white knight who rushes in to save the day."

He grunted, shaking his head like he wasn't going to even try to hear her out.

"Hey"—she put her hand on his arm—"I'm not your damsel in distress. I've been taking care of myself for years and I don't have any intention of stopping just because you decided to play house for a little while."

"You about done?" He jerked the steering wheel to the right and brought the truck to an abrupt stop on the side of the road.

"Maybe."

"I'm not trying to play house. I've never pretended to be anything beyond what I am."

"And what exactly is that? A guy who drops in when it's convenient? Who keeps things on his own terms? Who only cares about himself?" She'd raised her voice and practically yelled at him, even though they were only separated by the small space inside the cab of the truck.

"You really don't like me, do you?" He twisted his torso so he faced her. The spark of humor had left his eyes.

No. She didn't like him. She was falling in love with him. The realization made her gasp.

"What?" His brow crinkled with concern. "You okay?"

When had this happened? How had she not seen it coming? She stared at him, taking in the way his hair curled around his ears—a little too long but also just right. The tiny scar on the edge of his mouth—the one he'd gotten while diving off cliffs in the Caribbean. He craved adventure, adrenaline, action. There was no way he'd be satisfied spending his life in a place as boring and uneventful as Ido.

"I'm fine. I don't want to fight anymore."

"Good." The line between his brows softened. "There are much better things we could be doing with our time besides fighting."

She struggled to fill her lungs with air. He hadn't pretended to be anything different than what he was—a thrill seeker, a wanderer, someone who would always be incapable of settling down. That meant she had two choices— either put an end to whatever was growing between them. Or . . . take the temporary connection he could offer and enjoy it while it lasted.

Like she'd told him, she could take care of herself. She'd been doing it long before he showed up and would continue long after he left. "You're right."

"I am?" His eyebrows lifted. "Why do I get the feeling you don't say that to people very often?"

She let out a soft laugh. "Because I don't."

"But you did tonight." He looked like he was waiting for something to happen. Like she'd tricked him and was about to follow up with the knockout punch that would leave him tied up against the ropes.

"It seemed appropriate under the circumstances."

He leaned over, closing the distance between them. "What circumstances are those, Ms. Baxter?"

"The circumstances showing me that you're about to kiss me." Her hand went to his shoulder.

"Would you be receptive to a kiss from me?"

"What kind of kiss are we talking about?"

"What kind of kiss do you want?"

The kind that made her heart hammer in her chest, her stomach twist, and her panties seem to melt right off. "What kind are you offering?"

"Well"—his arm moved to the back of the seat behind her—"I could keep it soft and gentle like this." He closed the distance between them and placed a delicate kiss on her cheek. Her eyes closed and her pulse stuttered.

"That was . . . nice." She opened her eyes. His face was inches from hers. She could see the flecks of gold in the blue-green irises she'd come to love.

"Nice? That's tragic."

"There's nothing wrong with nice."

"Maybe something like this would be more appropriate."

Her heart hitched as he moved in again, kissing a trail from her cheek to her mouth. His tongue pressed against the seam of her lips and she opened for him. She wanted to lean into him, deepen the kiss, and climb over the center console that so inconveniently separated them.

"Better?" His voice sounded rough around the edges.

"Mm-hmm." She ran a finger around her lips, wiping away the traces of lip gloss she'd applied in anticipation of their burger date.

"What?" He sat back, his eyebrows drawn together.

"Nothing."

"Nothing, my ass. You've got to admit that was better than 'nice.'"

"Sure it was. It was *really* nice."

The edges of his mouth ticked up in a wicked grin. "You realize you're asking for it, don't you?"

Feigning innocence, she batted her eyelashes at him. Playing coy had never been her style. But she could see why some of her classmates had enjoyed it back in high school. "Asking for what exactly?"

He reached out, his hand going behind her neck. Pulling her toward him, he mumbled, "Really nice. I'll show you really nice."

Trying not to laugh, she let him pull her close. But when his lips touched hers, the gentleness disappeared. His mouth claimed hers in a hot, deep, hungry kiss. She responded with an urgency of her own. His hands ran over her shirt, tangled in her hair. She lifted herself up and over the console, eager to get her hands on him.

Her skin burned in the wake of his lips. *More, more, more.* Her entire body aligned in a singular purpose. She wanted him, no, needed him. Before she could tell him, he pulled back, practically ripping his mouth away from hers.

"Was that really nice?" The look in his eyes scared her a bit but also sparked something deep down inside. He looked tormented, like a man who bordered on the cusp between pleasure and pain . . . a line she was all too familiar with.

"Alex . . ." She placed her palm on his chest. "I don't know what we're doing here."

He wrapped his hand around hers and brought it to his lips. Kissing her fingertips, one by one, he listed off what exactly they were doing. "We're having fun. We're getting to know each other. We're working toward a common goal. We're helping each other." Only her pinkie remained. He held her gaze as he lowered his mouth toward the tip of her pinkie finger. "We might just be falling in love."

twenty-four

Love. He'd said *love*. Not in the three-little-word sense, but in the "we're moving toward three little words" sense. She hadn't been expecting it. He could tell by the way she gulped in a breath and coughed, choking on air.

"You okay?" He squeezed her hand.

"Um, yeah." She righted herself on her side of the cab.

"You sure?" He pushed a chunk of hair back over her shoulder. "Did I say something wrong?"

"No." Her head shook back and forth. "I think you just caught me by surprise."

"Do you disagree with me?" He could drop it right there. Leave it sitting between them like an oversized elephant on the center console. But if he'd learned one thing from his parents, it was that things left unsaid did far more harm than the shit that sat out in the open.

Her gaze met his. Those brown eyes held a world of hope. But something else mingled with it. Fear. He shouldn't have said anything. Maybe his parents had been right to keep secrets, even if it had torn the whole damn family apart in the end.

"I don't disagree with you." She turned to glance out the window. "But you're leaving soon and I guess I'd rather not open myself up to something that's not even an option."

Yeah, he could see that. "I get it." He did, too. No sense gearing up for something that wouldn't be. "But we can have a good time in the meantime, right?"

"I thought that's all this was."

"It is."

"But you said . . ."

"Hey, we're in charge here, right? We can call this whatever we want."

She nodded, her head moving up and down so slowly that he wondered if he'd imagined it. "Okay."

"Does this mean I can stop sleeping on the couch?"

Her laugh immediately lightened the mood. "We'll see about that."

"You ready for that burger?"

"Yeah. Let's get to it."

He cupped her cheek with his palm, taking one more look at her before her defensive shield slid back into place. Then he put his foot on the gas pedal and eased back onto the road.

Zina focused her gaze straight ahead. Her phone rang and she scrambled to dig it out of her purse. "It's Bodie."

Alex nudged his chin toward the phone. "Aren't you going to answer?"

She held the phone up to her ear. Alex couldn't hear the other end of the conversation, but Zina's side was filled with *mm*s and *oh*s until she finally ended the call.

"Everything okay?"

She closed her eyes and took in a long, deep breath.

"What's wrong?" Alex reached over and took her hand. Keeping one eye on the road and trying to make sure Zina wasn't having some sort of attack, he squeezed her hand. "Zina?"

Her head lolled to the side and she met his gaze. "Bodie found a puppy mill. The one he thinks is supplying the dog-fighting ring. I'm sorry to cancel dinner plans but can you take me back to my truck? I've got to meet up with him right away."

"Hell no." He put both hands back on the wheel.

"Excuse me?" She jerked her hand away from his. "I know this messes up your plans for dinner. But I've got to get over there."

"I know. I'm going with you. Just tell me where to go."

Forty-five minutes later they pulled off the main road onto what looked like an ATV trail through the woods. "You sure this is right?" Alex asked.

Zina had been sitting on the edge of her seat since Bodie's call. "I think so. Bodie said it was tucked way back in the woods. No wonder no one reported it before now."

"How did he find it?"

"An anonymous tip. Someone called the sheriff's office and said they were out on a trail ride and heard a bunch of dogs barking."

Tree limbs swatted at the truck as they forged on. Alex had to slow down to a crawl twice to cross two small streams. "This is crazy. How could someone live back in here?"

Zina's hand landed on his thigh as they pulled into a clearing. Bodie's truck sat in front of what could only be considered a compound of shacks. She hopped out of the truck before it even stopped moving. Alex pulled up behind Bodie's truck and took a good look around. The buildings looked like they might come tumbling down at any moment. He rushed over to where Zina stood, arms crossed over her middle, deep in conversation with Bodie and a woman Alex didn't recognize.

"What's going on?" He stopped when he reached them, and put a hand on Zina's back, trying to offer support.

"So far they've got two dozen dogs, six who appear to be pregnant, and two litters of puppies." Zina's hands wrung together. "We've got to get them out of here."

"Who owns this place?" Alex asked.

"We're looking into that now. Appears to be registered to a corporation, so I don't have a name. Whoever was staying here took off though. Doesn't look like anyone's been here in days." Bodie glanced toward the sheds. "Right now we've got to get these dogs out of here if they have any chance of survival."

"You think this is related to the guys from the restaurant?" Alex asked.

Zina twisted her head to look at him. "What guys?"

"Alex heard some men talking at the Burger Bonanza and mentioned it to me. I did see some double tire tracks over there, the same type we found over at your place." He glanced at Zina. "Know anyone who drives a black dually pickup?"

"Yeah, probably half a dozen people around town." She looked from Alex to Bodie and back again. "Obviously someone's trying to close down the dog shelter and shut me up in the process."

"Seems that way." Bodie jotted something down on his notepad. "The report came back on your roof, too. It was in bad shape to start with but evidence shows traces of some sort of acid. They probably used that to weaken the structure."

"Right now all I can do is worry about the dogs. Do they have kennels?" Zina asked. Her tone shifted from one of worry to one of take-charge action. "Let's get as many as we can and if I need to come back with crates for the rest, I can do it later."

"I'll come with you." Alex nodded. So much for having more room for the penguins. But they had to do something.

He hadn't seen a dog yet but even with his inexperienced eye, he could tell the dogs had lived through some sort of hell at this place.

"I ought to have a few more officers here in a bit. We'll clear the place, then help you get the dogs back to the warehouse." Bodie nodded.

Alex put an arm over Zina's shoulders and pulled her close as Bodie walked away. "You okay?"

She took in a jagged breath. "What kind of person does something like this?" Tilting her head up to meet his gaze, her bottom lip trembled. "People can be so cruel."

Alex nodded. He wasn't about to admit that he'd seen animals treated much worse on some of his travels around the world. "We'll get them situated. They'll be fine."

"But the warehouse . . ." She shrugged his arm off. "Where am I going to put them?"

"We'll figure it out. Together. Okay?" His thumb brushed over her knuckles. He pressed a kiss against her temple. "Trust me."

Nodding, she let her head drop to his shoulder. "Okay."

Bodie came back and they began to catalog the dogs. Alex's stomach tossed and turned as he took in the conditions the poor pups had been forced to live in. Some of the older dogs had scars on their muzzles. One was missing a leg. Zina had left her emotions checked at the door when they entered the first shed. She moved around the kennels, calling out markings and conditions like she was doing inventory at the warehouse, not detailing the travesties put upon dozens of dogs.

By the time they were done, the sun had almost set. Alex carried kennel after kennel out to the trucks, loading them as full as possible to eliminate the need to return. The whole place would be better off if someone took a torch to it. Bodie's other deputies arrived and they filled their truck beds with kennels as well. By the time they got the last pup loaded, Alex was ready for a shower and a whiskey. He wasn't even hungry anymore. Seeing how these animals had been treated had ruined his appetite for the night.

"Ready?" Zina appeared at his side, a clipboard in her hands.

"What's the plan, boss?"

"To the warehouse for now. I called one of our volunteers who's a vet. She's going to meet us there and check over all of the dogs."

For a moment Alex wished he'd finished college and pursued his veterinary degree. He'd feel a hell of a lot more useful if he could actually help treat the animals instead of just providing the muscle to move them around. But moving around was what he seemed to do best.

"You coming?" Zina asked, snapping him out of his thoughts.

"Yeah. I'm right behind you." He might not be able to change the past but he could do something about his future. Maybe he didn't need to take off when the wedding was over. Maybe he could find a job around town and give Char a hand for real instead of just tossing money and words at the situation.

There would be plenty of time to think about all of that later. Right now he needed to focus his efforts and attention on helping Zina with the dogs. He'd promised to help with the deductible on getting her that new roof and that meant he had to do whatever he could to make sure the Munyon wedding went off without a hitch. Even if he had to work around penguins and pit bulls to pull it off.

twenty-five

Over the next few days Zina found herself relying more and more on Alex. He'd made it clear he wouldn't be around for the long haul, but she needed help and he was there, so it made sense to let him pick up the slack. After the vet had gone over all of the dogs they'd seized from the puppy mill, she and Alex had tried to find other shelters to take in as many as they could. But even after a few volunteers drove some of them as far away as Kansas and Nebraska, she still had too many dogs on her hands.

At least she wasn't in it alone. Alex had been right by her side the entire time, doing everything he could to help right a very wrong situation. They hadn't had time to talk much since they'd brought the puppy mill dogs back, but she had let him back into the bedroom so at least when they fell into bed at the end of a nonstop day, they had each other to curl into.

With that thought in mind, she rolled over in bed and set her feet on the floor. Alex groaned and reached for her. "Just a few more minutes?"

She leaned over to brush the hair off his face. He wrapped an arm around her back and tugged her over. "Hey, we've got to get down to the warehouse."

"I know." He pulled her in for a kiss, and for a moment she was tempted to crawl back under the covers and get reacquainted with the parts of him that she hadn't had the luxury of enjoying for the past couple of nights.

"Later, okay? We'll make it an early night. I've got some volunteers coming in to do the night routine."

"Really?" He perked up, lifting his arm from over his head.

She almost laughed at the instant enthusiasm. "Really. We can order in and eat in bed and—"

"I don't even need food if you're promising you and me, a night with no interruptions." He propped himself up and nibbled on her neck.

"Trust me, you're going to need to eat something. You'll need your strength for what I've got in mind for later." She waggled her brows.

He flung the covers away and hopped off the bed. "By all means, let's get to it then."

Her heart pitter-pattered as he stalked toward the bathroom. She'd love nothing more than to climb back into bed and run her fingers over every sculpted inch of him. But duty didn't just call, it was yelling and screaming at her. They only had a couple of weeks left before the wedding party came to town, and she needed to do everything she could to get the rest of the dogs relocated before the bride and groom found out their wedding venue was being used as a temporary dog rescue shelter.

She tamped down the hunger pangs for Alex's touch and pulled on her clothes. As she clambered down the stairs to the kitchen, a new voice rang out. Who the hell was that? She paused outside the kitchen door. Maybe Morty had the television turned up too loud again.

Before she could push open the swinging door to the

kitchen, it sprang toward her. Zina barely jumped out of the way before the door opened wide and an explosion of color poured through.

"When did you say Mr. Sanders will be back?" A woman wearing a hot-pink fedora on top of her light pink hair strutted through the formal living room on three-, no, four-inch heels.

Morty followed. "Any minute. Let me give him a call and find out where he's at."

Zina cleared her throat, not quite able to speak yet from her close call with the door.

Morty and Pinkie turned toward her. Morty's face immediately relaxed. His shoulders slumped slightly and a smile of relief drifted over his mouth. "Oh, Zina. Meet Ms. Chyna. She's here to talk to Alex about the wedding."

Zina's gaze bounced back and forth between Morty's relieved grin and the expectant look on Pinkie's face. No, not Pinkie. Chyna. This was Chyna of wedding planner fame. Why in the world would she be standing in the front room of the Phillips House? She lived in California. LA, if Zina remembered correctly. That was over a thousand miles away. Yet, for some reason, Zina knew deep down that the petite woman with the shocking-pink hair was none other than the infamous wedding planner.

"Zina?" Chyna reached a hand toward her. "Are you helping Alex with the wedding?"

"Um, yes." Instinctively, Zina took her hand. "I mean, no."

"Well, which is it?" Chyna let her hand fall, then reached into the small clutch she'd tucked under her arm and sprayed something on her palm. "No offense, I've heard the allergies here are awful so I'm taking every precaution."

"No offense taken." Did she seriously feel the need to sanitize her hands after a simple handshake? Zina struggled not to react to Chyna's sudden appearance. All she could think about was the state of the warehouse. How would

Alex handle it? Surely Chyna would want to check in on the penguins. Her mind raced trying to come up with either an explanation for why the penguins were sharing their space or a solution to how to hide the dogs.

Before she could come up with anything, the man in question sauntered down the stairs.

"You know, I think maybe I need an appetizer this afternoon and then we can finish up the main course later on tonight. What do you say about—" He stopped in his tracks as he noticed the three of them watching his approach. "What's going on?"

"Alex, meet Chyna. The wedding planner from LA you've been working with." Zina sounded like a robot, even to her own ears.

Chyna offered her freshly sanitized hand. "Mr. Sanders, it's nice to meet you."

Alex took her hand in his but his gaze searched for Zina. What did he expect her to do? She gave a slight shrug and tilted her head toward the front door, trying to signal that she was going to head to the warehouse.

"It's nice to meet you, too. What do we owe the pleasure of this visit to?" He put his hands on his hips as Chyna pulled out the sanitizer and repeated the process of covering every square millimeter of her palm with the gel.

"I wanted to make sure we're on track for this wedding, so I took a red-eye to come check for myself."

"Well, that explains the early hour." Alex glanced at his watch. Zina could have told him it was just after seven. Too damn early to be entertaining an unwanted out-of-state visitor. "I wish you'd given us some notice. We would have been better prepared—"

"That's why I didn't call ahead." Chyna waved a hand in the air. The smell of artificial lemons wafted over to irritate Zina's nose. "I don't want you to prepare. I need to make sure you're prepared without having to prepare."

Alex nodded like that made sense. Clear as mud. Mud

that had been stepped in by a herd of Herefords and baked dry by the Texas sun.

"My flight leaves at two so I'd like to cut through the niceties and examine the venue. Can you lead the way?" She moved her gaze from Alex to the front door.

"Certainly." He glanced to Zina.

She lifted her shoulders, looking for guidance.

Alex pulled the door open and held it open for Chyna. She passed through first, giving them a moment to whisper between them.

"Hell, what do we do about the dogs?" Alex asked.

"I don't know. If we'd had some warning . . ."

"I know." Alex's hand gripped her shoulder. "We'll figure something out. Why don't you go do the breakfast routine and see if you can move some of them to the back while I stall her out front?"

Zina nodded. They'd constructed a temporary fence around a patch of grass behind the warehouse since they couldn't keep taking the dogs out on leashes. She could get most of the dogs outside while Alex took Chyna inside. It was worth a shot. Maybe the only shot they had to avoid her canceling the whole thing.

While Alex led Chyna around the porch, talking about the history of the building and property, Zina made her way to the warehouse.

"Wait up." Morty ambled after her.

She slowed her pace so he could catch up. "How long has she been here?"

"Not long, thank goodness. She just showed up on the front porch, so I let her in and offered her a cup of coffee."

Zina smiled. Morty brewed his coffee strong enough that it would "put hairs on your chest," his words, not hers. "How did she like that?"

"Took one sip, got the cup covered in that red shit she's

got on her lips, then turned up her nose. I don't know how Alex is going to be able to handle her. She's not his kind."

"Not his kind?" Zina pressed ahead, Morty on her heels.

"Nah. The makeup, the attitude, the snappiness."

"Yeah, she seems like she's used to getting what she wants, all right." Which made it even more imperative that her visit went well. Alex's job was riding on it and if that fell through, then her chance to get money to fix up the shelter would be gone and she'd have to figure out what to do with the poor dogs. Not coming through for Chyna's visit wasn't an option.

"What do you want me to do?" Morty paused, his breath labored, as they reached the door to the warehouse.

"We need to get as many dogs out back as we can. Hold back the troublemakers." Morty had been helping enough that he knew which dogs wouldn't get along with the others.

Morty nodded as he disappeared through the door. Zina followed. A chorus of barks broke out as they moved toward the kennels. The dogs kept better time than Alex's watch. They knew they should have had breakfast fifteen minutes ago. By the time Zina had let all of them out and filled up their dishes, Alex and Chyna were at the front door.

Zina held her breath as the door creaked open and the typical barks sounded. The jig was up. Chyna would realize they'd been using the wedding venue as a dog rescue and would pull the plug. No way was some oil baron's socialite daughter going to want to get married in a warehouse that smelled like sardines and wet dogs.

She fought the urge to disappear through the back door and hop in her truck. Lacey's was a relatively short drive. Or she could head over to the Burger Bonanza and drown her worries in an extra-large version of what they tried to pass off as a cappuccino and a breakfast full of enough grease to make sure her worries slid right away.

Instead, she took cautious steps toward the front of the building.

"That's actually a brilliant idea." Chyna slid the giant shades from her eyes and let them rest on top of her head. "I think the Munyon family will be very pleased with what you've put together."

The waves of panic that had been rolling through Alex's gut stilled. "Fantastic. We just want to make sure the bride has the wedding of her dreams."

"It will be. My staff will make sure." Chyna paused at the entrance to the warehouse. "Now, walk me through exactly how you envision the setup."

The waves gathered momentum, crashing into the sides of Alex's stomach. This was it, the moment where Chyna would realize he didn't have a plan. The moment everything would fall apart.

Zina came out of nowhere. "Actually, we thought it might be best to hold the ceremony and reception in tents."

Tents? Since when had they talked about tents? He blinked, hard, trying to figure out where that idea had come from.

She gave a slight shake of her head. He nodded, willing to see how it played out.

"Tents?" Chyna pulled her blouse away from her skin and fanned herself, even though the sun hadn't fully risen and the temperature lingered in the low seventies this early in the morning.

"Air-conditioned tents, of course." Zina nodded. "Alex mentioned that Mr. Munyon was willing to spare no expense."

"That's true, but tents?" Chyna eyed them both from under thick fake lashes. "Don't you think that's a bit, um, rustic?"

Alex bit back a laugh. Rustic? They were having a winter

wonderland wedding in the middle of nowhere with penguins. And she was worried about guests feeling like the location was too rustic?

"With a tent we can create whatever kind of environment we'd like. For the winter wonderland I was thinking a white tent with blue snowflakes projected on the walls and ceiling," Zina said.

Chyna nodded. "I can see it. The white sides of the tent will make guests feel like they're surrounded by a frosty winter wonderland."

"Right." Alex jumped into the conversation. "And we can have ice sculptures on the buffet tables—"

"No buffet. This will be a sit-down dinner." The look Chyna shot him could have turned him to ice.

At that point he decided to shut the hell up and let the two women figure out how best to set the scene. His job was to make sure the penguins played their part, no more, no less.

"And the penguins . . ." Chyna turned her attention on him. "I'd like to do a run-through so I can let Mr. Munyon know the birds are ready for their role in all of this."

"Um, sure." He glanced to Zina for direction.

"Why don't you head into town for breakfast while Alex and I set up? We'll mark off where the tents will be and then do a quick run-through with the penguins," Zina suggested.

"I could use a double espresso. That flight sucked the life force right out of me." Chyna spritzed something on her face from a small spray bottle she pulled out of her clutch. "I also need to hydrate. This heat and humidity is taking a toll on my skin. I can feel it already."

Zina put a hand on Chyna's back and directed her to the parking lot. "Give us at least an hour. We'll have everything ready to go when you get back."

"That sounds good." She paused when she reached the door of a white Mercedes. "I'll be back at nine sharp. I'd also love to have Mayor Cherish on the scene when I return. She's the one I've been dealing with on this."

Alex opened his mouth to tell her Lacey wouldn't be able to join them but Zina waved him off.

"I'll see if she's available on such short notice. She's very busy this time of year." Zina stepped next to him while the wedding planner situated herself inside the vehicle and slowly pulled away.

"What was that?" he asked. "How are we going to get Lacey here while she's on bed rest? Tents? Do you have any idea where we're going to get a tent big enough to hold the wedding and the reception?"

Zina waited until he finished spewing out rhetorical questions. "Would you rather have her mingle with the pit bulls and penguins? The whole warehouse smells like a sushi factory."

"I was going to work on that once we got the dogs out of there." Alex hung his head. "This whole thing is turning into a shit show."

"You're right about that." Zina bit her lip, a move that Alex had come to recognize as her thinking mode. "But this is going to be our shit show. Let me get Lacey on video and we'll figure this out. There's no way she can get over here. We'll say she's out of town or something. But she's the one who's put more work into this than any of us. She'll know what to do. Grab some of those stakes and a hammer. I'm going to look up tent rental places so we can mark off a perimeter. I figure you'll parade your penguins out, have them walk down the aisle, and then she'll be on her way."

"Yeah, okay." Alex left Zina standing in front of the warehouse while he went inside to find the hammer and stakes. One thing was certain. If he questioned their commitment to each other before this, it was clear they were now in this together, for better or for worse.

twenty-six

⟨♡⟩

"I told you not to come over here." Zina tried to stuff Lacey back in the truck. "You're supposed to be on bed rest."

"I can't miss out on this." Lacey pushed the door open, leaving Zina no choice but to step back or get sideswiped. "Why didn't she call ahead? Why didn't she tell me she was coming?" Lacey continued to shout questions even as she stomped toward the warehouse.

"I told you, she didn't tell anyone she was coming. She wanted it to be a surprise. I think she wanted to catch us totally unprepared to see how we'd react."

Lacey stopped and spun around. "That's just mean."

Zina couldn't agree with her more. "Just wait until you meet her."

"How much time do we have until she gets back?" Lacey propelled herself toward Alex like she had a rocket strapped to her hips. Zina had to jog to keep up with her.

"We told her to come back at nine but I wouldn't be surprised if she showed up a bit early."

"This is all we need. On top of being on bed rest, now I've

got the biggest wedding this town will ever see imploding around me." Lacey waved her hands over her head, mimicking the tornado she must imagine swirled around her.

"We've got this." Zina stopped, thrust her hands to her hips, and leveled her friend with her best glare. "Alex is marking off where the tents will go. I already called the place in Houston and reserved their two largest event tents for that day. Chyna seemed to like the idea, plus it means we won't have to worry about moving the dogs out of the warehouse so fast."

"Yeah, but how are you going to make sure they don't bark through the whole wedding?" Lacey rounded on her.

"I haven't made it that far yet."

"Hey"—Alex joined them and slung an arm over Zina's shoulders—"coming up with the tent idea on the spur of the moment was pure genius. I'm sure you'll think of something between now and the wedding."

Zina leaned against him, grateful for his show of support.

"Let me ask you this." Lacey's jaw clenched. "How did you go from hating the idea of turning this town into wedding central to running behind the scenes on our biggest wedding yet?"

Zina looked from Lacey to Alex and back again. "I guess I got pulled into it. You know I've got your back though. There's a ton riding on this, not just the reputation of Ido, but the dog shelter, too. We've all got a vested interest in pulling this off."

"You're right." Lacey reached for Zina's hand. "I'm sorry. The bed rest thing is stressing me out. I don't know what I'd do without your help."

"Relax. Alex and I have this all under control." Zina smiled up at Alex.

"Speaking of control, I'd better finish laying out the perimeter of the tents before she gets back."

Zina reluctantly let him go. It had been a long time since

she felt like part of a team, working toward a common goal. Granted, throwing the wedding of the century wasn't a common goal she would have picked if given the chance, but she'd missed that feeling of support she had when she'd been serving overseas. Like she was part of something bigger than herself and that everyone was just as committed to seeing it through.

By the time Alex had created a layout of where the tents would go, Chyna had pulled her rental car into the parking lot again.

"Let me handle this." Lacey ran a palm over her shirt. Zina noticed the tender way she curved it over her stomach. There was just the slightest hint of her pregnancy, but it was only a matter of time before baby Phillips would be bumping out that belly.

Zina and Alex hung back as Lacey met Chyna at her car. They exchanged a few words and then Chyna moved toward them, Lacey hot on her heels.

"Show me what you have in mind." It was more command than request.

Alex pointed to where the twine outlined the perimeter of the tent. "We'll set up a tent for the ceremony here. The wedding party will walk down the aisle, followed by the penguins. Then the bride will make her entrance."

"How many guests are you expecting?" Lacey held a pen poised over her notebook. "I want to make sure we have enough chairs."

Chyna barely glanced at her. "The penguins. Where will they be during the ceremony?"

"I, uh"—Alex shot a look to Zina, who shrugged—"Munyon just said he wanted them to waddle down the aisle. I figured I'd usher them out the back during the actual wedding."

"They need to be present." Chyna tapped a hot-pink talon against her lips. "We want them to lead the bride and groom back down the aisle after they exchange their vows as well."

Alex's mouth twisted like he was about to say something that would threaten the wedding.

"We'll be happy to make an adjustment to the procession," Lacey said.

"Can one of them hold a tiny basket?" Chyna walked the center of where the tent would be. "And sprinkle flower petals or maybe ice shavings down the aisle?"

Alex's eyes widened. "Penguins have flippers, not hands."

"I'm well aware of that. But seeing as how you're a penguin trainer, I'm assuming you can make some sort of accommodation."

Zina nodded. "We'll figure something out."

Apparently appeased, Chyna picked her way across the grass to the other wall of the imaginary tent. "Let's run through the ceremony. I'd like to see the flow."

"How exactly do you plan to do that?" Alex's gaze bounced between the three of them. "We don't have the bride and groom. We don't have a wedding party . . ."

Chyna let out a huff and checked her watch. "I have two hours before I have to leave for the airport. Rustle up some friends and make it happen."

A stifling silence settled between them, like even the crickets decided not to chirp for fear of angering the tiny dictator with the pink hair.

"Of course we will." Lacey scribbled something in her notebook. "Why don't you go grab a sweet tea from the house and we'll pull it together. Morty? Would you be so kind as to take our guest to the house for some tea?"

"I'd be happy to. Miss?" He held out an arm for Chyna. She tossed him a look, then proceeded across the lawn without him, her heels sinking into the grass with each step.

"Just do your best to keep her away until we're ready, will you?" Alex put a hand on his grandfather's shoulder.

"I'll do my best, but if you ask me, that woman's got a

lot of nerve showing up here and trying to take control of—"

"Good thing no one's asking you then, Gramps." Alex smiled.

Zina watched Morty hobble after the wedding planner as she struggled to come up with some sort of plan. How would they find enough people on such short notice to orchestrate a wedding walk-through? She'd been quick to come up with the idea of using tents, but that must have used up all of her spontaneous-thinking power. At a complete loss, she turned toward Lacey.

Lacey, who had that certain blend of cat-ate-the canary mixed with about-to-burst expression. Zina had seen that look before. Not often, but often enough to know that Lacey had one heck of an implausible plan up her sleeve. And that Zina wasn't going to like it. Not one tiny bit.

Alex must not have noticed the smug satisfaction Lacey wore like her favorite sweater. He shook his head, rolled his eyes, and shuffled the toe of his boot on the gravel.

"What are we going to do now? Where are we going to find a wedding party to walk through everything? The penguins aren't ready. We haven't even practiced what might come after the wedding, they've barely mastered just getting down the aisle." He paused long enough to shoot a glance at Zina.

She'd crossed her arms while she waited for his little tirade to end.

"What?" Alex asked.

Zina shook her head slightly. "Ask her." She nudged her chin toward where Lacey stood, her grin splitting her face in two.

"You have an idea?" Alex turned toward Lacey.

"Oh boy, do I." Lacey clapped her hands together, her enthusiasm leeching from every pore. "Here's what we're going to do."

* * *

Alex cleared his throat for the tenth time, maybe fifteenth. Who was counting? Then he glanced down the strip of red carpet they'd laid out to mark the aisle. A handful of men he barely knew stood to his left—the fake groomsmen Lacey had scrounged up at the last minute. Zeb on his left; then Jasper, the guy who'd adopted Buster; and Kirby, the aspiring limo business owner.

As he cleared his throat again, trying to dislodge the apprehension that appeared determined to prevent him from speaking during this sham of a rehearsal, he watched the never-ending stream of bridesmaid stand-ins drift down the aisle. Suzy smiled as she took her place. Then Char came down the aisle, followed by Jordan.

Lacey must have called in every favor ever owed to her. Seemed like the whole town had descended upon the Phillips House to run through the ceremony. And all for the benefit of the she-devil who sat in the front row.

The music changed. Lacey stood on the opposite side of the lawn and signaled to Bodie, who fiddled with his phone. A choppy rendition of the bridal march began and Gramps released the penguins. Alex couldn't hold back a smile as the dozen tuxedo-clad birds waddled toward him, half of them decked out in snowflake necklaces, the other half in bow ties. They knew he had a pocketful of fish waiting for them at the end of the carpet. He still hadn't figured out how to reward them for their trip down the aisle during the real ceremony. Odds were the groom probably didn't want to distribute a handful of fish right before he took his vows.

Thelma came first. She always was a greedy gal. Alex tossed a treat to each bird, then Izzy corralled them over to the side where Frankie and Dolly waited.

The music swelled. His gaze was drawn to Zina, who held a hastily gathered bouquet of long grass and wildflowers.

Even though everything about the moment was fake, orchestrated and totally inauthentic, seeing her at the opposite end of the aisle took his breath away. She hadn't even had a chance to shower that morning and she still radiated beauty. As she took small, tentative steps toward him, his pulse ticked up, his breath shortened, and his face heated. Her hair was swept off her face in a ponytail that swished behind her as she walked.

"Slower." Chyna stood in the front row, barking out directions. "The bride will be walking much slower than that."

Lacey's dad had even joined the charade, and was standing in for Munyon himself. He smoothed his hand over his T-shirt and mumbled something to Zina. She smiled at him and they resumed their trip down the aisle, at a turtle pace. A turtle who'd been fed a tranquilizer.

At this rate it might take all day for the two of them to reach him. Alex tried to take in a deep breath to slow down his heart rate. It didn't do any good. The sight of Zina walking toward him, posing as his bride, knocked the breath right out of him. He'd never been so uncomfortable and felt so confident in the same moment. For half a heartbeat he let himself imagine what it might be like if the two of them weren't just puppets going through the motions to satisfy the wedding planner of a couple of strangers.

Could he ever make this kind of commitment to someone? Hell, he'd never committed to anything much less anyone. But being around Zina, being part of the wedding plans, feeling like he was working with a team of people, it had gotten to him over the past several weeks. He'd found himself daydreaming about what it might be like to stay put for a change. Instead of making him feel like he wanted to run, for the first time in his life he thought he might be up for the challenge.

Because of her.

Zina reached him. Her gaze met his. Her eyes bright,

those full lips curved into a smile, Alex looked at her and everything else faded away. Lacey's dad mumbled something and then tucked Zina's arm into the crook of Alex's elbow.

"Bet you didn't see this coming," she muttered under her breath.

"Not in a million years." He grinned as they began to turn toward what would hopefully be where the officiant would stand to preside.

Lacey's voice came from the back. "Okay, they exchange vows, yada yada yada. Should we practice the exit now?"

"Not yet." Chyna rose from her chair. "I think we need to try this again. Can you add a little pep to the step of the penguins?"

Alex gritted his teeth.

"Easy now, she has to leave for the airport in just a bit. You can do this," Zina whispered.

He nodded, swallowing the backlash he'd been about to release on the wedding planner. "I'm not sure what you mean by 'pep to the step.' Care to demonstrate?"

Chyna put her hands to her sides, palms flipped out to mimic the penguins. "Not so much meandering, just have them walk a straight line down the aisle."

"You know penguins have a natural waddle to their stride, right?"

The pressure from Zina's hand tightened on his arm.

"They look drunk though. Can't you get them to waddle a little less?" Chyna demonstrated. Hands still at her sides like wings, she executed a graceful straight walk down the center of the aisle.

This had gone on long enough. The woman was beyond demanding now; her request was ridiculous. He opened his mouth to tell her just where she could shove the idea of his penguins non-waddling down the aisle. Before he could say a word, Zina clamped her hand over his mouth.

"We'll practice with the penguins to see if we can straighten their gait. Right, Alex?" Her eyes had taken on an almost maniacal shine. Like if he didn't play nice and agree with her, she might nip off his nose or something.

Clearing his throat, he reached up to move her hand away from his mouth and twined his fingers with hers.

"That's right." The smile he forced on his lips felt strained. "I'll see what I can do to de-waddle the birds."

Zina bit back a grin. He could tell she was about to lose it by the way her chest moved in and out, like she was trying to breathe without laughing.

"Very well." Chyna let her hands drop. "Now let's do the whole 'kiss the bride' and let me see how you manage to get yourselves back down the aisle."

Alex lifted a brow, and Zina linked her arm through his again. "She doesn't really mean for us to kiss, right?" he asked.

"No. Just turn around and we'll walk down the aisle. Slow, though."

They let their arms drop as they turned toward the front and then linked arms again.

Chyna had moved to the side, where she was trying to wrangle the penguins into a line to walk back down the aisle.

"I told you, we haven't practiced that part yet." Alex stepped toward her, passing his nieces, who still posed as bridesmaids.

"What do you do to get them to move?" Chyna asked.

"We'll work on it. I'll have it all pulled together by the time you come back for the real rehearsal."

"Stupid birds. No wonder you can't fly." She practically spit out the last word.

"Fly. Fly. Fly." The mimicked cry came from where Izzy stood. Her hands were still clasped in front of her, holding one of the scraggly last-minute bouquets Lacey had shoved in all of their hands.

How had he missed it? Hadn't she learned before not to bring the damn bird around? The pesky parrot in question poked his head out of the bag hanging from Izzy's shoulder.

"No." Alex made a move to stop him as Shiner Bock emerged from the bag and clambered up Izzy's arm.

"Fly. Fly. Fly," the damn bird called. Then he spread his wings and drifted from Izzy's shoulder to land on top of Chyna's head.

The scene unrolled as if in slow motion. As Chyna's hands grappled for him, he spooked, sailing back to Izzy, something hot pink in his grip.

Holy shit. Alex turned in horror to find Chyna with her hands on top of her head. The bird had stolen her hat.

Zina leapt toward Izzy, tossing her bouquet to the ground as she reached for the bird. Izzy must have freaked out because she whirled away from Zina and tried to run. But she tripped over the twine they'd used to mark the edges of the tent. Izzy screamed and clutched at her arm. Char yelled as her daughter went down.

All Alex could do was watch the scene unfold, massive disaster after massive disaster. Before the dust began to settle, one thing became sufficiently clear.

He was fucked.

twenty-seven

"It's going to be okay." If she said it enough times, it was bound to come true. That's what Zina kept telling herself as she muttered those five little words over and over again. They were in the emergency room, waiting to see if Izzy's arm was broken or just sprained. After Chyna's hat had been rescued from Shiner Bock and returned, the woman had retreated to her rental car and sped out of Ido so fast she left skid marks on the pavement.

Lacey had been admitted for observation due to high blood pressure, and Alex paced the small waiting room while they waited for news about poor Izzy. The bird had disappeared. Morty and the other girls had stayed at the scene to try to find him. How could things get any worse?

A few moments later Zina remembered why she never, ever asked that question. Lacey's face appeared on her phone wanting to video-chat. How the hell was that possible seeing as how Lacey was supposed to be under medical observation in a room upstairs?

"I thought you were admitted for high blood pressure," Zina said as the video call connected.

"I was. I'm still here. But I just got a call from Chyna and I had to tell someone."

Zina braced herself for the news. The wedding planner had probably called the whole thing off. Alex's penguins would go back to the aquarium, the roof of the shelter would never get repaired . . . in a blink of an eye her entire future dissolved right before her.

"Zina?" Lacey barked into the phone.

"What?"

Alex shifted on the orange vinyl bench next to her. He'd been sick with worry over his niece. Zina stood and moved toward the door in an attempt to give him some space and also gain a little privacy. She didn't want her world to crash in on her in the waiting room of the Swynton Memorial Hospital.

"She said she'd never been more humiliated or mistreated in her entire life." Lacey's furrowed brow told Zina everything she needed to know. She may as well hang up now and not put herself through hearing the rundown of how they'd all failed. "Zina? Are you paying attention?"

"Yeah. I'm sorry. Alex had no idea his niece brought the bird to the rehearsal. He's sorry. I'm sorry. Everyone is so sorry."

"Listen. She was pissed. So incredibly pissed. I mean, I've been mayor now for over a year and have dealt with some pretty angry constituents, but this woman could put all of them to shame. She used four-letter words I've never even heard of."

If Lacey was trying to make Zina feel even worse than she already did, it was working. A weight like a ton of bricks, no, make that a ton of bricks encased in a ton of concrete, wedged in her chest. "I wish it had gone differently, I really do."

"But that's just it. She said despite all of the issues with the penguins being too waddly, the dirt being too dirty, and the bird being too damn birdy, she absolutely loves the venue."

"Huh?" Zina's heart skipped a beat. Then another. "Did you just say she loves it here?"

"Yes." Lacey's head bobbed up and down. "She said she's going to recommend us to another wedding she's got coming up. But this one's a bride who wants a western theme. Can you imagine? Horses and a chuck wagon dinner for five hundred guests."

The weight pressing down on Zina's chest doubled, then tripled as she imagined trying to talk everyone in town into loaning their horses to a fake western wedding setup. "I don't know about that, Lacey. How far away is that wedding?"

"Oh, it's not until next spring. But we're getting there. Ido is really creating a name for itself in the destination wedding business. Isn't it fabulous?"

"Fabulous," Zina agreed. What else could she do? She wasn't about to argue with Lacey that she was in over her head. Wouldn't do any good. The most she could hope for was that when the western wedding world descended upon Ido, she'd be squared away in her newly repaired building, far away from what surely would become another incredible fiasco. "I've got to go. We're still waiting to hear if Izzy's arm is broken."

"Oh, that poor sweet little girl. Find out what her favorite kind of ice cream is. I'm going to send over a care package later, okay?"

"Will do." Zina disconnected and made her way back to Alex. Char had taken the seat next to him. She must have news.

Alex reached for her hand as she joined them on the bench. "Izzy's arm is broken but it's a clean break."

"How's she doing?" Zina asked.

Char smiled, a welcome change from the worry and fear she'd been carrying with her since they arrived at the hospital. "She's asking for a pink cast and wants to know if the penguins can somehow sign it for her."

"That must mean she's not in too much pain." Zina relaxed against Alex's chest. One less thing to worry about.

"She'll be okay. I don't know what she was thinking trying to have that bird with her."

Alex hung his head. "Yeah, that might be partly my fault. She said she missed Shiner Bock, so I told her she could visit him if she helped with the wedding run-through."

"Did you tell her she should stuff him in that bag and make him part of the wedding party?" Char asked.

"Well, no. But I still feel a bit responsible."

"Good," Char said. "It wasn't your fault, and you have nothing to apologize for."

"Then why's that good?" Alex looked up.

"It's good because that's the first time I've ever heard you say you feel responsible for something." Char stood while Alex appeared to let that statement settle in. "Now why don't the two of you get out of here? I'm sure Gramps could use some help finding the bird. And you know the pain of a broken arm won't be anything compared to a broken heart if Shiner Bock doesn't come back."

"Way to make a guy feel good." Alex reached out and pulled Zina to her feet next to him. "Let's head back to party central, shall we?"

The last thing Zina wanted to do was go back to the warehouse. All she wanted was a few moments alone to figure out how to get through this wedding once and for all. Playing bride and groom had stirred up something inside her. Something not altogether unpleasant, but something she wasn't prepared for or interested in dealing with now. Maybe not ever. But she pasted a happy-go-lucky smile on her face anyway. Alex needed her.

"I've got to get back and check on the dogs before I help you look for the bird." That would give her time to catch her breath and provide a much-needed break from Alex. He wasn't the problem so much as what he represented. Walking down the aisle earlier had brought possibilities into focus. Crystal clear focus. And Alex was in the center of it all. She'd never imagined herself getting married, tying her fate to someone else's for the rest of her life.

Especially not someone like Alex, who seemed to crave adventure. He never stayed in one place long enough to make any kind of promise or see anything through. But maybe he was changing. If his sister thought so, it might be happening.

The last thing Zina wanted to do was get her hopes up, but that's exactly what she'd been doing all along. Ever since that night they found the puppies. She'd been unintentionally letting her guard down, letting Alex in, little by little until it hit her smack-dab in the center of her chest. She liked him. Really, really liked him. Maybe even loved him.

As they walked into the early afternoon heat, she turned slightly so she could take a good look at the man who'd stolen her heart. The afternoon sun glinted off the scruff on his chin. He'd slid his shades in place when they walked outside, so she couldn't get a read on what he might be thinking. He tightened his grip on her hand when he caught her staring.

"You okay?"

"Yeah, just thinking."

"Oh, don't do that." His lips parted into a teasing grin.

"What? Think?"

Alex nodded. "Yeah, isn't that what got everyone into trouble in the first place? Lacey thinking about how she could change Ido, then me thinking about how I could fix your roof, then you thinking about . . ." He stopped and turned slightly toward her. "Well, damn, I don't know what you've been thinking about."

She tapped on his chest with her pointer finger. "I think plenty, I just don't need to share my thoughts with the world."

"What are you thinking about now?" He gripped her finger and brought it to his lips.

Her stomach twisted and turned like a wet dishrag being wrung out to dry. She'd never be able to tell him what she'd actually been thinking. "I'm just wondering if we're still on for that early night tonight."

"Of course. Right after we find Shiner Bock and de-waddle the penguins."

Zina took a step toward the truck and he followed. "Lacey said Chyna loved everything. I expected her to cancel the whole wedding but it sounds like we're offi-cially a go."

"Shoot. I forgot I've got to run Gramps over to Water's Edge today. They had an opening come up so I scheduled a tour."

Zina took in a slow, calming breath. She and Morty had talked about this. He didn't want to go to a home and she didn't blame him. "You know he's really been bonding with Herbie. I noticed working with the dogs has made a differ-ence in his attitude. Have you picked up on that at all?"

"If you mean have I noticed he's not as grumpy and ea-ger to bite my head off every day, then the answer is yes." He twined his fingers with hers and let their hands swing between them as they crossed the lot.

"When my brother came home from his last tour, he wasn't the same. I tried everything to help him: therapy, meds, trying to talk to him about it, giving him space . . ." Her heart twinged as she remembered how hollow her brother had seemed when he returned. Like a shell of the man she'd grown up with, he wasn't the same.

"That's too bad. I remember him as being a total baller on the football field."

"He was." A shiver ran through her as she thought of how different Zeb was now than he'd been in his glory days as a high school football star. He wouldn't go near the sta-dium now. It was too unpredictable. He needed to be in familiar surroundings where he could anticipate the activity level at any given moment.

Alex squeezed her hand. "He's lucky he had you looking out for him. I know you had to leave the Army to take care of him. He's fortunate he had someone like you to help him."

"He's family. That's what family does . . . we help each other out." She hadn't meant to be so obvious, but even after laying it out like that, she wasn't sure Alex had picked up on the similarities in their situations.

He stopped a few feet away from the truck. "I see what you're trying to do here."

"Really? What's that?"

"Compare Zeb to Gramps. You were willing to put your own life aside for him and come back to take care of him. You're saying I ought to do that for Gramps."

"No, that's not what I'm trying to—"

"It's different. Your brother survived something no one should have to. He came back with a medical diagnosis of PTSD. Look, my grandfather is a good man and you're right, he doesn't deserve to get shoved into some home. But he's lived a full life. It's a totally different situation, not like comparing apples to . . . oh hell. I've got to go."

"But—"

His quick kiss to her cheek silenced her protest. What happened? Was he so set on leaving that he couldn't even consider what might be best for his own family?

"I've got to find Shiner Bock and get Gramps to that tour. I'll catch up with you later, okay?"

She nodded. What else could she do? If Alex didn't want to stay, she certainly couldn't make him. All she could do was try to protect her heart because it was already breaking at the thought of having to let him go.

Alex banged his head against the headrest of the truck once, then twice, trying to either knock some sense in or knock some bullshit out. Either way, he'd be better off than where he'd been earlier that afternoon. When he'd shut Zina down and bailed on her. At least they'd found the bird while he was at the hospital. One bright spot in an otherwise dark string of events.

Gramps cleared his throat in the passenger seat. "You okay over there?"

"Yeah." Alex let his frustration seep out on a long sigh and tried to gloss over any emotion. "You sure you don't like it here? That one bedroom seems like a perfect option." Plenty of natural light, no steps to contend with. A walking path right outside the front door.

"I told you, I'm going home."

"Gramps, it doesn't work like that. If Char and I don't think you'll be able to take care of yourself, we can't let you move back to the ranch on your own."

"I'm not asking for permission."

Alex groaned. Great, that's all he needed. He'd come home with the intention of helping Char. Now he was going to leave her with an even bigger mess on her hands. "What makes you think you're well enough to live in the middle of nowhere on your own?"

"I won't be on my own."

"Really? You planning on renting out a room to someone I don't know about?"

"I talked to Zina. I'm going to adopt Herbie."

"Herbie the pit bull?" Alex studied his grandfather's profile. The older man seemed calm, not pissed off like he'd been when Alex first came back to town. "Zina said that was okay?"

"She said as long as he had a home to go to I could take him. Water's Edge won't let me bring a dog, so I don't have a choice but to go to the ranch. I don't know why you think you have a say anyway. It's my life. I can do what I want with it."

"It doesn't work like that, Gramps."

"Why not? I've been talking to her brother, too. Zeb said he'd like being out in the country, so I'm going to see if he wants a place to live rent-free. I don't see you asking me for permission to do anything. That's how you live your life."

Alex opened his mouth to fire off a quick response. But dammit, Gramps was right. Alex had done the same damn thing. All the years he stayed away, he'd been putting his own needs first.

"Hell, by the time I was your age I had a wife, a stable nine-to-five, and two kids to feed. Don't try to talk to me about my choices."

"I'm not. You made choices. You saddled yourself with a wife and kids before you had a chance to have fun. Dad did the same thing. Then his life blew up in front of his face and he didn't have time to do all the things he put off while he raised a family."

"You talked to your dad about this?" Gramps asked. His salt-and-pepper eyebrows knit together.

"Just once."

"And that's what your dad told you? That he wished he'd made different choices?"

"No, of course not. He told me what he thought I wanted to hear. That Char and I were the most important things in the world to him. That even if he had it all to do over again, he'd have done the same thing." Alex glanced over at his grandfather. His father's eyes looked back at him. Why hadn't he inherited the same eyes as his dad and his gramps? It was spooky how similar his dad looked to Gramps. So similar that at times Alex almost mistook the older man for his father.

"He told you that because it's true." Gramps's gaze drilled into Alex's.

Alex looked away first.

"You listen to me and listen good," Gramps warned. "Your dad loved you and Charlene more than anything. It's true he had different plans, plans that didn't involve marrying your mama and becoming a dad at such a young age. But he wouldn't have changed a thing. Y'all were the most important people in the world to him."

Alex blinked back the threat of any emotion forcing its way through. "You don't think he would have been happier if he hadn't gotten bogged down with a wife and a baby right out of high school?"

"No," Gramps said. He meant it, too. Alex could tell by the way his grandfather held his gaze. Nothing but truth shone through those blue eyes.

"You think I should stay here then. Help out with Char and the girls?"

Gramps laid a weathered hand over his. "No, son. But I think you need to take a long look at what you want out of life. Because right now I think you're just trying to run away from your daddy's past mistakes."

Alex stared straight ahead, past the dashboard of the truck, past the stretch of asphalt in front of him. He'd been on the go for so long he'd almost forgotten what made him start running in the first place. All of it came back now. The fear of getting trapped in a life he didn't want. The threat of someone having a claim to him. The feeling of being suffocated by the expectations of the ones he loved most.

"You think about it." Gramps removed his hand and faced forward. Evidently the heart-to-heart had ended.

They rode the rest of the way back to the Phillips House in silence. Alex tried to think of a way to justify his decisions over the past few years. Nothing came to mind. Gramps was right. Here he thought he'd been so brave by charting new territory, exploring places he'd only read about in books as a kid, playing off his never-ending trips as an adventure and a lifestyle choice. Why had it taken him so long to realize the only thing he'd been doing was running away from his fear of turning out just like his dad?

twenty-eight

The afternoon passed in a whirlwind of taking care of dogs, making phone calls to other rescue centers near and far, and trying to calm down Lacey, who'd received three other wedding referrals from Chyna. Zina took a final walk-through of the warehouse before she turned toward the house and let the volunteers take over for the night.

She was beat. The ordeal with the wedding planner, the fake rehearsal, the strange conversation with Alex . . . it had all taken its toll. All she wanted was to grab a quick bite and turn in early. So when she stepped into the house, she was unprepared for the scent of something bubbling away on the stove. A combination of spices tickled her nose and made her stomach growl in appreciation.

"Zina, is that you?" Alex called from the kitchen.

She followed his voice, determined to find the source of the deliciousness. "What are you doing?"

Alex pulled the kitchen door open, and the smell of cumin, ginger, and garlic swirled around her, making her mouth water. With all of the excitement this morning she hadn't had a chance to grab lunch.

"Hungry?" Alex asked. He held a giant spoon in one hand and a pot holder in the other. He looked like a very scruffy, younger version of Jamie Oliver, ready to take on the world, one spice at a time.

"What's this?" She glanced around the kitchen, her gaze resting on a pot of something delectable simmering on the stove.

"I figured you'd be tired so I went ahead and whipped up some dinner for us. How spicy do you like your curry? One pepper? Two?" He stepped in front of the stove and lifted the lid off the stockpot.

"You made curry for dinner?" She could tell just by the way it smelled that it was going to be delicious.

"Chicken tikka masala. It's not really curry. A friend of mine who owns a restaurant in England taught me how."

"And how did you meet a restaurant owner in England?" It shouldn't surprise her. Alex had all kinds of stories about the people he'd met while traveling the world. The only place she'd been outside of Texas in the past ten years was her stint in Afghanistan. And she didn't have much of a chance to sample the local cuisine or make a lot of friends while she was there.

"I met him while diving in the Maldives. He said he was opening a restaurant outside of London and told me to stop by if I ever found myself on that side of the world."

"I should have known better than to ask."

"Why do you say that?"

"Because you've been so many places. I can only imagine the kinds of experiences you've had traveling the world."

"Ready to eat?"

"Dish it up. I'm starving."

She took a seat at the table while Alex spooned rice and whatever it was he'd made into two bowls. By the time he grabbed a plate full of naan and brought it to the table, she was ready to pass out from hunger.

"I went a little easy on the spice for you."

"For me?" With her fork poised at the edge of her bowl, she eyed him. "I was born and raised in Texas. What makes you think I can't handle my spice?"

"It's a different kind of spice. Trust me." He dug into his dish and slid a bite into his mouth.

At that point Zina wasn't going to argue over how much heat she could handle. She took a big bite and let the flavors roll over her tongue. It wasn't fair that someone could be blessed with his good looks and his skills between the sheets, and still be able to put a delicious meal on the table. Not when he was planning on leaving.

"What do you think?" His eyebrows lifted. He wanted to impress her and it showed.

"It's okay." No need to let him know how much she enjoyed it. The man clearly didn't suffer from a bruised ego. He knew his strengths.

"Just okay?" He grinned, obviously aware she was trying to pull one over on him.

"No, it's not just okay. It's freaking fantastic. When do you even get a chance to practice your cooking skills? I mean, you travel all the time. How often do you find yourself somewhere with a stocked kitchen?"

"So you do like it." The side of his mouth quirked up in a smug smile.

"I don't like it, I love it." She slid another melt-in-your-mouth bite past her lips. "Actually, I more than love it. What's more than love?"

"Hmm. You adore it?"

She nodded, her mouth full.

"Or maybe you just adore the man who introduced you to this culinary phenom?" He rested his elbows on the table and leaned toward her.

She tried not to laugh with her mouth full. It would serve

his cocky ass right if he ended up with a face full of whatever awesomeness he'd concocted.

"Call it what you want, but I seriously need this in my life. You need to show me how to make it so I can have it while you're . . ." Her voice trailed off and it hit her. When the wedding was over, Alex was going. All of this, everything they'd shared over the past several weeks, would be nothing but a memory. A temporary pause on his neverending journey. She was a pit stop. Nothing more than a chance to rest, refill, and move on.

"While I'm what?" His voice dropped lower. In the short time she'd known him, she'd come to love the way his tone grew deeper when they started to discuss something serious.

"You know." She let her fork rest against the side of her dish. Two minutes ago she'd been ravenous. But now, with the promise of his eventual departure hanging between them, she'd lost her appetite. Not even the mouthwatering blend of spices and sauce could sway her to eat another bite.

"What if I didn't?"

"Didn't what?" Her heart skittered like a needle scratching across an old record.

"Didn't . . . you know."

"Wait, are we both talking about the same 'you know' here?"

His shoulders rose and fell in a shrug. An adorable smile danced across his extremely kissable lips. He knew exactly what she meant. He was playing with her, stringing her along.

She placed a palm on his chest and gave him a playful push. "Don't tease."

He wrapped his hand around hers, demanding her attention. Her gaze met his. "I'm not teasing. At least not about this. What if I stayed?"

The question wedged itself into the sliver of space between them. She didn't know how to respond. If she acted too excited, would she scare him off? If she were too nonchalant, would he change his mind?

"Well?"

"I'd love it if you'd . . . you know." A grin threatened to split her serious expression in two.

"All right then. It's settled." He wrapped an arm around her shoulders and pulled her close. "After the wedding, I'll find a place to stay. We can try this on for real."

"Just like that?"

"Doesn't need to be more complicated, right?"

She didn't trust herself to react with anything but a nod. The thought of him sticking around for a bit gave her hope. Maybe she wasn't destined to be alone. Maybe the universe had some magical, mystical plan that would set her up with a chance for happiness.

The mood lightened and they joked around while they ate the rest of their dinner. Alex did a spot-on imitation of Chyna after she lost her hat. Zina almost fell out of her chair from laughing. After the dishes had been washed, dried, and put away, he held out a hand. "You want to try out that tub?"

"What are you going to do while I'm soaking?" She took the hand he offered and they moved toward the stairs.

"What do you mean? I measured and there's plenty of room in that tub for two."

They didn't make it to the bathtub. Alex had barely shut the bedroom door behind them when Zina whirled around and pressed him up against the wall. Her lips were hungry, as eager for him as his were for her. The length of her body aligned with his, her soft curves a perfect fit against his hard planes. He'd been anticipating this night for weeks. Every time she'd brushed against him, every time they'd accidentally touched, every time she'd looked at him with that combination of heat and hope in her eyes, it had stoked the fire she'd ignited when he first set eyes on her.

He pushed off the door and backed her toward the bed. The need to feel every bare inch of her against his skin drove his hands under her shirt. His fingers trailed up and over her ribs while goose bumps pebbled her skin. Her hands worked his shirt up while she continued nipping and sucking at his lips.

When the backs of her legs hit the bed, she fell backward, pulling him down on top of her. He shifted to the side so he didn't hurt her, although Zina had shown him on more than one occasion that she wasn't fragile or delicate or one who'd be so easily overcome. The woman was strong, capable, and not afraid to take what she wanted.

His hands roamed over her full hips, kneading the roundness of her ass. She moaned into his mouth, breaking contact just long enough for him to flip her on her back.

He got to his hands and knees and hovered over her. "How about you lose the shirt?" Her chest rose and fell with her breath, making him eager to get his hands on her.

Her brow edged up. "I will if you will."

"Done." He reached over his shoulder and jerked his shirt up and over his head in one smooth move.

She laughed. "Someone's feeling frisky tonight." Then she slowly unfastened the bottom button on her shirt, her gaze never leaving his. A sliver of sun-kissed skin peeked through the slit.

He wanted to bend over and slide his tongue against her, but he didn't want to rush things; he was enjoying the way the heat continued to build between them.

Her tongue flicked out, gliding over her upper lip as she pushed the next button through the hole, exposing another few inches of her stomach.

"You okay there, Captain Jaybird? You're looking a little hot under the collar. I don't want you to melt."

Tempted to growl out his frustration, he kept his cool. "You're a tease."

"Hmm." She moved her hands to the next button. "You say that like it's a bad thing."

Heat coiled in his gut as he held himself back, resisting the overwhelming urge to pop the buttons right off her shirt and let himself run his tongue down the center of her breastbone. He couldn't wait to taste her skin and show her the real meaning of what it meant to be a tease.

Another button slid through its hole, revealing the bottom band of her bra.

"You draw this out any longer and I might just change my mind," he teased.

"Oh yeah?" Her fingers gripped the sides of her shirt and pulled them together, cutting off his view of her rib cage. "You have something better to do tonight?"

He shrugged. "Astros are playing pre-season. Maybe I want to check out the game."

Her mouth split into a knowing grin. "You'd rather watch a bunch of sweaty men toss their balls around than have me fondling yours?"

His dick responded to that comment, growing even thicker and harder as he imagined her doing just that. Faking a direct hit to the heart, he fell onto his side, adjusting himself on the way down. "You're killing me, Baxter."

She shed her shirt and straddled him, centering herself directly over his crotch. Her hips glided forward, creating the lightest, sweetest amount of pressure along his growing hard-on. "Well we can't have that. At least not until I'm done with you."

Gazing up at her, the light from the bedside lamp casting a glow behind her head, she looked like an angel. An angel whom he'd very much like to strip naked and drive to the brink of madness with his mouth.

He reached behind her and unclasped her bra. Her eyes

narrowed as he moved his hands around her rib cage and slid them up to cup her breasts. "Who's fondling who now?" he whispered.

Her mouth quirked up in a lopsided grin. She had him exactly where she wanted him; he could tell by the way she brushed over his hips, using her body to taunt him. Her breasts were heavy in his hands, and he swept the pads of his thumbs over her nipples. She bit her lower lip and lowered her hips, increasing the pressure, grinding against him.

He'd had enough. He cupped his hands under her ass and lifted up from the bed. Her legs wrapped around his middle, and he held her with one hand while he fumbled with his belt buckle. She didn't make it easy—her tongue circled his ear, her hands tunneled through his hair. Dammit. Why did he have to wear the button-fly jeans today?

"Having trouble?" She pulled back enough to meet his gaze.

Hell, she drove him crazy. He'd been holding back, wanting to be gentle, wanting to keep himself in check and make sure she was taken care of before he took control. But now . . . now he wanted to claim her, wipe that smug smirk off her face, and show her what happened when she played with fire.

He dumped her on the bed and jerked his pants down his legs along with his briefs. As he kicked his feet loose, he wrapped a hand around his length. "Is this what you want?"

She licked her lips. If anything, the shift in power turned her on. She let her bra fall forward while she took her time unbuttoning her jeans and slowly sliding them down her legs. While she watched, he grabbed the box he'd stored in the drawer, ripped open a packet, and unrolled a condom.

Stripped down to her birthday suit, she lay back on the bed and propped herself up on an elbow. Then she patted the space next to her and arched a brow. "What are you waiting for?"

* * *

The look on his face might have made her a little nervous if it were anyone but Alex. She may have pushed him too far, but she was enjoying herself and he could take it. In fact, he seemed to thrive on her smartass remarks and looked like he wanted her just as much as she wanted him.

He crept onto the bed like an animal stalking its prey. She couldn't suppress the giggle that escaped when she rolled toward the indentation he made on the bed.

"You think this is funny?" His tone dipped low, but the hint of humor in his eyes showed her he wasn't taking anything too seriously.

"No. I think it's about time we got on with it. What if I want to watch the Astros play?"

He ducked his head, his mouth connecting with her throat while his palm splayed across her navel. "You'd rather watch baseball?" he murmured against the pulse pounding away in her neck.

There was absolutely nothing she'd rather be doing in this moment than be devoured by this man. Body, mind, and spirit, he'd infiltrated her very soul. But damn, he was fun to tease, so she hitched up a knee and flung her leg over his hip, aligning her core with his tip.

"I do love to watch a man fondle his bat."

He chuckled. "I'd rather you fondle my bat."

"Why do I have to be the one to do all of the work around here?" She let out a breathy sigh as her fingers crept down his abs.

"I've always been an equal opportunist."

She grinned as she shifted on top of him again. His hands went to her hips and he lifted her up. Positioning herself directly over his cock, she eased her way down onto him, relishing the way she stretched to accommodate him, the way he filled her.

His chest expanded as breath flowed into his lungs. They stilled, locked together in the most intimate way. Then he moved, thrusting a bit deeper. She'd been teasing him, playing with him, but now she was the one who was lost. As they moved together, finding their rhythm, she let herself go. His hands moved over her, cupping her breasts, squeezing her hips, and zeroing in on her need. She'd never felt so connected to someone before, so powerful and vulnerable at the same time.

Then he shifted, rising to a seated position. The angle changed and her release swelled. He dipped his head down to suck her nipple into his mouth and she was gone. She rode him, taking everything she needed until the momentum crashed over her. Slumped against him, her arms around his neck, he lifted her up and laid her down.

"Roll over, sport."

"Sport?" She could barely speak as aftershocks continued to spark through her.

"Hey, you're the one who wanted to talk baseball."

She flipped onto her stomach, not sure her knees would be able to support her. Her limbs had turned to jelly.

His arm scooped under her stomach and he helped her up to her hands and knees. "You okay?"

Nodding her head, she pushed her ass back into him. "Come on, slugger."

His laugh sent a blast of warm breath over her lower back and she shivered. "You're something else, you know that?"

"Mm-hmm. But I sure do like hearing you say it." She felt him line up against her backside and then push into her. The pressure sent her reeling again. He pulled back and pushed in farther. Nice and slow, gentle, like he was afraid he might hurt her.

His hand curved around her hip, splaying over her curls, his finger stroking her as he slid in and out. She moaned, tightening around him while another orgasm built.

He increased the pace. She met him thrust for thrust,

both of them straining, eager for something just out of reach. Then she slumped down, angling her back end higher in the air as his fingers finished what he'd started. He gave a final thrust, straining, his hand holding her hip so tight she was sure he'd leave a bruise. One she'd cherish as a mark of what could only be described as the most intense night of her life.

Spent, he rolled to the side, pulling her against him. "You're amazing."

She nestled her backside into his front. "You're not so bad yourself."

"I love you, Zina." His finger moved a chunk of her hair away from her ear. Then he pressed a gentle kiss against her neck.

Her heart glowed. She could actually feel it warming inside her chest. "I love you, too."

"Good. And now I know what to get you for Christmas."

"What's that?" The idea of him being around to give her anything for Christmas was gift enough.

"Hell, now that I know how turned on you get by baseball talk, I think I'll see if I can get on the list for season tickets."

She let out a laugh and realized that for once in her life she knew what it felt like to be content. Truly, happily, completely content.

twenty-nine

The next few weeks flashed by in a haze of wedding preparations, rehabilitating the puppy mill dogs, and spending as much time as possible with Alex. Bodie was certain the dog-fighting ring had moved out of town, so he'd given Zina the go-ahead to move back into her place. But Alex insisted she stay at the Phillips House with him. He used all kinds of logical reasoning to make his point: it was closer to where the dogs were staying, she could help with the wedding, and the most convincing argument of all . . . it would give them more time to be together.

It didn't seem fair for one person to have so much happiness but Zina was trying hard to enjoy it. She'd been dreading the upcoming wedding not only because of all the work but because of what it represented. But now, based on what Alex said, it was no longer a looming date signaling the end of whatever had been growing between them, just a milestone marking the end of his job with the penguins and when he'd have to start looking for something else that would keep him nearby.

She didn't know what kind of opportunity he might be able to find or how far he might have to go from Ido. But he seemed committed to sticking around and that was good enough for her.

"You ready for this afternoon?" Lacey fluffed the pillow behind her and sat up straighter.

Zina had stopped by to get last-minute instructions for the wedding weekend. Poor Lacey. The biggest event Ido had ever hosted and the woman who'd made it all possible was stuck in bed. She was her own worst enemy, though, since she kept pushing herself too hard and ending up right back on bed rest.

"We've gone over it at least a dozen times. Don't worry, I've got this." Zina took the folder Lacey held out to her. "What's this?"

"I took the liberty of doing a little research on all of the members of the wedding party. Those are just some helpful hints. You know, like the bride's mother prefers her cosmos with a twist of orange instead of lemon. Little things that will make a difference."

"You cyberstalked the Munyon family?"

"No, I did the groom's family, too. His grandma is allergic to hairy caterpillars, so I've asked your brother to do a sweep of the tents before everyone arrives."

Zina shook her head. "How long did it take you to pull this together?"

Lacey waved her hands. "What else am I supposed to do? Between you and Bodie I've barely been allowed to walk to the bathroom. I'm bored out of my mind."

"I'll pass the info along. I'm sure everyone will find it extremely helpful." She tucked the folder into her bag. "Anything else you need to fill me in on?"

Lacey shook her head. "Nope. Just be nice. I know you're not one hundred percent on board with the whole wedding destination thing. Try not to piss anyone off, okay?"

"Piss anyone off? What exactly do you think I'm going

to do out there?" Zina pressed a hand to her heart in mock offense.

"Nothing." Lacey reached for her hand and gave it a squeeze. "You're just not as warm and fuzzy as . . ."

"As you?" That was the gospel truth. And thank God for that. She could tell by the way Lacey's shoulders drooped that she'd hit the proverbial nail on the head.

"You know I love you, Z. Just channel your soft side. These people are going to be demanding and probably push every hot button you've got. I'm just asking you to keep the needs of Ido in mind before you fly off the handle because of some stupid request."

Zina could appreciate her concern. Lacey had always been the mushy, gushy one. Zina was more calculating, a lot less enthusiastic, and had a history of dissing people who came up with outlandish expectations.

"Don't worry. I'll be so accommodating they won't know what hit them."

Lacey smiled but her brows drew together, showing she didn't fully believe the promise.

"What now?" Zina pulled her hand away and picked up her bag. "Make it quick. I've got to get over to the Phillips House to make sure they've got those garlands installed just like you wanted."

"Nothing. I know you'll be great. Just . . ."

"What?"

"Thanks." Lacey wiped a tear from the corner of her eye. The pregnancy hormones must be jacking with her emotions. Even as the emotional one in their relationship, she was rarely reduced to tears.

"Oh, honey, you're welcome." Zina perched on the edge of the bed and pulled her bestie in for a gentle hug. "We'll get through this weekend and then you can stop worrying about everything and focus all of your attention on growing that baby."

"You're the best. And I know you're not the hard-ass you

pretend to be. At least not so much now that you've got a certain birdman in your life."

"Do *not* call him a birdman. That strips away any kind of attractiveness."

"It's true though. Alex said he might be sticking around for a while, maybe even for good?"

She was digging for info. Zina hadn't had the time or desire to fill Lacey in on the plans she and Alex had discussed. Partly because she hadn't had a chance. But mostly because she still wasn't totally sure he meant it. Once they got through the wedding from hell, she'd have a better idea if he would follow through.

"We'll see. Can we talk about this after I spend all weekend working my ass off?"

"Of course. Call me if you need anything. I might not be allowed to leave my bed but I can still make calls or follow up on things or look stuff up online."

"Try to get some rest." Zina slid the strap of her bag into place. "Alex and I have everything under control. I promise."

A half hour later she wished she hadn't uttered such a ridiculous assurance. As Zina pulled in to the drive leading to the Phillips House, she came across the florist stringing garland along the low wooden fence. She pulled over and rolled down the window.

"Hey, Suzy, how's it going?" Had Lacey approved the clash of colors currently being installed on the fence? Based on what they'd talked about she clearly remembered the bride's request of using only white flowers in all of the decor.

"Great. Almost done here, then I'll go over and set up the centerpieces for the reception dinner tomorrow."

"I thought Lacey talked to you about using white flowers in all of the decor?" Zina reached for the three-inch-thick notebook Lacey had saddled her with so she could confirm the floral order.

Suzy shook her head. "The wholesaler didn't have enough, so he had to make some substitutions. Besides, that would be so boring. With all of the gorgeous colors available this time of year, don't you think it's better to amp up the display?"

"Suzy." Zina lowered her voice. She remembered how the florist had botched Lacey's own wedding last year. Since then Lacey had warned her about taking creative liberties and she'd been following the flower orders to a T. Until now.

"You've got to agree, this is a lot more welcoming for all of those Hollywood types heading our way." Suzy stepped back and crossed her arms as if she needed to take a minute to admire her own creation.

Zina groaned as she climbed out of the truck. "You can't just change things on a whim. The wedding planner wants all white flowers. It's our job to give them to her."

Suzy barely came up to Zina's chin, but she carried herself with such power that even Zina took a step back when the vertically challenged spitfire turned her attention Zina's way.

"I tried. The order didn't come in and now it's too late to get new flowers anyway."

This wasn't a good way to start the weekend events. "What are we going to do?"

"I spent the past two days stringing these garlands together. There's no way you're going to be able to change them out before that hoity-toity wedding lady with the pink hair gets here." Suzy turned her attention back to the flowers.

"We have to do something." Zina forced her hands to her hips, ready to stand her ground. She'd gone up against much fiercer opponents in the military. Ones who weren't taxidermists posing as wedding florists.

"It's your funeral, sweetie." Suzy dropped the garland she held in her hand and stalked back to where she'd pulled her truck onto the side of the road. "Good luck."

"It's not a funeral, it's a wedding," Zina muttered under her breath. Or at least she hoped it wouldn't turn into a funeral. Because right now it was her head on the chopping block. She consulted the minute-by-minute schedule Lacey had printed out, detailing the weekend's events. Chyna and the bridal party would be arriving in three hours. That gave her one hundred eighty minutes to figure out a way to magically transform the colorful garland into winter wonderland white.

With the threat of a headache twinging at her temples, she gritted her teeth and climbed back into her truck. She'd figure out a way to make this work. She didn't have another choice.

thirty

 ⌒♡⌒

Alex tossed a sardine in the air for Louise to catch. "Good girl." Now if she could just keep her cool and execute her walk up and down the aisle tomorrow as smoothly as she'd done today, they'd have nothing to worry about. Too bad there were so many ifs in that statement. Why did so much of their success have to depend on a bunch of birds?

The wedding photographer Chyna hired snapped a few more shots. "Thanks for letting me sit in on your training session."

"Not a problem. You get what you need?"

"Sure did. I think the bride and groom will appreciate the behind-the-scenes shots of the prep work." He sat down in the front row and began to disassemble his camera.

"Just remember, no flash at the ceremony. The penguins will freak out."

"Got it."

Alex waited for the photographer to leave, then turned back to the penguins, ready to have them take another turn down the aisle. Before he had a chance, Zina rushed into the tent.

"I've got a problem, and I need help."

"What's up?" They'd anticipated issues and had spent the better part of the past three days coming up with plans B, C, D, and all the way down to N. He was confident that whatever issue she was dealing with was one they'd already worked out a solution for.

"The flowers didn't come in. Suzy didn't question it and now we don't have time to get all white like Chyna wanted." Zina set her bag down on a table that hadn't been draped with linens yet. The caterer was holding off on setting out the white tablecloths until the last moment lest the wind kick up and cover everything in a nice coat of dusty grit.

"Calm down. We'll figure it out together." He racked his brain trying to remember what their alternate plan was for a florist gone rogue. Surely they'd talked about that.

"It looks like a circus threw up on the fence. What are we going to do?"

"How much time do we have?"

Zina checked her watch. "Two hours and forty-eight minutes until Chyna arrives."

Alex bit his lip and took in a deep breath through his nose. The smell of paint hit him. Of course. "Come on, I've got an idea."

He rushed to the front of the tent where one of Zina's volunteers was touching up the paint on the front of the warehouse.

"No. That's not going to work." Zina crossed her arms over her chest.

"You're right. We won't have time to brush it on." He turned to the guy wielding the paintbrush. "Y'all got a paint sprayer?"

Fifteen minutes later he stood over the bright garland of flowers. *Here goes nothing.* He squeezed the trigger and sprayed a light coating of white paint over a particularly large sunflower. "What do you think?" he shouted to Zina over the roar of the compressor.

She shrugged. "You've committed now. I say go for it."

He nodded, then continued to coat the entire garland with a light layer of white. It almost looked like snow. Snow that had fallen in the middle of April, coating a crazy clash of colors in a soft layer of white. Who the hell would buy that? He dug in, continuing to layer light coat upon light coat until the entire garland sparkled in the sun.

Zina cut the compressor and stalked toward him. "I think that's all we can do under the circumstances. How long will it take you to do the rest?"

Alex eyed the fence line. "Give me an hour. It ought to dry fast in this heat and then we'll string them up long before she gets here. Sound good?"

Zina nodded, then pressed a kiss to his cheek. "Thanks. Have I told you how much I love you? I'd be totally lost without you right now."

He gave her a half hug in return as he wielded the sprayer. For some reason her confidence in him tugged at him this morning, and not in a good way. He shook it off. "Don't you have something more important to do than watch paint dry?"

"I do. I'm going to head over to the house and make sure they've got the buffet for the rehearsal dinner set up. Catch up with you in a few?"

"You bet." He waited until she walked away before he fired up the sprayer. He'd been the happiest he'd ever been over the past few weeks. Spending time with Zina, working on a common goal, it had been fantastic being so close to her and taking on such a huge role in her life. But he'd also been getting a little freaked out. What if he ruined it? Everything was so good. What if he screwed it up like he always did? What if he failed her?

He finished the flowers and returned the sprayer to the

warehouse. As he made his way back to ensure the penguins had been secured, he caught a glimpse of Gramps. The old man had Herbie on a leash and was heading his way.

"Hey, Gramps. You've got to kennel the dog." Even though Zina had done her best to find new homes or shelters for the pups they'd had on-site, they still had a few that needed to remain out of sight and out of earshot over the next couple of days.

"It's okay. This one's coming up to the house with me." Gramps stopped when he reached Alex. "I've been telling Herbie all about the pastures we've got at the ranch."

"That's great. I'm sure he's been enjoying the stories." Everyone had a part to play this weekend. Gramps needed to get it in gear and start working on his. He was in charge of helping with the penguins and making sure the remaining rescue dogs stayed under the radar.

"He sure is. I can't wait to see him running loose out there." Gramps reached down and ruffled Herbie behind the ears. The dog rewarded him by jumping up and swiping his tongue across the older man's chin.

"Can you take him out of here? We don't need anyone catching sight of the dogs when the wedding party arrives, right?"

"We're going. Any idea when we'll be moving out to the ranch? Zeb's in. I told him he could take your grandmother's old sewing room. We'll have our work cut out for us fixing the place up. I figure you'll need a few days to ship the penguins back, but—"

"What?" Alex had already turned his back but now his grandfather had his full attention.

Gramps patted his forehead with a hanky. They'd sacrificed the portable air conditioner so Zina could run it out to the tent. The humidity hung in the air, making everyone glisten with a fine sheen of sweat. "When we move. You said you were going to stick around. I assumed you'd be moving into the ranch house with me. I suppose if Zeb's there it'll satisfy your sister, but where are you going to stay then?"

Alex closed his eyes and counted to three in his head. When he opened them again, he hoped he'd realize he'd inhaled too many paint fumes and was hallucinating. But no, Gramps stood in the same spot, the same furrow bisecting his brow. "We don't have time to talk about this right now. Let's just get through the wedding and then we'll figure out a plan, okay?"

"I know it's going to take some cash to make the improvements. I've got a little bit of money saved. Is it about the cash?"

"Gramps. You've got to get the dog out of here. We'll have to talk about it later." What was going on with everyone? First Zina confided how lost she'd be without him. Now Gramps wanted to talk about having Zeb move in with them and remodeling the ranch house.

Gramps shook his head and stomped toward the warehouse. Alex gritted his teeth and started to move toward the tents.

"There you are." Char caught up to him as he reached the larger of the two tents, the one they'd designated as the reception area.

"What do you need?" He didn't mean to lash out, but he was feeling backed into a corner. All of a sudden it seemed like everyone had plans for him, everyone but him.

"Nothing. Geez, what's wrong with you today?" Char grinned as she elbowed him in the side. "I figured you'd be in a good mood seeing as how you're almost ready to give up the penguins and get back to normal."

Normal. His normal had been globe-trotting around the world. Meeting new people and taking part in amazing adventures. "What do you mean 'normal'?"

"You know, sending the penguins packing, settling down . . ."

His stomach twisted into knots. Why was everyone assuming he was going to be settling down? "Settling down?"

"Yeah. Gramps told me you decided to move out to the ranch with him. With the way things are going between you and Zina, it seems like there might be another wedding in the not-so-distant future if you know what I mean."

The edges of his vision went fuzzy. Like he was staring down a long tunnel and Char stood at the end, yapping her mouth. But no words came out. A buzzing rang in his ears. He shook his head to try to knock it, but all he could think about was how everyone had already seemed to figure out his future. Everyone but him.

"I've gotta go." He wasn't even sure if he'd managed to utter the words out loud but he didn't wait around for Char to respond. His boots crunched on the gravel as he stalked toward the truck. Every fiber of his being urged him to do one thing . . . flee.

"Where's Alex?" Zina checked her watch. He should be there by now. Chyna would be on-site in less than ten minutes and the first thing they'd planned to do was show a united front by meeting her in person and walking her through the events of the weekend. Zina had checked every detail herself. The only update she needed was from Alex regarding the penguins.

At least that was one area she didn't need to worry about. Alex had surprised her by how dedicated he was to making sure the wedding went off without a hitch. It was nice to not have to do everything all alone and be able to depend on someone for a change.

While she waited, her phone rang. Lacey. She'd lost count of how many times Lacey had called, but it had to be in the high double if not triple digits by now.

"What now?" Zina asked.

"Please tell me you didn't give Kirby the go-ahead to pick the wedding party up at the airport in his hearse."

"What?" Zina gasped. "Of course not. Why would you think that?"

"Because he just tagged the Phillips House on social media saying he was waiting for the bride and groom."

"No." All the breath left her lungs. Why would Kirby have taken it upon himself to fetch the bride and groom? "I set it up with an outfit from Houston. Let me give them a call and I'll call you back."

Lacey disconnected and Zina tried to take a few deep breaths as she looked up the phone number for the limo service she'd booked.

By the time they answered and explained someone had canceled the limo service, Lacey was calling again. Zina clicked over, with no idea how to explain that Kirby had gone rogue.

"He's got them," Lacey shrieked through the phone. "He just updated his status and he's on his way. What's going on?"

"I'm sure it will be fine. Kirby knows how important this is. He's not going to do anything to put the wedding in danger."

"Danger?" Chyna's voice rang out from the back of the tent. "We're all going to be in danger if we can't turn the air up in here. The whole wedding party will roast."

"Chyna's here." Zina eyed the wedding planner as she made her way down the center aisle. "Can you call Kirby and see what's happening? I've got to go."

"So help me, if he ruins this for us, Bodie may have to book me for manslaughter." Lacey groaned.

"Everything's going to be fine. Text me and let me know what you find out." Zina disconnected and took in a breath, trying to center herself. She'd been in war zones before, she could handle a little last-minute chaos for a wedding. Then she pasted the most patronizing smile on her face she could summon under the extenuating circumstances and turned to face Chyna.

"Chyna, I'm so glad you made it. How was your flight?"

"Fine. Now fill me in. The Munyons will be here soon." She looked striking as always, in a designer ensemble complete with a trendy pillbox-style hat she wore over a new shade of bright pink hair.

"All right then. Here's the schedule." Zina ran through the timeline of events, starting with the arrival of the wedding party and ending with the fireworks they'd arranged to go off as the bride and groom departed the next night.

Chyna nodded along, adding a comment here and there until they reached the end of the itinerary. "Looks good. I have to say, I had my doubts about this place but you and your boss came through."

Zina didn't bother to set the record straight that Lacey was not, in fact, her boss nor was she employed in any way, shape, or form by the town. What mattered was that the next two days were the happiest, most joyful days of the lovebirds' lives.

Chyna cleared her throat. A tall man in dark jeans, cowboy boots, and a straw Stetson appeared at the entrance of the tent.

"Tad, darling." Chyna floated down the aisle, her hands already reaching for his. "Come in, let me show you what I've done to create your daughter's dream winter wonderland."

"Who's this?" Tad smiled at Zina. "Are you one of Chyna's helpers?"

Before she could answer, Chyna beat her to it. "She's local staff."

"In that case, well done." Tad held his phone out. "My daughter just sent me a text of the limo y'all sent to pick them up. I've gotta say, I've never seen anything like it."

Zina clutched her hands together. She didn't want to look.

"Genius." Chyna's excitement made her voice vibrate.

Kirby had revamped the hearse into a convertible limo with a clear dome on top. It looked just like the popemobile she'd seen on TV. The new white paint job sparkled. Zina bowed her head. She couldn't wait to tell Lacey that Kirby had come through for them.

"Let me show you around. Zina, can you find the man who trained the penguins? Tad's going to want to see a demonstration. They are, after all, besides the bride and groom, the main attraction."

"Sure, let me see what I can do." Zina exited through a flap in the back of the tent while Chyna prattled on about all the plans she'd put into place. Lacey might not mind sharing the spotlight with the presumptuous wedding planner, but it irked Zina to the core to hear the woman claim responsibility for all the hard work they'd put into the event.

Didn't matter now. She fired off a text to Lacey to set her mind at ease. The only thing that mattered was getting through the next two days.

Alex had just secured the penguins when Zina entered the warehouse.

"Where have you been? Mr. Munyon's here. He wants to meet you." Zina reached for his hand and twined her fingers with his.

He'd usually welcome her touch but with everyone dumping demands on him, he was feeling the stress of the culmination of weeks of preparation and not even Zina's presence seemed to make him feel better.

"Yeah, of course. Just wrapping up and getting the penguins settled. Where is he?"

"In the main tent. I was going to go check on the food for the rehearsal dinner up at the house. Want me to come with you?"

He shook his head. "I've got it."

"Have you officially turned down his offer of employment yet?" She clasped her hands around the back of his neck and rose to her tiptoes. "He doesn't look like the kind of man who likes to be refused."

Alex pulled her against him as he pressed a kiss to her forehead. "I figured I'd wait until the wedding was over. Don't want to rock the boat, right?"

"Good call." She ran her fingers through the hair at the nape of his neck.

He could stand there for hours, lost in her touch, the way she looked up at him with love and hope and the promise of a future in her eyes. But that wouldn't get him through the next two days. "I'll see you up at the house later?"

"Later." She let her hands slide down his body before she turned away. "Good luck."

"Thanks." Luck was something he'd been without for a very long time. If ever there was a time he could use it, today was that day.

He entered the tent where the ceremony would be taking place. A few of the townspeople were making last-minute preparations. Chyna and Mr. Munyon stood at the front of the tent, where the bride and groom would say their vows.

"Here he is." Chyna sprang toward him, a huge smile pasted on her lips. "Tad, I'd like you to meet Alex Sanders, your penguin handler."

Tad thrust his hand forward. "Nice to meet you, Alex."

"It's nice to meet you too, sir." The man looked younger than Alex expected.

"Call me Tad. We're going to be working together, aren't we?"

Alex inclined his head. Now wasn't the time to bring that up.

"I'm so glad you're coming on board. I've got plans for the international arm of my business. Big plans." He pumped Alex's hand a few times, then let it go. "Chyna tells me you've been doing an incredible job with this event."

"It's been a pleasure working for you, and the penguins, well, they've been a very accommodating group."

"That's good to hear. Listen, about that job we talked about. I need someone on the ground right away. Think you can leave Sunday morning and head down to the Caymans to take a look at a property?"

"Um, sure." Alex wanted to politely decline. But he didn't want to piss off the father of the bride right before the wedding. Besides, the thought of sinking his toes into the sand forced everything else out of his head. For the first time in days his problems seemed to fall by the wayside as he pictured the white sandy beaches of the Caribbean.

"Great. I'll have my assistant set it up. Can't wait to see those penguins in action tomorrow." He turned a smile on Chyna. "Can you show us where we're staying? I'd like to get settled in before the rest of the wedding party arrives."

"I've got a fleet of luxury RVs parked just down the road. Right this way." Chyna linked her arm through Tad's, leaving Alex standing in the middle of the aisle, wondering why he hadn't said no.

thirty-one

❤

Strains of classical music drifted over the state-of-the-art sound system Chyna had brought in for the event. Zina stood just outside the front of the tent. Ushers from the wedding party had closed the flaps while the bride and her dozen bridesmaids got themselves arranged in the order they'd walk down the aisle.

The past twenty-four hours had been a whirlwind of last-minute crises. Zina was dead on her feet and couldn't wait to get through the ceremony. She hadn't even seen Alex since the night before. The only thing standing between her being off duty was the quick exchange of the vows. After the penguins finished their procession up and back down the aisle, she'd be off the hook for the rest of the night. Chyna had flown enough staff in with her from LA to handle the party portion of the evening.

While she waited for the music to change and the first bridesmaid to start down the aisle, Alex led the penguins over, the clicker he used to train the birds in his hand.

"How are you holding up?" he whispered.

Zina blinked a long, slow blink and shook her head. "Ready for this to be over. How about you?"

Chyna shushed them. The flaps of the tent opened long enough for the first bridesmaid to walk through, then closed behind her.

Alex leaned closer. "Finish line's in sight."

She nodded, hoping he was right. One by one the bridesmaids entered the tent to Chyna's precise count until only the bride and the penguins remained. Alex signaled Zina that he was going to walk around to the back of the tent like they'd practiced. Thanks to Chyna and her insistence that the penguins take part in the entrance and exit processions, they'd had to find some way to keep the penguins interested in hanging out while the vows were exchanged. Having Alex behind the tent with a bucket of fish had worked during their practice sessions. She had no reason to think it wouldn't work when it mattered the most.

Zina arranged the birds in pairs by height just as the flaps of the tent reopened. She cast a quick glance at Chyna, who nodded. With her fingers crossed, Zina gave the signal for the first pair of penguins to start down the aisle. A chorus of oohs and aahs rose from the assembled guests as each pair of birds waddled into the tent. Chyna's lips pursed and Zina couldn't help but wonder if the wedding planner still disapproved of how waddly the penguins waddled.

The guests didn't seem to mind. In fact, they began to stand, trying to get a closer look at the birds. Then, just as the music changed to the classic "Here Comes the Bride," the photographer stepped into the center aisle. He raised his camera to his eye, adjusted the lens, and pressed the button. Bursts of light flashed through the tent, bouncing off the glittery silver and iridescent snowflakes Alex's nieces had helped Zina string across the ceiling, blinding everyone and everything.

Zina's heart slammed into her throat. The no she tried to yell didn't make it past the lump in her esophagus. The

penguins hated the light. Alex had specifically requested
no flash photography while the penguins were present. Instead of retreating, the photographer actually moved closer
to the birds and took another shot. Two of the penguins
dove into the chairs. Guests screamed and tried to get away
from the blinded birds.

Gilligan raced toward the photographer as fast as his
flippers would carry him. He rammed into the man's midsection and the photographer went down, his equipment
catching on the tulle netting they'd swooped between rows
to line the aisle. Chairs crashed to the ground. Zina tried to
keep an eye on the birds, but they scattered like buckshot
fired through a cannon and she couldn't track them all.

Chyna climbed on top of a chair, her face pinker than
her new hair color. With her hands waving in the air, she
tried to stop the swell of people moving toward the exit.
"Please return to your seats."

It was too late for that. Zina swept into the tent and
fought the current of the crowd until she reached the front
of the aisle. Alex and Morty must have ducked in when the
commotion broke out and had corralled several of the birds
to a safe spot behind the harpist.

Alex yelled over the chaos. "Where are the others?"

Zina did a quick count. Ten birds were accounted for,
including the two that had nose-dived into the guest section. Who was missing? Was it odd she knew all twelve
birds by name and could recognize them on sight? After
counting them off again, she knew who'd made a break
for it. Thelma and Louise were on the loose. They couldn't
get far.

"Thelma and Louise are missing," she said.

Alex turned to Morty. "Can you go get this group settled
in the warehouse?"

He nodded.

"Let's go find the others," Alex said.

Confident that Morty could handle the tamer ten, Zina

ducked out of the side of the tent and scoped out the yard. Guests milled around, not sure what the emergency contingency plan was on how to handle rogue penguins. She couldn't offer any suggestions because this was one unforeseen circumstance they hadn't taken into account when they'd worked up their contingency plans.

How had she let Lacey talk her into this in the first place? Her phone rang. How could Lacey know she'd lost control? It hadn't even been two minutes since all hell had broken loose.

"I'm handling it," Zina barked into the phone.

"By handling it you mean you've salvaged the wedding and I shouldn't be afraid to look at the front page of the paper tomorrow?"

"Now's not a good time." Zina caught a flash of white off in the distance. She broke into a jog, hoping beyond all hope it was Thelma or Louise.

"I'm coming over." Lacey grunted like she was heaving herself out of bed. "I don't care what the doctor says. If we can't pull this back together, we may as well shut down the whole wedding operation. No one will want to book with us after tonight."

Zina stepped into the flower bed. An azalea bush shook as something brushed past it. "Gotcha." Her hand closed around Thelma's floral necklace.

"Are you there?" Lacey asked.

"One bird down, one to go. Can I call you back?" She didn't have the bandwidth to handle Lacey right now.

"Don't bother. I'll be there in twenty minutes. Fifteen if Bodie will turn on the lights and siren."

"That's not necess—" The line went dead.

Zina kept a loose grip on Thelma's flipper as she marched her back to the warehouse. She caught a glimpse of Chyna out of the corner of her eye. What the woman lacked in stature, she made up for in attitude. She'd produced a bullhorn and barked directions at the crowd. Zina managed to catch the tail end of it. Sounded like they were taking a ten-minute break to reset the tent and would call everyone in when it was ready. At least the Munyons hadn't pulled out . . . yet. There was still a chance to save Lacey's reputation.

She herded Thelma into the warehouse, where the rest of the penguins playfully dove into the water and stood around chattering.

"Hey, Zina. Come see this." Morty called her from the other side of the makeshift wall.

Zina rounded the corner to find Louise snuggled up on a blanket with Aurora, the pit bull that Dolly had named. "How did this happen?"

"Found her over here when I brought the others in."

"She nearly gave me a heart attack. I thought we were going to have to put out an APB on a missing penguin." Zina moved closer to where the two animals cuddled. "I can't believe it."

As if to make a point that yes, pit bulls and penguins could be the best of friends, Aurora's tongue whipped out of her mouth and swept over Louise's cheek. The penguin shivered, sending a wave of chills down to the tips of her flippers.

"Well I'll be. I think I've seen it all now." Morty put a hand to his heart like he was about to say the pledge.

"Seen what?" Alex's voice cut through the tender moment.

"We found them. Everything's going to be fine now." Zina reached for Alex but he brushed past her to check on the bird.

"I told that guy not to use the flash."

"Yes, you did. He made a mistake. It's fine now. We'll get the penguins settled, get everyone back into the tent, and get this wedding done. You with me?" She held out her hand.

"We need to talk." Alex glanced up at her. There was

something going on with him, something she couldn't quite put her finger on.

"Well that was fun." Chyna's shrill voice could have peeled wallpaper from the walls. "Can we get this show on the road? I've reset the wedding tent. Are you ready to go?"

"Yes, we sure are. Alex is just getting the penguins calmed down and we'll be right over."

"Zina, come with me. The bride's mother needs a cosmo before we start up again and she says you're the only one who knows how to make it." Chyna held out a hand.

Zina wanted to find out what Alex meant. She couldn't walk away while there was something left unsaid. But he waved her off.

"Go. Let's get through this. I'll be there in a few minutes."

"Okay." She smiled, hoping she'd infused it with enough encouragement to get him through the ceremony when they'd have a chance to chat. Then she turned to Chyna. "Let's go."

Two hours, three kegs, and four cases of champagne later, the fireworks exploded right on cue. Zina breathed out a sigh of relief that had been forty-eight hours in the making. The party was over. She hadn't seen Alex since he'd sent the penguins down the aisle and couldn't wait to find him so they could celebrate with a toast of their own.

"Congratulations on a job well done." Chyna stepped beside her as the bride and groom ducked into the waiting hearse turned popemobile–style limo. With all of the sparkles and twinkle lights, it looked like they'd just stepped into their own custom snow globe.

"Thanks." She'd consider "a job well done" as high praise coming from someone like Chyna.

"You ever consider going into event planning?" Chyna asked.

"No. Definitely not." After the last several weeks the only thing she wanted to do was get back to working with the dogs. There'd been a reason she'd chosen to work with animals over humans. Having to fill in for Lacey and be the "go to" gal had reminded her how much she disliked having to put on a front and play nice with everyone.

"Well if you change your mind, look me up." Chyna handed her a hot-pink card with a number printed on it. "That's my cell."

Zina took it, with absolutely no intention of ever using it. But the thought was nice. And maybe if push came to shove and she found herself without a way to earn a living, maybe then she'd give Chyna a call and . . . On second thought, no, not even then.

"I'm going to go check in at the house and make sure they've got all the food packed up for the family." Zina offered her hand. "Thanks for everything and have a safe trip back to LA tomorrow."

Chyna barely touched her fingertips to Zina's. "Take care."

Zina forgot the woman was somewhat of a germophobe. She'd been holding herself together all day, all weekend, when all she wanted to do was hide out somewhere with Alex and celebrate. As she reached the porch of the house, Lacey called to her from the swing.

"What are you still doing here?" Zina turned toward her friend, who was most definitely not on bed rest. "I thought you went home."

"I couldn't leave without seeing how it all turned out." Lacey patted the cushion next to her. "Come and sit for a few minutes. I poured you a sweet tea."

If she sat down now, Zina wasn't sure she'd get back up again. Plus, she needed to find Alex. He deserved to share in the celebration. "Have you seen Alex?"

"No, but he can wait a few minutes, can't he?" Lacey held out a full glass of tea. It even had a slice of lemon perched on the rim.

Zina carefully settled on the edge of the swing and took the glass. "What's going on?"

Lacey put an arm around Zina's back and gave her a squeeze. "I owe you big-time for this."

"For almost destroying your high-profile event? I think we're even."

"Not even close. You know how much I wanted to be part of this wedding, how much it meant to me that we had such a huge opportunity in Ido."

"Yeah, I know."

"But you did better than I could have imagined. You're amazing, Z. You really came through for me, even with the . . . well, even with the issue with the penguins. I talked to Mr. Munyon and he doesn't blame us for any of it. He said the photographer admitted he'd agreed not to use his flash. He's taking full responsibility."

"Well that's good news."

"It is, isn't it? Now where's your boyfriend? He ought to be celebrating with us, too." Lacey clinked her glass of tea against Zina's.

"I don't know. Will you be here for a bit? I'm going to see if I can track him down."

"Sure. I'll wait."

Zina gave Lacey a one-armed hug, then left her sitting on the porch. Alex was probably doing a final check on the penguins before turning in for the night. She reached the door to the warehouse just as Morty was coming out.

"Hey, have you seen Alex?" she asked.

"No, I was coming to ask you the same thing. I haven't seen him for a couple of hours."

She swallowed. Hard. He wasn't in the house. He wasn't at the warehouse. There had to be an explanation. She pulled out her phone again and checked for a text. Nothing. She pulled up his picture on her phone, the one she'd snapped the night they found the puppies. The call connected. It rang three, four, five times before voice mail kicked in.

"He's not picking up." She pulled the phone away from her ear.

"Yeah, I tried calling a few times and wasn't able to reach him. I hope he's not still mad."

"Mad?" She grabbed hold of Morty's arm. "Why would he be mad?"

Morty grimaced. "We were talking about after the wedding. When I said something about moving out to the ranch, it seemed to set him off. It'll be okay though. He'll cool off."

"So the two of you had a little falling-out and you think he's gone off somewhere to calm down?"

"I'm sure that's what happened. Just give him some time."

"What kind of time are we talking about here? An hour or two?"

Morty sighed. "I don't understand that boy. Last time we argued like this it took him ten years to circle back."

Panic clawed its way up her throat. This was Alex they were talking about. Alex, who even up until that morning had been willing to do anything and everything to save the wedding. He'd even spray-painted flowers for her. And then she'd told him she loved him. And he hadn't said it back. And then he'd got that deer-in-the-headlights look that she'd dismissed as nerves.

"Oh hell."

"What's wrong, dear?" Morty peered up at her, his eyes extra round through the thick lenses of his glasses.

She slid her phone out of her pocket to see an incoming text from Alex. Hope that he'd left to run an errand filled her heart. It was all a misunderstanding. He was probably driving one of the servers home or chasing down a dog that accidentally got loose.

But as she read the first few words, her heart stopped beating. She reached for the handrail of the steps to steady herself.

> I'm at the airport. I decided to take the job with Munyon. I thought I could settle in but I just can't. I'm sorry.

thirty-two

Alex waited to see if Zina would respond. It would serve him right if she never spoke to him again. He felt awful about walking out but he couldn't help it. All the plans, the commitments, the pressure to do what everyone else thought he should had piled up on him until he couldn't take it anymore. Walking away had been one of the hardest things he'd ever done but he didn't have a choice.

At least that's what he kept telling himself as he stood in front of the departure board at Houston's international airport. The vise around his heart tightened as he searched for the gate for his departure. His usual MO when he got overwhelmed or it seemed like someone was backing him into a corner was to get the hell out as fast as possible. Why wasn't it working this time?

Once he got where he was going, far away from the epicenter of it all, he was sure he'd feel better. With a resigned shrug, he made his way to the gate area, ready to take off on a new adventure and clear his head and hopefully his heart.

Snagging a last-minute ticket on a relatively full flight put him in a middle seat between an older man and a woman who seemed to be a few years younger than him. He wished he'd had enough time to make arrangements for an emergency exit row. With his long legs, the idea of spending the next couple of hours squeezed into a middle seat almost made him reconsider. But the alternative of postponing and waiting for a later flight was even less appealing, so he stowed his backpack in the overhead compartment and sat down.

"You going all the way to the Caymans?" the older man asked.

Alex nodded, hoping his silence might deter the man from further conversation. It didn't.

"It's been a long time since I've been back."

"Oh yeah? That's nice." Alex plumped the pillow that had been sitting on his seat and tried to get comfortable.

"Last time I was there I got married."

"Mmm." The thought of engaging in conversation all the way until they made the stop in Miami made his stomach clench. Surely the guy would get the hint.

"She died last year."

The woman on Alex's left leaned over. "I'm so sorry. How long were you together?"

"Forty-three years. Never saw it coming but it was the most impulsive, best decision I've ever made. I'm heading back to spread her ashes."

"I'm sorry for your loss." The woman reached past Alex and patted the man on the arm. Then she glared at Alex, an expectant look on her face.

"I'm sorry, too." The whole reason he left Ido was to outrun his emotions. He couldn't provide a shoulder for the guy next to him to cry on all the way to the Caymans. Maybe he could switch seats. There had to be an aisle or window seat open somewhere. He sat up straighter and craned his neck to look for an opening.

"You ever been married?" the man asked Alex.

"What, me? No. Hard no to that." Alex lowered himself back into his seat. There weren't any openings in the surrounding rows, and the flight attendant was about to close the aircraft door. Looked like he was stuck. At least for the next two and a half hours. He vowed to check in at the ticket counter when they landed in Miami and see if he could get a row to himself on the next leg.

"That's too bad. You're still young though. You've got plenty of time."

"Oh, I'm not the marrying kind." Alex didn't mean to speak up, he actually preferred not to engage in conversation if the guy wanted to talk about commitment.

"I didn't think I was, either. Funny what meeting the right person will do to long-held beliefs."

Alex nodded as he slid his earbuds in place. If the guy couldn't take a subtle hint, maybe he'd get a more direct message. He closed his eyes and tried to focus on the playlist he'd created a couple of years ago. A little heavy metal usually got him psyched up for his next trip. But for some reason, after playing the eighty-four-minute list of tracks all the way through twice, he still hadn't lost that nagging feeling in his gut that he was doing the wrong thing.

He ran through the events that led up to his departure. Spending time with Zina had been amazing. A vision of her snuggling one of the tiny rescue pups drifted through his mind. Then what happened later when they'd finally stopped arguing and decided to give in to the attraction between them and take a chance on each other. She gave so freely of herself. And the whole time he'd had one foot halfway out the door. He didn't deserve her trust. She was better off without him. She'd be pissed as hell for a while but she'd realize it was for the best. He'd always been up front with her that he wasn't a man who liked to stay put.

Someone tapped him on the shoulder. Alex cracked an eyelid to see the older man next to him signaling for him to take his earbuds out. "Last call for snacks. Figured a young guy like you might not want to miss out."

"Thanks." Alex tucked his earbuds into the case and lowered his tray. He hadn't eaten a thing since he'd snagged a quick snack before the wedding. Zina had brought him a made-from-scratch muffin she'd picked up on a run into town the day before. She said she wanted to make sure he got through the ceremony on a full stomach.

He checked his watch. She'd probably be sound asleep right now. For a moment he let himself think about how it had felt to wake up with her in his arms. He'd never have that again. Not now.

"You grow up in Texas, son?" The guy next to him gestured to Alex's boots. Alex hadn't thought to change into his sneakers before taking off for the airport. He'd probably stick out like a sore thumb once he landed in Miami. Maybe he could trade the handcrafted boots for something else. Something that didn't remind him of his roots or everything he'd left behind in Texas.

"Yes. Though I've been away for a long time. I was just home for a quick visit."

"You ranch?"

"We used to. My grandfather owns a place with some acreage just outside of Ido." Or at least he would for a little while longer. Hopefully Char would make good on Alex's promise to let Gramps move back out to the ranch. For a moment Alex's heart ached as a sliver of regret lodged deep.

The man chuckled. "Ido, huh? I saw a piece in the paper about the wacky wedding stuff they had going on over there this weekend. You see any of that?"

"A little bit." Alex didn't like the turn of conversation. Although, to be fair, he hadn't liked the conversation from the start.

"Oh, I think it sounded like fun," the gal on his left piped in. "I mean, penguins at a wedding is kind of a stretch. I hope they're not mistreating those birds at all."

"They're not." Alex couldn't let some rumor get started about how Ido was exploiting penguins for their own profit.

"How do you know that?" she asked.

"I just do." Alex glanced ahead. The flight attendant still had a few rows to go before she reached them.

"Were you involved in that at all?" the man asked.

"Here and there. I can tell you the penguins are being cared for by a qualified professional under the supervision of the aquarium in Houston. They're handling everything on the up-and-up."

"Good to know." The woman turned back to her magazine but Alex wondered at his own comment.

The penguins *were* being taken care of by a somewhat qualified professional. But now? Now it was up to Zina and Gramps to see to their every need before they moved back to their habitat. He hadn't considered that his abrupt departure might put them at risk of criticism. He'd only been thinking about himself. Again.

"You don't happen to have a copy of that article, do you?" Alex asked.

"Sure. I'm finished with the paper if you want to hang on to it." The man reached into the seat pocket in front of him.

"Thanks." Alex flipped through it until he came to the article about Ido and the high-profile wedding they were hosting at the Phillips House. The reporter didn't know what the hell he was talking about. The article mentioned the penguins, then went on to talk about the wedding planner flying all the way in from LA. At the bottom it said something about how the penguins were being housed with dogs from For Pitties' Sake. That part was true, but not the paragraph that followed. Alex read the short bit twice. According to the reporter, the original shelter had been condemned and was going to be torn down. It went on to say the director of the rescue was unavailable for comment but that they'd be following up to make sure visitors to the Phillips House weren't at risk.

At risk of what?

Alex had heard Zina talk about how the dogs at the rescue were misunderstood. He'd been around them for weeks and hadn't seen a single reason to be wary of the breed. What was she going to do without the shelter? She couldn't keep the rescue dogs at the warehouse forever. With everything else going on, did she even know about not being able to move back to the shelter yet?

His heart thudded, a deep, hollow pounding in his chest. She'd be devastated when she found out. He needed to be there for her. Thoughts of hiding away in the Caymans dissipated. He needed to get back to Ido, and the sooner the better.

"You okay?" The older man glanced over, probably wondering what had gotten into Alex in the past couple of minutes.

"I will be." Alex took in a shaky breath. He'd never been so certain of anything. "Once I get back to Ido and prevent myself from making the biggest mistake of my life."

thirty-three

Alex hadn't slept in over thirty hours. As soon as he'd landed in Miami, he tried to get the next flight back to Houston. Everything was full, which meant he had to wait until the next day to try again.

Zina must have turned off her phone because every time he called, it went straight to voice mail. He'd screwed up. Big-time. He'd been so afraid of getting stuck and feeling trapped that he'd let it get in the way of enjoying what they'd been building together. When he heard about the shelter being condemned all he wanted to do was go to her, offer some comfort, and figure out a way to help.

Spending twenty-four hours bouncing around airports had given him plenty of time to think. He'd never wanted to turn out like his dad. His parents hadn't been together very long when his mom got pregnant with Char. He'd always figured his dad felt trapped into marriage and given up his dream of traveling the world to get a job and support his unexpected family. Hearing his dad talk about the places he'd always wanted to visit, with that wistful tone in his voice, made Alex vow that he'd never let his dreams get derailed by a moment of emotion.

But now, he realized what he didn't know way back then. It didn't have to be an all-or-nothing choice. He could have both. Alex realized he didn't have to push Zina away. She wasn't the one trying to trap him. He'd done that to himself by being so shortsighted he couldn't see what a good thing they had going between them.

That's why he had to get back to her. He had to tell her how he felt. Before it was too late.

The truck he'd retrieved at the airport bounced over the dips and divots in the gravel drive leading up to the Phillips House. The garland he'd spray-painted still graced the front fence line. Had that just been a couple of days ago when he and Zina were working together?

He pulled into the lot and headed toward the Phillips House. With any luck Zina would be cleaning up after the wedding and he'd find her inside. If not, he had no idea what he'd do next.

The front door opened and he made his way to the kitchen. Gramps stood at the sink with Herbie on the rug next to him.

"Hey." Alex set his keys down on the counter and Gramps turned to face him. Suds covered his lower arms, up to his elbows.

"Well, I'll be."

"Zina around?" Alex asked. He could catch up with Gramps later. Right now there was only one person he needed to see.

Gramps shook his head. "Not that I know of. I haven't seen her since yesterday."

"She hasn't been in to check on the dogs?" Alex asked.

"No. I told her she deserved a few days off and that I'd keep an eye on them. If she's not at home, I don't know where she'd be. Speaking of, where the hell have you been?"

"It's a long story, Gramps." Alex reached down and ran a hand over Herbie's head. "Can we catch up later?"

"I suppose. Your sister's coming day after tomorrow to check me in to that jail for old people. Said no way would she honor a promise you made." Gramps turned around and muttered, "Figures."

Alex shook his head. "Everything's going to change."

"What do you mean?"

"No Water's Edge for you. We'll move out to the ranch, just like you wanted."

Gramps turned, his pale blue eyes starting to water. "Herbie, too?" The dog returned to his side, tail wagging.

Alex swallowed the lump in his throat. "Herbie and the damn bird can come as well. Zeb, too, if he wants."

"Damn bird, damn bird," the annoying parrot said.

Alex glanced over to where Shiner Bock perched on the swing hanging from the middle of his wire cage.

"Well it's about time you got your head out of your ass." Gramps dropped the pan he'd been scrubbing into the soapy water. A deluge of suds flew up and covered him in bubbles. "Give me a hug."

Alex fought back a rise of emotion as Gramps came at him covered in suds. He wrapped his arms around the older man's shoulders and held him close for a beat. This was what it meant to be there for family . . . to hold tight, even when it meant letting go of things that didn't seem to matter so much anymore. "Now I've got to go find Zina. If all goes well, Herbie will have a lot of company out at the ranch."

"What are you waiting for? Go." Gramps flung a hand toward the door, sending bubbles everywhere.

Alex grinned, happy to be back in the good graces of his grandfather. That had gone better than he expected. One down, one to go. He feared sucking up to Zina would require quite a bit more effort.

After checking the warehouse and driving by her place,

he had no idea where to go next. It was getting late. She had to be somewhere close. Unless she'd pulled a move like he had and tried to run away at the first sign of trouble. Zina wasn't like him though. That's what he loved most about her.

He hadn't wanted to open himself up to major criticism yet, but with no other choice, he pulled up Lacey's number. If anyone knew what was going on with Zina, it would have to be her best friend.

"What do you want?" Lacey's tone didn't just hold an edge of a chill. He felt like the tip of his ear might actually suffer from frostbite, just from hearing her speak.

"I'm looking for Zina. Do you know where she is?"

"No. But even if I did, why would I tell you?"

He sighed. "I messed up."

"Yeah, you did."

"But I'm back and I want to fix things."

"You're back in town? I thought you took off. Your sister said you were headed to Cuba or something."

"Grand Cayman. But then I came to my senses and hopped the next flight back. Now I need to find Zina and apologize."

"You hurt her, asshole. She's better off without you."

"I know." Lacey spoke the truth on both counts. He'd been a giant dick and he didn't deserve her. But he had to try.

His agreement must have caught Lacey a bit off guard. Her voice wasn't quite so frosty when she asked, "So, if you know, why do you want to find her?"

"Because I need to apologize and see if she'll give me another chance." He was wasting time. "Do you know where she is or not? I've checked the house and she's not at the warehouse. It's late and I'm worried."

Lacey let out a huff. "Don't make me regret telling you. If you hurt her again, I'll hunt you down. I'll rip out your heart and feed it to the penguins for breakfast."

Alex chuckled. "Aren't you on strict bed rest?"

"I'll send Bodie. If you're not scared of me, you ought to be scared of him."

"I have no intention of hurting her. She deserves an apology. After that, what happens next will be entirely up to her." He'd already decided if she told him to leave her the hell alone he'd abide by her wishes. But he planned on doing his best to convince her that they needed a second chance.

The silence seemed to drag on forever. Finally, Lacey sighed. "Did you check the shelter?"

"I thought it was condemned."

"Yeah. But if I know Zina, she's probably over there trying to salvage what she can before they bulldoze it to the ground."

Alex hit the heel of his hand against his forehead. Of course. "I haven't been over there but I'm going to swing by now. If you hear from her, will you let me know?"

"Yes. And, Alex?"

"Yeah?" He was already moving toward the door.

"Don't be a dick."

"I promise." He disconnected and shoved his phone in his pocket. If he wanted to make things right with Zina, he'd need to show her he was willing to commit. She wouldn't believe him if he made more hollow promises.

With the tiniest seedling of an idea sprouting in his mind, he headed back to the warehouse to grab a few things before he tracked her down.

"Come on, Aurora." Zina still couldn't believe she'd let Alex's niece talk her into naming the dog after a princess, especially a cartoon princess. Thankfully, she'd cleared most of the supplies from the shelter over the past few weeks. Once the announcement they were condemning the building and going to raze it to the ground came out, someone must have broken in and taken anything left worth saving. The walls were still standing, at least for now, but the spirit of the rescue had disappeared when she had to move the dogs.

She knew in her heart she'd done her best to rehome and relocate as many of the dogs as possible, but she still felt like she'd failed them. She'd spent so much time and effort on that wedding that she'd neglected what really mattered. Being around Alex had blinded her. She'd been so caught up in finally feeling like she had something worth working toward with him that she'd lost track of her priorities.

With Alex out of the picture and the loss of the shelter, it was too much. Her brother seemed to be in a good enough place now that maybe they could find somewhere else to go. Listening to Alex talk about his adventures made her realize she didn't have to stay put. She could load up the couple of pups she had left and she and Zeb could try to find a job somewhere, anywhere, as long as it was far from Ido and gave her the chance to work with animals.

Bottom line was, there wasn't anything or anyone but Lacey holding her to Ido now. And with her and Bodie about to have their first kid, Zina wouldn't even have a chance to spend much time with them anyhow. Seemed as good a time as any to pick up her shallow roots and try to plant them somewhere else.

She'd almost finished gathering the few things worth saving when a noise came from out front. Sounded like someone was pulling into the lot. There was no need for anyone to be out here, especially this late. She crept to the front office and felt around in a desk drawer for something she could use to defend herself. Coming up empty, she wrapped her hand around the first thing she grabbed—a stapler—and held it at the ready.

"What now?" Zina whispered to the dog. Aurora's ears perked, and she cocked her head one way, then the next. "Some watchdog you are."

Something scuffled on the gravel outside. Aurora let out a bark, and the sound receded. Armed with the stapler and her phone's flashlight app, Zina peered through the window. No one was there. Feeling like a fool, she pulled open the door and looked outside. She glanced to her right, then swung her gaze to the left. Nothing. Then her gaze came to rest on the ground.

A stuffed penguin sat two feet in front of her . . . not more than a foot tall. Was this someone's idea of a joke? She almost slammed the door but then noticed a tag hanging from around the stuffed animal's neck. She reached for it and read the handwritten note.

I made a mistake and now I know. How wrong I was to let you go.

Zina let the penguin drop to her side. Alex? He wasn't that cheesy, was he? A quick glance around didn't reveal anything out of place. She stepped outside. Aurora ran toward something in the darkness up ahead.

"Aurora, come back." The dog leapt up, jumping at something, no, make that someone.

Alex came toward the front door, triggering the motion sensor to activate the front floodlight. He dropped to one knee in front of her and reached for her hand.

She jerked it away before he could touch her. "What are you doing here?" Her pulse kicked up so high it felt like a percussion section had started playing a private concert inside her chest.

"I'm literally on my knees, begging you to forgive me." He looked like shit. Shit that had sat out all day and warmed up in the Texas sun. His hair shot out in all directions like he'd been running his hands through it all day. Dark circles stood out under his eyes.

"Get up." She turned her back on him and headed toward

the door, wanting to put some sort of barrier between them. She supposed the glass door would have to do.

He struggled to his feet and caught her hand. "Please give me a chance to explain."

"There's nothing to explain." She turned toward him and crossed her arms over her chest. "You bailed."

Biting his lip, he nodded. "You're right. There's no excuse for me leaving. Especially not the way I did. I'm sorry about the shelter."

"I guess you heard. Joke's on me, isn't it? The whole reason I went into this was to try to save the shelter. And now they're tearing it down anyway." It was too much. She hadn't begun to process Alex walking out on her and now she had to deal with losing the shelter, too. She slumped against the doorway and let the tears finally come.

"Come here." Alex opened up his arms. She didn't want to lean on him. He'd done nothing but cause pain, but he moved closer, and before she could turn away, she'd plastered herself against him, holding on for dear life as waves of grief washed over her.

It was an ugly cry. A snot-running-down-the-nose, T-shirt-soaking outpouring of emotion.

"It's okay." His palm smoothed over her back while he murmured soothing words against her ear. "It's all going to be okay."

She fought with herself between wanting to knee him in the groin and leave him writhing on the floor and needing to take the comfort he offered. When it seemed like she could pull back and face him without bursting into tears again, she broke the embrace.

"You okay?" he asked.

She wanted to tell him she'd never be okay again but instead she nodded, not wanting to let him see her in her weakened, pathetic state. "I'll be fine. Don't you have a plane to catch?"

"No. I did. I mean, I got a ticket to Grand Cayman and flew to Miami but then it hit me."

She'd like to hit *him*. But she also wanted to find out what big revelation he thought he'd experienced. "And?"

He took her hands in his. "And I don't want to run. Not this time. Not from you."

Her lungs failed her and she took in a shaky breath. "But you did."

"I know. I spooked." He shrugged. "I felt stuck, like I'd backed myself into a corner."

"Are you trying to make me feel better or worse?"

"That's just it." He squeezed her hands. She'd missed the contact. Even though he'd been gone less than forty-eight hours, it felt like forever since they'd touched. "It was all me. I've spent my whole life trying not to get attached. I watched my dad give up his dreams because he got trapped. I didn't want that to happen to me."

"God forbid you find love. You're right, what a horrible way to make sure you're miserable for the rest of your life."

"Would you let me finish apologizing? Someone told me once that it doesn't count unless I say the actual words."

For the first time, the crushing feeling around her heart eased. "Whoever said that sounds super smart."

"She is." He squeezed her hands together. "Zina Baxter, I failed you and I'm so incredibly sorry. You're the best thing that's ever happened to me. Will you please accept my apology and give me another chance?"

"What happens if you get spooked again?"

He pressed something into her hands. "Here's my passport. I want you to hang on to it for as long as it takes for you to feel like I'm not going to run out on you again."

"Alex, I can't take this. I don't want it. You shouldn't feel bound to me because you can't leave. If you want to make this work, you have to make the choice every day that you want to stay."

"I figured you might say something like that so I brought you this, too." He held out a clicker, just like the one he'd used to train the penguins. "Let's work on this together. Anytime I get out of hand you can put me back in my place with a click." He demonstrated by pressing on the thin metal strip.

"Can I train you to feed the dogs and pooper scoop by clicking on the magic clicker?"

He smiled and it sent a shock of warmth straight through her. "That's the other thing. Here."

"What's this?" He'd handed her a key. "I don't get it."

"That's a key to one of the climate-controlled outbuildings on my granddad's property. I'm going to be living in the ranch house with him. He's been wanting to move home for a while now but Char hasn't been able to swing it. There's plenty of room out there for you to set up the shelter."

"You're kidding." But a look at his face told her he wasn't.

"Plenty of room in the house for you and Zeb, too, if you want to be close to the dogs." He lowered his voice and stepped closer. "And close to me."

"Are you asking me to move in with you?"

He nodded.

"And my brother and your granddad?"

He winced and nodded again.

"I believe that's the most unromantic offer I've ever had."

"Really?" His nose nuzzled into her hair, and his lips pressed against a sensitive spot behind her ear. "I make fantastic breakfast quesadillas."

"Oh, well, if there will be breakfast quesadillas, I might consider it."

"There's one thing I'm even better at than making breakfast."

"Is that special talent part of your offer as well?" She knew what one thing he was referring to and even if she hated his guts and never wanted to set eyes on him again, she'd still have to admit how good he was at that.

"It can be."

"Well, I think we'd have to negotiate that into the arrangement. How long will that offer stay open?"

He leaned down and put an arm behind her knees, sweeping her off her feet and into his arms. "There's no expiration date. It's good for a lifetime."

"A lifetime?"

He nodded, his gaze meeting hers. Love shone through. He was telling the truth. She might not have seen it coming and probably would have run the other way if she had. But somewhere over the past several weeks she'd fallen hard for Alex Sanders. He'd changed the way she looked at the world, changed the way she looked at herself. And most of all, he'd taught her that a love like theirs was worth a second chance.

She smiled at him, the kind of smile that an amazing man like him deserved. "A lifetime sounds good. I think we can definitely start with that."

epilogue

Zina raced along the walkway leading to the entrance of the aquarium. She should have been there fifteen minutes ago, but she'd gotten caught up in traffic after stopping by to check on one of the puppy mill pups who'd been settling in with her new family just outside of Houston.

Alex was going to strangle her if she missed the dedication for the new penguin habitat. Especially since it was the first time they'd get a chance to visit with Thelma, Louise, and the rest of the Ido dozen who'd been part of the Munyon wedding. She shook her head as she thought about what a crazy mess that had been. Over seven months later and she could still remember how it felt to think her whole life was over because he'd spooked.

Since then she and Lacey had worked with over a dozen brides to give them the weddings of their dreams. Well, mostly her since Lacey was still pushing herself too hard and the doc kept putting her back on bed rest. But today wasn't about weddings or events or pit bulls. It was all about Alex.

He'd been invited to participate behind the scenes this week and help move the colony into their new habitat, so it was just as easy for her to meet him there. Plus he'd promised her dinner at the exclusive Cattleman's restaurant after the quick dedication ceremony. She'd be a fool to turn down that kind of an offer.

The aquarium had gone all out with the holiday decorations. Christmas was still over a month away, but as she entered the front door and made her way to the penguin exhibit, twinkle lights sparkled overhead. Alex had warned her it would be a pretty small affair. The public dedication would be happening the next day but since he'd been instrumental in coordinating the makeover, the aquarium had extended an invite to their private ceremony. She hadn't seen much of him since he'd started the veterinary program at the University of Houston in September. Even though he'd arranged all of his classes so he only had to drive into the city a few times a week, she was ready for the holiday break so they'd have more time to spend together.

Her heels clicked on the tile as the first strains of music drifted from the sound system down the empty hall. The low hum of chatter made her think the party might be bigger than she thought. She smoothed a hand over the skirt of her dress, suddenly wondering if she should have worn something nicer.

As she turned the corner, eager to get her first glimpse of the new exhibit and even more excited to wrap her arms around the man who'd made it possible, she stopped in her tracks.

What was her brother doing here? Zeb stood off to the side, Semper at his feet. Lacey sat at a small bar top table with Bodie's arm draped over her back. Char spotted her and rushed over, a flute of champagne in her hand.

"She's here." Dolly wrapped her arms around Zina's legs, preventing her from moving any farther.

"What's going on?" Zina let her gaze rest on each person in attendance.

"Cue the penguins," a deep voice boomed out over the room. Morty glanced over, catching Zina's eye.

"What in the world is happening? Where's Alex?"

It only took a moment for her to catch sight of him. Two rows of penguins waddled toward her, Alex bringing up the rear. Thelma and Louise stopped when they reached her and took turns lifting their flippers for a high five. Zina laughed as she tapped her palm against them.

"How did you finally teach them that trick?" She smiled at Alex. He'd been working on that one for weeks when the penguins had been staying in the warehouse.

"Turns out you can get anyone to do pretty much anything if you provide the right incentive." He dropped down onto one knee in front of her.

Her stomach flip-flopped while her heart seemed to swan dive to her feet. "What are you doing?"

"I'm hoping I'm about to make you an offer you can't refuse." He grinned, the same sexy, smug grin she'd come to love.

"Well, get on with it then." The steady tone of her voice didn't betray the mishmash of emotions that swirled around inside.

He reached for her hand. "Zina Baxter, you're the strongest, most beautiful, most capable woman I've ever met. I don't know what you see in me but I start off every day so thankful that you're a part of my life."

Dammit, he was going to make her cry. The threat of tears swelled. She focused on her breath, trying not to lose it before he finished saying what he wanted to say.

"We haven't known each other all that long in human years but we've been together longer in penguin years."

She laughed, spilling a tear over the rim of her lashes.

"That's three and a half years in dog years, too. Plenty

of time for me to know that you're the one for me. I hope you feel the same way."

She nodded, the tears no longer a threat now, but an inevitable outcome.

"I love you. Will you marry us?"

"'Us'?" She'd been ready to literally bowl him over with an enthusiastic yes, but that last word caught her off guard.

"Yeah, us." He stood and gestured around him. "You're not just getting me. You're getting the family I came with and the one we've created. Penguins, dogs, people, hell, even the damn bird."

"Damn bird. Damn bird." Shiner Bock piped up from his perch on Morty's shoulder.

"Is he supposed to be in here?" She pointed to the bird.

"He's part of the family. For better or for worse. What do you say?"

Alex held an open jewelry box out to her. A large aquamarine stone nestled against a white velvet background. "An aquamarine?"

"Yeah, like the ocean." He took the ring and slid it onto her finger. "I figured that's technically what brought us together."

She centered the stone on her finger and looked up at him. Her cheeks already hurt from smiling.

"So?" he asked.

"So what?"

"You didn't actually say yes yet. It doesn't count if you don't say the words."

She bit her lip, loving the fact that he'd turned her own argument against her. "Fair point. I say yes. Yes to this motley, ragtag crew we've brought together. Yes to you."

"Good." He caught her up in his arms and spun her around. When his lips met hers, everything else faded into the background.

Until someone tapped her on the shoulder. A firm, persistent tap that didn't let up.

"Yes?" Zina pulled away from Alex to find Lacey invading her personal space.

"We need to get started right away. I'm picturing a winter wonderland dogsledding wedding so we can incorporate both the penguins and the dogs."

"Oh no." Zina shook her head and held tight to Alex. "We're going to have a small ceremony. No fuss. No fireworks. No ice."

"Aw, honey, are you sure?" Alex squeezed her hand.

She nudged her nose against his, her hair falling around them like a curtain, blocking out the rest of the room. "Actually, I have an even better idea."

"What's that?"

"Let's elope."

acknowledgments

Huge thanks to Berkley and their team of editors and artists for making me look so good on paper. Especially my editor, Kristine Swartz, who didn't blink an eye when I wanted to put penguins in the middle of Texas. Hugs and smooches to my agent, Jessica Watterson, for always believing in me (or at least faking it) even when she thinks I've gone off the deep end with one of my ideas. And I couldn't have written this book without the support of my reader group, Crushin' It Crew, and the amazing readers and authors in both Must Love Cowboys and Romance Chicks Partypalooza. I always hate listing names because I'm terrified I'm going to forget someone, but special thanks to Christina Hovland, Jody Holford, Renee Ann Miller, Serena Bell, Brenda St. John Brown, Aidy Award, LeAnne Bristow, Dawn Luedecke, and Sandra Marine for being a fabulous sounding board and support system. And finally, to my family, especially Mr. Crush, HoneyBee, GlitterBee, and BuzzleBee. You'll always be my why.

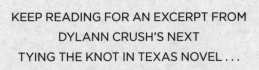

one

Delilah Stone removed her rhinestone tiara as she ducked into the vintage trailer she'd been living in for the past few months. As the reigning Miss Lovin' Texas, her most pressing official duty was judging the state tourism board's search for the most romantic small town in Texas. Thirty days had been more than enough time to determine the tiny town of East, which ironically happened to be located in the westernmost corner of the state, wasn't going to win. She'd already been to Hartwood, a charming little town located in the Hill Country and the clear favorite to take the title.

With only one more town to judge, she was looking forward to putting her time as Miss Lovin' Texas behind her. Living in the hot pink branded trailer provided by the pageant's main sponsor was getting old. She just had to spend the next thirty days in Swynton—the final contender—before she could trade in the trailer for her condo and get back to pursuing something more meaningful than deciding which town would secure the title.

"Well that was a nightmare." Delilah's manager, who also happened to be her mother, or "momager" in pageant terms, came in behind her and pulled the door shut.

"Two stops down, one to go." Delilah lifted her sash over her head and hung it in the tiny closet.

"Just think, a couple of months from now, and this will all be behind you." Her mother unfastened the eye hook at the back of Delilah's dress and slid the zipper down to where she could reach it. "Next time you might want to smile more and talk less."

"Thanks for the feedback, Stella." Delilah had been banished from calling her mother anything but her given name. God forbid someone actually mistake her mom for anything but her older sister—a game Delilah had grown tired of playing.

Her fingers closed around the zipper, and she stepped into the tiny bedroom area to change into something a little more comfortable and a lot less sparkly. Tonight's final farewell appearance marked the end of her time in East. Tomorrow they'd start the trek to the southeast Texas town of Swynton where she'd spend the next month evaluating their efforts to win the title.

She'd be glad when this jig was up. Not only could she use some time away from Stella, but she was also ready to move on to bigger and better things. Once she wrapped up her stay in Swynton, she'd just have one final appearance to make—the award ceremony where the board would award the title to the most romantic small town in Texas.

At twenty-five, she was ready to retire from pageant life and use her connections to make a difference in the world. Some of her competitors might not believe in the causes they promoted on their personal platforms, but Delilah did. And once her current reign came to a glittering end, she had plans to put her money where her mouth was and start doing something to support her cause of empowering young girls instead of just talking about it all the time.

She carefully slipped the glittery gown onto a hanger then pulled on her dressing robe. As she slid a headband in place to start her long makeup removal routine, her cell rang.

"Want me to pick up for you?" Stella asked. Even with the door between the bedroom and the living area closed, it sounded like her mother was standing right next to her.

"I'll get it." Delilah moved through the trailer and reached for her phone. "Hello. Miss Lovin' Texas speaking."

"Good evening, Ms. Stone. It's Marty Plum. We've had a change of plans as to your travel itinerary tomorrow."

"Oh? What kind of change?" Delilah had only spoken to the contest chair a few times since she started her term.

Stella leaned against the counter next to her. "What's going on?"

Delilah shrugged. "I don't know yet," she whispered.

Mr. Plum cleared his throat. "Seems Swynton has been disqualified from the competition."

"Disqualified?" Delilah shot a glance to Stella. "What did they do?"

"That's right. They've been accused of bribing a member of the committee. We can't have any kind of scandal touch the competition, so we've taken them out of the running."

"I'm sorry to hear that." Delilah couldn't care less about Swynton, Texas. Didn't matter to her which town they sent her to, as long as she'd be done by the date her contract specified.

"What's happening?" Stella asked.

Delilah held up a finger. "Does that mean my judging obligations are complete? It's just between Hartwood and East?"

"Not exactly." Marty cleared his throat again. "The committee wants to let the runner-up town take Swynton's place. It's actually a fairly convenient swap since it's right across the river. Instead of spending thirty days in Swynton, we're going to have you spend the next month in Ido."

"Ido? Where's that?" Delilah had never heard of the town and as a lifelong pageant participant, she'd traveled back and forth across the great state of Texas more times than the pony express had in its heyday.

Stella whipped her head back and forth, turning her giant earrings into weapons. "No. You're not going there."

"I'm sorry, Mr. Plum. Could you hold for just a moment?" She put her hand over the mouthpiece and studied her mother. "What's in Ido?"

"It's where I grew up. You're not spending any amount of time in that place. I barely escaped alive, I'm not sending my only child back there. Traveling to Swynton was close enough. No, you can't do it."

"Ms. Stone, are you there?" Marty asked. "Is there a problem?"

"I'm still here." She motioned for her mother to sit down at the small dinette. "Can you please send over the information? I need some time to talk to my manager about the change of plans."

"Of course. E-mail okay?"

"That would be just fine. Thank you. I'll give you a call in the morning."

By the time Delilah disconnected, Stella sat at the tiny table with her head in her hands. "They can't just trade out a town like that."

"What's the big deal? Whether I go to Swynton or Ido or Timbuktu, one of my official duties is judging their contest. I can't back out now." Stella was the one who'd insisted she sign up for the Miss Lovin' Texas pageant in the first place. Why the change of heart?

"I have such bad memories."

Delilah slid onto the bench seat across from her mom. "Whatever you ran from in Ido, Texas, is long gone. You don't have to come with me, you can go back to—"

"Not go with you?" Stella lifted her head, her blue eyes

taking on a haunted, wounded look. "You don't want me to travel with you anymore?"

"That's not what I said." Delilah couldn't win, not where her mother was concerned. If she wanted her to go with her, Stella would call her demanding. If she didn't want her to come, then she'd be insensitive. She'd navigated the tricky interpersonal relationship with her mother her whole life. "I want you to do what's best for you even though I have to follow through on the commitment I made when I won this title."

Stella placed a hand over her heart. "If I'd have known they'd be sending you to Ido, I never would have encouraged you to enter that pageant."

Not wanting to argue, Delilah nodded. "This will be good though. You can head back to Dallas and keep things moving on our new cosmetics line while I serve out the rest of my sentence."

"Are you sure that's what you want to do?" Stella's frown switched into a hopeful smile. "We could still make a run for the big title. With your looks and my pageant know-how, we're a good team."

"We *have* made a good team, but weren't you the one who said I should quit while I was ahead?" Winning a national-level title was her mother's dream. Even though they'd worked their tails off, winning local and regional competitions across the south, the big title had remained elusive.

"I know we agreed Miss Lovin' Texas would be your last pageant, but don't you want to try one more time?" Stella bit her lip, her forehead creased.

"You're going to give yourself wrinkles if you keep frowning," Delilah pointed out, tossing her mother's own wisdom right back in her lap.

Stella immediately relaxed her expression. "Are you sure your contract doesn't say anything about what happens if they switch locations on you at the last minute?"

"Nope. I'm pretty much at their mercy until we get through the final ceremony when they name the winner." Stella would know that if she actually read the contracts. But she tended to be more involved on the front-end side of things . . . picking out the dresses and offering unsolicited advice on makeup and hairstyle trends. Her mother might drive her crazy at times, but she never steered her wrong when it came to appearances. She also had an amazing knack for business, hence the new line of cosmetics that she and Delilah would be launching after her reign came to an end. Delilah's mentor, Monique McDowell, the first African American woman to win multiple national titles, was also on board and Delilah couldn't wait to get started.

Thankfully, Monique had stepped in early on in Delilah's pageant career and provided the guidance she'd been missing from her mother. Stella might have big dreams, but she lacked personal experience. Delilah had heard the story of how her mother chose love over pageant wins and sacrificed everything to get married and become a mother. She never actually came out and said it, but somehow the sense that Delilah owed her mother a big win had been implied since the first time she stepped on a stage.

"I don't care what they say. It's ridiculous. They can't make you go to Ido." Stella's mouth set in a grim line.

"Actually, they can, and it looks like they are." Delilah held her phone out. "Mr. Plum's new itinerary has me arriving on Friday in time for their kick-off celebration. That gives me three days to get there."

"Oh, honey, how are you going to manage all by yourself?" Stella's brow furrowed again.

Delilah pointed at her forehead. "Keep that up and you'll be taping your forehead while you sleep." Stella had often threatened to make Delilah sleep with clear tape holding her skin taut, saying it was a tried-and-true way to prevent fine lines and wrinkles.

"So, you'll go to Swynton and I'll go back to Dallas?" Stella asked, her face devoid of any expression.

"I guess so. You said you wanted to get started on that line of cosmetics. What else were you looking into?" Delilah couldn't keep it all straight. Her mother had more projects in the works than the Texas Department of Transportation and that was saying a lot.

Stella brightened. "Monique and I are finalizing with that cosmetics company on your signature line. Plus, we've got those fashion faux pas fixers in the works. Don't you worry, Texas won't forget Delilah Stone, even if you're no longer competing."

Staying in the public eye was her mother's dream, not Delilah's. But when Mama was happy, everyone else was happy so Delilah was content to let her mother work on whatever projects she wanted to. As long as it kept her busy and gave her something else besides her daughter to focus her overwhelming attention on, it was a win-win.

"I'll tell Mr. Plum to let Ido know they can expect me on Friday then."

Stella nodded, her attention already shifting away from the contest. "Do you think you can drop me at the airport on the way? I'll just take a flight back to Dallas. You'll be fine, won't you?"

"Absolutely." Delilah left her mother at the tiny built-in dinette and resumed her nighttime routine. She loved her mother dearly but was eager for a break. They'd been traveling together for the past two months and anyone who'd ever spent any time around Stella Stone would have agreed that was about two months too long.

Suddenly having to spend the next thirty days in Ido, Texas, didn't seem so bad. She'd have a bit of respite from the breakneck schedule she'd been keeping for the past several years. Without having to entertain her mother, she'd have plenty of time to think about what she wanted to do next, beyond the launch of all of the products Stella and Monique had in the works.

For the first time in a long time, Delilah felt the knot in her chest loosen just a smidge. Having to spend a month in Ido, Texas, might just be the best thing that had ever happened to her.

two

Jasper Taylor drew in a breath as he walked through what remained of his family's pecan orchard. The twister that had blown through last month had skipped over their neighbor's cattle ranch but had unleashed its wrath on Taylor Farms. Less than a quarter of the trees from their hundred-year-old orchard remained, not nearly enough to fulfill the orders they'd already committed to from this year's harvest.

"We're doomed." Jasper's dad, Frank, hung his head. "I shouldn't have taken out a loan against the farm. We're going to lose it all."

Jasper chewed on the inside of his cheek and tried to come up with a reassuring word. Truth was, they *were* doomed. Unless he could find a way to conjure pecans out of thin air, they weren't going to be able to dig themselves out this time.

"Your poor mama. She's going to skin me alive when she finds out what I've done." Dad ran a calloused hand behind his neck. "If only Colin were around. It's about time you two made up, don't you think?"

According to his parents, the absence of his older brother was the reason everything had gone to shit. Jasper had been tempted to tell them the truth on more than one occasion, but it would break their hearts. So instead he let them go on believing what they would while he tried to hold things together on his own.

"I might have an idea." Jasper hadn't wanted to bring it up. He'd been shot down too many times in the past for trying to buck tradition and expand beyond the family trade. But look where doing things the same had got them— wiped out by a fickle late summer storm. If he didn't figure out a way to literally save the family farm, there wouldn't be any traditions left to buck because they'd be forced to sell their land and figure out a new way of life.

"Don't start spoutin' off about that woman's crazy wedding ideas again," Dad warned.

"Do you want to have to tell mom you're moving the family into town?"

"She'd leave me." Dad sighed.

"She'd never leave you. But she might not talk to you for the rest of your lives." Jasper had seen his mama hold a grudge and it wasn't pretty. She still had trouble looking him in the eye since she blamed him for Colin's departure.

"Tell me what you have in mind. I suppose it's worth a listen."

"Mayor Cherish said she's looking for complementary businesses to help expand Ido's hold on the wedding market. I told you years ago that people pay big bucks to rent out barns for wedding receptions. And we've got the oldest barn in the state of Texas, that ought to be good for—"

"You can't tell me some hoity-toity bride all dressed in white is going to want to say her vows while standing in a pile of horse shit." Dad shook his head.

"You're missing the point." His dad had almost run their business into the ground thanks to his narrow-minded ways. If he didn't come around to trying something new, they'd all suffer.

"What's the point then? Enlighten me." They'd stopped at the edge of the ring where Jasper's younger sister, Abby, put her favorite mare through her paces. Dad hooked the heel of his boot on the lowest board of the fence.

"We move the horses to the smaller barn and renovate the big one. You're right, no bride is going to want to use it like it is now. But with the insurance money we have coming in, we could use that to—"

"Have you lost your mind? That insurance money's got to buy trees to replace the ones we lost. What good is a pecan farm without pecan trees?"

Jasper tried to keep his cool. "You know it's going to take at least five years, probably seven or eight to get those trees back to producing something we can sell. But if we revamp the barn, we could be making money hand over fist by next spring."

Dad shook his head. "That's crazy talk. Your mama would never go for such a crackpot idea."

Jasper's chest tightened. Now was his shot. "She thinks it might work."

"What?" Dad's eyes went wide, and his mouth hung open.

"I talked to Mayor Cherish about it last week, just to gauge her reaction. She thinks it's a great idea. Then I mentioned it to Mom."

"You went behind my back." Dad's voice dropped into a growl. "You talked to your mama, you went to visit the mayor, all without saying a word to me?"

Jasper let out a long sigh. "Because I knew you wouldn't even consider it. But we've got to do something to make some money over the next few years. Even if we replant half the trees we lost, can't you try something else to supplement in the meantime?"

Dad rested his hands on the top rail of the fence and let his head drop between his shoulders. "Over a hundred years. This farm's been operating under the Taylor name for four generations. I can't lose it."

"Then let me help you save it." Jasper clapped a hand on his dad's shoulder. "I only want what's best for all of us."

"If that's true, you'd best be going to find your brother and convince him to come back."

"Dad . . ." Jasper closed his eyes for a long beat, trying to battle away the tension in his jaw at the mention of his brother. He wished he had it in him to come clean, but it would make things so much worse. It was easier to let them believe what they wanted to.

"Whatever happened between the two of you, you're family." Dad squinted. "You can't avoid him forever."

Jasper nodded. "I know."

"I'm going to have to talk to your mama about this." Dad adjusted his hat and squared his shoulders.

"I understand." The phone in his back pocket started to vibrate. He reached for it and saw Mayor Cherish's number light up his screen. "Hey, it's the mayor. I ought to take this."

His dad didn't respond so he took several long strides toward the shade of one of the oldest pecan trees they had on the property and answered the call. "Hello?"

"Jasper, it's Lacey Cherish. Something's come up. Are you still interested in trying to make a go of it with your idea on using your barn for weddings?"

"I'm not quite sure yet." Jasper's chest tightened. "I mentioned it to Dad, and he needs some time to get used to the idea."

"Well, I'm in a bind. I just got word that the state tourism board gave us a spot to compete for the most romantic small town in Texas."

"That's great. But what does that have to do with turning the barn into a wedding venue?"

"I need someone to represent Ido as our hospitality host . . . be the point of contact for the judge while she's here in town. Is that something you'd be able to do?"

"Oh, I don't know. I've got a lot to do around here. We still haven't cleaned everything up from the storm, and—"

"I'm in a real jam. We weren't supposed to be competing in this contest but Swynton got disqualified and we got their spot. I don't have time to come up with another plan. If we can claim the title of the most romantic small town in Texas we could increase the wedding business we've already got. It would give you a chance to really make a go of it with the barn idea."

Jasper sensed a golden opportunity within his grasp. Mayor Cherish was right. If Ido claimed the title, there would be a huge influx of tourists. Not only brides, but they could do anniversary parties, maybe even corporate outings with trail rides. If he could turn things around and save their land, how could he refuse?

"What would you need me to do?"

"They're sending Miss Lovin' Texas over to judge. From what I understand, she'll live here in town for a month, and then they'll hold a big shindig in Houston in November where they'll announce the winner. We're the last stop. She's already been to Hartwood and East. What do you say? Will you be Ido's hospitality host?"

"You want me to entertain a beauty queen for a month?" His gut rolled. "There's got to be someone else better qualified for the job."

"I wish," Lacey muttered.

"What's that?"

"I wish we had time to find someone, but there's no one else. Believe me, I've tried to come up with ideas on who might be best to fill this role. You've got incentive. If Ido wins, you win. Plus, you can't argue that right now you've got the time."

No, he couldn't argue with that. Harvesttime was coming up and with seventy-five percent fewer trees to pick, not even the busiest time of year would keep him all that occupied.

"What would I have to do?"

"Easy peasy. Just shuttle her around and introduce her to the folks in town. Make sure she sees the best of Ido and gets to all the events on time. Should be a piece of cake."

A piece of cake. In his experience, most things folks thought would be a piece of cake ended up being more like a cake fight. He clenched his jaw, trying to think of another solution. But he'd spent the past month running through every scenario he could come up with to save the orchard. Turning the barn into some sort of event venue and taking advantage of the town's strategy to become the most romantic small town in Texas might be the best option. Maybe even the only option. But what did he know about romance?

"I don't know. I'd be happy to pitch in, but I don't think I'm the right man for the job."

Lacey sighed. "Some help is better than none. Can you swing by my office this afternoon? We need to get started right away."

"Sure thing. I thought you said you were pretty busy this week with that big wedding coming up. Maybe we should wait until next week?" That would give his dad a chance to further warm up to the idea.

"We don't have time to spare. She'll be here Friday."

"Friday? As in the day after tomorrow?" His stomach flipped.

"Yes, Friday. We've got to put together some sort of kickoff event in less than forty-eight hours."

"Wow." Dammit. How was he going to convince his dad

to get on board that fast? Dad was deliberate in his decisions. He took time to weigh the options and examine his moves from every angle before he committed to taking any kind of action. He'd never get behind an idea this wild in such a short time frame.

"Can I count on you?"

Jasper took in a deep breath. Helping the town would be the best way to help his family, even if they didn't see it that way yet.

"Let me get cleaned up, and I'll be over in a bit."

"Thanks, Jasper. I'll see you soon."

He ended the call and rejoined his dad by the fence.

"What did the mayor want?" Dad asked.

Jasper hooked his fingers over the top rail. "She asked if I wanted a job."

"What kind of job?"

"Seems Ido is in the running for most romantic small town in Texas and she needs a hospitality host."

Dad let out a deep laugh. "No offense, son, but I hope you turned her down. You don't really know much about either, do you?"

"What's that supposed to mean?"

"When's the last time you went on a date? Shouldn't someone who's in charge of romance and hospitality know something about one or the other?"

"I did turn her down but told her I'd be willing to help. If Ido wins that title, it would mean a bunch of publicity for something like a wedding barn."

"Tell you what." Dad turned and faced him. The humor had faded from his eyes. "You and Lacey get that title for Ido and I'll let you try that wedding idea with the barn."

Jasper grinned. "You sure you want to make that deal?"

His dad thrust out his hand. "I'm sure, but how about you? If you fail, we're going to have to make some difficult decisions around here." He glanced to where Abby slowed the mare to a walk. "Some of those horses we've got are worth quite a bit. I'm not afraid to make some hard decisions to do whatever it takes to save this place."

Jasper wrapped his hand around his dad's. "If all goes well, you won't have to."

Ready to find
your next great read?

Let us help.

Visit prh.com/nextread

Penguin
Random
House